6 SIDEKICKS OF TRIGGER KEATON

CREATED BY KYLE STARKS & CHRIS SCHWEIZER

WRITER

KYLE STARKS

ART, COLORS, LETTERING

CHRIS SCHWEIZER

COLORING ASSISTANT

LIZ TRICE SCHWEIZER

EDITOR

JON MOISAN

LOGO DESIGN

ANDRES JUAREZ

PRODUCTION DESIGN

CARINA TAYLOR

SKYBOUND ENTERTAINMENT | ROBERT KIRKMAN Chairman | DAVID ALPERT CEO | SEAN MACKIEWICZ SVP, Editor-in-Chief | SHAWN KIRKHAM SVP, Business Development | BRIAN HUNTINGTON VP, Online Content | ANDRES JUAREZ Art Director | ARUNE SINGH Director of Brand, Editorial | ALEX ANTONE Senior Editor | JON MOISAN Editor | AMANDA LAFRANCO Editor | CARINA TAYLOR Graphic Designer DAN PETERSEN Sr. Director, Operations & Events | Foreign Rights & Licensing Inquiries: contact@skybound.com | SKYBOUND.COM

IMAGE COMICS, INC. | TODD MCFARLANE President | JIM VALENTINO Vice President | MARC SILVESTRI Chief Executive Officer | ERIK LARSEN Chief Financial Officer | ROBERT KIRKMAN Chief Operating Officer | ERIC STEPHENSON Publisher / Chief Creative Officer | NICOLE LAPALME Controller | LEANNA CAUNTER Accounting Analyst | SUE KORPELA Accounting & HR Manager | MARLA EIZIK Talent Liaison | JEFF BOISON Director of Sales & Publishing Planning | DIRK WOOD Director of International Sales & Licensing | ALEX COX Director of Direct Market Sales | CHLOE RAMOS Book Market & Library Sales Manager | EMILIO BAUTISTA Digital Sales Coordinator | JON SCHLAFFMAN Specialty Sales Coordinator | KAT SALAZAR Director of PR & Marketing | DREW FITZGERALD Marketing Content Associate | HEATHER DOORNINK Production Director | DREW GILL Art Director | HILARY DILORETO Print Manager | TRICIA RAMOS Traffic Manager | MELISSA GIFFORD Content Manager | ERIKA SCHNATZ Senior Production Artist | RYAN BREWER Production Artist | DEANNA PHELPS Production Artist | IMAGECOMICS.COM

SIX SIDEKICKS OF TRIGGER KEATON VOLUME ONE. Second Printing. Published by Image Comics, Inc. Office of publication: PO BOX 14457, Portland, OR 97293. ISBN: 978-1-5343-2008-6

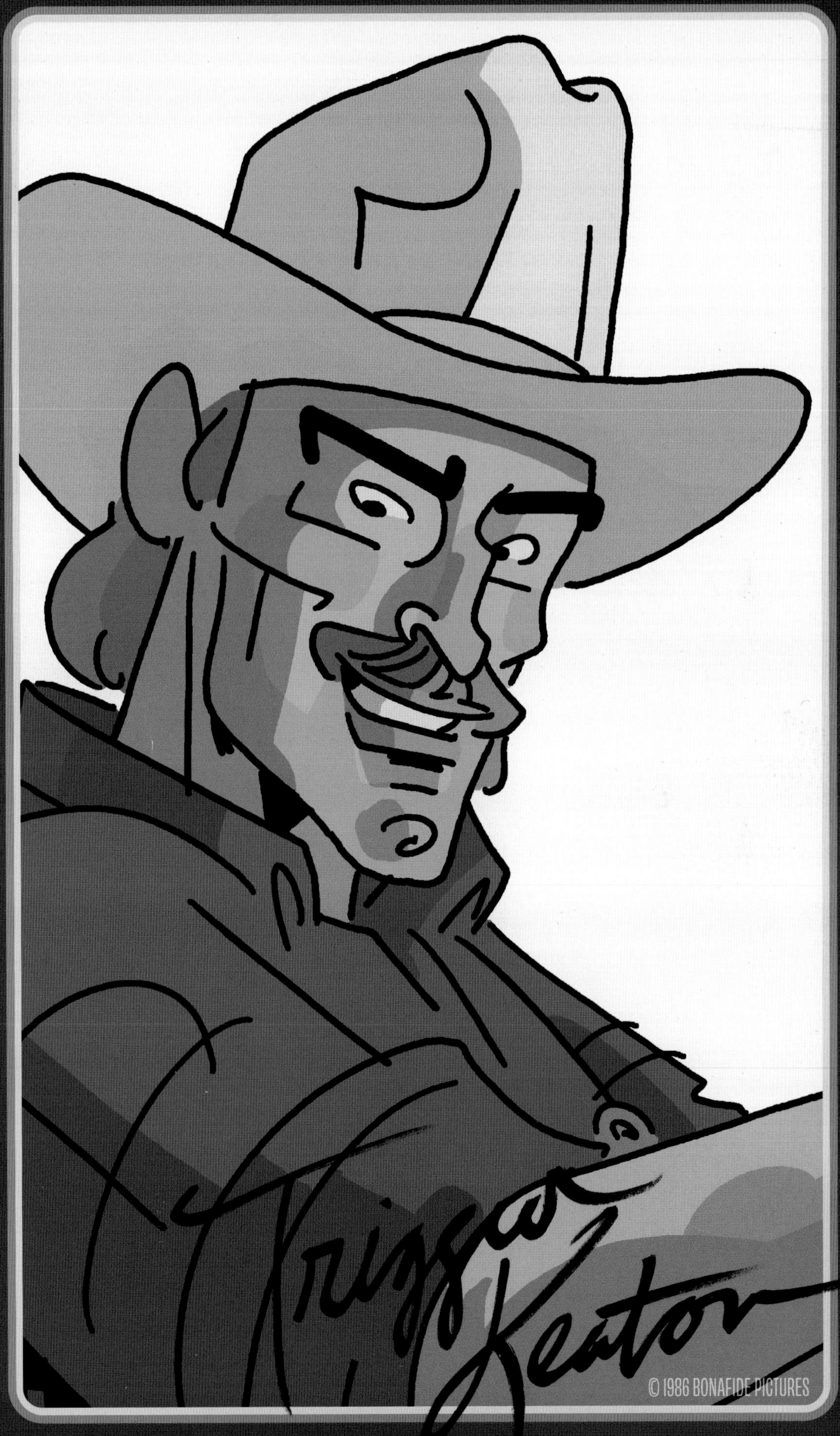
Trigger Keaton
© 1986 BONAFIDE PICTURES

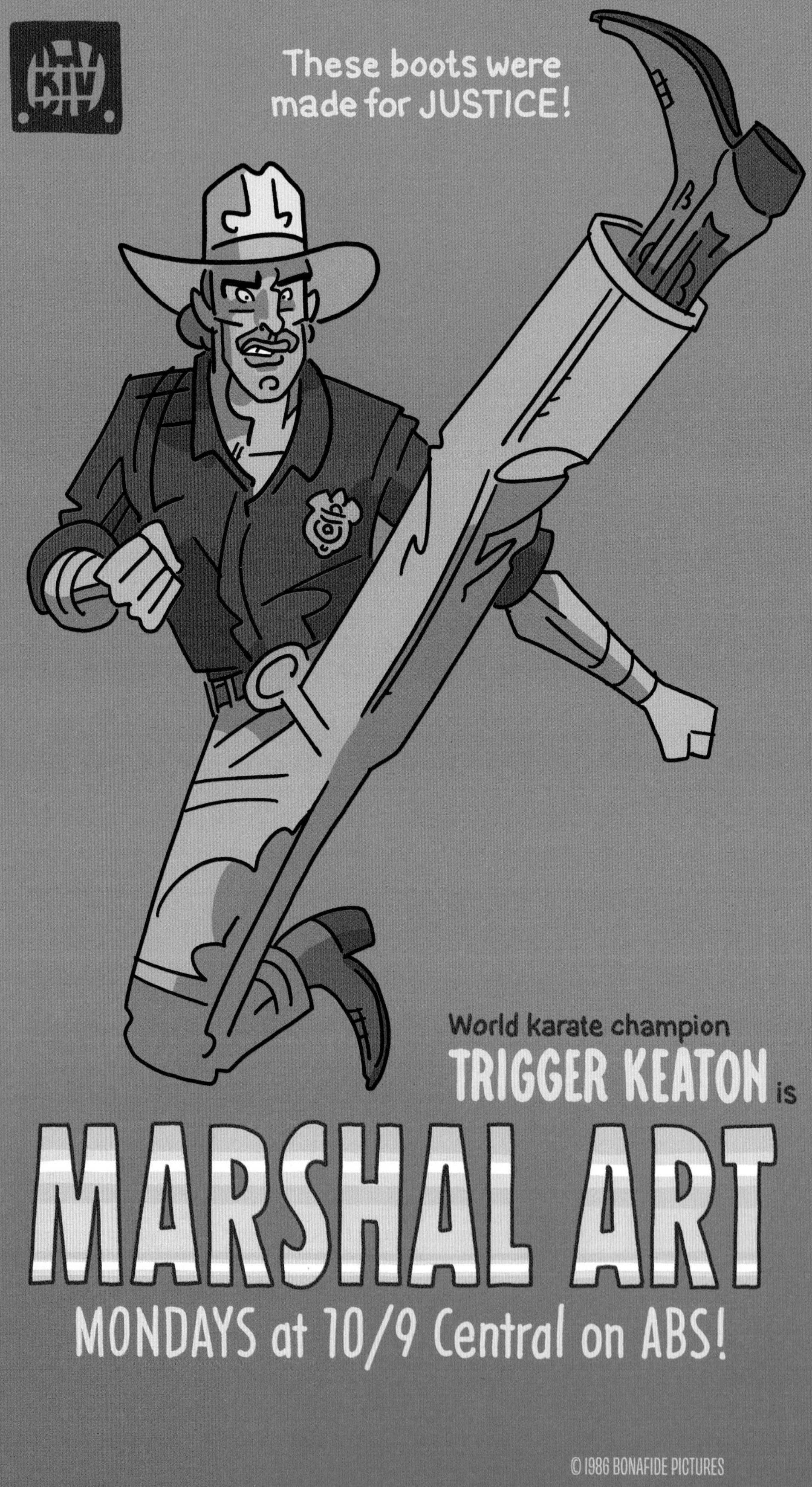

These boots were made for JUSTICE!
World karate champion
TRIGGER KEATON is
MARSHAL ART
MONDAYS at 10/9 Central on ABS!
© 1986 BONAFIDE PICTURES

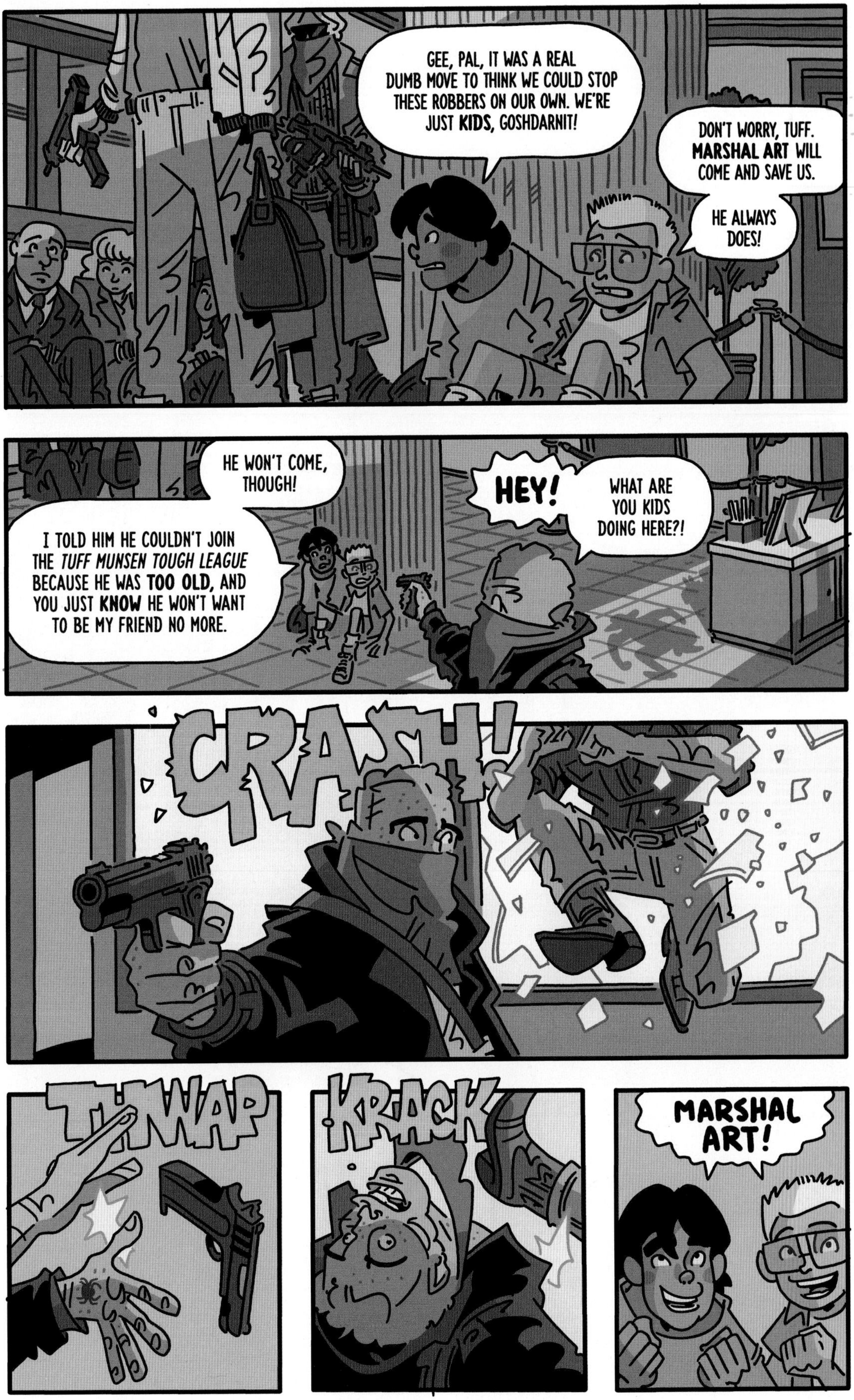
GEE, PAL, IT WAS A REAL DUMB MOVE TO THINK WE COULD STOP THESE ROBBERS ON OUR OWN. WE'RE JUST **KIDS**, GOSHDARNIT!
DON'T WORRY, TUFF. **MARSHAL ART** WILL COME AND SAVE US.
HE ALWAYS DOES!
HE WON'T COME, THOUGH!
I TOLD HIM HE COULDN'T JOIN THE *TUFF MUNSEN TOUGH LEAGUE* BECAUSE HE WAS **TOO OLD**, AND YOU JUST **KNOW** HE WON'T WANT TO BE MY FRIEND NO MORE.
HEY!
WHAT ARE YOU KIDS DOING HERE?!
CRASH!
THWAP
KRACK
MARSHAL ART!

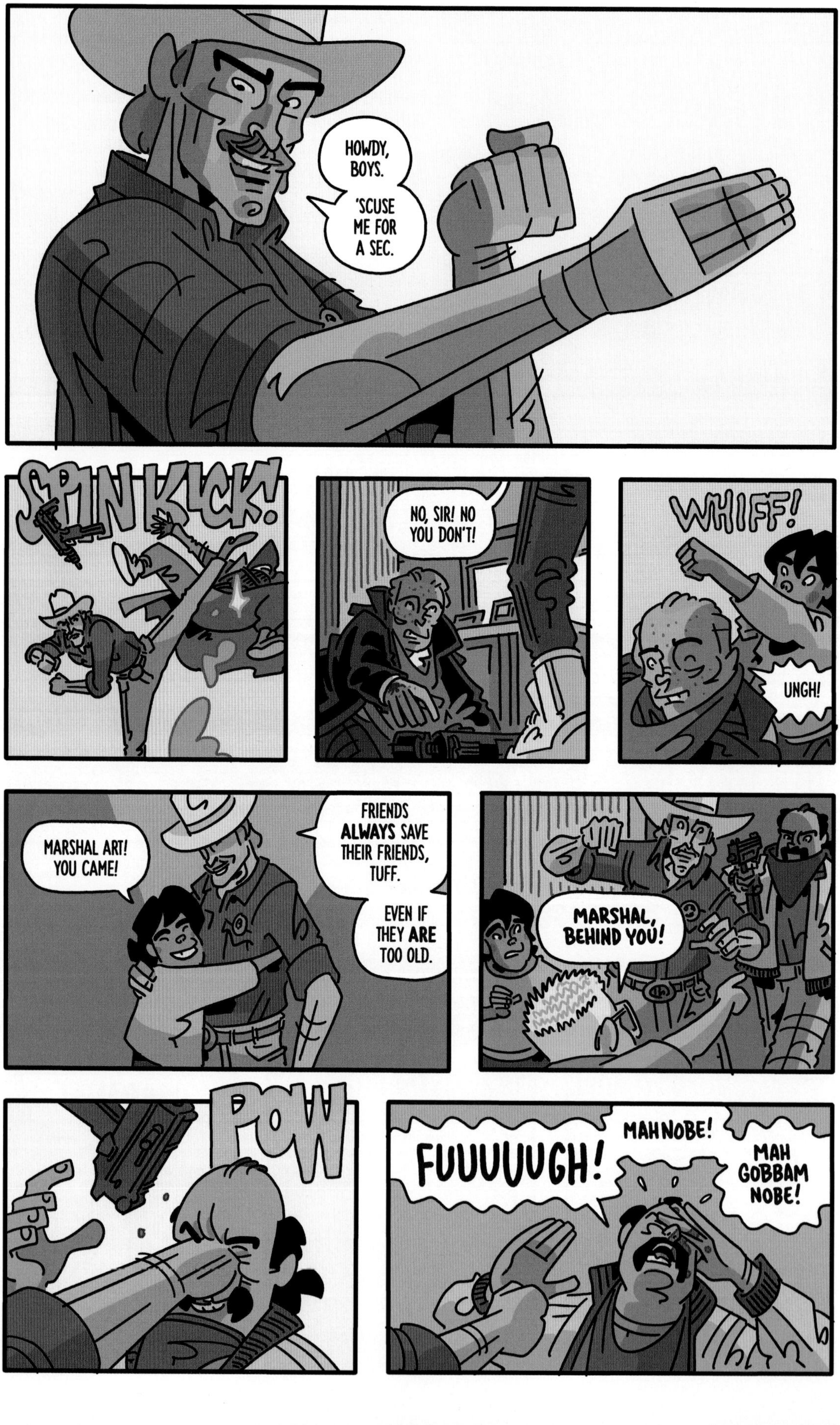
HOWDY, BOYS.
'SCUSE ME FOR A SEC.
SPIN KICK!
NO, SIR! NO YOU DON'T!
WHIFF!
UNGH!
MARSHAL ART! YOU CAME!
FRIENDS **ALWAYS** SAVE THEIR FRIENDS, TUFF.
EVEN IF THEY **ARE** TOO OLD.
MARSHAL, BEHIND YOU!
POW
FUUUUUGH!
MAHNOBE!
MAH GOBBAM NOBE!

DABBIT, TRIGGER!

CUT. **CUT!**

KEATON, FOR GOD'S SAKES, YOU **HAVE** TO STOP FOR-REAL PUNCHING THE STUNT PEOPLE.

THAT'S THEIR **JOB**, DIPSHIT.

YOU KEEP SIDELINING STUNTMEN, THEY'RE STICKING **US** WITH THEIR HOSPITAL BILLS, OUR INSURANCE PREMIUMS ARE SKYROCKETING—

PEOPLE ARE WATCHING *MARSHAL ART* BECAUSE THEY **KNOW** I'M THE MOST DANGEROUS MAN ON THE GOL'DAMNED **PLANET**.

I DIDN'T MASTER SEVEN MARTIAL ARTS AND DO ALL MY OWN STUNTS JUST TO HAVE BULLSHIT-LOOKIN' FIGHTS ON MY SHOW.

ALAZAR, FOLKS HAVE **EXPECTATIONS** FOR A TRIGGER KEATON SHOW. WE HAVE TO GIVE THE PEOPLE WHAT THEY **WANT**.

THAT'S NO REASON TO GIVE THIS CRUDE BUFFOON SO MUCH ROPE. IT'S LIKE THIS INSANE **TWENTY-FIVE YEAR CONTRACT** YOU GAVE HIM.

BEFORE TRIGGER KEATON CAME ALONG, BONAFIDE PICTURES WAS BARELY MORE THAN PUBLIC ACCESS.

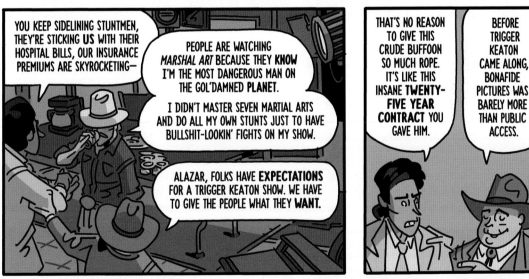

NOW WE'RE A GENUINE PRODUCTION COMPANY. HE'S MONEY IN THE BANK.

H-HEY, MISTER KEATON, I'VE REALLY BEEN PRACTICING. D-DID MY PUNCHES LOOK BETTER THIS—

LEG SWEEP

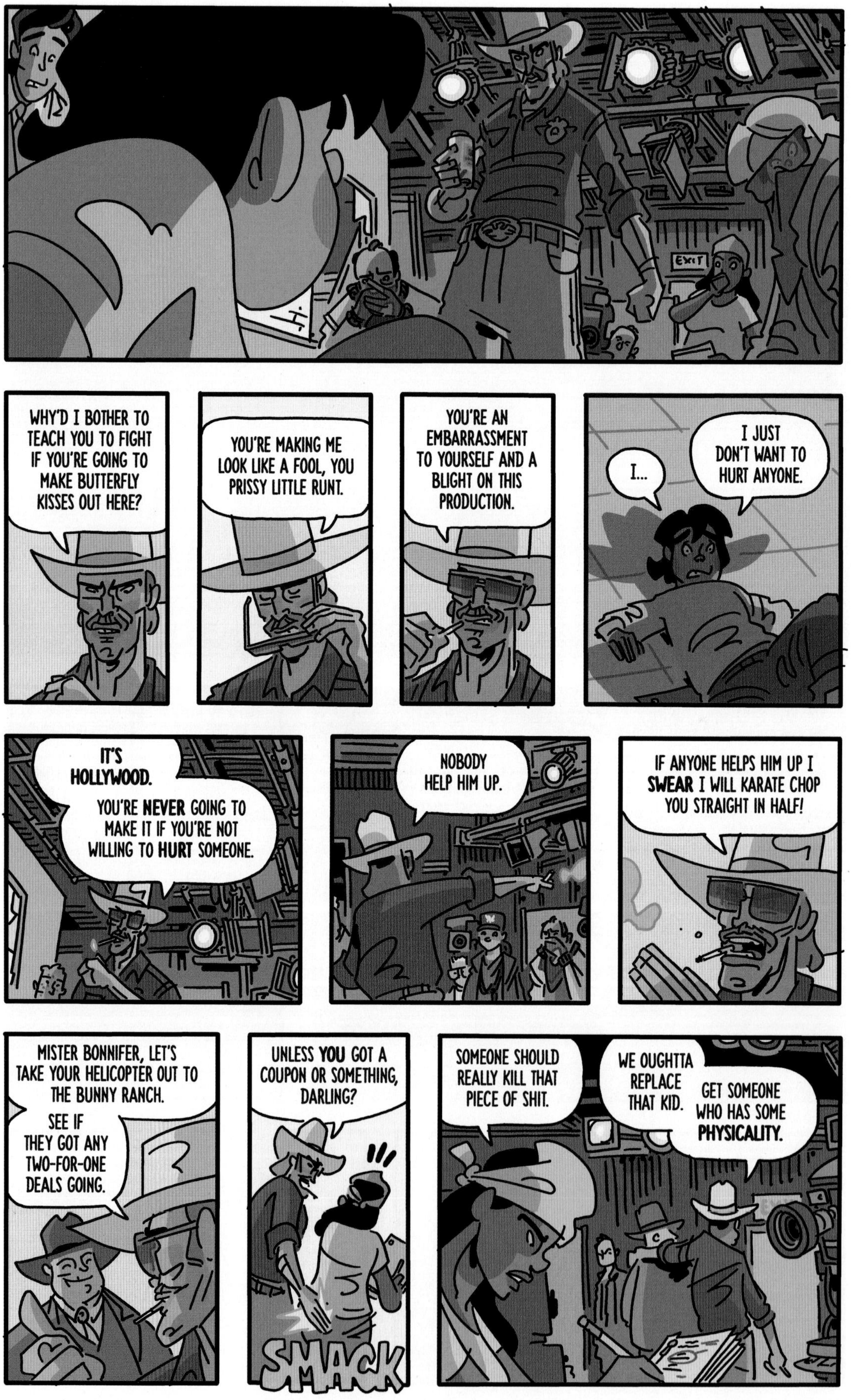

EXIT
WHY'D I BOTHER TO TEACH YOU TO FIGHT IF YOU'RE GOING TO MAKE BUTTERFLY KISSES OUT HERE?
YOU'RE MAKING ME LOOK LIKE A FOOL, YOU PRISSY LITTLE RUNT.
YOU'RE AN EMBARRASSMENT TO YOURSELF AND A BLIGHT ON THIS PRODUCTION.
I...
I JUST DON'T WANT TO HURT ANYONE.
IT'S HOLLYWOOD.
YOU'RE NEVER GOING TO MAKE IT IF YOU'RE NOT WILLING TO HURT SOMEONE.
NOBODY HELP HIM UP.
IF ANYONE HELPS HIM UP I SWEAR I WILL KARATE CHOP YOU STRAIGHT IN HALF!
MISTER BONNIFER, LET'S TAKE YOUR HELICOPTER OUT TO THE BUNNY RANCH.
SEE IF THEY GOT ANY TWO-FOR-ONE DEALS GOING.
UNLESS YOU GOT A COUPON OR SOMETHING, DARLING?
SMACK
SOMEONE SHOULD REALLY KILL THAT PIECE OF SHIT.
WE OUGHTTA REPLACE THAT KID.
GET SOMEONE WHO HAS SOME PHYSICALITY.

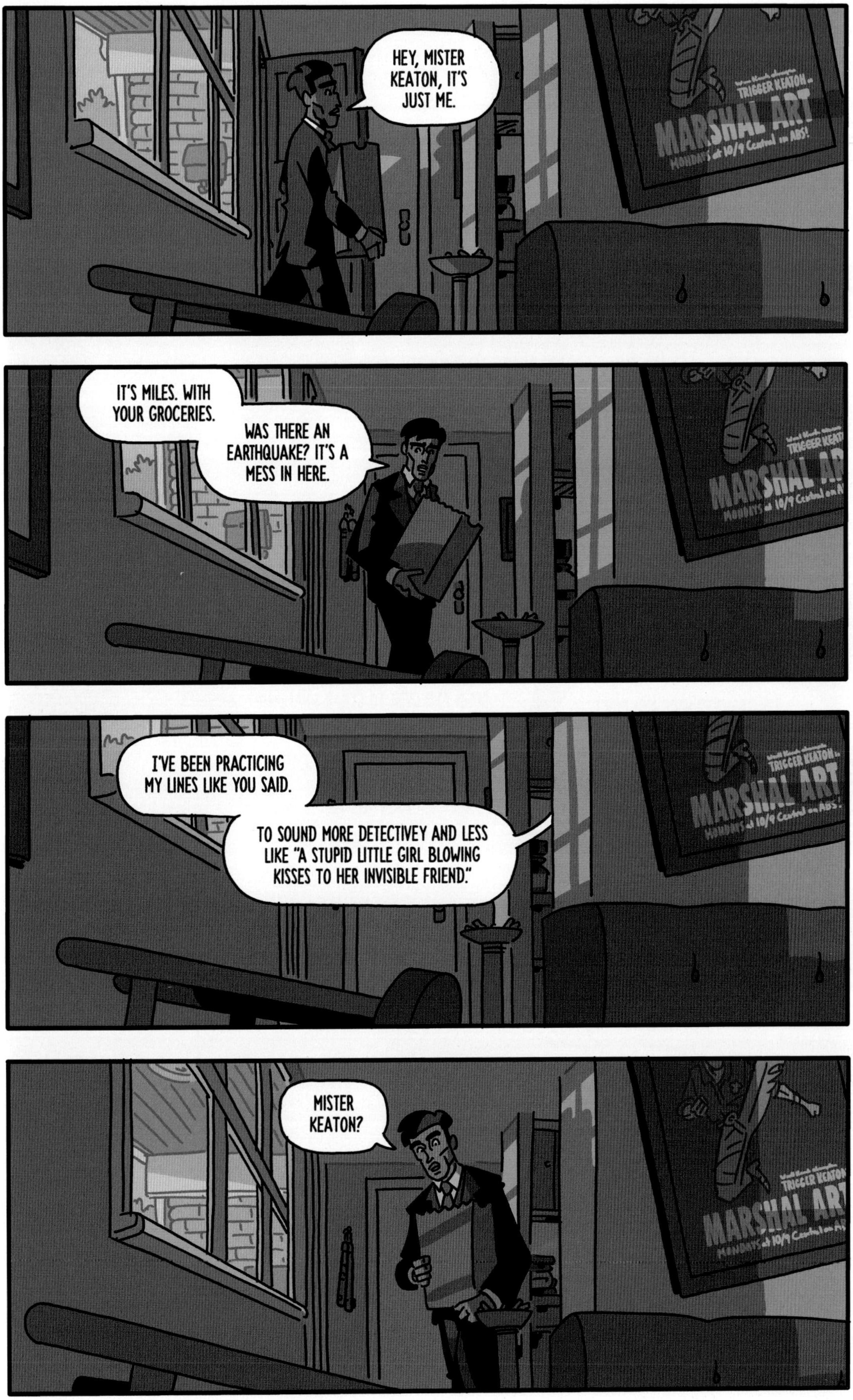
HEY, MISTER KEATON, IT'S JUST ME.
TRIGGER KEATON
MARSHAL ART
MONDAYS at 10/9 Central on ABS!
IT'S MILES. WITH YOUR GROCERIES.
WAS THERE AN EARTHQUAKE? IT'S A MESS IN HERE.
I'VE BEEN PRACTICING MY LINES LIKE YOU SAID.
TO SOUND MORE DETECTIVEY AND LESS LIKE "A STUPID LITTLE GIRL BLOWING KISSES TO HER INVISIBLE FRIEND."
MISTER KEATON?

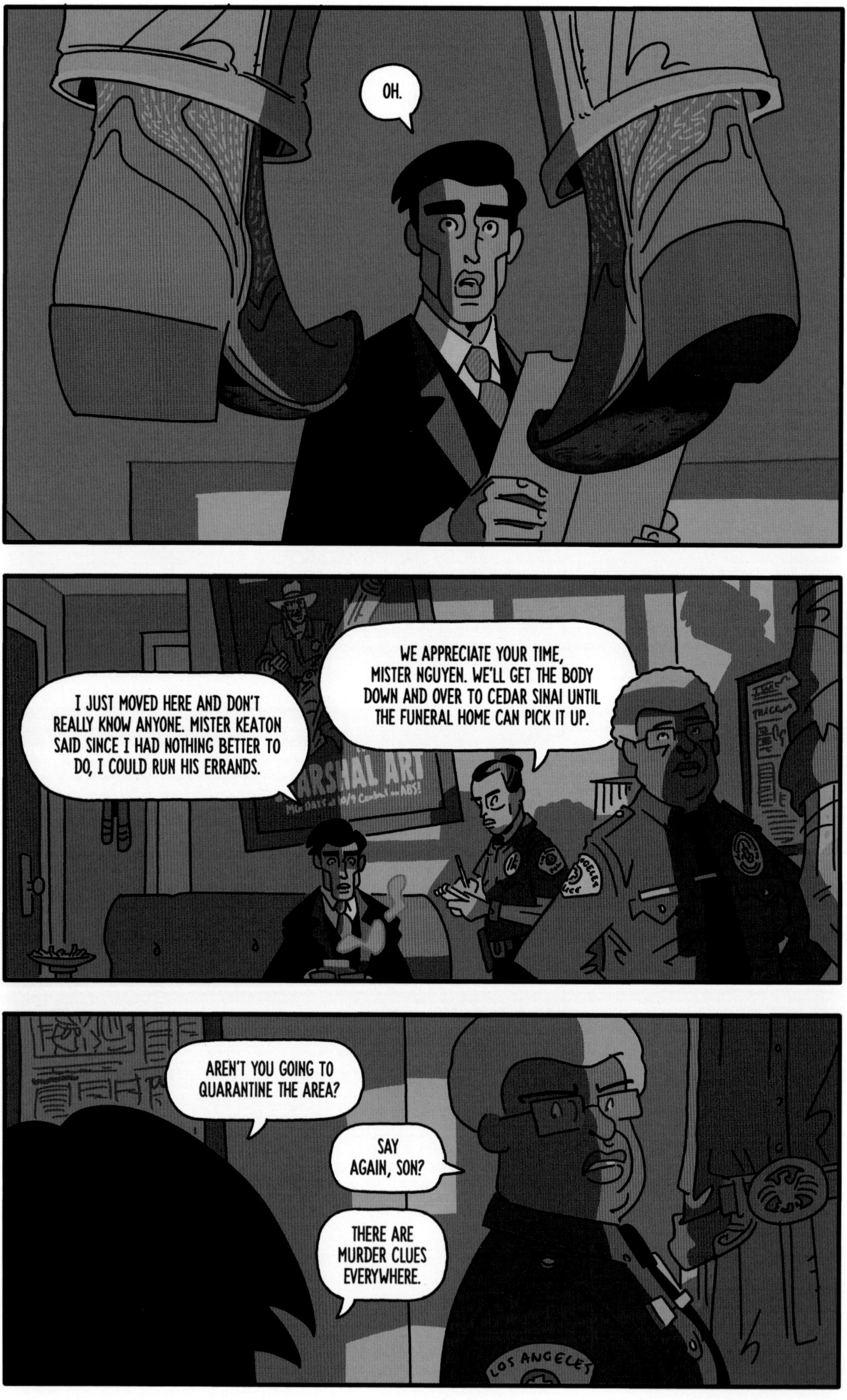
OH.
I JUST MOVED HERE AND DON'T REALLY KNOW ANYONE. MISTER KEATON SAID SINCE I HAD NOTHING BETTER TO DO, I COULD RUN HIS ERRANDS.
MARSHAL ART
WE APPRECIATE YOUR TIME, MISTER NGUYEN. WE'LL GET THE BODY DOWN AND OVER TO CEDAR SINAI UNTIL THE FUNERAL HOME CAN PICK IT UP.
AREN'T YOU GOING TO QUARANTINE THE AREA?
SAY AGAIN, SON?
THERE ARE MURDER CLUES EVERYWHERE.
LOS ANGELES

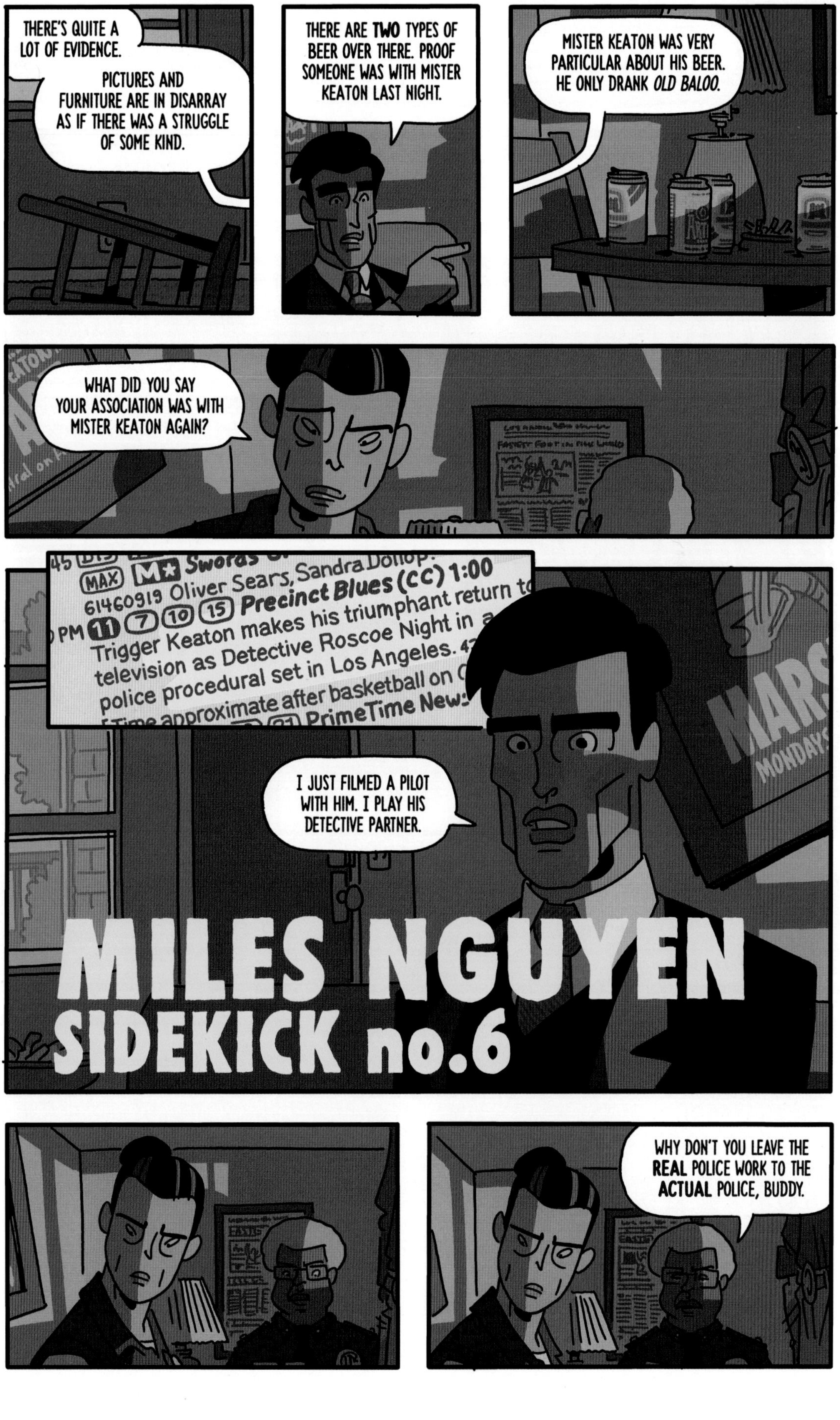
THERE'S QUITE A LOT OF EVIDENCE.
PICTURES AND FURNITURE ARE IN DISARRAY AS IF THERE WAS A STRUGGLE OF SOME KIND.
THERE ARE **TWO** TYPES OF BEER OVER THERE. PROOF SOMEONE WAS WITH MISTER KEATON LAST NIGHT.
MISTER KEATON WAS VERY PARTICULAR ABOUT HIS BEER. HE ONLY DRANK *OLD BALOO.*
WHAT DID YOU SAY YOUR ASSOCIATION WAS WITH MISTER KEATON AGAIN?
MAX
61460919 Oliver Sears, Sandra Dollop.
Precinct Blues (CC) 1:00
PM 11 7 10 15 Trigger Keaton makes his triumphant return t
television as Detective Roscoe Night in a
police procedural set in Los Angeles.
Time approximate after basketball on
PrimeTime New
I JUST FILMED A PILOT WITH HIM. I PLAY HIS DETECTIVE PARTNER.
MILES NGUYEN
SIDEKICK no.6
WHY DON'T YOU LEAVE THE **REAL** POLICE WORK TO THE **ACTUAL** POLICE, BUDDY.

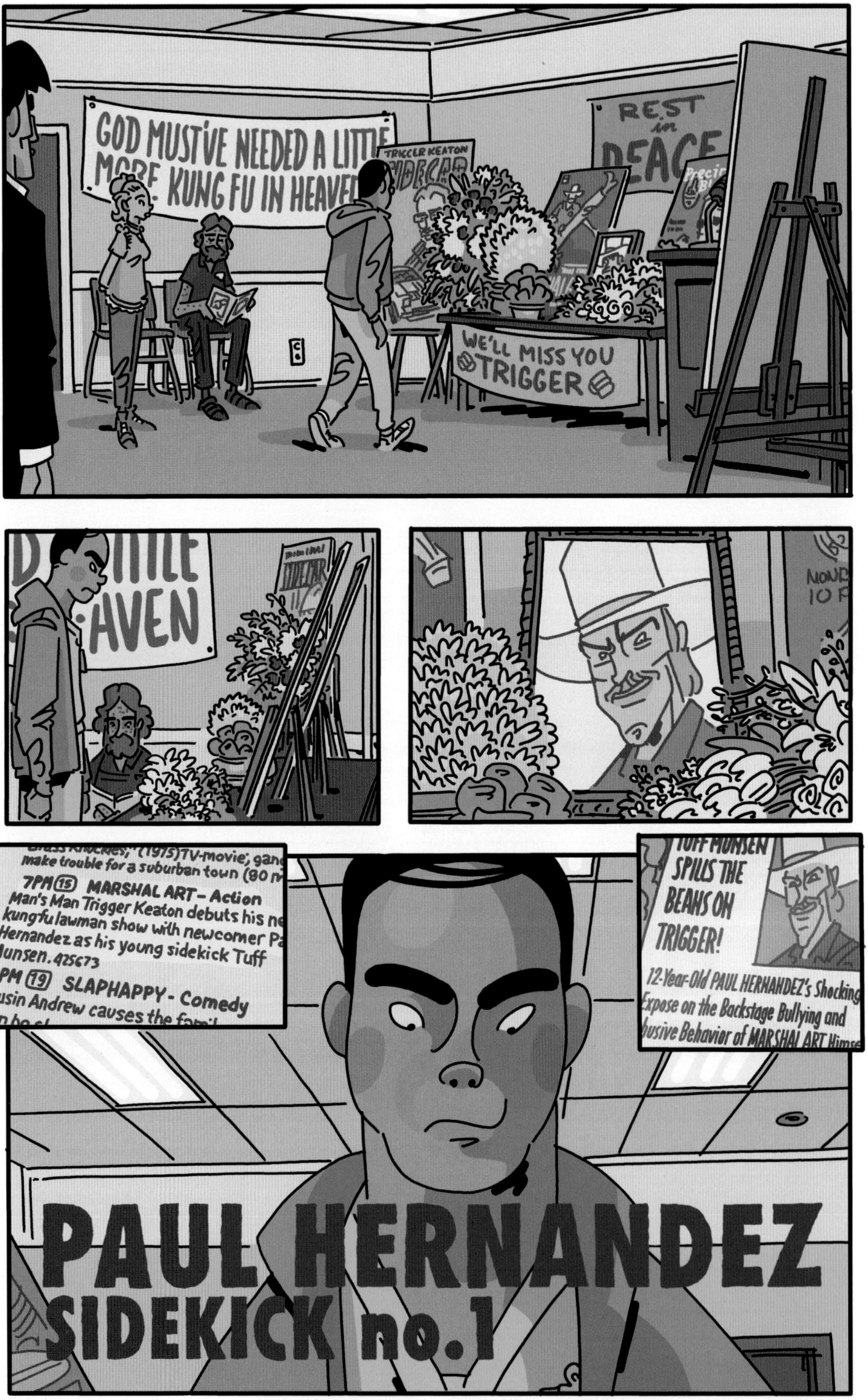
GOD MUST'VE NEEDED A LITTL
MORE KUNG FU IN HEAVE
TRIGGER KEATON
REST in PEACE
WE'LL MISS YOU TRIGGER
AVEN
make trouble for a suburban town (90 m
7PM 15 MARSHAL ART – Action
Man's Man Trigger Keaton debuts his ne
kungfu lawman show with newcomer Pa
Hernandez as his young sidekick Tuff
Munsen. 425673
7PM 19 SLAPHAPPY - Comedy
usin Andrew causes the fam
TUFF MUNSEN SPILLS THE BEANS ON TRIGGER!
12-Year-Old PAUL HERNANDEZ's Shocking Expose on the Backstage Bullying and busive Behavior of MARSHAL ART Himse
PAUL HERNANDEZ
SIDEKICK no.1

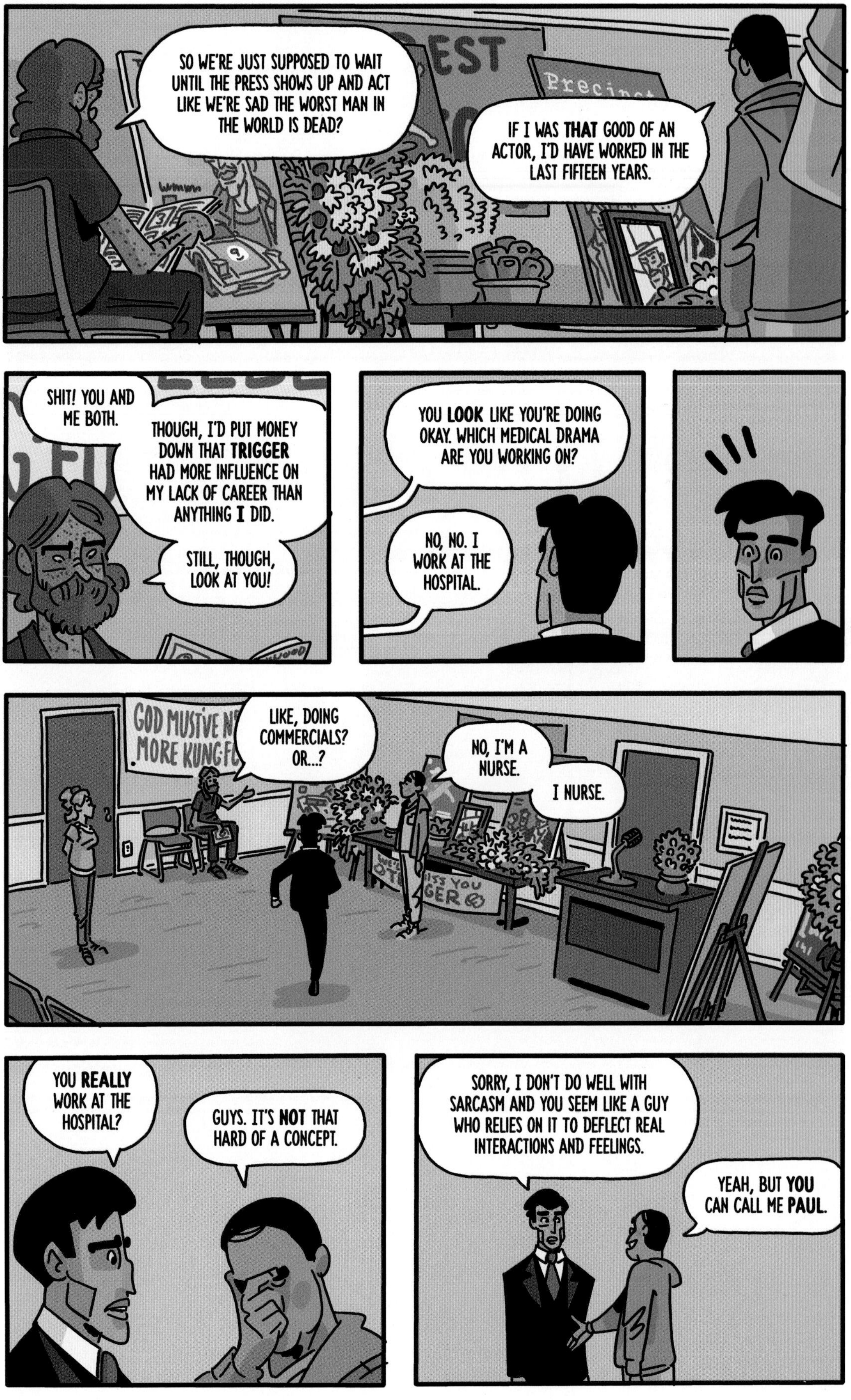
SO WE'RE JUST SUPPOSED TO WAIT UNTIL THE PRESS SHOWS UP AND ACT LIKE WE'RE SAD THE WORST MAN IN THE WORLD IS DEAD?
IF I WAS THAT GOOD OF AN ACTOR, I'D HAVE WORKED IN THE LAST FIFTEEN YEARS.
SHIT! YOU AND ME BOTH.
THOUGH, I'D PUT MONEY DOWN THAT TRIGGER HAD MORE INFLUENCE ON MY LACK OF CAREER THAN ANYTHING I DID.
STILL, THOUGH, LOOK AT YOU!
YOU LOOK LIKE YOU'RE DOING OKAY. WHICH MEDICAL DRAMA ARE YOU WORKING ON?
NO, NO. I WORK AT THE HOSPITAL.
GOD MUST'VE N... MORE KUNG-F...
LIKE, DOING COMMERCIALS? OR...?
NO, I'M A NURSE.
I NURSE.
YOU REALLY WORK AT THE HOSPITAL?
GUYS. IT'S NOT THAT HARD OF A CONCEPT.
SORRY, I DON'T DO WELL WITH SARCASM AND YOU SEEM LIKE A GUY WHO RELIES ON IT TO DEFLECT REAL INTERACTIONS AND FEELINGS.
YEAH, BUT YOU CAN CALL ME PAUL.

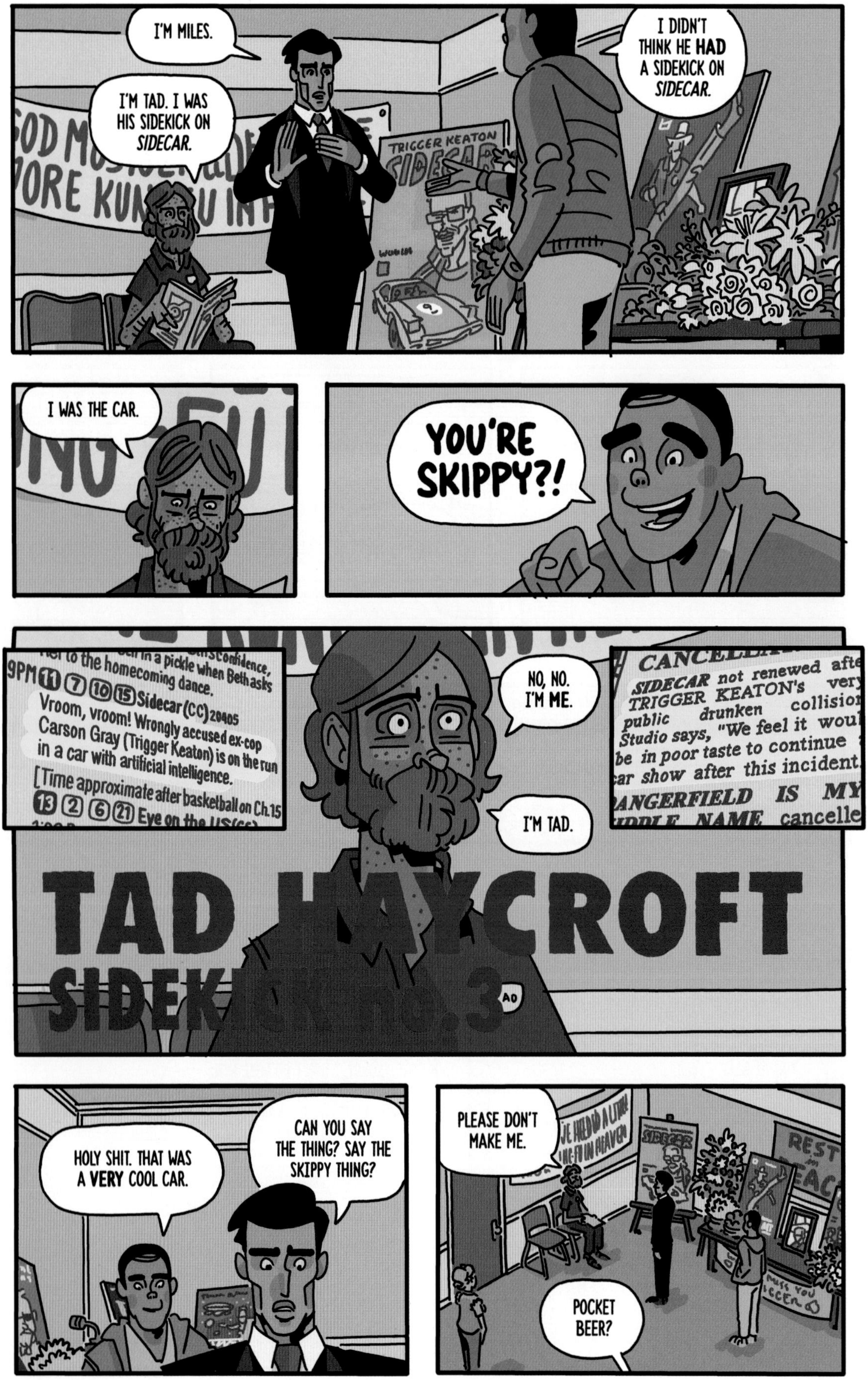
I'M MILES.
I'M TAD. I WAS HIS SIDEKICK ON *SIDECAR.*
I DIDN'T THINK HE **HAD** A SIDEKICK ON *SIDECAR.*
TRIGGER KEATON
I WAS THE CAR.
YOU'RE SKIPPY?!
9PM 11 7 10 15 Sidecar (CC) 20405
Vroom, vroom! Wrongly accused ex-cop Carson Gray (Trigger Keaton) is on the run in a car with artificial intelligence.
[Time approximate after basketball on Ch.15
NO, NO. I'M **ME**.
I'M TAD.
SIDECAR not renewed afte TRIGGER KEATON's very public drunken collisio Studio says, "We feel it woul be in poor taste to continue car show after this incident.
TAD HAYCROFT
SIDEKICK NO. 3
HOLY SHIT. THAT WAS A **VERY** COOL CAR.
CAN YOU SAY THE THING? SAY THE SKIPPY THING?
PLEASE DON'T MAKE ME.
POCKET BEER?

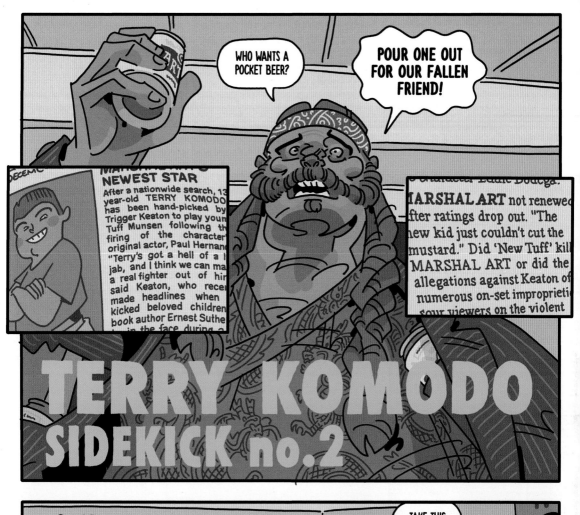

WHO WANTS A POCKET BEER?

POUR ONE OUT FOR OUR FALLEN FRIEND!

NEWEST STAR

After a nationwide search, 13 year-old TERRY KOMODO has been hand-picked by Trigger Keaton to play youn[g] Tuff Munsen following th[e] firing of the character['s] original actor, Paul Hernan[dez] "Terry's got a hell of a [...] jab, and I think we can ma[ke] a real fighter out of hi[m]," said Keaton, who rece[ntly] made headlines when [he] kicked beloved children['s] book author Ernest Suthe[...] [...] in the face during a [...]

MARSHAL ART not renewe[d] [a]fter ratings drop out. "The [n]ew kid just couldn't cut the [m]ustard." Did 'New Tuff' kill[ed] MARSHAL ART or did the allegations against Keaton of numerous on-set improprietie[s] [s]our viewers on the violent

TERRY KOMODO
SIDEKICK no.2

POCKET BEER?

POCKET BEER?

POCKET BEER.

POCKET BEER?

TAKE THIS, DIPSHIT.

POCK—

WHOA. **NOPE!**

I'M NOT DOING THIS IF **THIS** GUY IS HERE.

THIS GUY IS THE JUDAS ISCARIOT OF CHILD ACTORS AND **I** REFUSE TO TOLERATE HIS PRESENCE.

YOU KNOW WHAT? IT WAS A MISTAKE FOR ME TO COME HERE. I SHOULD GET BACK TO THE HOSPITAL ANYWAY.

OH, **I** CAN MAKE SURE YOU END UP IN THE HOSPITAL, ALRIGHT!

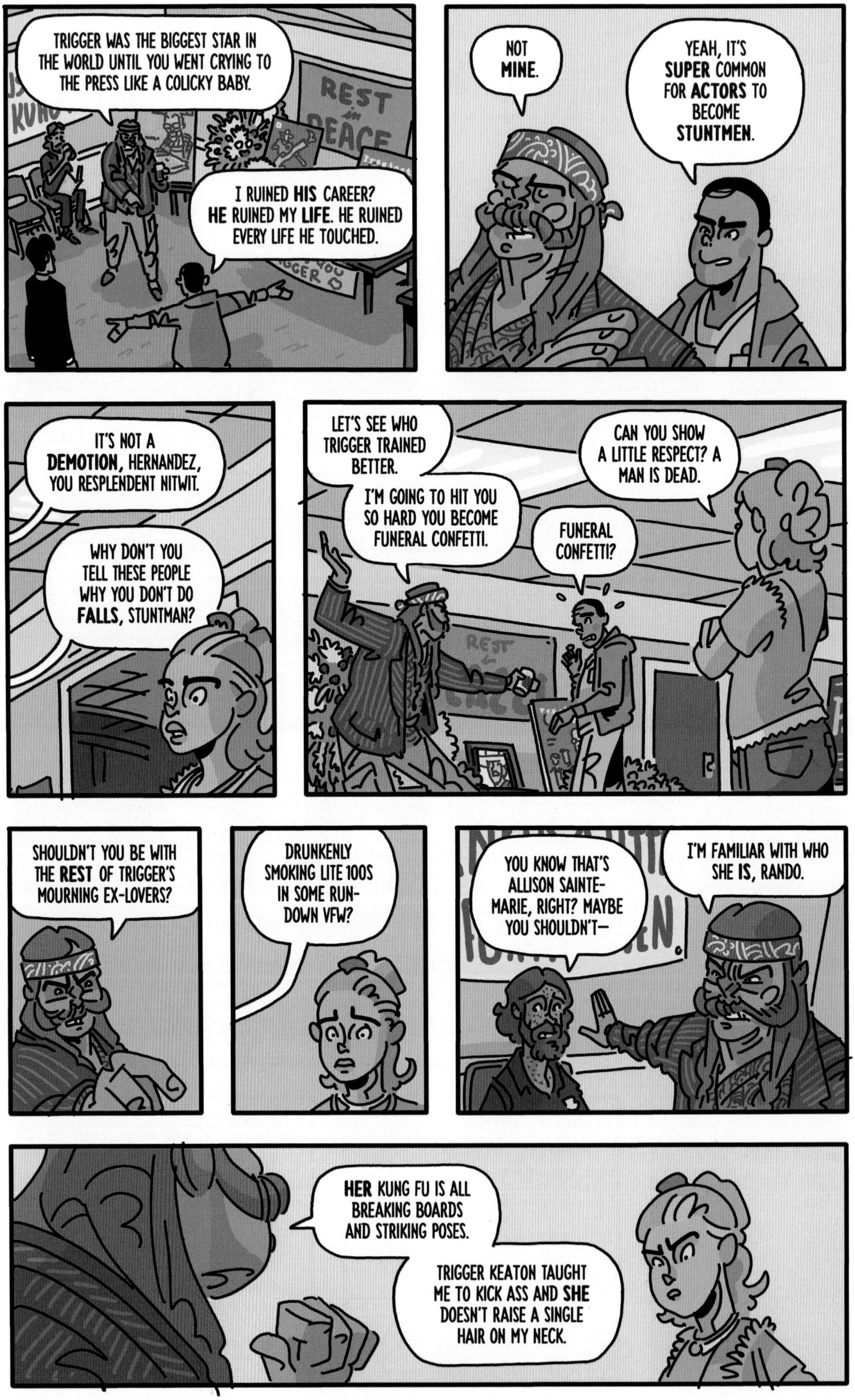
TRIGGER WAS THE BIGGEST STAR IN THE WORLD UNTIL YOU WENT CRYING TO THE PRESS LIKE A COLICKY BABY.
REST in PEACE
I RUINED **HIS** CAREER? **HE** RUINED MY **LIFE**. HE RUINED EVERY LIFE HE TOUCHED.
NOT **MINE**.
YEAH, IT'S **SUPER** COMMON FOR **ACTORS** TO BECOME **STUNTMEN**.
IT'S NOT A **DEMOTION,** HERNANDEZ, YOU RESPLENDENT NITWIT.
WHY DON'T YOU TELL THESE PEOPLE WHY YOU DON'T DO **FALLS**, STUNTMAN?
LET'S SEE WHO TRIGGER TRAINED BETTER.
I'M GOING TO HIT YOU SO HARD YOU BECOME FUNERAL CONFETTI.
FUNERAL CONFETTI?
CAN YOU SHOW A LITTLE RESPECT? A MAN IS DEAD.
SHOULDN'T YOU BE WITH THE **REST** OF TRIGGER'S MOURNING EX-LOVERS?
DRUNKENLY SMOKING LITE 100S IN SOME RUN-DOWN VFW?
YOU KNOW THAT'S ALLISON SAINTE-MARIE, RIGHT? MAYBE YOU SHOULDN'T—
I'M FAMILIAR WITH WHO SHE **IS**, RANDO.
HER KUNG FU IS ALL BREAKING BOARDS AND STRIKING POSES.
TRIGGER KEATON TAUGHT ME TO KICK ASS AND **SHE** DOESN'T RAISE A SINGLE HAIR ON MY NECK.

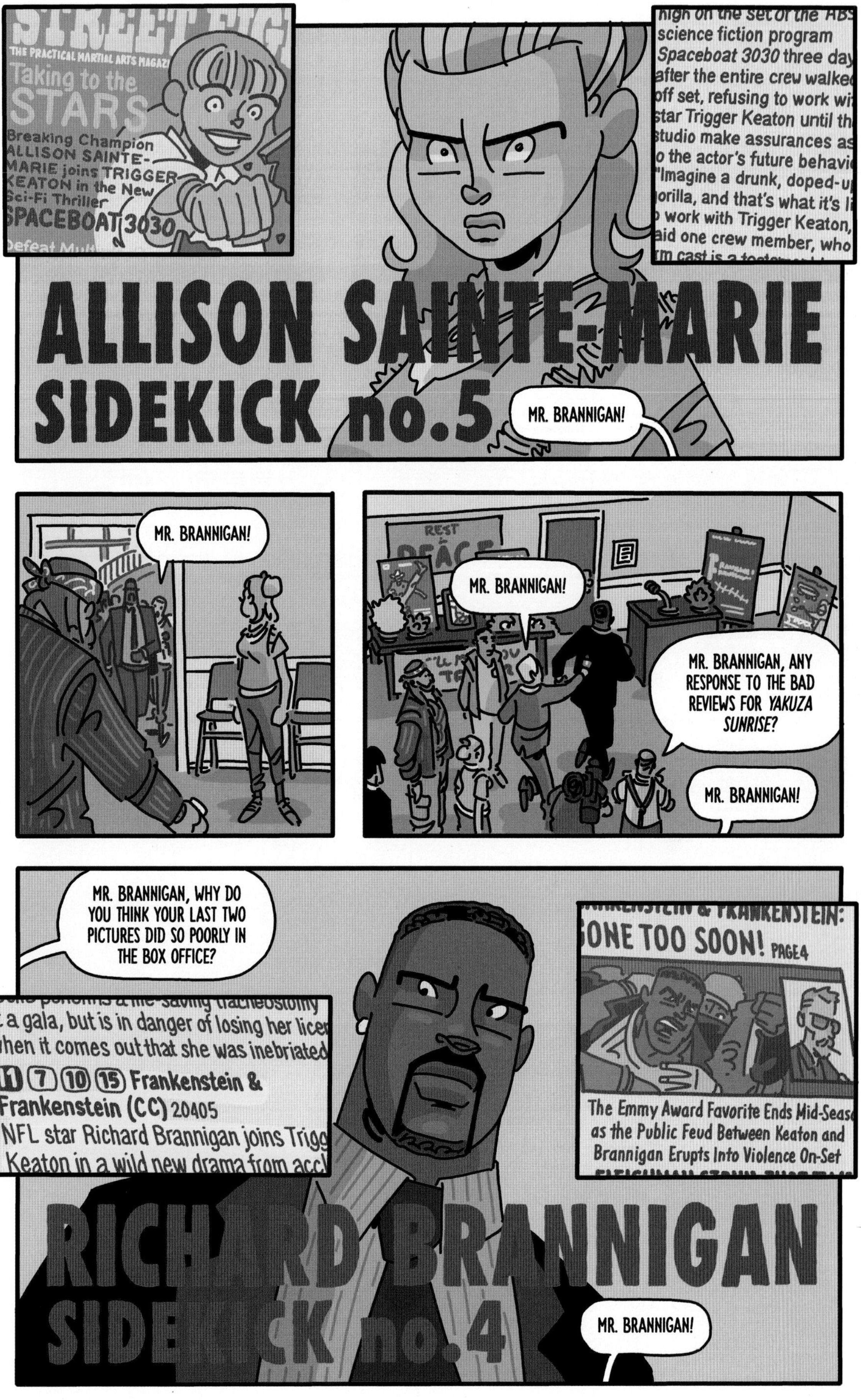

THE PRACTICAL MARTIAL ARTS MAGAZI
Taking to the STARS
Breaking Champion ALLISON SAINTE-MARIE joins TRIGGER KEATON in the New Sci-Fi Thriller SPACEBOAT 3030
science fiction program Spaceboat 3030 three day after the entire crew walked off set, refusing to work wi star Trigger Keaton until th studio make assurances as o the actor's future behavi "Imagine a drunk, doped-u gorilla, and that's what it's l o work with Trigger Keaton, aid one crew member, who
ALLISON SAINTE-MARIE
SIDEKICK no.5
MR. BRANNIGAN!
MR. BRANNIGAN!
REST in PEACE
MR. BRANNIGAN!
MR. BRANNIGAN, ANY RESPONSE TO THE BAD REVIEWS FOR *YAKUZA SUNRISE*?
MR. BRANNIGAN!
MR. BRANNIGAN, WHY DO YOU THINK YOUR LAST TWO PICTURES DID SO POORLY IN THE BOX OFFICE?
t a gala, but is in danger of losing her lice when it comes out that she was inebriated
11 7 10 15 Frankenstein & Frankenstein (CC) 20405
NFL star Richard Brannigan joins Trigg Keaton in a wild new drama from acc
GONE TOO SOON! PAGE4
The Emmy Award Favorite Ends Mid-Seas as the Public Feud Between Keaton and Brannigan Erupts Into Violence On-Set
RICHARD BRANNIGAN
SIDEKICK no.4
MR. BRANNIGAN!

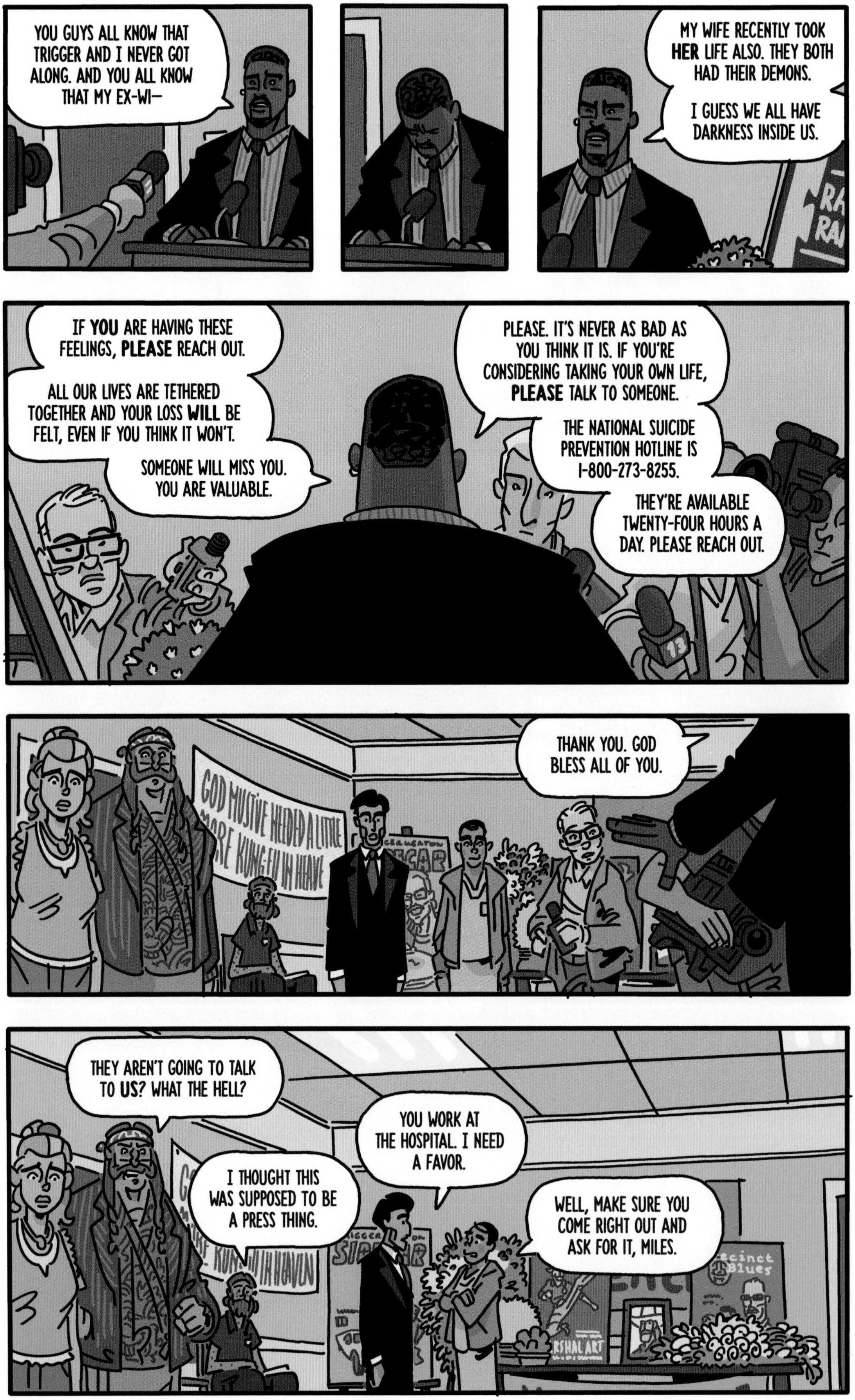
YOU GUYS ALL KNOW THAT TRIGGER AND I NEVER GOT ALONG. AND YOU ALL KNOW THAT MY EX-WI—
MY WIFE RECENTLY TOOK **HER** LIFE ALSO. THEY BOTH HAD THEIR DEMONS.
I GUESS WE ALL HAVE DARKNESS INSIDE US.
IF **YOU** ARE HAVING THESE FEELINGS, **PLEASE** REACH OUT.
ALL OUR LIVES ARE TETHERED TOGETHER AND YOUR LOSS **WILL** BE FELT, EVEN IF YOU THINK IT WON'T.
SOMEONE WILL MISS YOU. YOU ARE VALUABLE.
PLEASE. IT'S NEVER AS BAD AS YOU THINK IT IS. IF YOU'RE CONSIDERING TAKING YOUR OWN LIFE, **PLEASE** TALK TO SOMEONE.
THE NATIONAL SUICIDE PREVENTION HOTLINE IS 1-800-273-8255.
THEY'RE AVAILABLE TWENTY-FOUR HOURS A DAY. PLEASE REACH OUT.
THANK YOU. GOD BLESS ALL OF YOU.
THEY AREN'T GOING TO TALK TO **US**? WHAT THE HELL?
I THOUGHT THIS WAS SUPPOSED TO BE A PRESS THING.
YOU WORK AT THE HOSPITAL. I NEED A FAVOR.
WELL, MAKE SURE YOU COME RIGHT OUT AND ASK FOR IT, MILES.

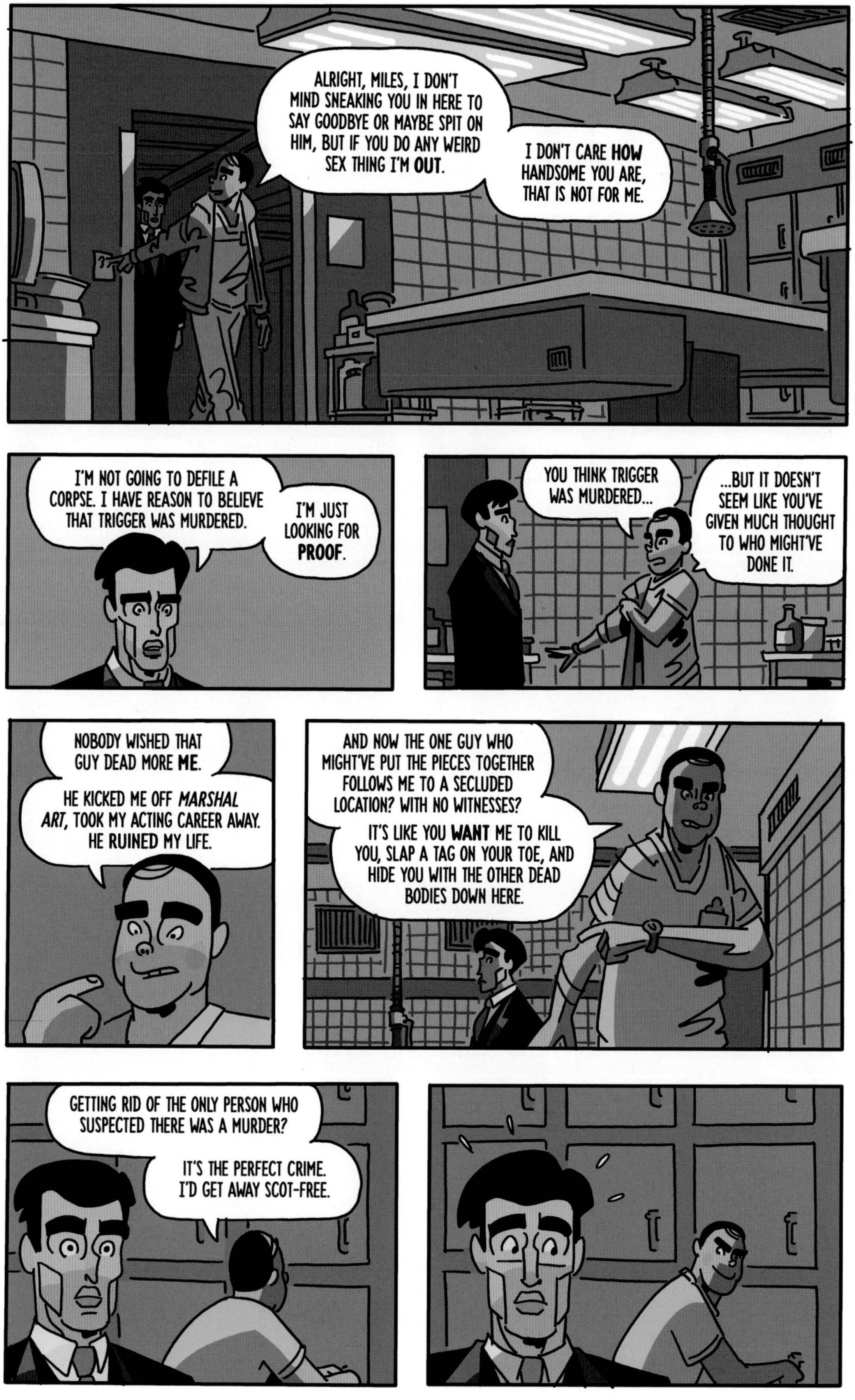
ALRIGHT, MILES, I DON'T MIND SNEAKING YOU IN HERE TO SAY GOODBYE OR MAYBE SPIT ON HIM, BUT IF YOU DO ANY WEIRD SEX THING I'M **OUT**.
I DON'T CARE **HOW** HANDSOME YOU ARE, THAT IS NOT FOR ME.
I'M NOT GOING TO DEFILE A CORPSE. I HAVE REASON TO BELIEVE THAT TRIGGER WAS MURDERED.
I'M JUST LOOKING FOR **PROOF**.
YOU THINK TRIGGER WAS MURDERED...
...BUT IT DOESN'T SEEM LIKE YOU'VE GIVEN MUCH THOUGHT TO WHO MIGHT'VE DONE IT.
NOBODY WISHED THAT GUY DEAD MORE **ME**.
HE KICKED ME OFF *MARSHAL ART*, TOOK MY ACTING CAREER AWAY. HE **RUINED** MY LIFE.
AND NOW THE ONE GUY WHO MIGHT'VE PUT THE PIECES TOGETHER FOLLOWS ME TO A SECLUDED LOCATION? WITH NO WITNESSES?
IT'S LIKE YOU **WANT** ME TO KILL YOU, SLAP A TAG ON YOUR TOE, AND HIDE YOU WITH THE OTHER DEAD BODIES DOWN HERE.
GETTING RID OF THE ONLY PERSON WHO SUSPECTED THERE WAS A MURDER?
IT'S THE PERFECT CRIME. I'D GET AWAY SCOT-FREE.

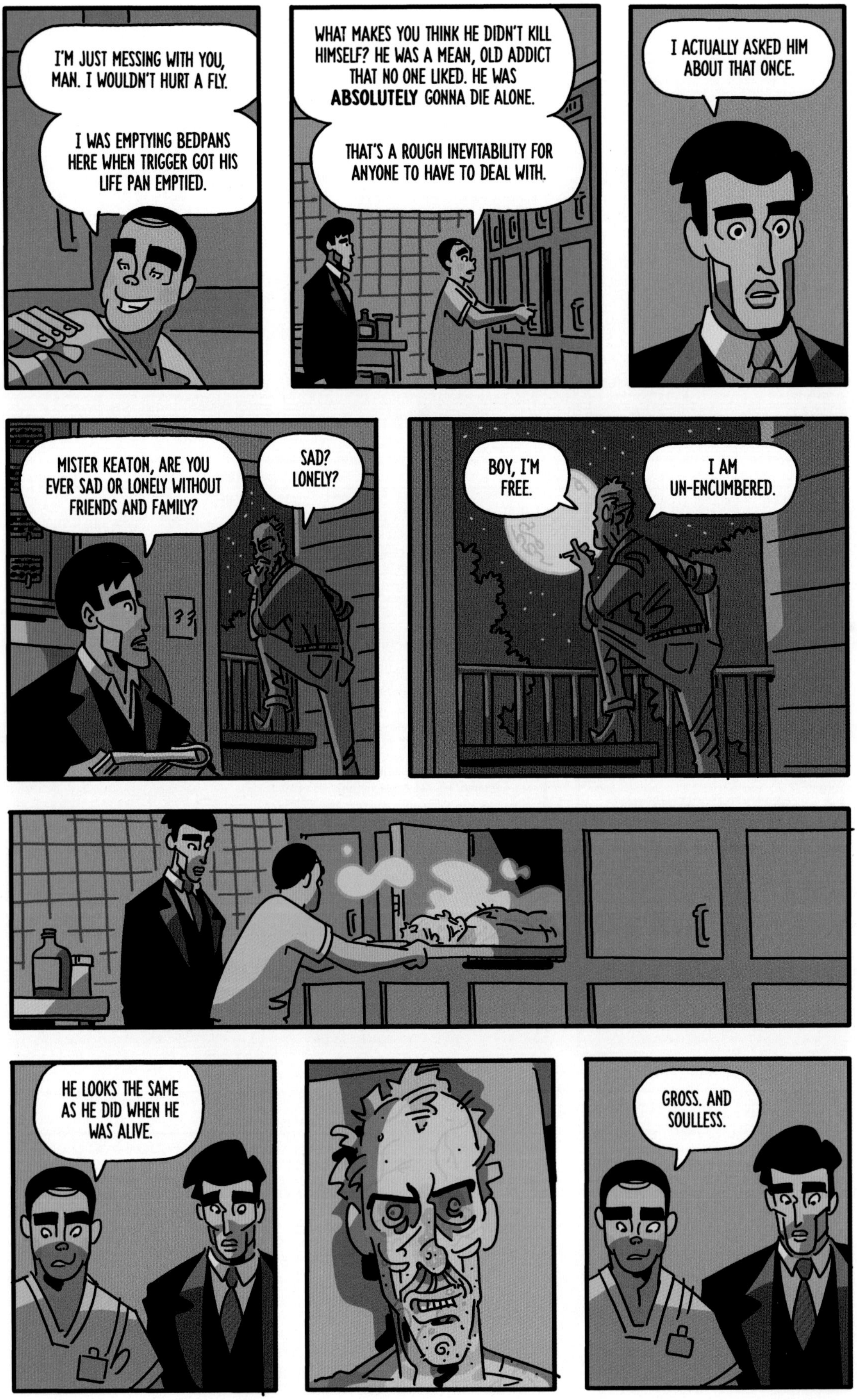
I'M JUST MESSING WITH YOU, MAN. I WOULDN'T HURT A FLY.
I WAS EMPTYING BEDPANS HERE WHEN TRIGGER GOT HIS LIFE PAN EMPTIED.
WHAT MAKES YOU THINK HE DIDN'T KILL HIMSELF? HE WAS A MEAN, OLD ADDICT THAT NO ONE LIKED. HE WAS **ABSOLUTELY** GONNA DIE ALONE.
THAT'S A ROUGH INEVITABILITY FOR ANYONE TO HAVE TO DEAL WITH.
I ACTUALLY ASKED HIM ABOUT THAT ONCE.
MISTER KEATON, ARE YOU EVER SAD OR LONELY WITHOUT FRIENDS AND FAMILY?
SAD? LONELY?
BOY, I'M FREE.
I AM UN-ENCUMBERED.
HE LOOKS THE SAME AS HE DID WHEN HE WAS ALIVE.
GROSS. AND SOULLESS.

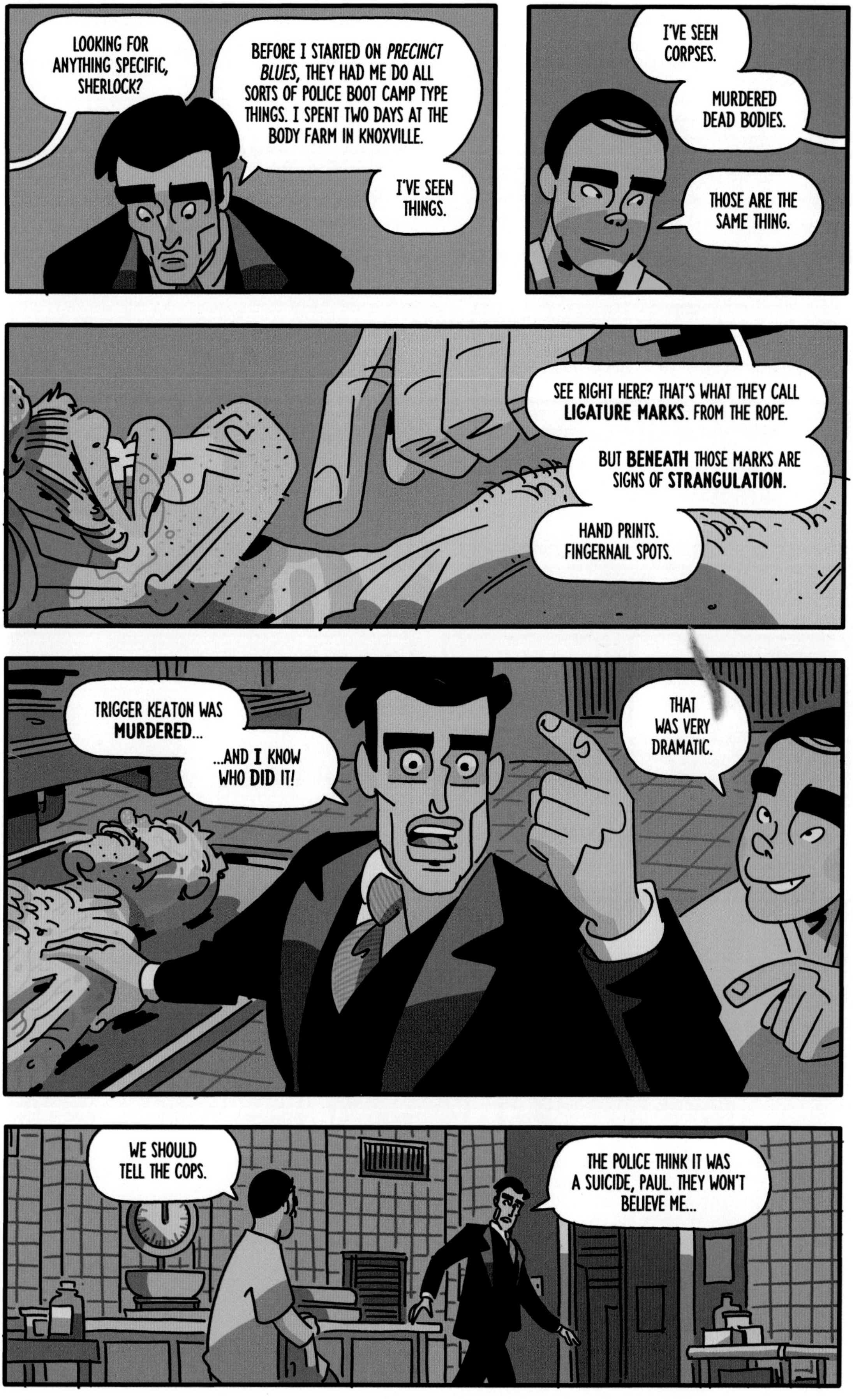
LOOKING FOR ANYTHING SPECIFIC, SHERLOCK?
BEFORE I STARTED ON *PRECINCT BLUES*, THEY HAD ME DO ALL SORTS OF POLICE BOOT CAMP TYPE THINGS. I SPENT TWO DAYS AT THE BODY FARM IN KNOXVILLE.
I'VE SEEN THINGS.
I'VE SEEN CORPSES.
MURDERED DEAD BODIES.
THOSE ARE THE SAME THING.
SEE RIGHT HERE? THAT'S WHAT THEY CALL **LIGATURE MARKS**. FROM THE ROPE.
BUT **BENEATH** THOSE MARKS ARE SIGNS OF **STRANGULATION**.
HAND PRINTS. FINGERNAIL SPOTS.
TRIGGER KEATON WAS **MURDERED**...
...AND **I** KNOW WHO **DID** IT!
THAT WAS VERY DRAMATIC.
WE SHOULD TELL THE COPS.
THE POLICE THINK IT WAS A SUICIDE, PAUL. THEY WON'T BELIEVE ME...

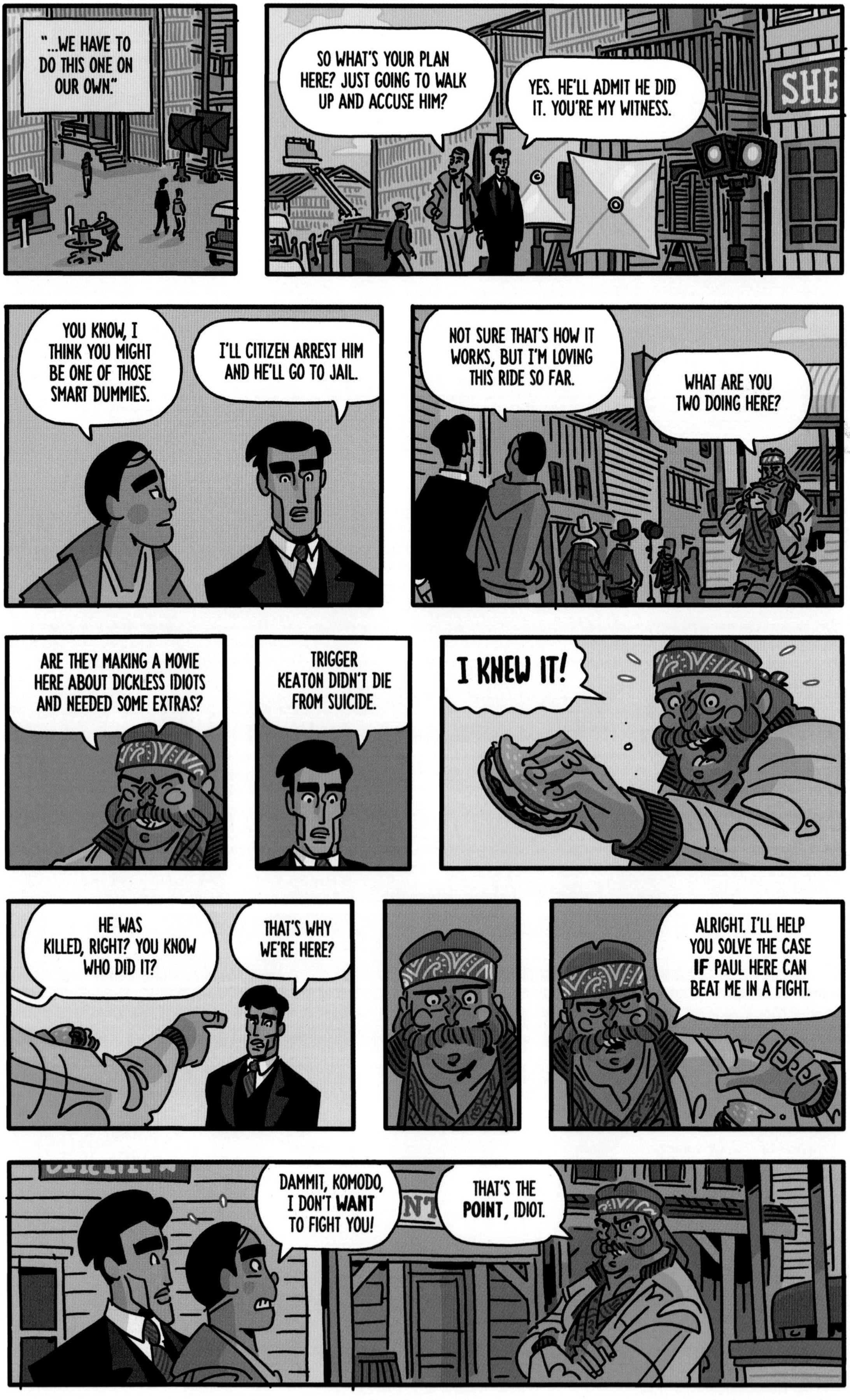

"...WE HAVE TO DO THIS ONE ON OUR OWN."
SO WHAT'S YOUR PLAN HERE? JUST GOING TO WALK UP AND ACCUSE HIM?
YES. HE'LL ADMIT HE DID IT. YOU'RE MY WITNESS.
SHE
YOU KNOW, I THINK YOU MIGHT BE ONE OF THOSE SMART DUMMIES.
I'LL CITIZEN ARREST HIM AND HE'LL GO TO JAIL.
NOT SURE THAT'S HOW IT WORKS, BUT I'M LOVING THIS RIDE SO FAR.
WHAT ARE YOU TWO DOING HERE?
ARE THEY MAKING A MOVIE HERE ABOUT DICKLESS IDIOTS AND NEEDED SOME EXTRAS?
TRIGGER KEATON DIDN'T DIE FROM SUICIDE.
I KNEW IT!
HE WAS KILLED, RIGHT? YOU KNOW WHO DID IT?
THAT'S WHY WE'RE HERE?
ALRIGHT. I'LL HELP YOU SOLVE THE CASE **IF** PAUL HERE CAN BEAT ME IN A FIGHT.
DAMMIT, KOMODO, I DON'T **WANT** TO FIGHT YOU!
THAT'S THE **POINT**, IDIOT.

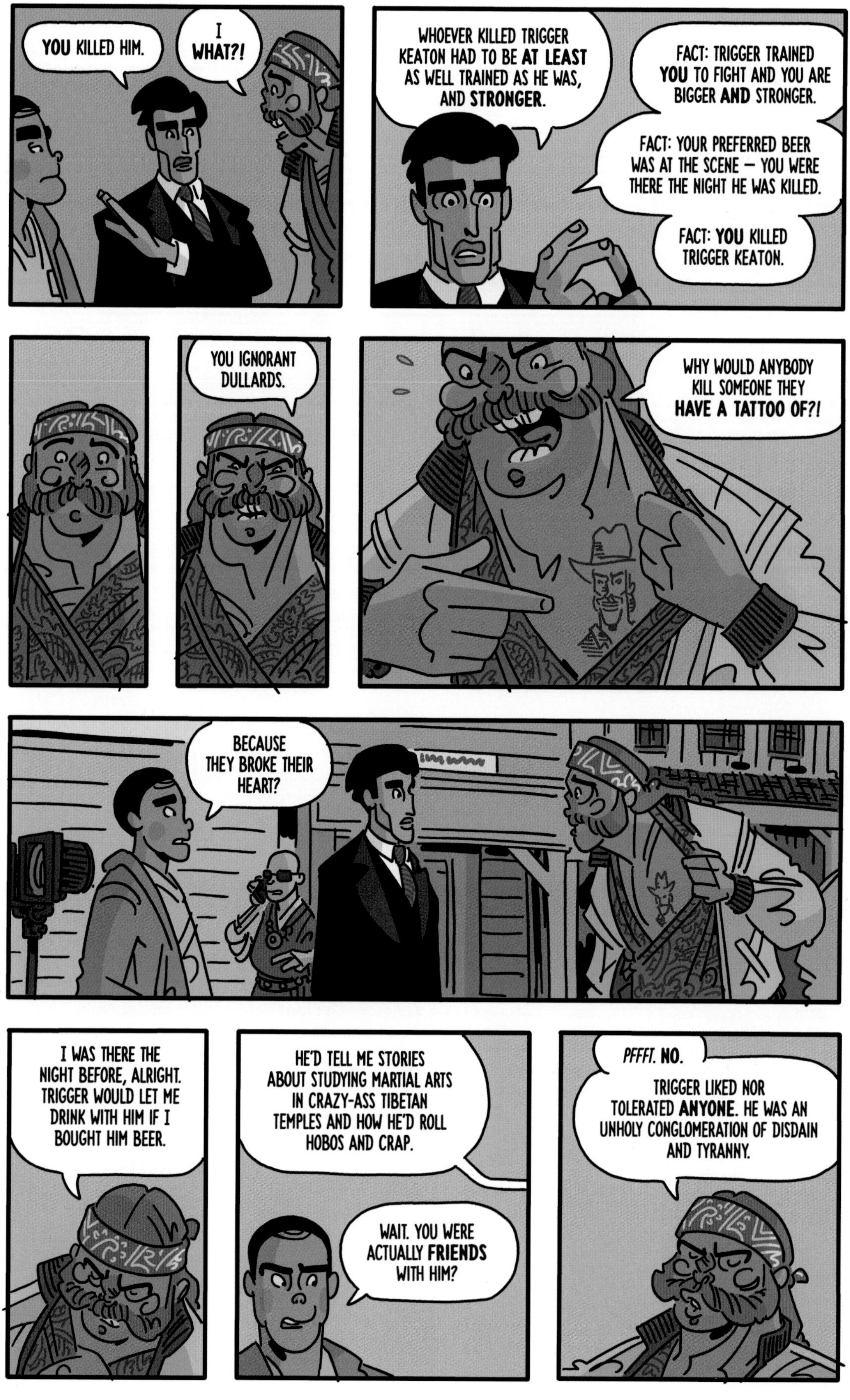
YOU KILLED HIM.
I WHAT?!
WHOEVER KILLED TRIGGER KEATON HAD TO BE AT LEAST AS WELL TRAINED AS HE WAS, AND STRONGER.
FACT: TRIGGER TRAINED YOU TO FIGHT AND YOU ARE BIGGER AND STRONGER.
FACT: YOUR PREFERRED BEER WAS AT THE SCENE — YOU WERE THERE THE NIGHT HE WAS KILLED.
FACT: YOU KILLED TRIGGER KEATON.
YOU IGNORANT DULLARDS.
WHY WOULD ANYBODY KILL SOMEONE THEY HAVE A TATTOO OF?!
BECAUSE THEY BROKE THEIR HEART?
I WAS THERE THE NIGHT BEFORE, ALRIGHT. TRIGGER WOULD LET ME DRINK WITH HIM IF I BOUGHT HIM BEER.
HE'D TELL ME STORIES ABOUT STUDYING MARTIAL ARTS IN CRAZY-ASS TIBETAN TEMPLES AND HOW HE'D ROLL HOBOS AND CRAP.
WAIT. YOU WERE ACTUALLY FRIENDS WITH HIM?
PFFFT. NO.
TRIGGER LIKED NOR TOLERATED ANYONE. HE WAS AN UNHOLY CONGLOMERATION OF DISDAIN AND TYRANNY.

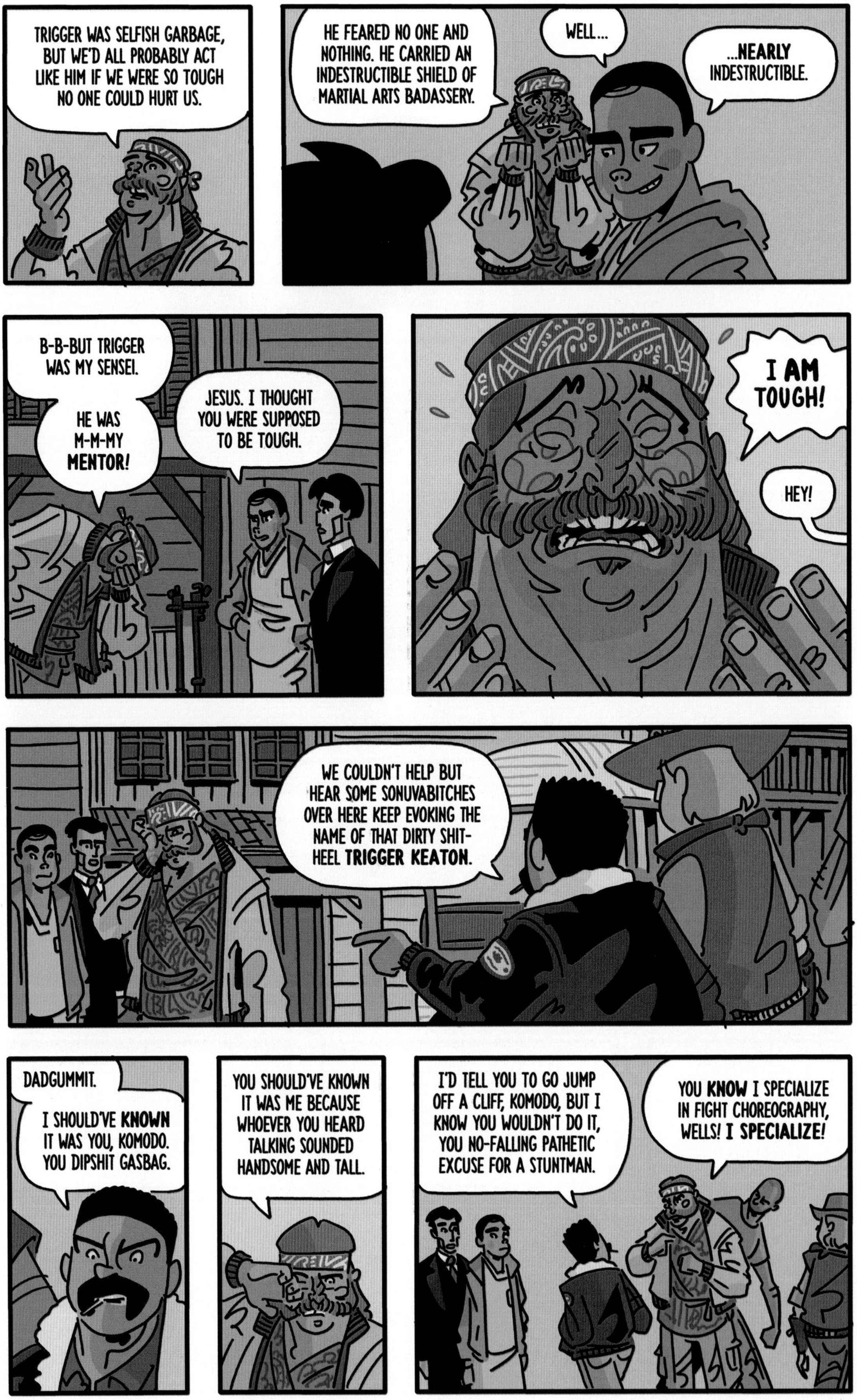
TRIGGER WAS SELFISH GARBAGE, BUT WE'D ALL PROBABLY ACT LIKE HIM IF WE WERE SO TOUGH NO ONE COULD HURT US.
HE FEARED NO ONE AND NOTHING. HE CARRIED AN INDESTRUCTIBLE SHIELD OF MARTIAL ARTS BADASSERY.
WELL...
...**NEARLY** INDESTRUCTIBLE.
B-B-BUT TRIGGER WAS MY SENSEI.
HE WAS M-M-MY **MENTOR!**
JESUS. I THOUGHT YOU WERE SUPPOSED TO BE TOUGH.
I AM TOUGH!
HEY!
WE COULDN'T HELP BUT HEAR SOME SONUVABITCHES OVER HERE KEEP EVOKING THE NAME OF THAT DIRTY SHIT-HEEL **TRIGGER KEATON.**
DADGUMMIT.
I SHOULD'VE **KNOWN** IT WAS YOU, KOMODO. YOU DIPSHIT GASBAG.
YOU SHOULD'VE KNOWN IT WAS ME BECAUSE WHOEVER YOU HEARD TALKING SOUNDED HANDSOME AND TALL.
I'D TELL YOU TO GO JUMP OFF A CLIFF, KOMODO, BUT I KNOW YOU WOULDN'T DO IT, YOU NO-FALLING PATHETIC EXCUSE FOR A STUNTMAN.
YOU **KNOW** I SPECIALIZE IN FIGHT CHOREOGRAPHY, WELLS! I **SPECIALIZE!**

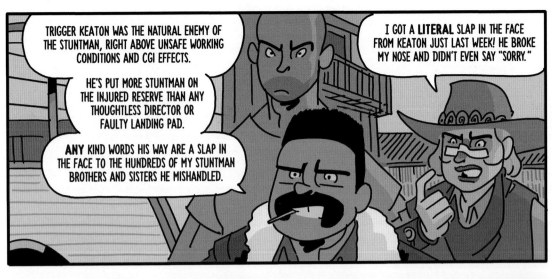

TRIGGER KEATON WAS THE NATURAL ENEMY OF THE STUNTMAN, RIGHT ABOVE UNSAFE WORKING CONDITIONS AND CGI EFFECTS.

HE'S PUT MORE STUNTMAN ON THE INJURED RESERVE THAN ANY THOUGHTLESS DIRECTOR OR FAULTY LANDING PAD.

ANY KIND WORDS HIS WAY ARE A SLAP IN THE FACE TO THE HUNDREDS OF MY STUNTMAN BROTHERS AND SISTERS HE MISHANDLED.

I GOT A **LITERAL** SLAP IN THE FACE FROM KEATON JUST LAST WEEK! HE BROKE MY NOSE AND DIDN'T EVEN SAY "SORRY."

I WILL **NOT** STAND HERE AND LISTEN TO TRIGGER BEING DEFAMED THIS WAY.

TRIGGER KEATON WAS AN AMERICAN ICON. HE DID **WHAT** HE WANTED, **WHEN** HE WANTED.

HELL, HE **WAS** AMERICA!

HE WAS AN ASSHOLE. YOU SAYING AMERICA IS AN **ASSHOLE**, KOMODO?

WE'RE **GLAD** HE'S DEAD!

ANYBODY SAYS ONE MORE THING ABOUT TRIGGER AND I'M GOING TO GO APE SHIT CRAZY ON ALL OF YOU.

I'M SERIOUS. I WON'T BE ABLE TO CONTROL MYSELF.

TRIGGER KEATON WAS A NO-GOOD—

KRAK!

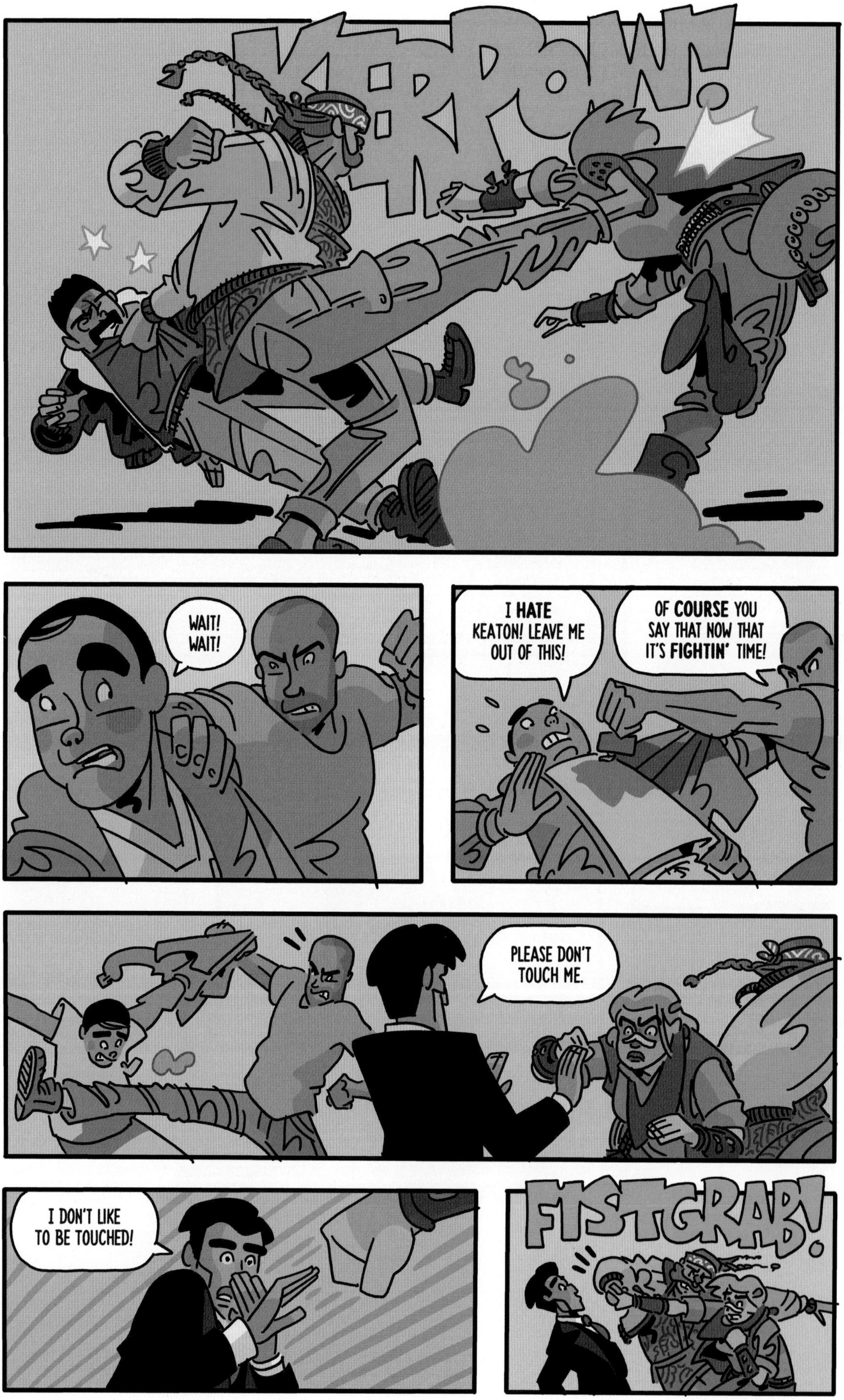
KERPOW!
WAIT! WAIT!
I HATE KEATON! LEAVE ME OUT OF THIS!
OF COURSE YOU SAY THAT NOW THAT IT'S FIGHTIN' TIME!
PLEASE DON'T TOUCH ME.
I DON'T LIKE TO BE TOUCHED!
FISTGRAB!

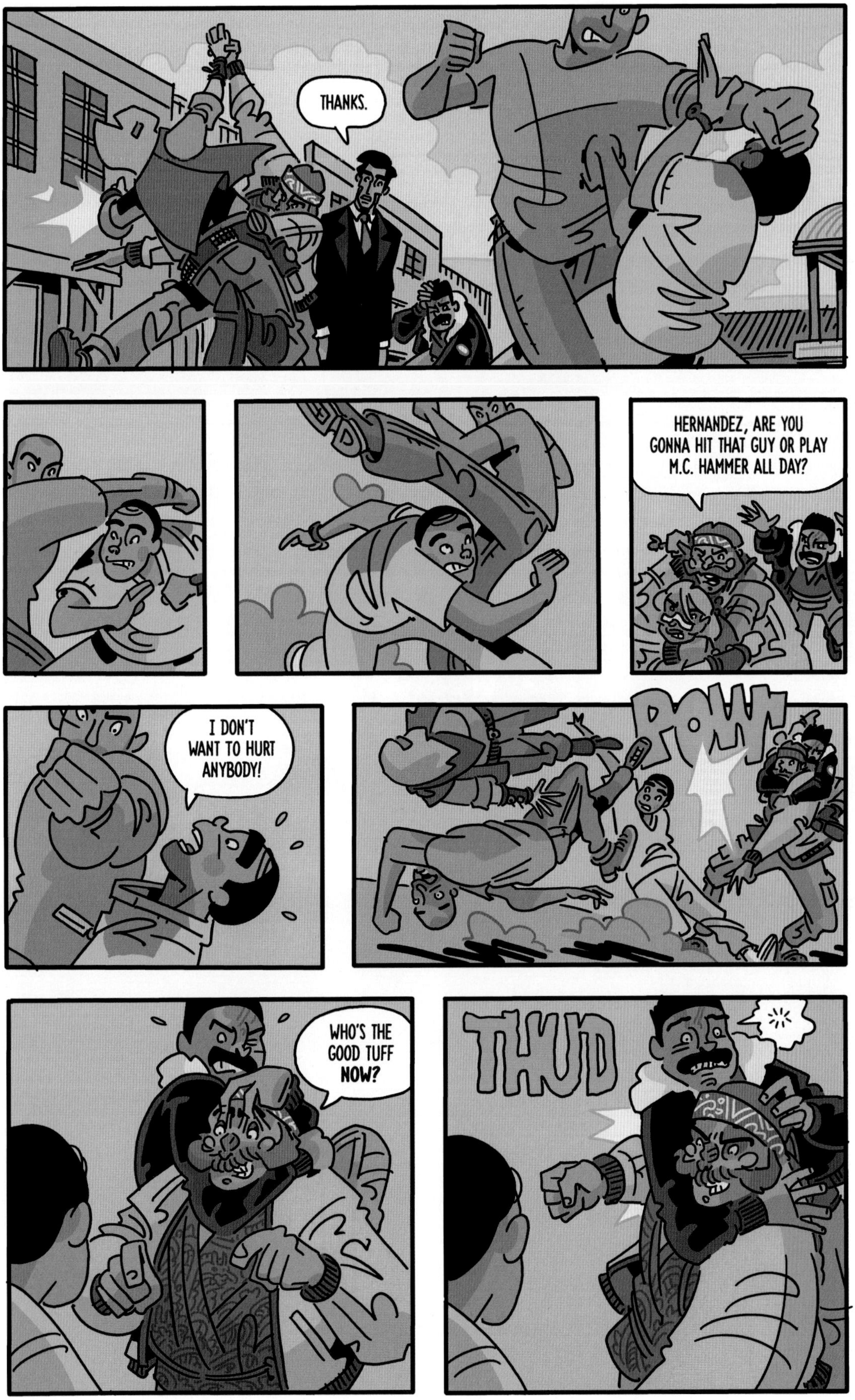
THANKS.
HERNANDEZ, ARE YOU GONNA HIT THAT GUY OR PLAY M.C. HAMMER ALL DAY?
I DON'T WANT TO HURT ANYBODY!
POW
WHO'S THE GOOD TUFF NOW?
THUD

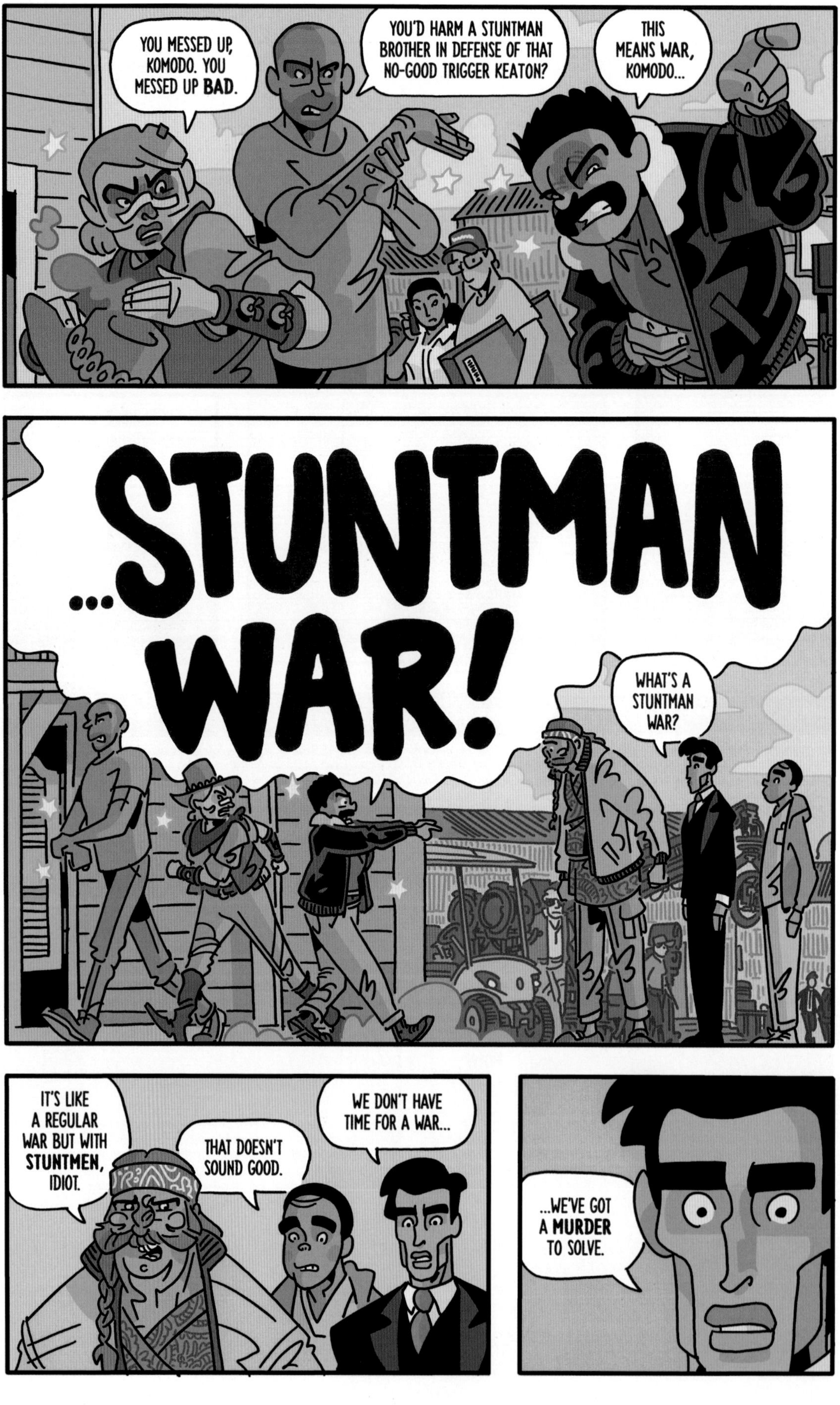
YOU MESSED UP, KOMODO. YOU MESSED UP **BAD**.
YOU'D HARM A STUNTMAN BROTHER IN DEFENSE OF THAT NO-GOOD TRIGGER KEATON?
THIS MEANS **WAR**, KOMODO...
...STUNTMAN WAR!
WHAT'S A STUNTMAN WAR?
IT'S LIKE A REGULAR WAR BUT WITH **STUNTMEN**, IDIOT.
THAT DOESN'T SOUND GOOD.
WE DON'T HAVE TIME FOR A WAR...
...WE'VE GOT A **MURDER** TO SOLVE.

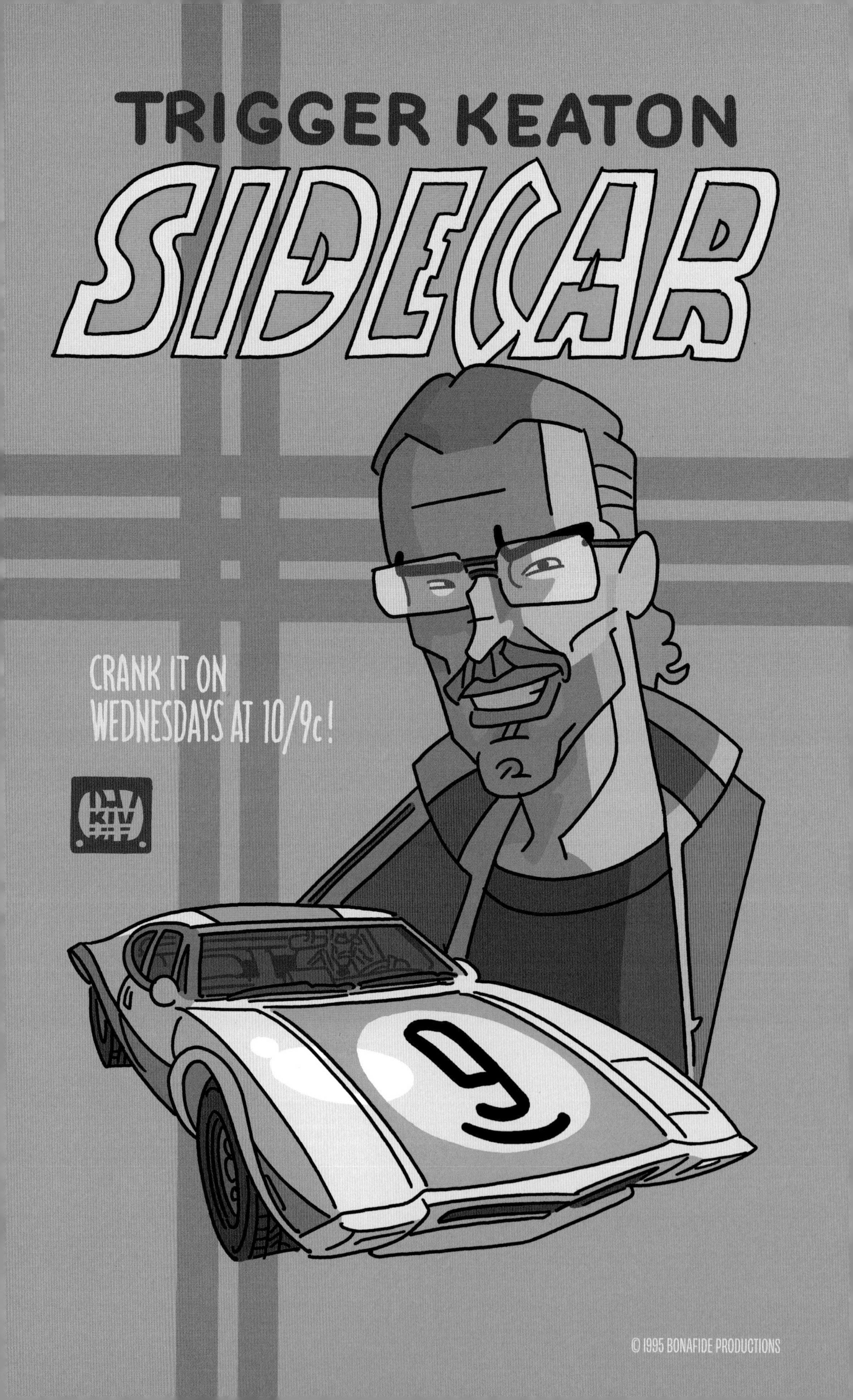
TRIGGER KEATON
SIDECAR
CRANK IT ON
WEDNESDAYS AT 10/9c!
9
© 1995 BONAFIDE PRODUCTIONS

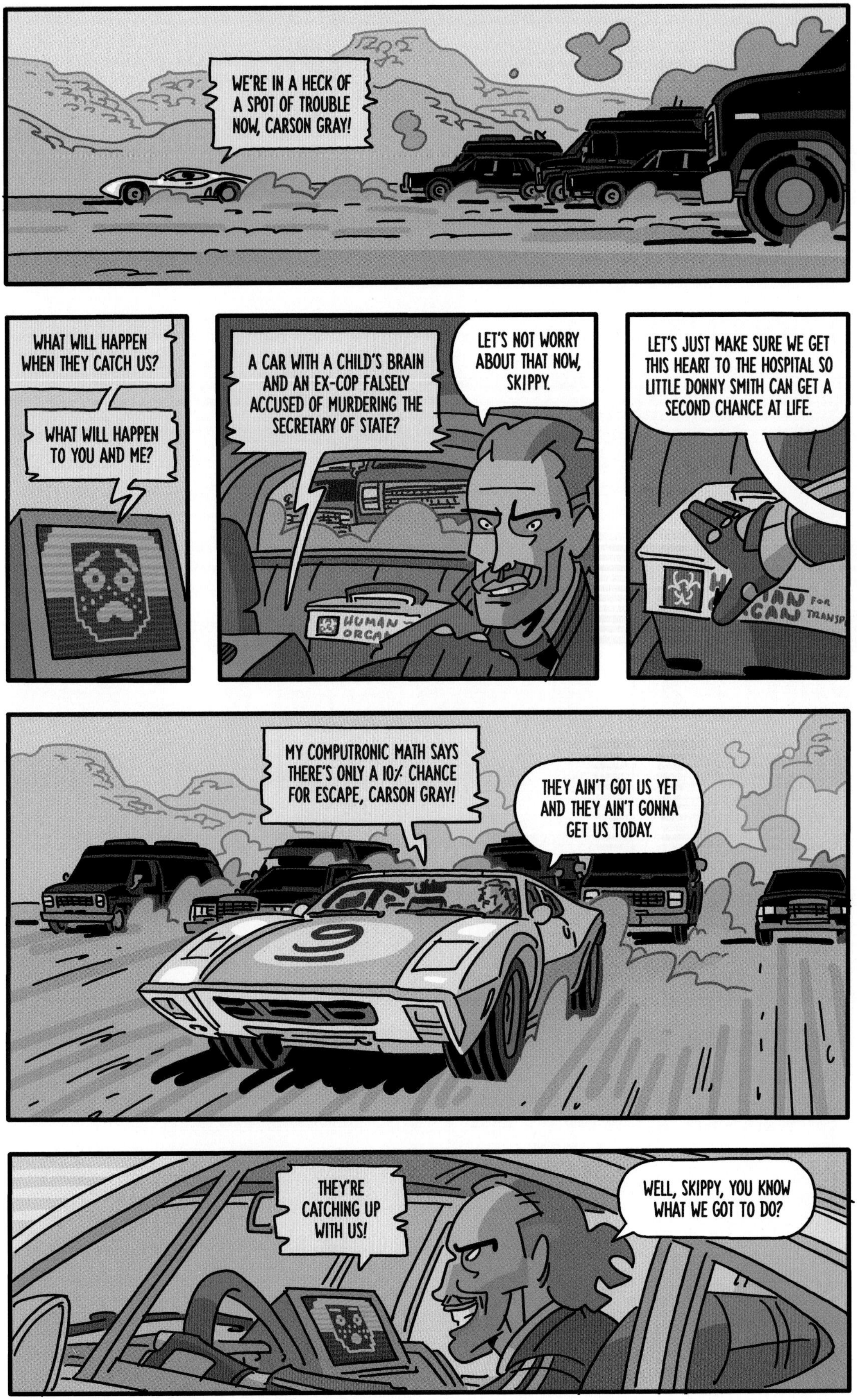
WE'RE IN A HECK OF A SPOT OF TROUBLE NOW, CARSON GRAY!
WHAT WILL HAPPEN WHEN THEY CATCH US?
WHAT WILL HAPPEN TO YOU AND ME?
A CAR WITH A CHILD'S BRAIN AND AN EX-COP FALSELY ACCUSED OF MURDERING THE SECRETARY OF STATE?
LET'S NOT WORRY ABOUT THAT NOW, SKIPPY.
HUMAN ORGAN
LET'S JUST MAKE SURE WE GET THIS HEART TO THE HOSPITAL SO LITTLE DONNY SMITH CAN GET A SECOND CHANCE AT LIFE.
FOR TRANSP
MY COMPUTRONIC MATH SAYS THERE'S ONLY A 10% CHANCE FOR ESCAPE, CARSON GRAY!
THEY AIN'T GOT US YET AND THEY AIN'T GONNA GET US TODAY.
THEY'RE CATCHING UP WITH US!
WELL, SKIPPY, YOU KNOW WHAT WE GOT TO DO?

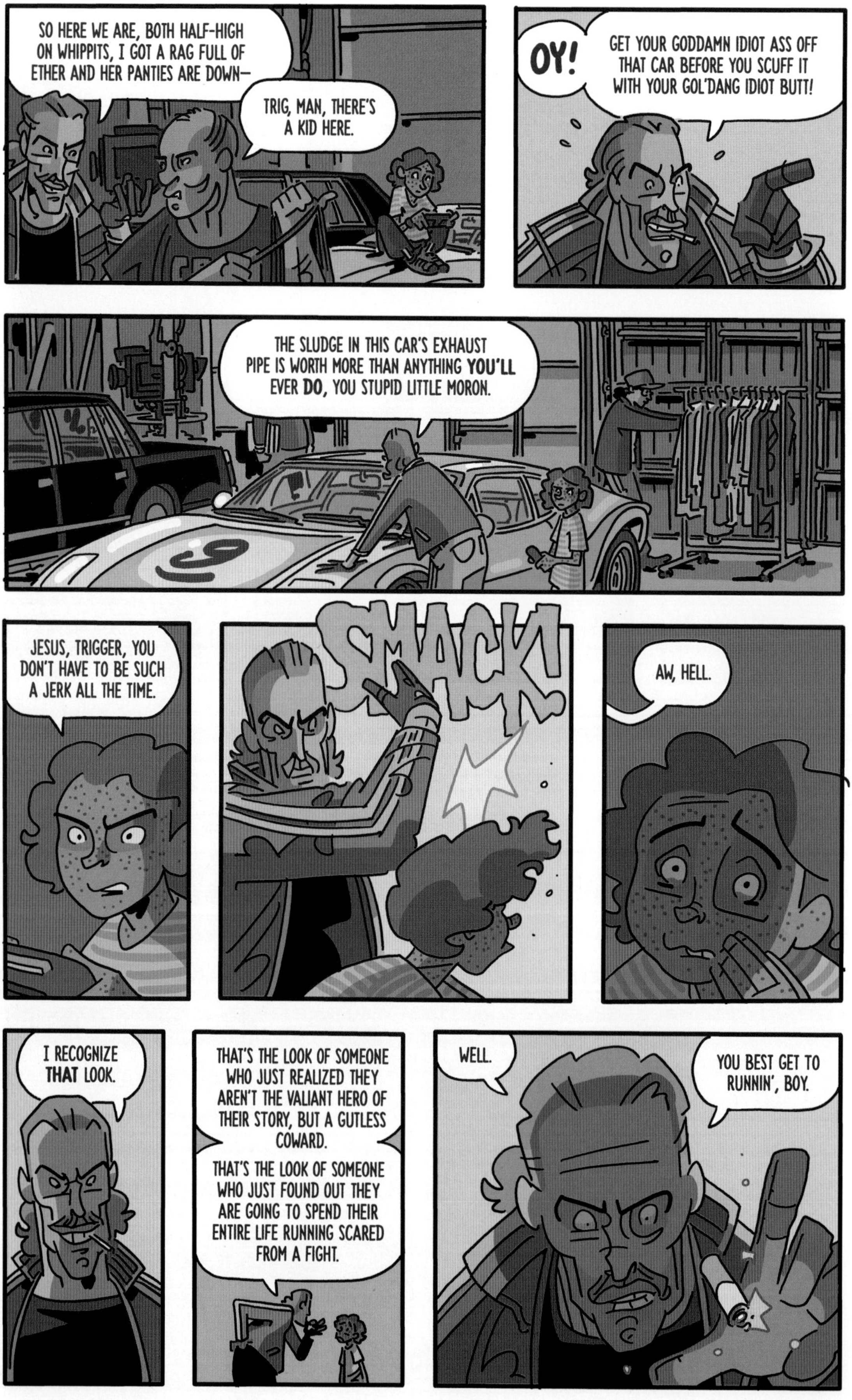
SO HERE WE ARE, BOTH HALF-HIGH ON WHIPPITS, I GOT A RAG FULL OF ETHER AND HER PANTIES ARE DOWN—
TRIG, MAN, THERE'S A KID HERE.
OY!
GET YOUR GODDAMN IDIOT ASS OFF THAT CAR BEFORE YOU SCUFF IT WITH YOUR GOL'DANG IDIOT BUTT!
THE SLUDGE IN THIS CAR'S EXHAUST PIPE IS WORTH MORE THAN ANYTHING **YOU'LL** EVER **DO**, YOU STUPID LITTLE MORON.
JESUS, TRIGGER, YOU DON'T HAVE TO BE SUCH A JERK ALL THE TIME.
SMACK!
AW, HELL.
I RECOGNIZE **THAT** LOOK.
THAT'S THE LOOK OF SOMEONE WHO JUST REALIZED THEY AREN'T THE VALIANT HERO OF THEIR STORY, BUT A GUTLESS COWARD.
THAT'S THE LOOK OF SOMEONE WHO JUST FOUND OUT THEY ARE GOING TO SPEND THEIR ENTIRE LIFE RUNNING SCARED FROM A FIGHT.
WELL.
YOU BEST GET TO RUNNIN', BOY.

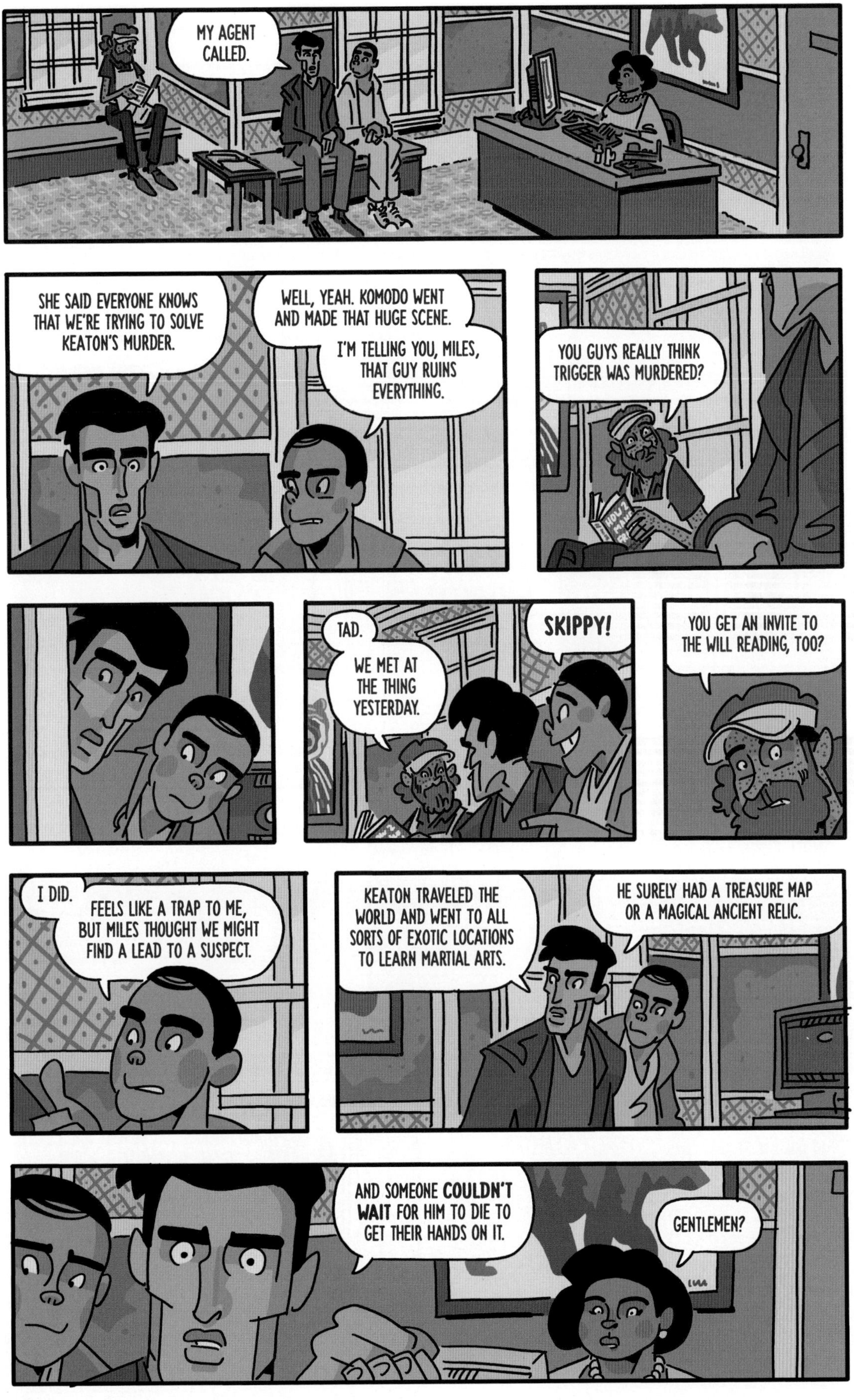
MY AGENT CALLED.
SHE SAID EVERYONE KNOWS THAT WE'RE TRYING TO SOLVE KEATON'S MURDER.
WELL, YEAH. KOMODO WENT AND MADE THAT HUGE SCENE.
I'M TELLING YOU, MILES, THAT GUY RUINS EVERYTHING.
YOU GUYS REALLY THINK TRIGGER WAS MURDERED?
TAD.
WE MET AT THE THING YESTERDAY.
SKIPPY!
YOU GET AN INVITE TO THE WILL READING, TOO?
I DID.
FEELS LIKE A TRAP TO ME, BUT MILES THOUGHT WE MIGHT FIND A LEAD TO A SUSPECT.
KEATON TRAVELED THE WORLD AND WENT TO ALL SORTS OF EXOTIC LOCATIONS TO LEARN MARTIAL ARTS.
HE SURELY HAD A TREASURE MAP OR A MAGICAL ANCIENT RELIC.
AND SOMEONE COULDN'T WAIT FOR HIM TO DIE TO GET THEIR HANDS ON IT.
GENTLEMEN?

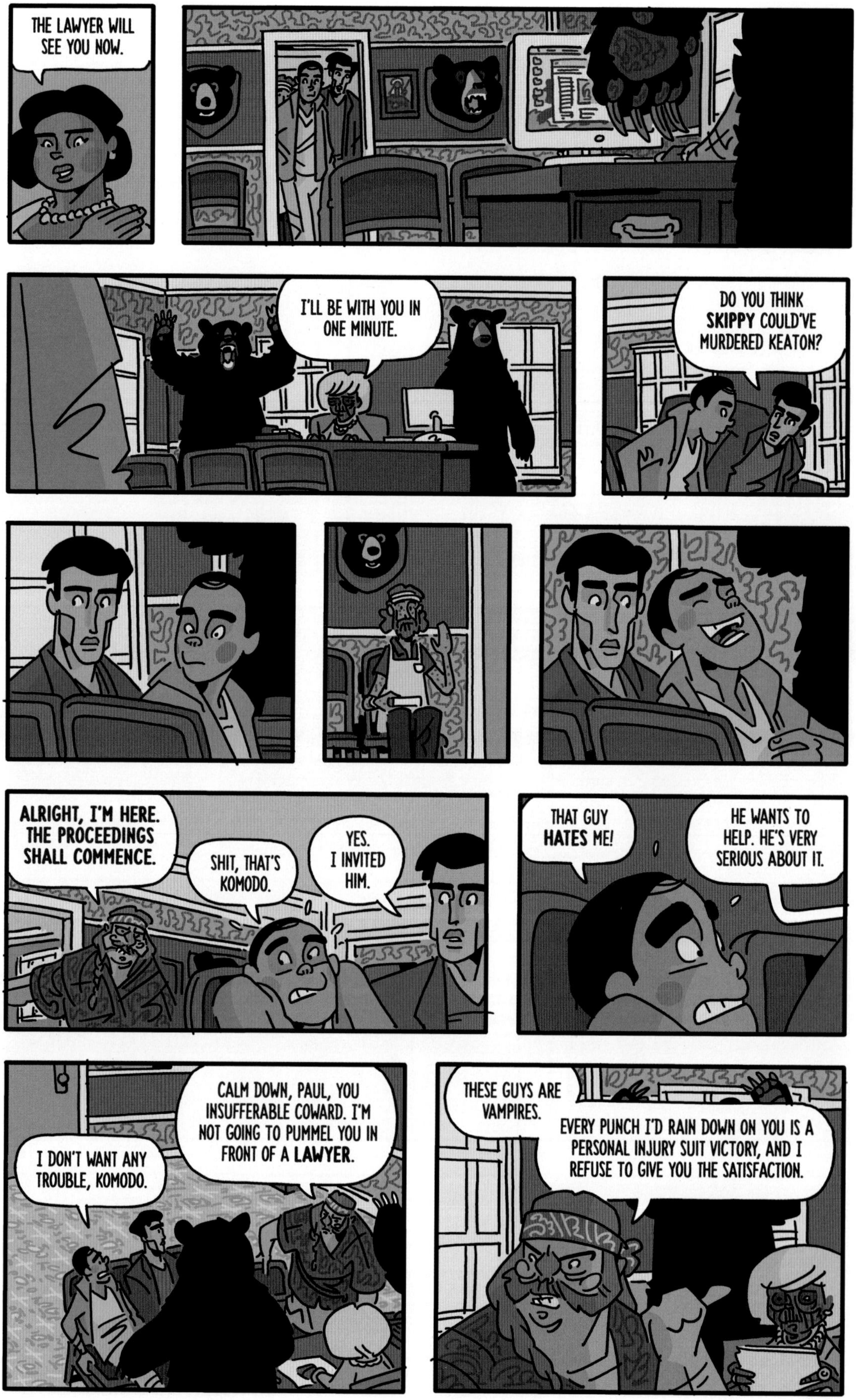
THE LAWYER WILL SEE YOU NOW.
I'LL BE WITH YOU IN ONE MINUTE.
DO YOU THINK **SKIPPY** COULD'VE MURDERED KEATON?
ALRIGHT, I'M HERE. THE PROCEEDINGS SHALL COMMENCE.
SHIT, THAT'S KOMODO.
YES. I INVITED HIM.
THAT GUY **HATES** ME!
HE WANTS TO HELP. HE'S VERY SERIOUS ABOUT IT.
CALM DOWN, PAUL, YOU INSUFFERABLE COWARD. I'M NOT GOING TO PUMMEL YOU IN FRONT OF A **LAWYER**.
I DON'T WANT ANY TROUBLE, KOMODO.
THESE GUYS ARE VAMPIRES.
EVERY PUNCH I'D RAIN DOWN ON YOU IS A PERSONAL INJURY SUIT VICTORY, AND I REFUSE TO GIVE YOU THE SATISFACTION.

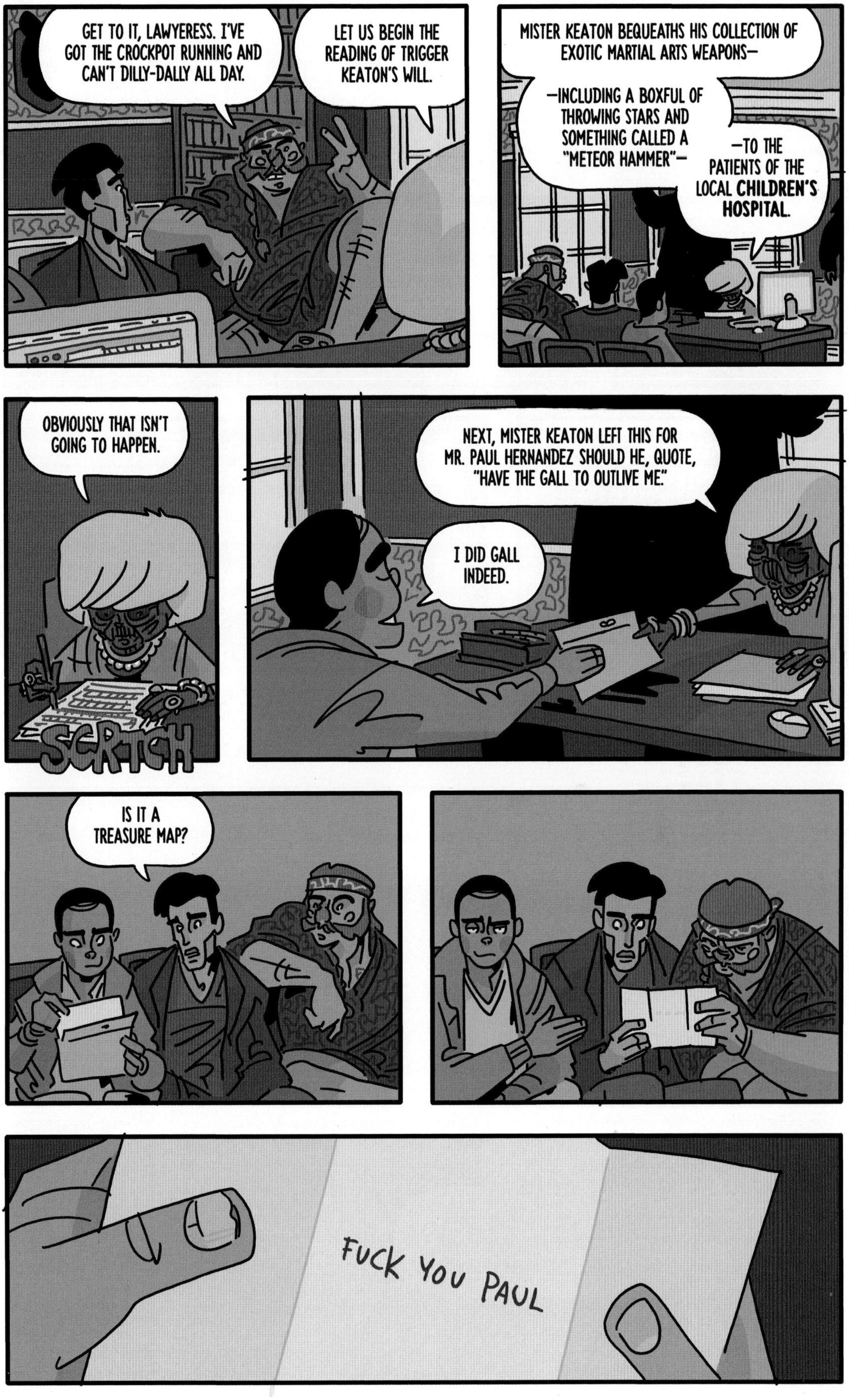
GET TO IT, LAWYERESS. I'VE GOT THE CROCKPOT RUNNING AND CAN'T DILLY-DALLY ALL DAY.
LET US BEGIN THE READING OF TRIGGER KEATON'S WILL.
MISTER KEATON BEQUEATHS HIS COLLECTION OF EXOTIC MARTIAL ARTS WEAPONS—
—INCLUDING A BOXFUL OF THROWING STARS AND SOMETHING CALLED A "METEOR HAMMER"—
—TO THE PATIENTS OF THE LOCAL **CHILDREN'S HOSPITAL**.
OBVIOUSLY THAT ISN'T GOING TO HAPPEN.
SCRTCH
NEXT, MISTER KEATON LEFT THIS FOR MR. PAUL HERNANDEZ SHOULD HE, QUOTE, "HAVE THE GALL TO OUTLIVE ME."
I DID GALL INDEED.
IS IT A TREASURE MAP?
FUCK YOU PAUL

MR. KEATON INSISTED I READ THE FOLLOWING MESSAGE WHEN PRESENTING THE FINAL ASSET.

"TO THADDEUS HAYCROFT, I LEAVE MY 1973 AMC AMX/3 PROTOTYPE MUSCLE CAR. A STUPID CAR FROM A STUPID SHOW."

THE SIDECAR?!

WHO THE FUCK IS THADDEUS HAYCROFT?

"MAY YOU FOREVER BE REMINDED THAT YOU'LL NEVER BE ANYTHING BUT A REPLACEABLE PART OF THIS THING THAT'S BETTER THAN YOU IN EVERY WAY. LET IT SERVE AS A REMINDER OF YOUR OWN INCONSEQUENCE.

"ENJOY DRIVING THIS IMPECCABLE MONUMENT TO YOUR LIFE'S FAILURE."

DON'T TAKE THAT CAR, TAD!

REFUSE!

IT'S AN INSULT. A HUMILIATION FROM BEYOND THE GRAVE.

I REALLY NEED A CAR, THOUGH.

WAIT. I DIDN'T EVEN GET A FUCK YOU LETTER?

UM, MRS. GROZBAN? I'M SORRY TO INTERRUPT, BUT I HAVE SEVERAL ANGRY PEOPLE OUT HERE HOLDING WHAT APPEAR TO BE BOXES OF, UM—

—HUMAN FECES?

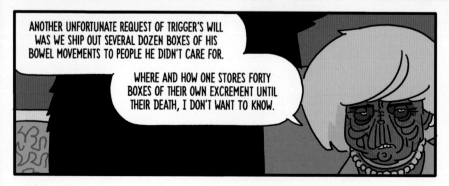

ANOTHER UNFORTUNATE REQUEST OF TRIGGER'S WILL WAS WE SHIP OUT SEVERAL DOZEN BOXES OF HIS BOWEL MOVEMENTS TO PEOPLE HE DIDN'T CARE FOR.

WHERE AND HOW ONE STORES FORTY BOXES OF THEIR OWN EXCREMENT UNTIL THEIR DEATH, I DON'T WANT TO KNOW.

BZZP

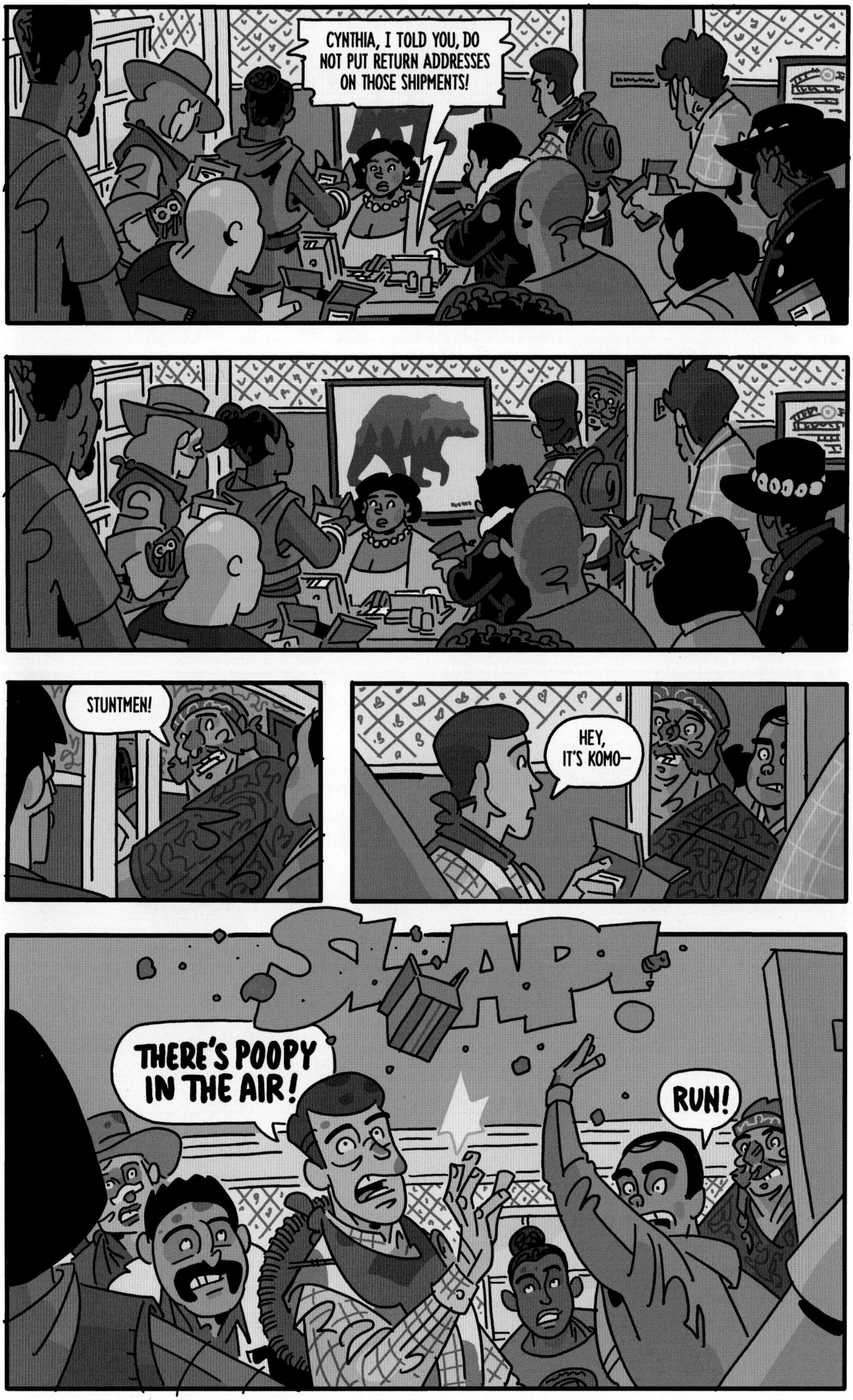
CYNTHIA, I TOLD YOU, DO NOT PUT RETURN ADDRESSES ON THOSE SHIPMENTS!
STUNTMEN!
HEY, IT'S KOMO—
SLAP!
THERE'S POOPY IN THE AIR!
RUN!

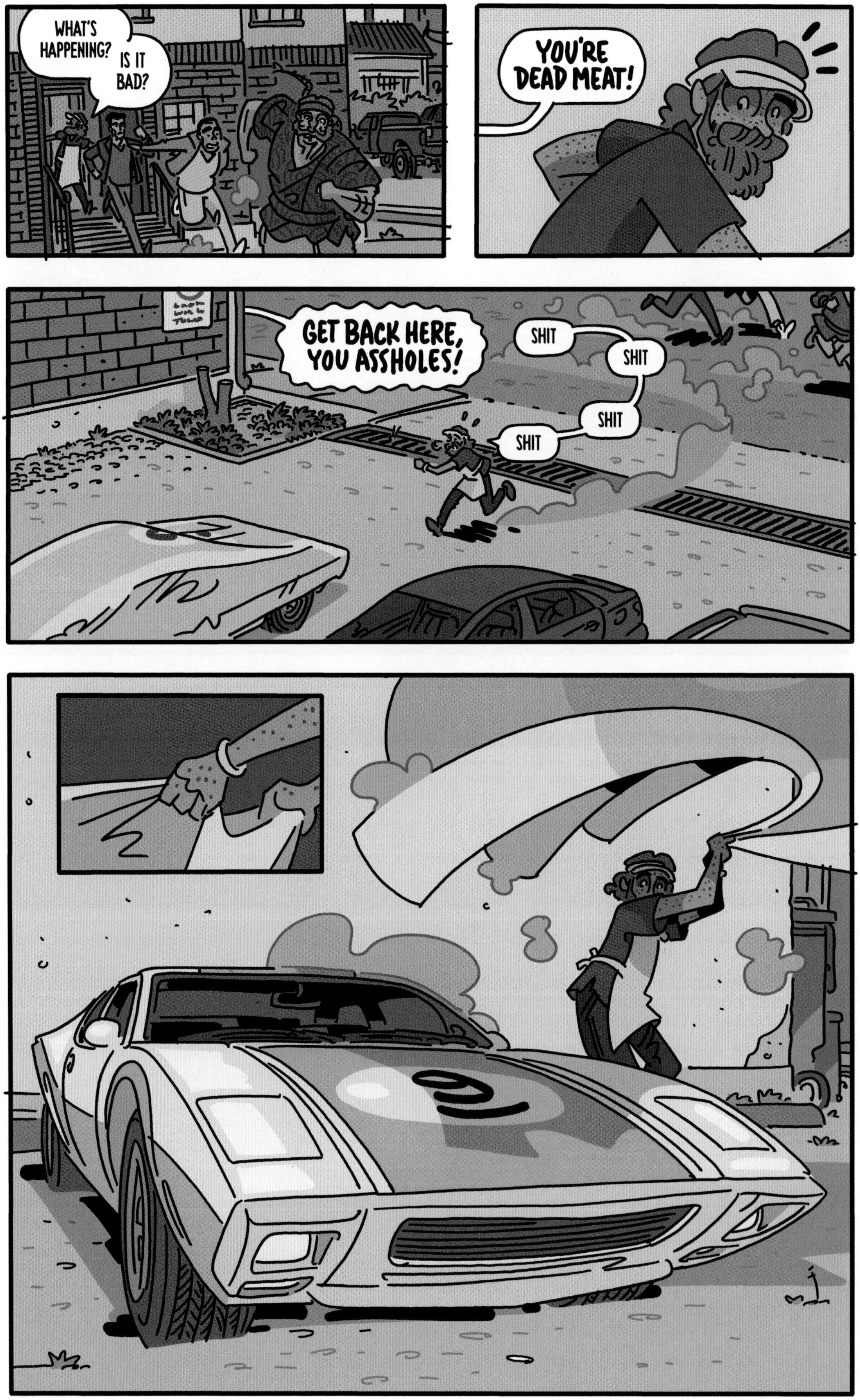

WHAT'S HAPPENING?
IS IT BAD?
YOU'RE DEAD MEAT!
GET BACK HERE, YOU ASSHOLES!
SHIT
SHIT
SHIT
SHIT

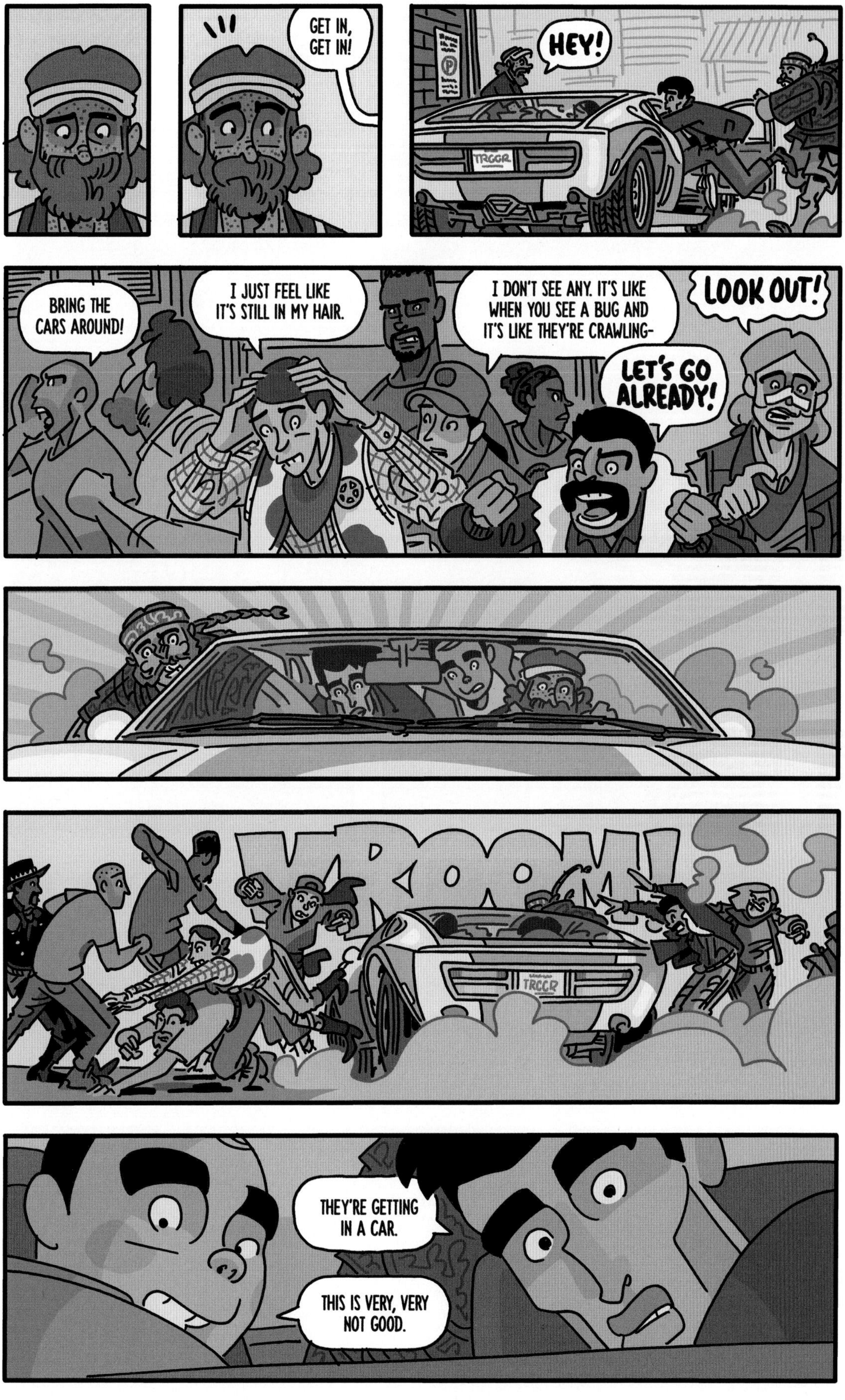
GET IN, GET IN!
HEY!
BRING THE CARS AROUND!
I JUST FEEL LIKE IT'S STILL IN MY HAIR.
I DON'T SEE ANY. IT'S LIKE WHEN YOU SEE A BUG AND IT'S LIKE THEY'RE CRAWLING-
LOOK OUT!
LET'S GO ALREADY!
VROOM!
THEY'RE GETTING IN A CAR.
THIS IS VERY, VERY NOT GOOD.

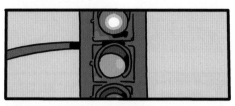

SCRREEEEE~~~

WHAT ARE YOU DOING?!

IT'S A RED LIGHT!

DON'T STOP! GO!

THEY STOPPED AT **THEIR** RED LIGHT!

THERE ARE RULES TO AN ENGAGEMENT!

WHAT'S GOING TO HAPPEN WHEN THEY CATCH UP TO US, KOMODO?

WHAT HAPPENS IN **ANY** WAR?

THEY'RE GOING TO KILL US.

NOT IN A THUMB WAR.

SHIT!

JUST GET US OUT OF HERE, SKIPPY!

YOU CAN'T RUN A RED LIGHT.

OF COURSE YOU CAN! RUN THE RED LIGHT!

MAYBE YOU GUYS JUST GET OUT? THESE GUYS DON'T WANT **ME**.

YOU'RE DEAD MEAT, KOMODO!

YOU AND **ALL** YOUR DRAMATURGICAL FRIENDS!

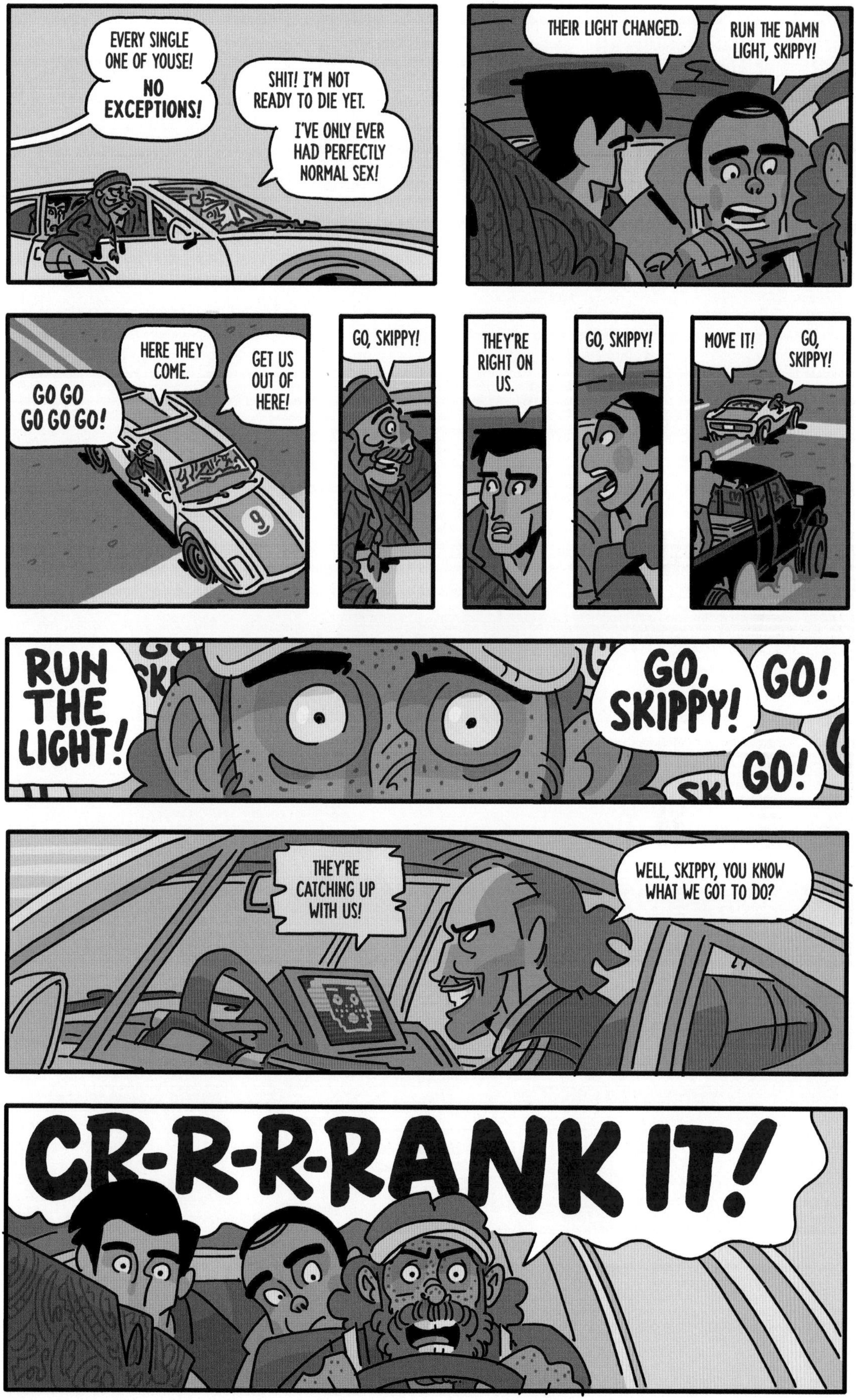
EVERY SINGLE ONE OF YOUSE! NO EXCEPTIONS!
SHIT! I'M NOT READY TO DIE YET.
I'VE ONLY EVER HAD PERFECTLY NORMAL SEX!
THEIR LIGHT CHANGED.
RUN THE DAMN LIGHT, SKIPPY!
HERE THEY COME.
GO GO GO GO GO!
GET US OUT OF HERE!
GO, SKIPPY!
THEY'RE RIGHT ON US.
GO, SKIPPY!
MOVE IT!
GO, SKIPPY!
RUN THE LIGHT!
GO, SKIPPY!
GO!
GO!
THEY'RE CATCHING UP WITH US!
WELL, SKIPPY, YOU KNOW WHAT WE GOT TO DO?
CR-R-R-RANK IT!

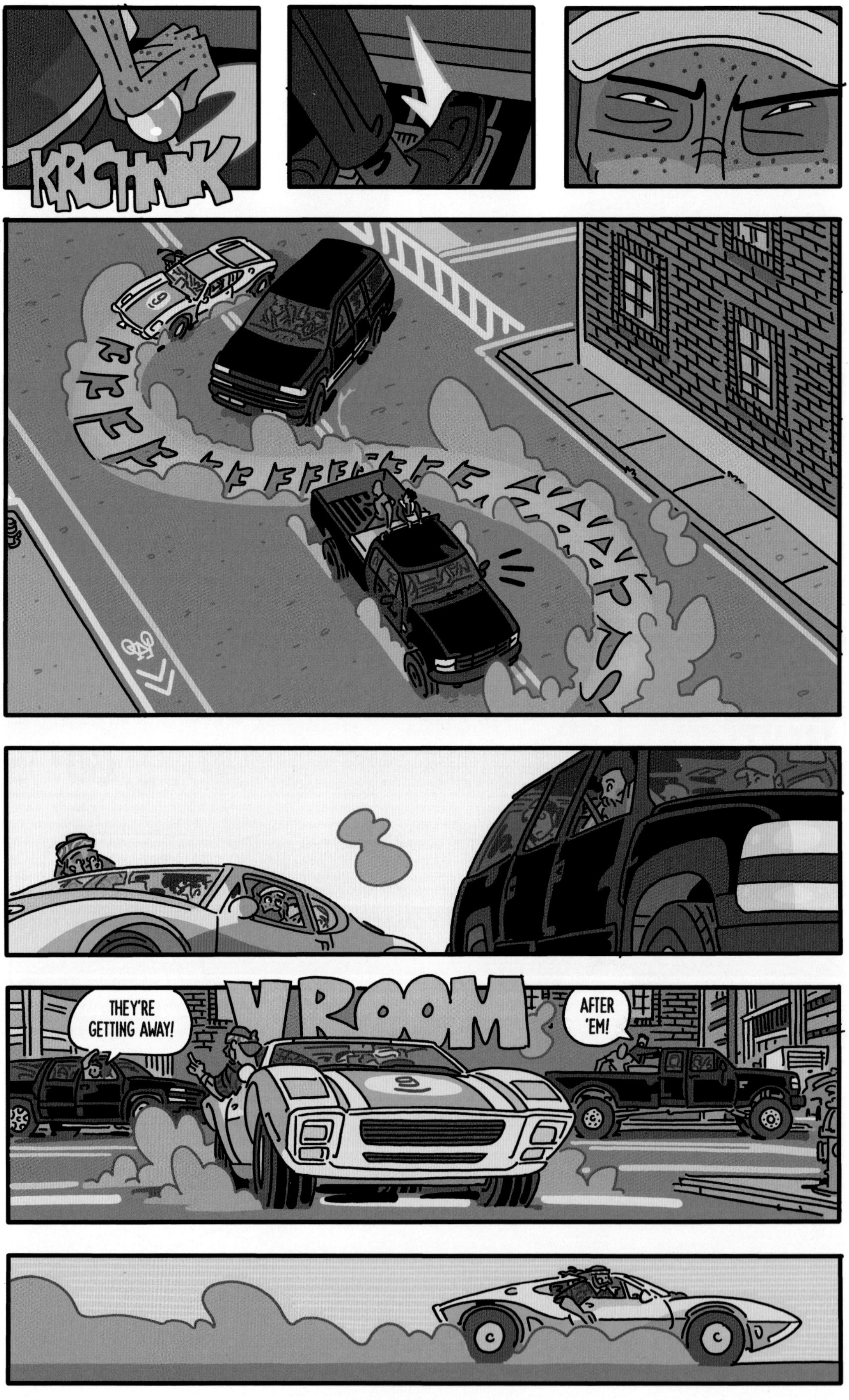
KRCHNK
THEY'RE GETTING AWAY!
VROOM
AFTER 'EM!

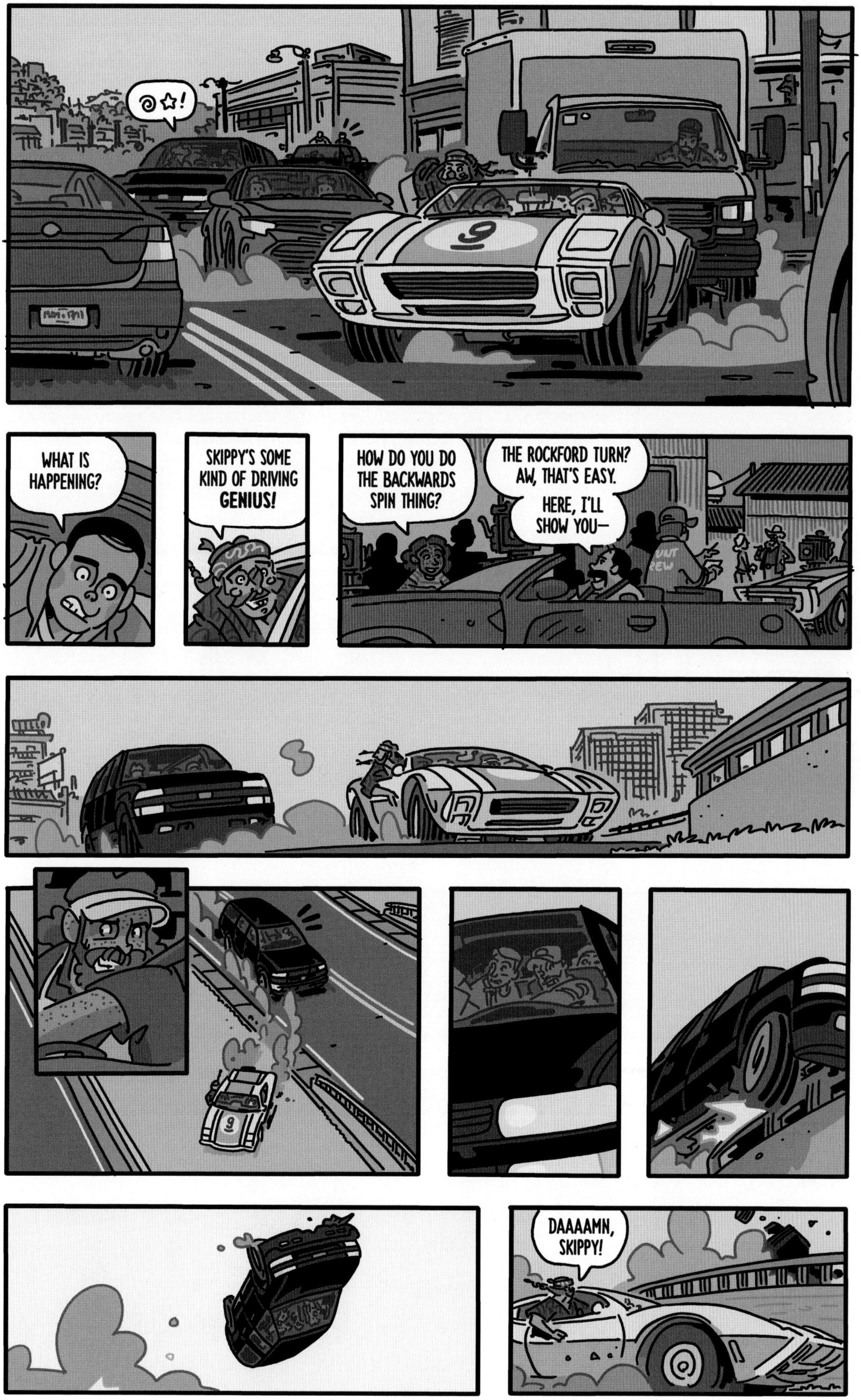
@☆!
WHAT IS HAPPENING?
SKIPPY'S SOME KIND OF DRIVING **GENIUS!**
HOW DO YOU DO THE BACKWARDS SPIN THING?
THE ROCKFORD TURN? AW, THAT'S EASY.
HERE, I'LL SHOW YOU—
DAAAAMN, SKIPPY!

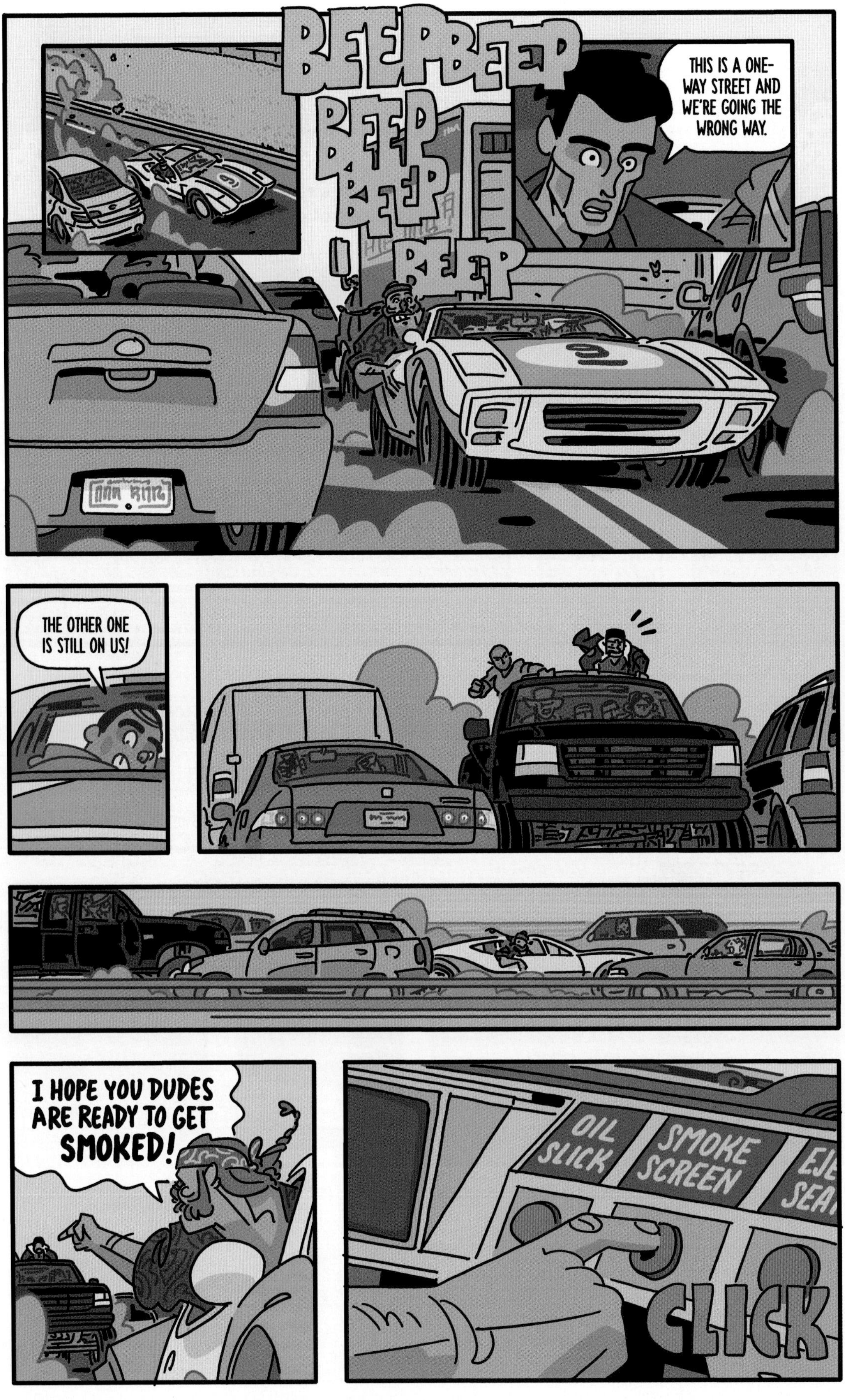
BEEPBEEP
BEEP
BEEP
BEEP
THIS IS A ONE-WAY STREET AND WE'RE GOING THE WRONG WAY.
THE OTHER ONE IS STILL ON US!
I HOPE YOU DUDES ARE READY TO GET SMOKED!
OIL SLICK
SMOKE SCREEN
CLICK

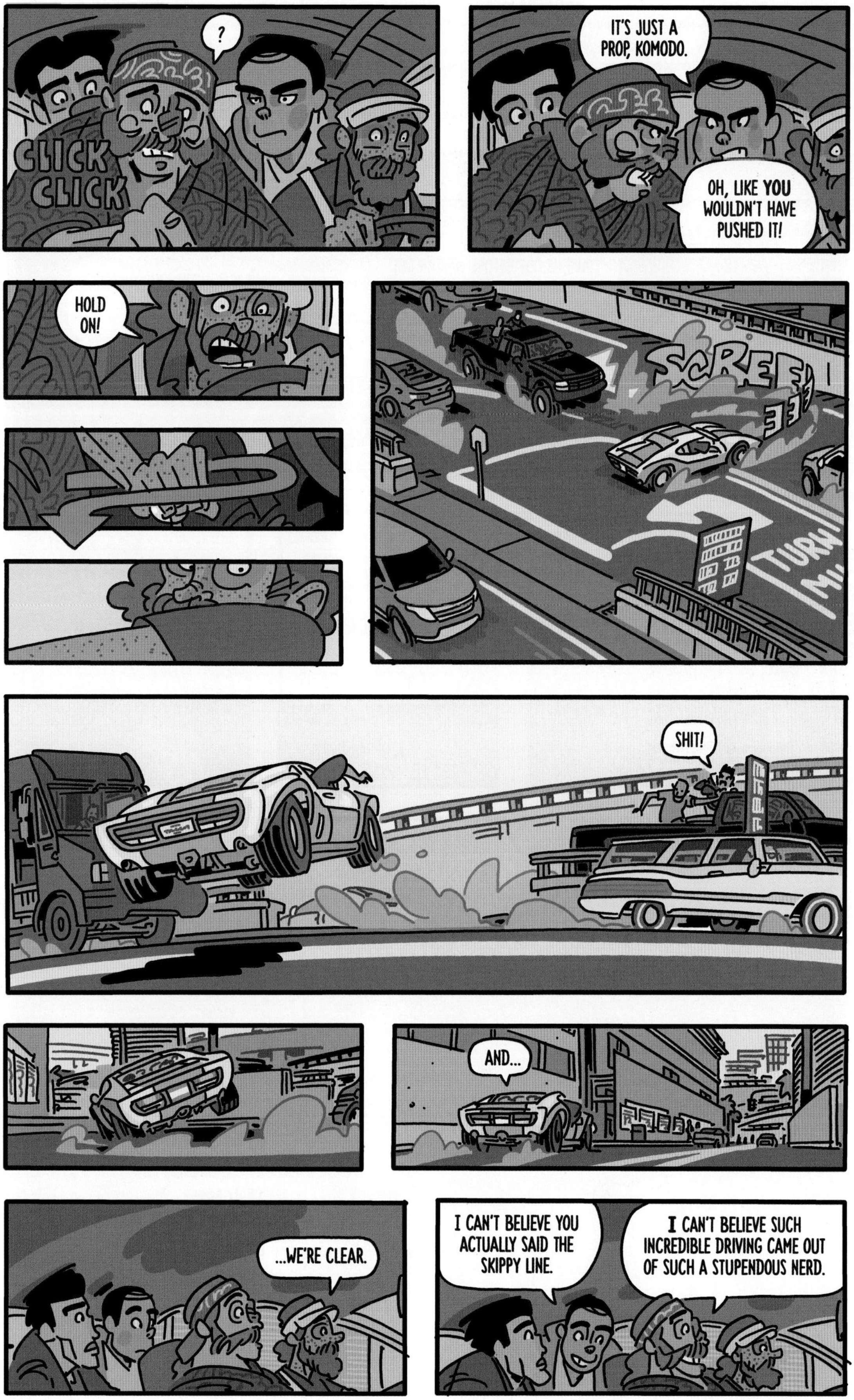
?
CLICK CLICK
IT'S JUST A PROP, KOMODO.
OH, LIKE YOU WOULDN'T HAVE PUSHED IT!
HOLD ON!
SCREEE
SHIT!
AND...
...WE'RE CLEAR.
I CAN'T BELIEVE YOU ACTUALLY SAID THE SKIPPY LINE.
I CAN'T BELIEVE SUCH INCREDIBLE DRIVING CAME OUT OF SUCH A STUPENDOUS NERD.

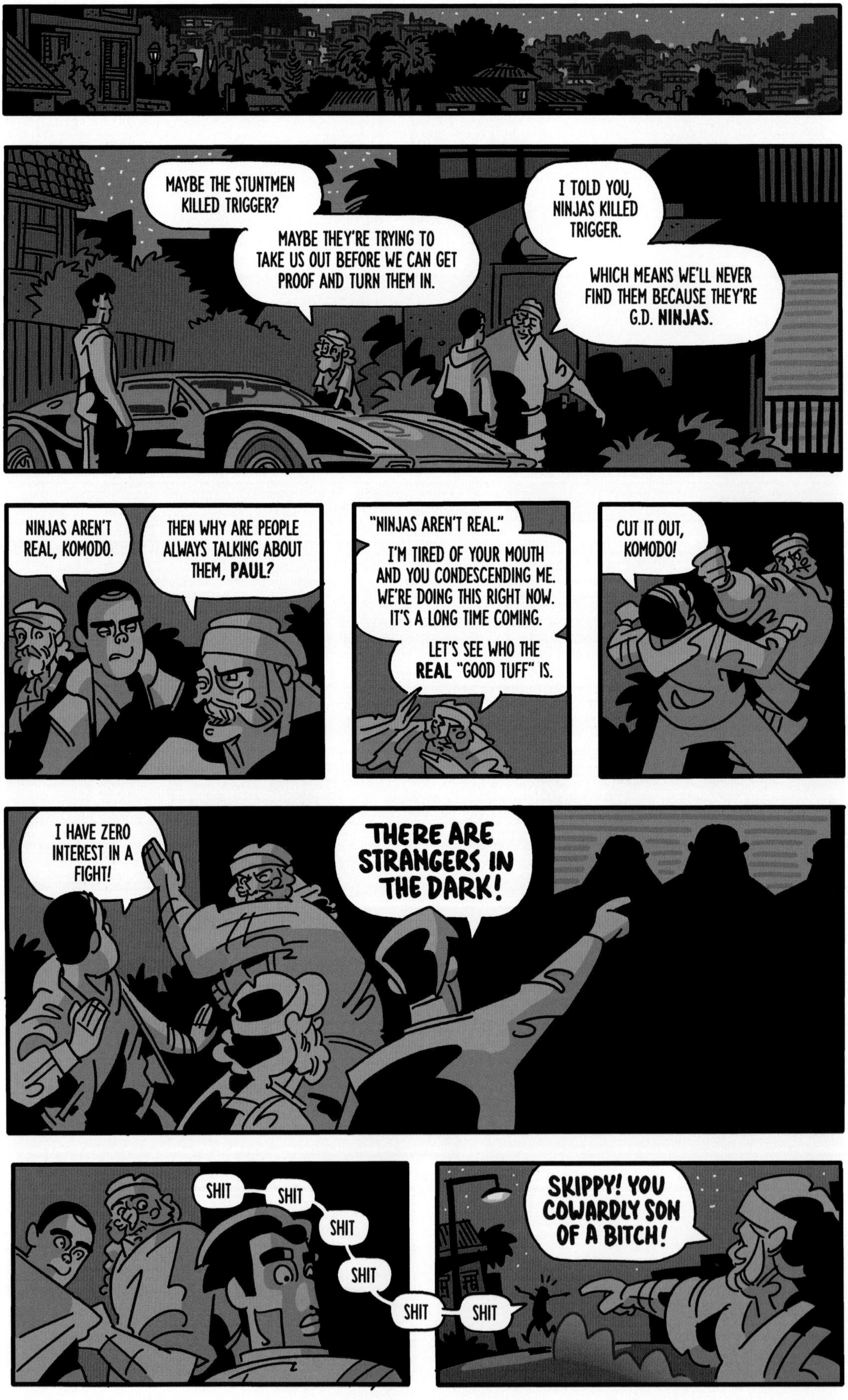
MAYBE THE STUNTMEN KILLED TRIGGER?
MAYBE THEY'RE TRYING TO TAKE US OUT BEFORE WE CAN GET PROOF AND TURN THEM IN.
I TOLD YOU, NINJAS KILLED TRIGGER.
WHICH MEANS WE'LL NEVER FIND THEM BECAUSE THEY'RE G.D. **NINJAS**.
NINJAS AREN'T REAL, KOMODO.
THEN WHY ARE PEOPLE ALWAYS TALKING ABOUT THEM, **PAUL**?
"NINJAS AREN'T REAL."
I'M TIRED OF YOUR MOUTH AND YOU CONDESCENDING ME. WE'RE DOING THIS RIGHT NOW. IT'S A LONG TIME COMING.
LET'S SEE WHO THE **REAL** "GOOD TUFF" IS.
CUT IT OUT, KOMODO!
I HAVE ZERO INTEREST IN A FIGHT!
THERE ARE STRANGERS IN THE DARK!
SHIT
SHIT
SHIT
SHIT
SHIT
SHIT
SKIPPY! YOU COWARDLY SON OF A BITCH!

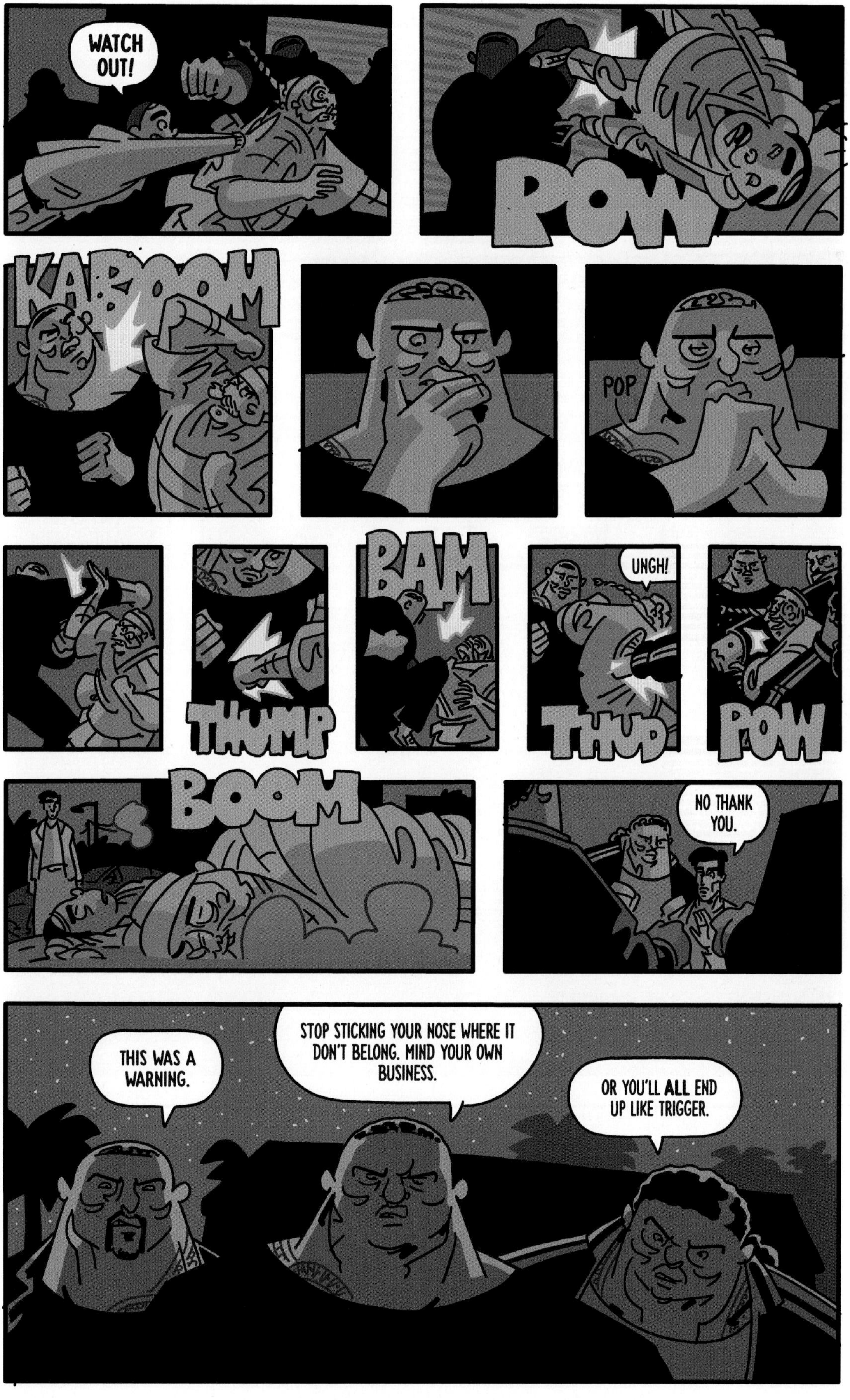
WATCH OUT!
POW
KABOOM
POP
THUMP
BAM
UNGH!
THUD
POW
BOOM
NO THANK YOU.
THIS WAS A WARNING.
STOP STICKING YOUR NOSE WHERE IT DON'T BELONG. MIND YOUR OWN BUSINESS.
OR YOU'LL **ALL** END UP LIKE TRIGGER.

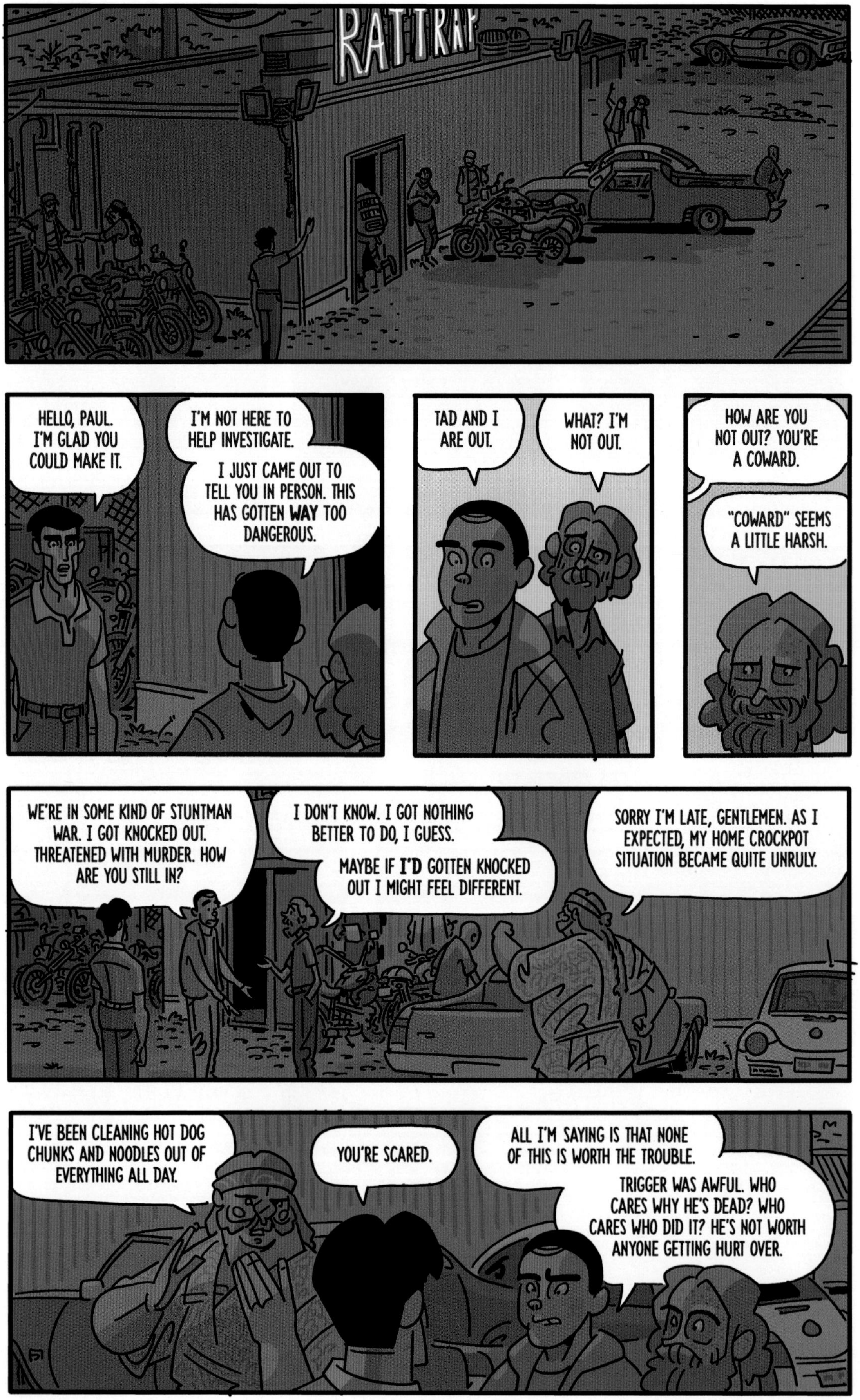
RATTRAP
HELLO, PAUL. I'M GLAD YOU COULD MAKE IT.
I'M NOT HERE TO HELP INVESTIGATE.
I JUST CAME OUT TO TELL YOU IN PERSON. THIS HAS GOTTEN **WAY** TOO DANGEROUS.
TAD AND I ARE OUT.
WHAT? I'M NOT OUT.
HOW ARE YOU NOT OUT? YOU'RE A COWARD.
"COWARD" SEEMS A LITTLE HARSH.
WE'RE IN SOME KIND OF STUNTMAN WAR. I GOT KNOCKED OUT. THREATENED WITH MURDER. HOW ARE YOU STILL IN?
I DON'T KNOW. I GOT NOTHING BETTER TO DO, I GUESS.
MAYBE IF **I'D** GOTTEN KNOCKED OUT I MIGHT FEEL DIFFERENT.
SORRY I'M LATE, GENTLEMEN. AS I EXPECTED, MY HOME CROCKPOT SITUATION BECAME QUITE UNRULY.
I'VE BEEN CLEANING HOT DOG CHUNKS AND NOODLES OUT OF EVERYTHING ALL DAY.
YOU'RE SCARED.
ALL I'M SAYING IS THAT NONE OF THIS IS WORTH THE TROUBLE.
TRIGGER WAS AWFUL. WHO CARES WHY HE'S DEAD? WHO CARES WHO DID IT? HE'S NOT WORTH ANYONE GETTING HURT OVER.

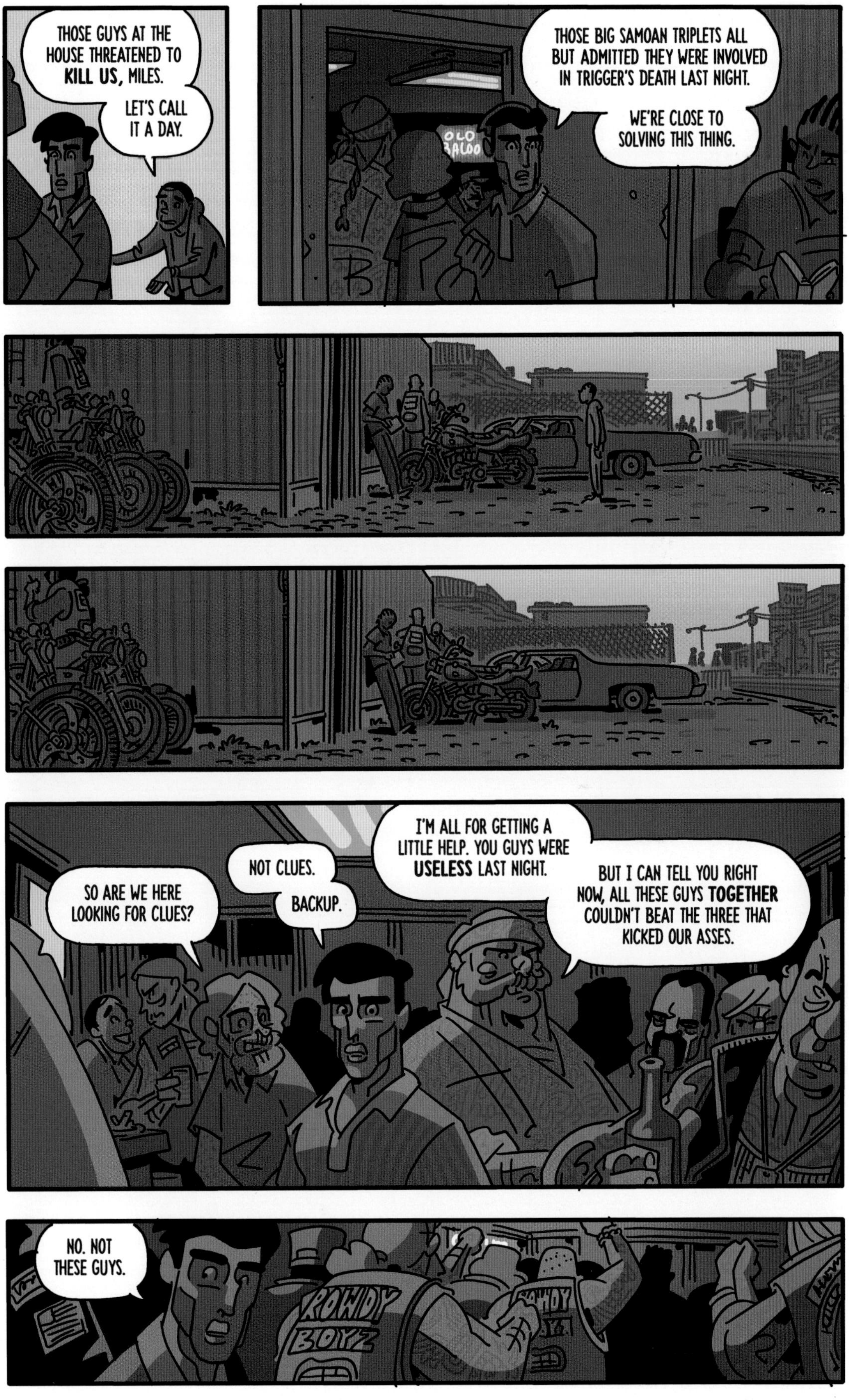
THOSE GUYS AT THE HOUSE THREATENED TO KILL US, MILES.
LET'S CALL IT A DAY.
THOSE BIG SAMOAN TRIPLETS ALL BUT ADMITTED THEY WERE INVOLVED IN TRIGGER'S DEATH LAST NIGHT.
WE'RE CLOSE TO SOLVING THIS THING.
SO ARE WE HERE LOOKING FOR CLUES?
NOT CLUES.
BACKUP.
I'M ALL FOR GETTING A LITTLE HELP. YOU GUYS WERE USELESS LAST NIGHT.
BUT I CAN TELL YOU RIGHT NOW, ALL THESE GUYS TOGETHER COULDN'T BEAT THE THREE THAT KICKED OUR ASSES.
NO. NOT THESE GUYS.
ROWDY BOYZ

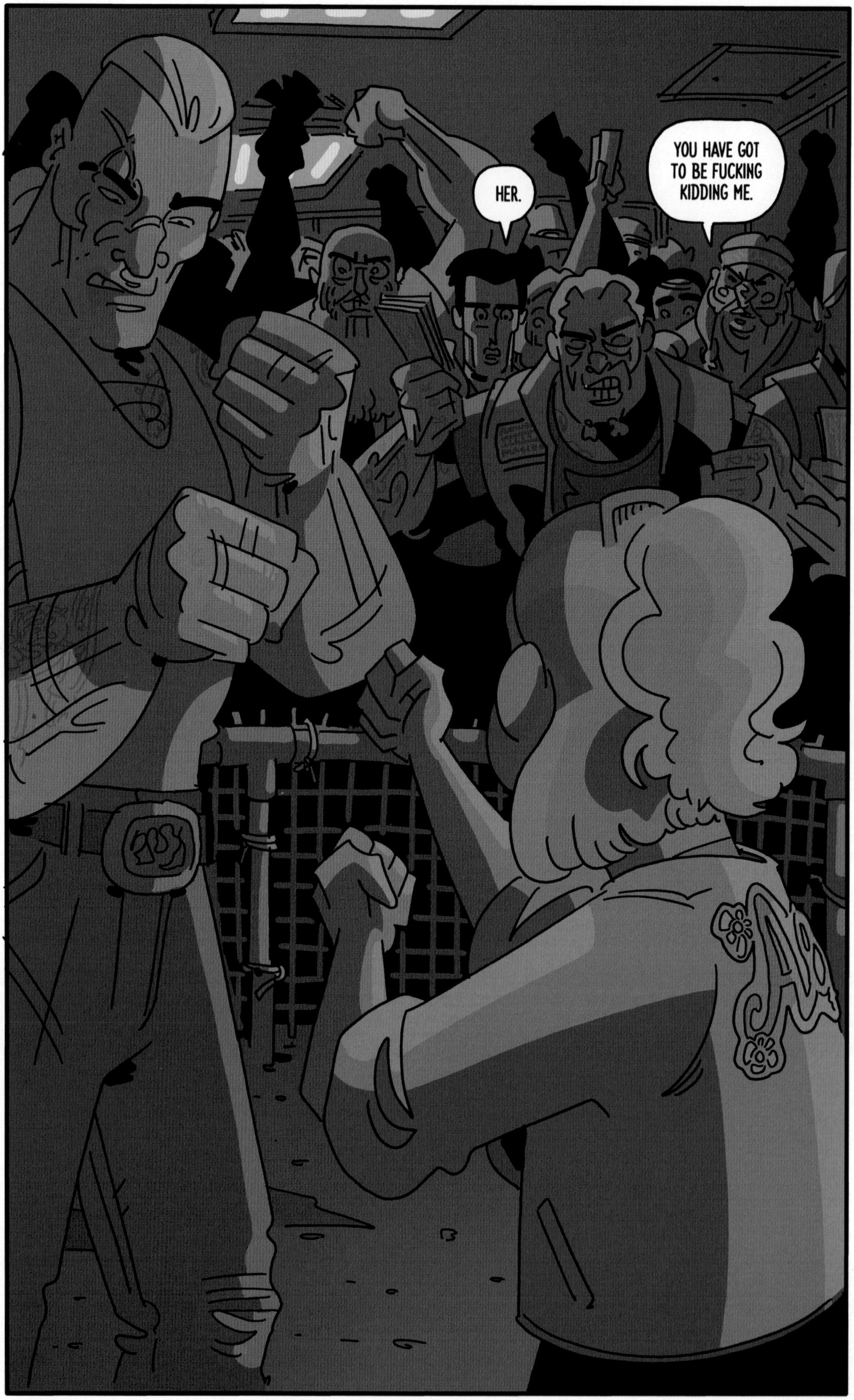
HER.
YOU HAVE GOT TO BE FUCKING KIDDING ME.

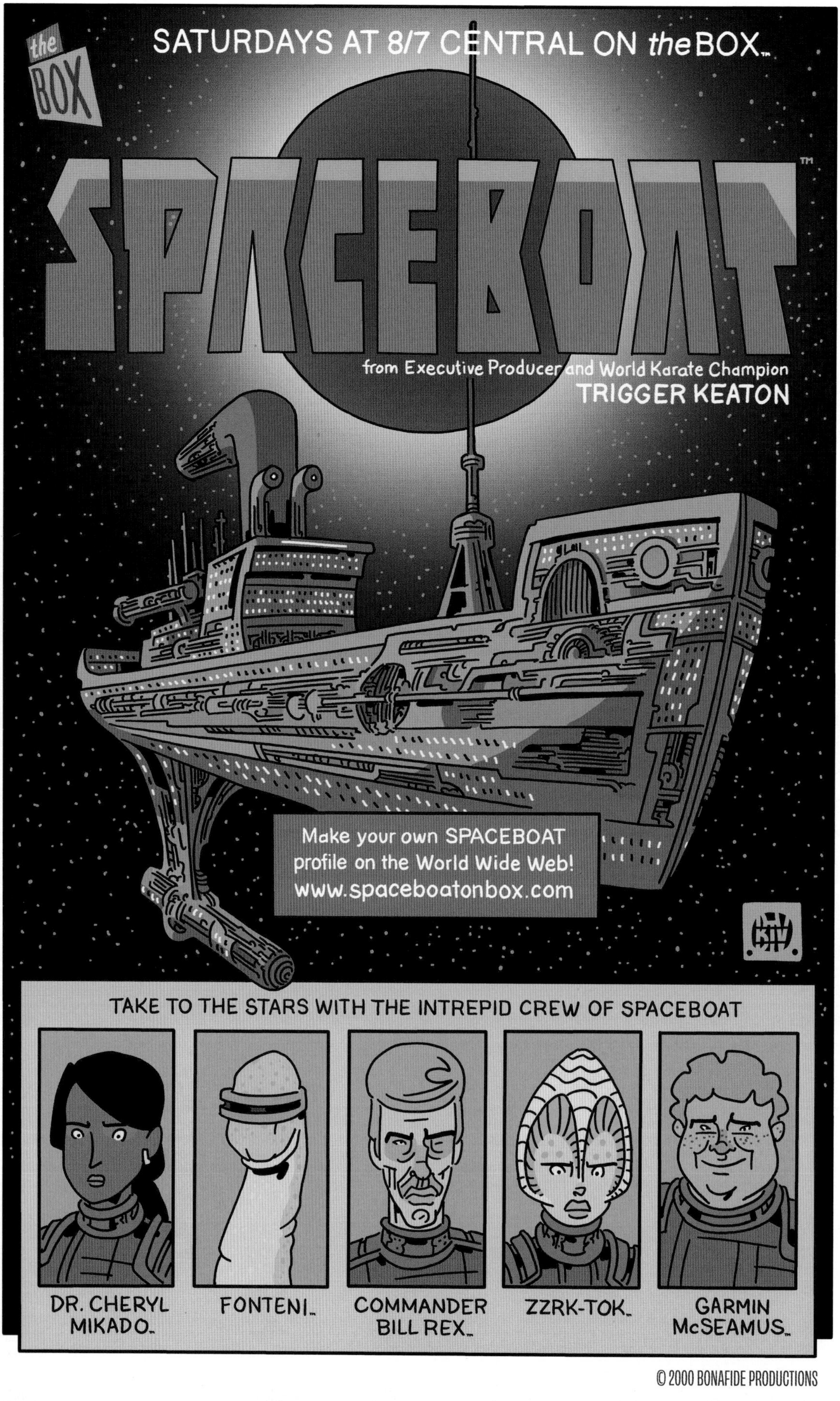
the BOX
SATURDAYS AT 8/7 CENTRAL ON the BOX™
SPACEBOAT™
from Executive Producer and World Karate Champion
TRIGGER KEATON
Make your own SPACEBOAT
profile on the World Wide Web!
www.spaceboatonbox.com
TAKE TO THE STARS WITH THE INTREPID CREW OF SPACEBOAT
DR. CHERYL MIKADO™
FONTENI™
COMMANDER BILL REX™
ZZRK-TOK™
GARMIN McSEAMUS™

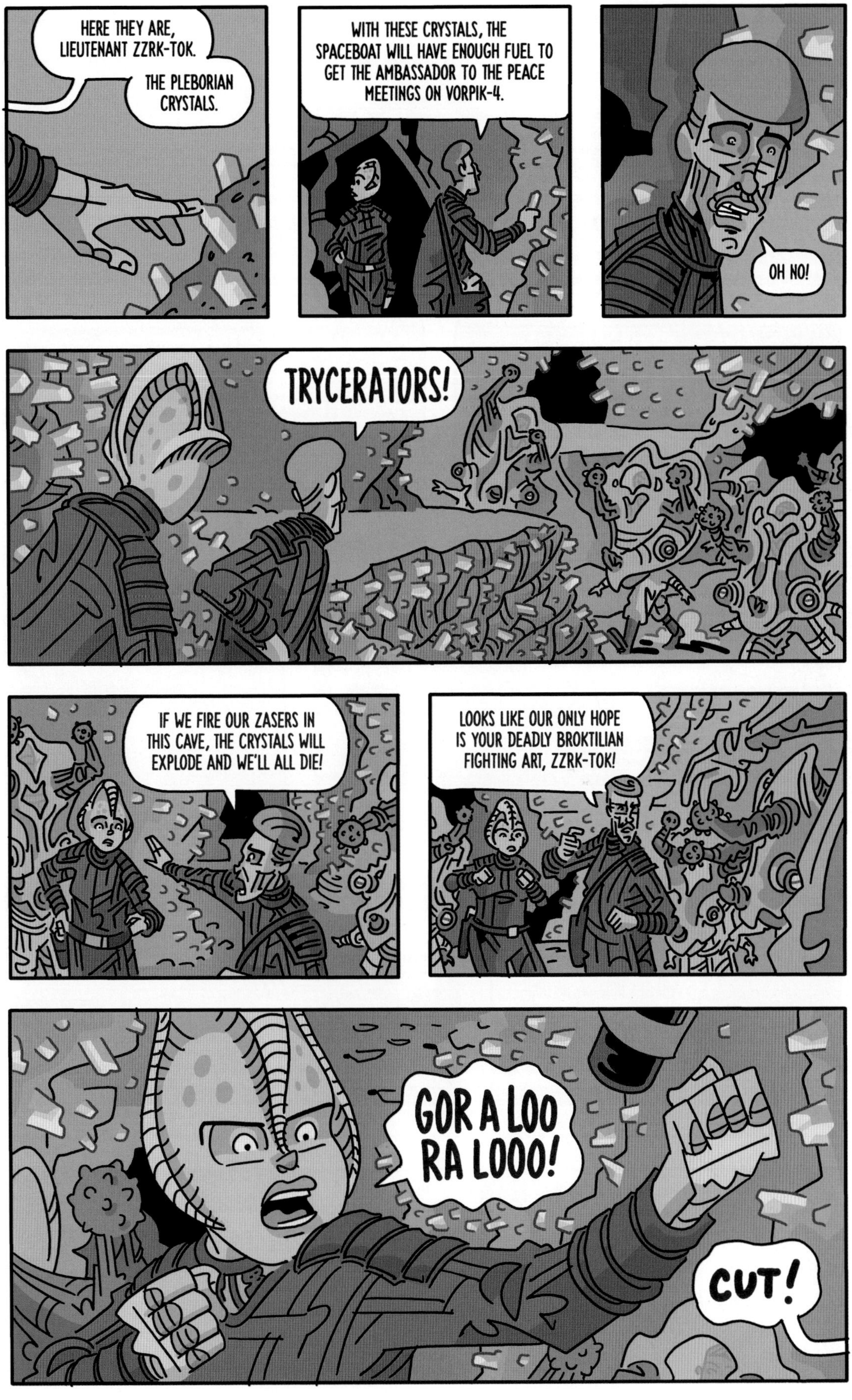
HERE THEY ARE, LIEUTENANT ZZRK-TOK.
THE PLEBORIAN CRYSTALS.
WITH THESE CRYSTALS, THE SPACEBOAT WILL HAVE ENOUGH FUEL TO GET THE AMBASSADOR TO THE PEACE MEETINGS ON VORPIK-4.
OH NO!
TRYCERATORS!
IF WE FIRE OUR ZASERS IN THIS CAVE, THE CRYSTALS WILL EXPLODE AND WE'LL ALL DIE!
LOOKS LIKE OUR ONLY HOPE IS YOUR DEADLY BROKTILIAN FIGHTING ART, ZZRK-TOK!
GOR A LOO RA LOOO!
CUT!

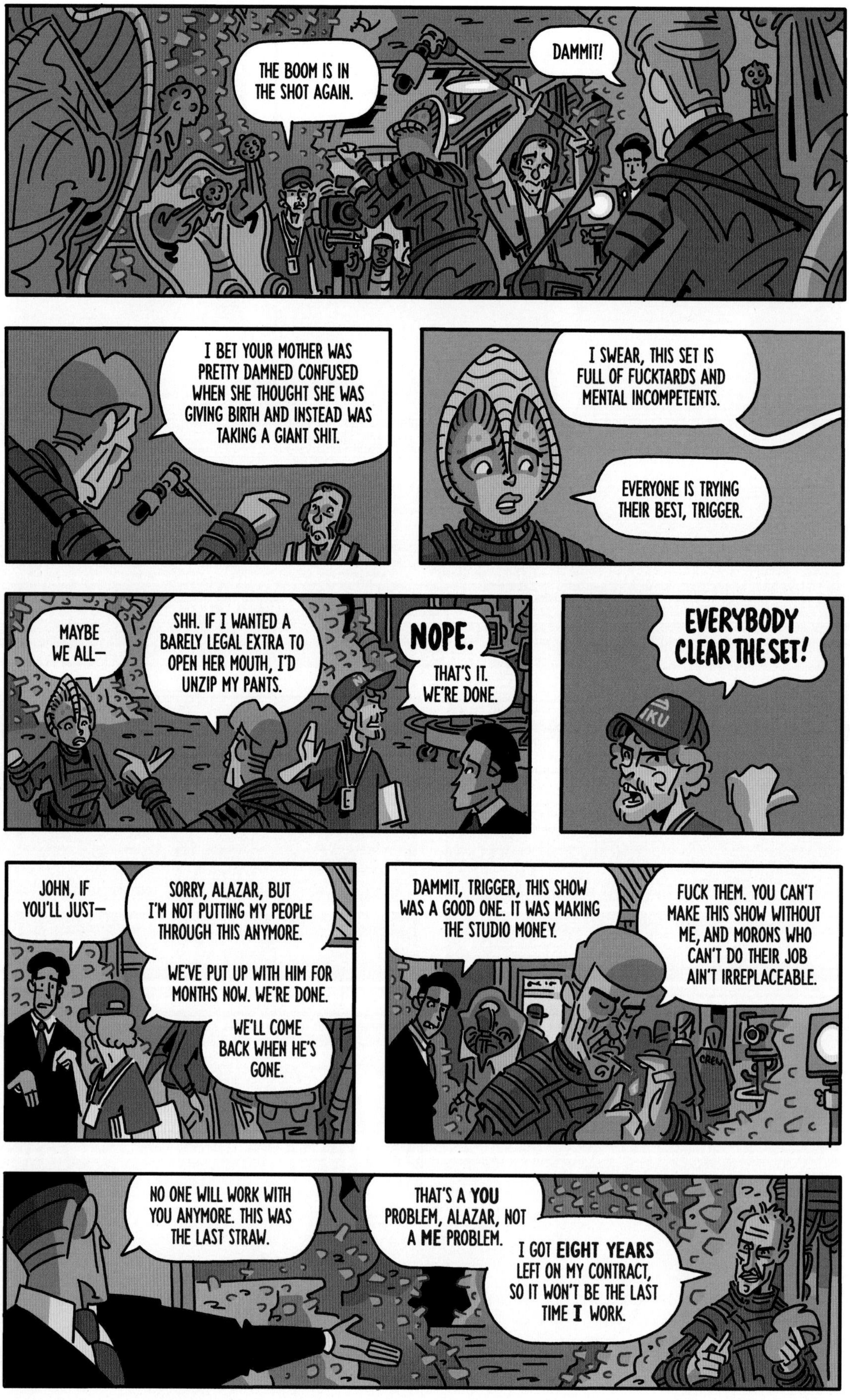
THE BOOM IS IN THE SHOT AGAIN.
DAMMIT!
I BET YOUR MOTHER WAS PRETTY DAMNED CONFUSED WHEN SHE THOUGHT SHE WAS GIVING BIRTH AND INSTEAD WAS TAKING A GIANT SHIT.
I SWEAR, THIS SET IS FULL OF FUCKTARDS AND MENTAL INCOMPETENTS.
EVERYONE IS TRYING THEIR BEST, TRIGGER.
MAYBE WE ALL—
SHH. IF I WANTED A BARELY LEGAL EXTRA TO OPEN HER MOUTH, I'D UNZIP MY PANTS.
NOPE.
THAT'S IT. WE'RE DONE.
EVERYBODY CLEAR THE SET!
JOHN, IF YOU'LL JUST—
SORRY, ALAZAR, BUT I'M NOT PUTTING MY PEOPLE THROUGH THIS ANYMORE.
WE'VE PUT UP WITH HIM FOR MONTHS NOW. WE'RE DONE.
WE'LL COME BACK WHEN HE'S GONE.
DAMMIT, TRIGGER, THIS SHOW WAS A GOOD ONE. IT WAS MAKING THE STUDIO MONEY.
FUCK THEM. YOU CAN'T MAKE THIS SHOW WITHOUT ME, AND MORONS WHO CAN'T DO THEIR JOB AIN'T IRREPLACEABLE.
NO ONE WILL WORK WITH YOU ANYMORE. THIS WAS THE LAST STRAW.
THAT'S A YOU PROBLEM, ALAZAR, NOT A ME PROBLEM.
I GOT EIGHT YEARS LEFT ON MY CONTRACT, SO IT WON'T BE THE LAST TIME I WORK.

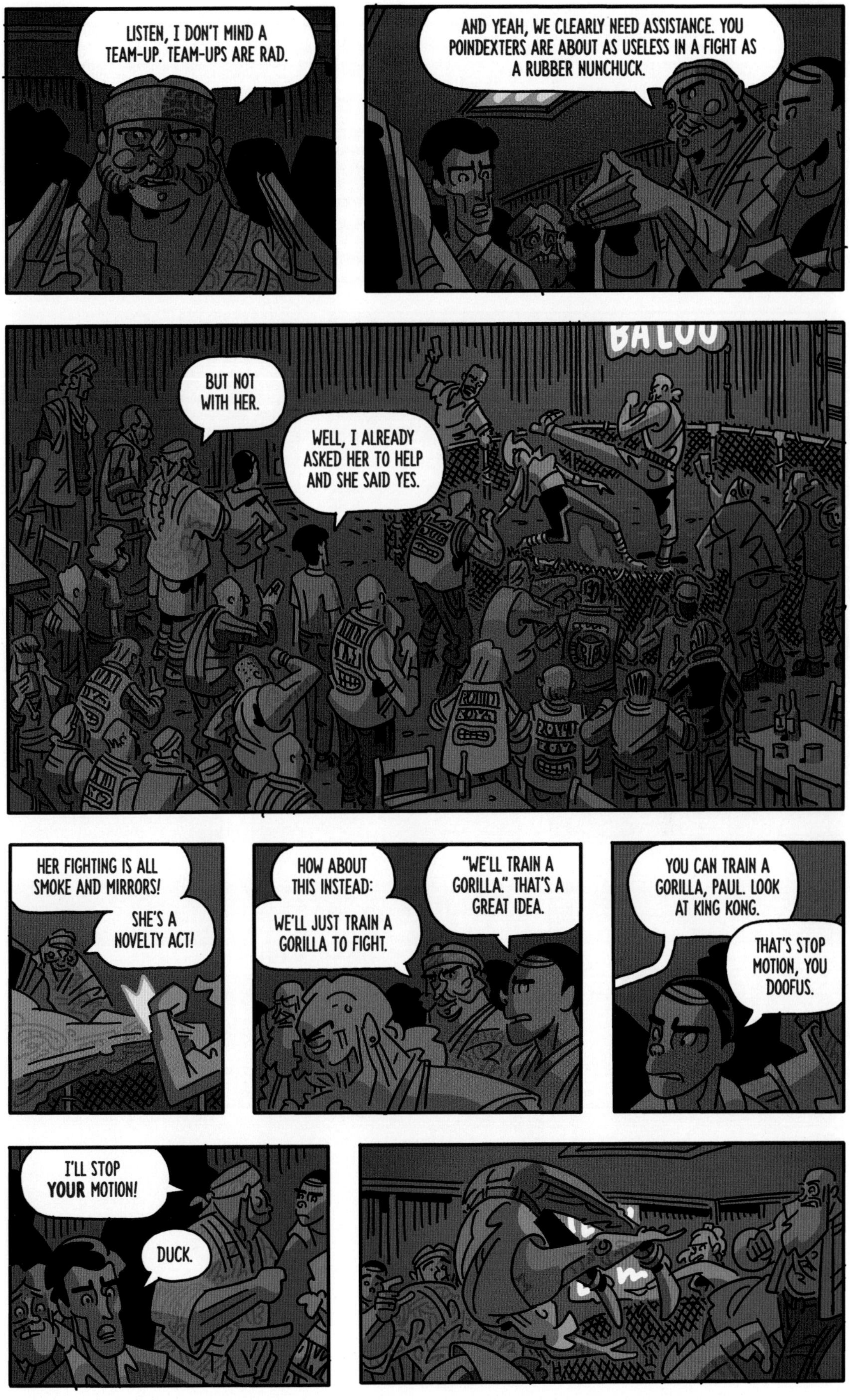
LISTEN, I DON'T MIND A TEAM-UP. TEAM-UPS ARE RAD.
AND YEAH, WE CLEARLY NEED ASSISTANCE. YOU POINDEXTERS ARE ABOUT AS USELESS IN A FIGHT AS A RUBBER NUNCHUCK.
BUT NOT WITH HER.
WELL, I ALREADY ASKED HER TO HELP AND SHE SAID YES.
HER FIGHTING IS ALL SMOKE AND MIRRORS!
SHE'S A NOVELTY ACT!
HOW ABOUT THIS INSTEAD:
WE'LL JUST TRAIN A GORILLA TO FIGHT.
"WE'LL TRAIN A GORILLA." THAT'S A GREAT IDEA.
YOU CAN TRAIN A GORILLA, PAUL. LOOK AT KING KONG.
THAT'S STOP MOTION, YOU DOOFUS.
I'LL STOP YOUR MOTION!
DUCK.

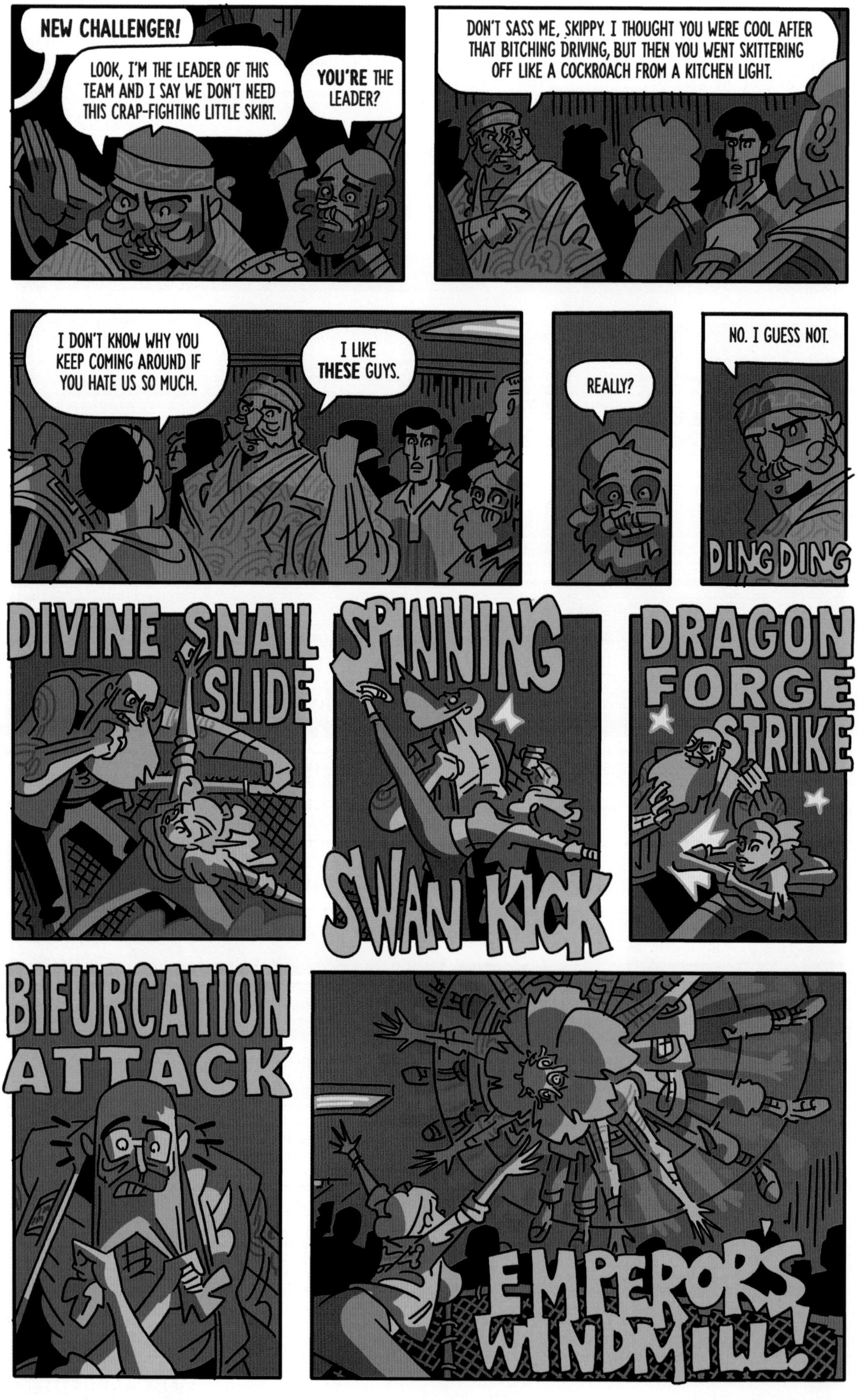
NEW CHALLENGER!
LOOK, I'M THE LEADER OF THIS TEAM AND I SAY WE DON'T NEED THIS CRAP-FIGHTING LITTLE SKIRT.
YOU'RE THE LEADER?
DON'T SASS ME, SKIPPY. I THOUGHT YOU WERE COOL AFTER THAT BITCHING DRIVING, BUT THEN YOU WENT SKITTERING OFF LIKE A COCKROACH FROM A KITCHEN LIGHT.
I DON'T KNOW WHY YOU KEEP COMING AROUND IF YOU HATE US SO MUCH.
I LIKE THESE GUYS.
REALLY?
NO. I GUESS NOT.
DING DING
DIVINE SNAIL SLIDE
SPINNING SWAN KICK
DRAGON FORGE STRIKE
BIFURCATION ATTACK
EMPEROR'S WINDMILL!

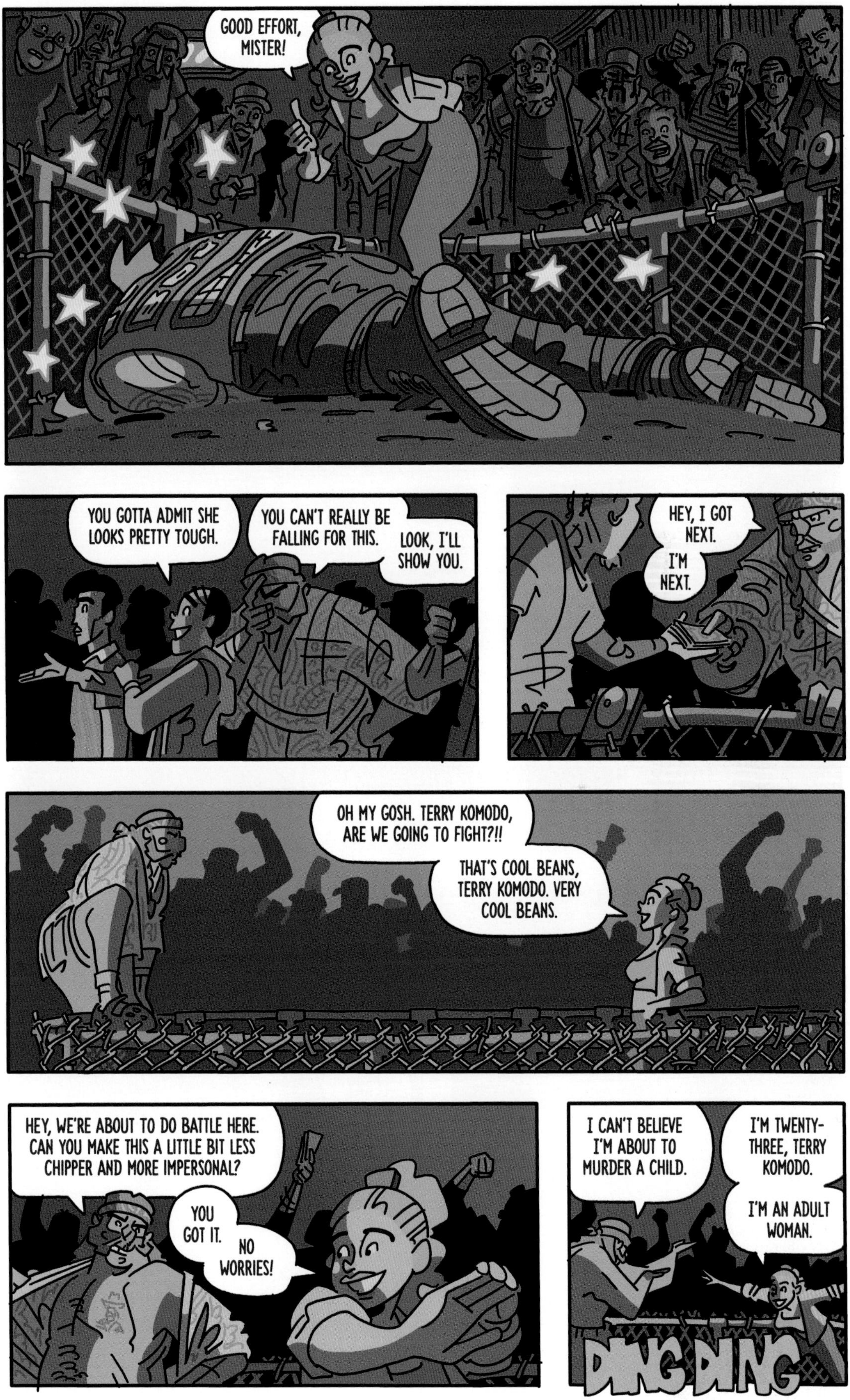
GOOD EFFORT, MISTER!
YOU GOTTA ADMIT SHE LOOKS PRETTY TOUGH.
YOU CAN'T REALLY BE FALLING FOR THIS.
LOOK, I'LL SHOW YOU.
HEY, I GOT NEXT.
I'M NEXT.
OH MY GOSH. TERRY KOMODO, ARE WE GOING TO FIGHT?!!
THAT'S COOL BEANS, TERRY KOMODO. VERY COOL BEANS.
HEY, WE'RE ABOUT TO DO BATTLE HERE. CAN YOU MAKE THIS A LITTLE BIT LESS CHIPPER AND MORE IMPERSONAL?
YOU GOT IT.
NO WORRIES!
I CAN'T BELIEVE I'M ABOUT TO MURDER A CHILD.
I'M TWENTY-THREE, TERRY KOMODO.
I'M AN ADULT WOMAN.
DING DING

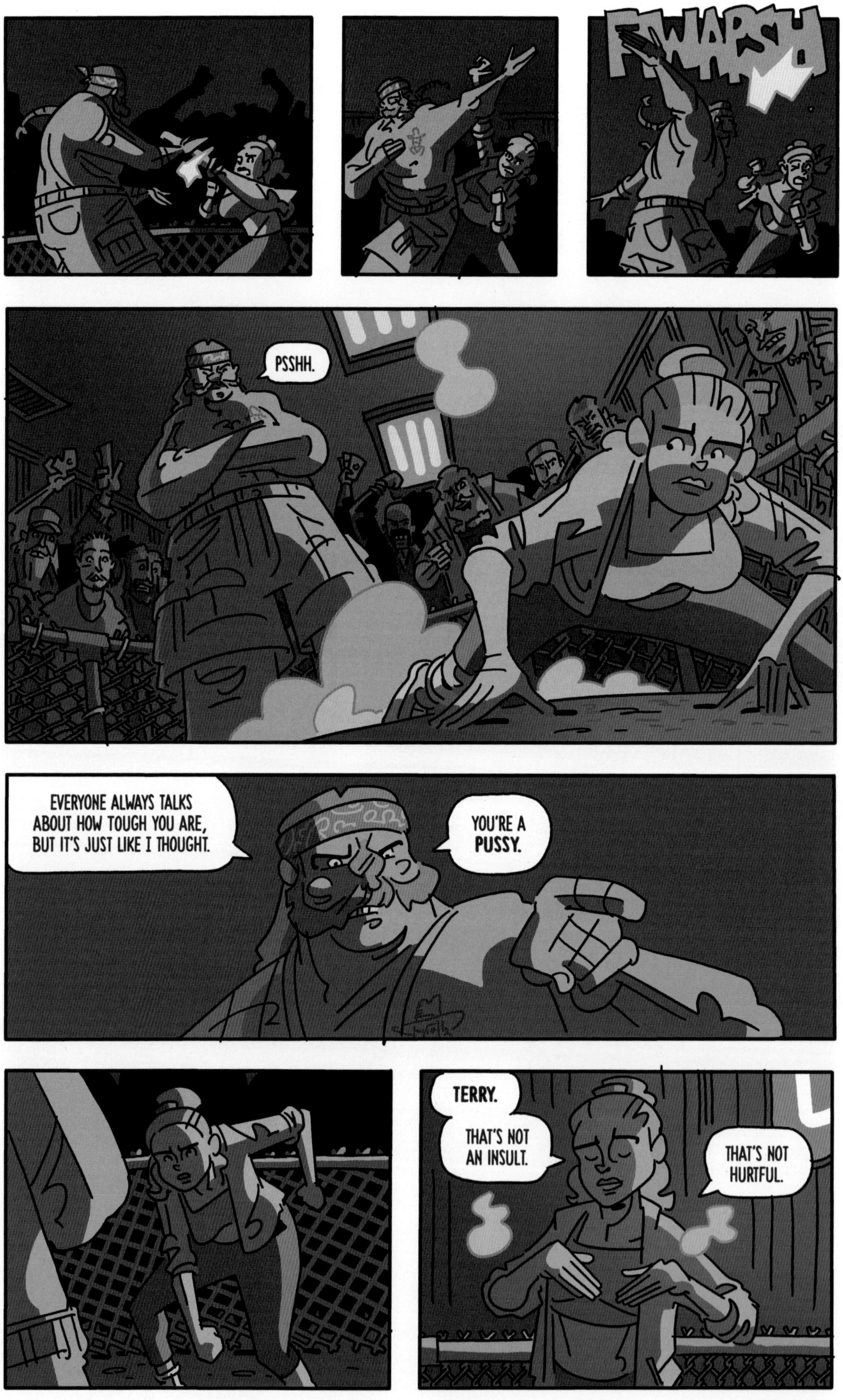
FWAPSH
PSSHH.
EVERYONE ALWAYS TALKS ABOUT HOW TOUGH YOU ARE, BUT IT'S JUST LIKE I THOUGHT.
YOU'RE A PUSSY.
TERRY.
THAT'S NOT AN INSULT.
THAT'S NOT HURTFUL.

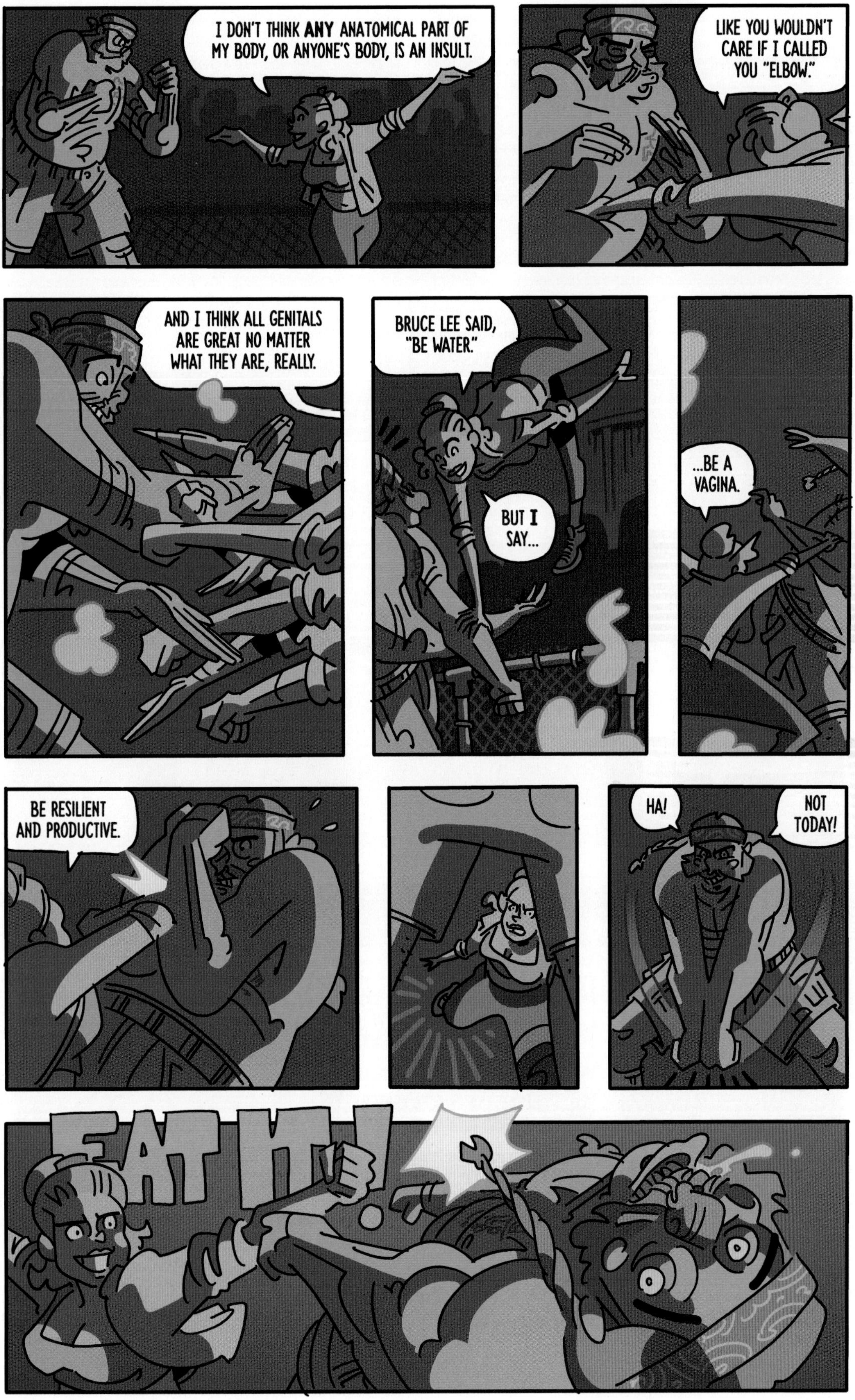
I DON'T THINK **ANY** ANATOMICAL PART OF MY BODY, OR ANYONE'S BODY, IS AN INSULT.
LIKE YOU WOULDN'T CARE IF I CALLED YOU "ELBOW."
AND I THINK ALL GENITALS ARE GREAT NO MATTER WHAT THEY ARE, REALLY.
BRUCE LEE SAID, "BE WATER."
BUT **I** SAY...
...BE A VAGINA.
BE RESILIENT AND PRODUCTIVE.
HA!
NOT TODAY!
EAT IT!

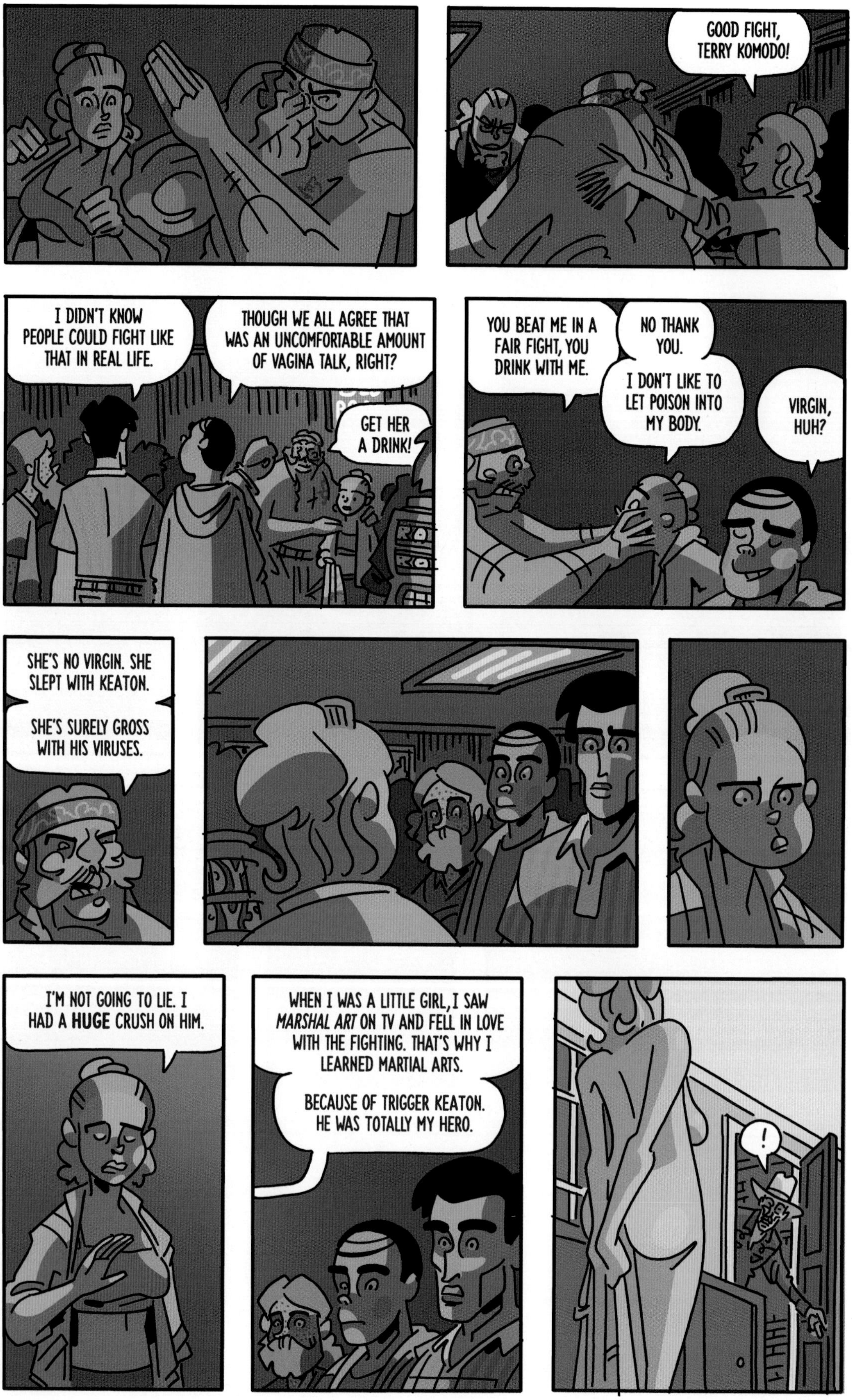
GOOD FIGHT, TERRY KOMODO!
I DIDN'T KNOW PEOPLE COULD FIGHT LIKE THAT IN REAL LIFE.
THOUGH WE ALL AGREE THAT WAS AN UNCOMFORTABLE AMOUNT OF VAGINA TALK, RIGHT?
GET HER A DRINK!
YOU BEAT ME IN A FAIR FIGHT, YOU DRINK WITH ME.
NO THANK YOU.
I DON'T LIKE TO LET POISON INTO MY BODY.
VIRGIN, HUH?
SHE'S NO VIRGIN. SHE SLEPT WITH KEATON.
SHE'S SURELY GROSS WITH HIS VIRUSES.
I'M NOT GOING TO LIE. I HAD A **HUGE** CRUSH ON HIM.
WHEN I WAS A LITTLE GIRL, I SAW *MARSHAL ART* ON TV AND FELL IN LOVE WITH THE FIGHTING. THAT'S WHY I LEARNED MARTIAL ARTS.
BECAUSE OF TRIGGER KEATON. HE WAS TOTALLY MY HERO.
!

GIRL, TAKING YOU TO BONETOWN WOULDN'T BE NOTHING TO ME.

BUT I GOT A POLICY OF NEVER GETTING NAKED AROUND **ANYONE** WHO COULD TAKE ME IN A FIGHT.

THAT'S HOW YOU LOSE A PECKER.

ANYWAY, I REALLY DODGED A BULLET THERE BECAUSE HE WAS A NASTY, NASTY MAN.

I'LL DRINK TO THAT.

THIS IS DELICIOUS!

LIKE EVEN IF TRIGGER WAS MURDERED—

—AND I'M NOT DOUBTING THAT—

I'M NOT REAL SURE WHY **WE'RE** SUPPOSED TO DO ANYTHING ABOUT IT.

JUSTICE.
A CRIME WAS COMMITTED AND THE PERPETRATOR IS GOING TO GET AWAY WITH IT UNLESS WE DO SOMETHING.

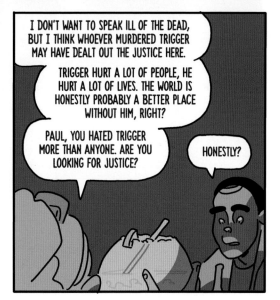

I DON'T WANT TO SPEAK ILL OF THE DEAD, BUT I THINK WHOEVER MURDERED TRIGGER MAY HAVE DEALT OUT THE JUSTICE HERE.

TRIGGER HURT A LOT OF PEOPLE, HE HURT A LOT OF LIVES. THE WORLD IS HONESTLY PROBABLY A BETTER PLACE WITHOUT HIM, RIGHT?

PAUL, YOU HATED TRIGGER MORE THAN ANYONE. ARE YOU LOOKING FOR JUSTICE?

HONESTLY?

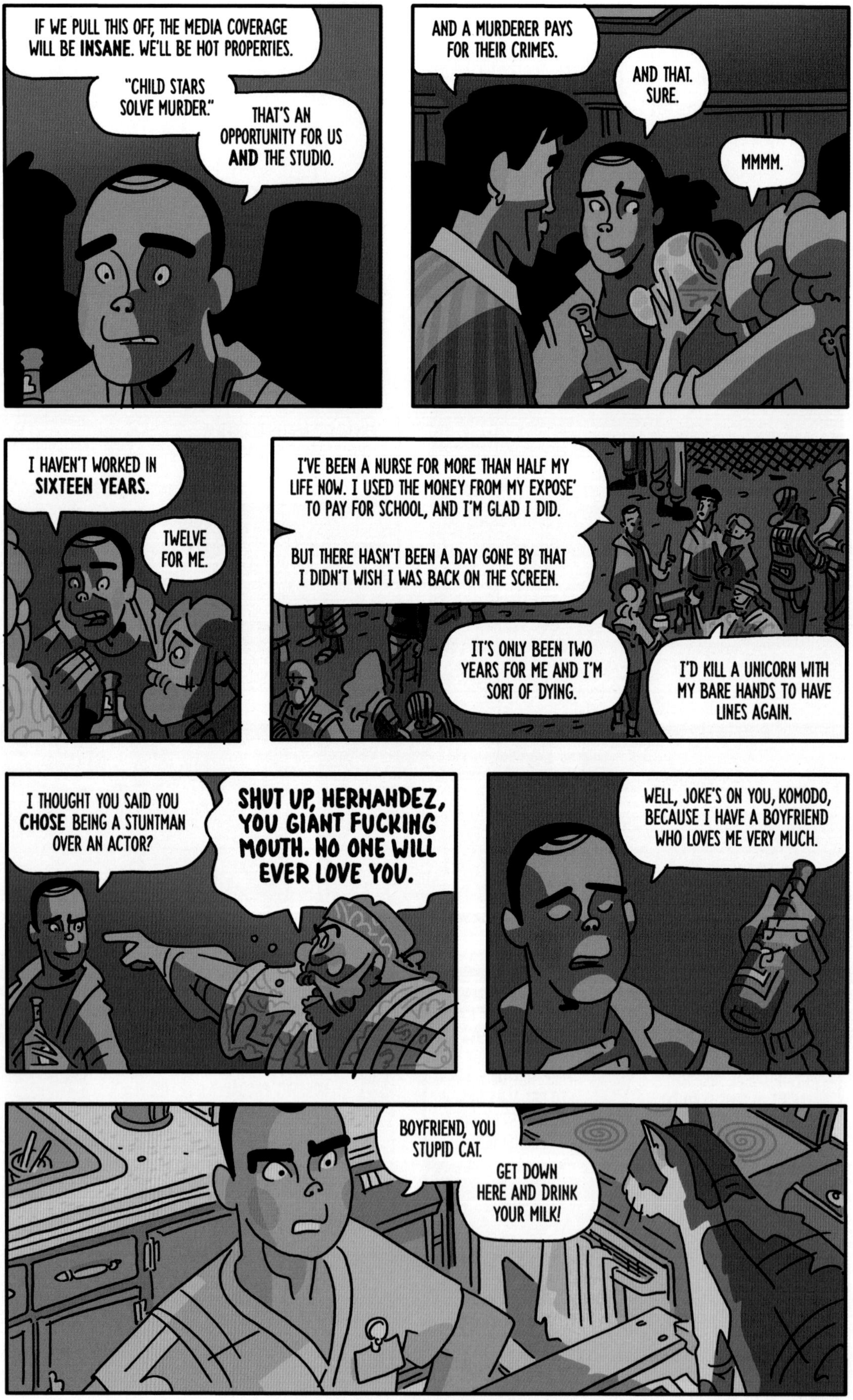
IF WE PULL THIS OFF, THE MEDIA COVERAGE WILL BE **INSANE**. WE'LL BE HOT PROPERTIES.
"CHILD STARS SOLVE MURDER."
THAT'S AN OPPORTUNITY FOR US **AND** THE STUDIO.
AND A MURDERER PAYS FOR THEIR CRIMES.
AND THAT. SURE.
MMMM.
I HAVEN'T WORKED IN **SIXTEEN YEARS.**
TWELVE FOR ME.
I'VE BEEN A NURSE FOR MORE THAN HALF MY LIFE NOW. I USED THE MONEY FROM MY EXPOSE' TO PAY FOR SCHOOL, AND I'M GLAD I DID.
BUT THERE HASN'T BEEN A DAY GONE BY THAT I DIDN'T WISH I WAS BACK ON THE SCREEN.
IT'S ONLY BEEN TWO YEARS FOR ME AND I'M SORT OF DYING.
I'D KILL A UNICORN WITH MY BARE HANDS TO HAVE LINES AGAIN.
I THOUGHT YOU SAID YOU **CHOSE** BEING A STUNTMAN OVER AN ACTOR?
SHUT UP, HERNANDEZ, YOU GIANT FUCKING MOUTH. NO ONE WILL EVER LOVE YOU.
WELL, JOKE'S ON YOU, KOMODO, BECAUSE I HAVE A BOYFRIEND WHO LOVES ME VERY MUCH.
BOYFRIEND, YOU STUPID CAT.
GET DOWN HERE AND DRINK YOUR MILK!

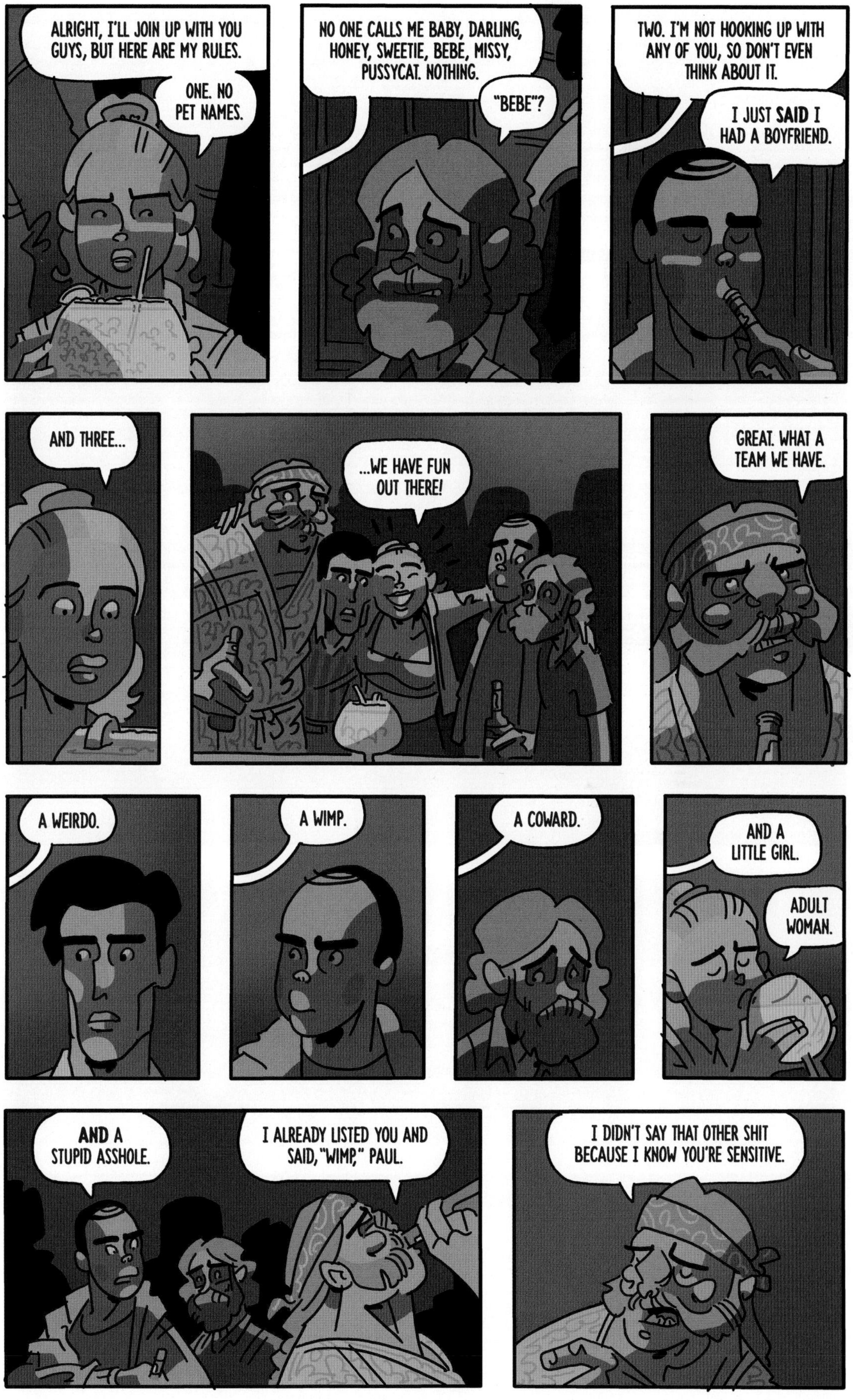
ALRIGHT, I'LL JOIN UP WITH YOU GUYS, BUT HERE ARE MY RULES.
ONE. NO PET NAMES.
NO ONE CALLS ME BABY, DARLING, HONEY, SWEETIE, BEBE, MISSY, PUSSYCAT. NOTHING.
"BEBE"?
TWO. I'M NOT HOOKING UP WITH ANY OF YOU, SO DON'T EVEN THINK ABOUT IT.
I JUST **SAID** I HAD A BOYFRIEND.
AND THREE...
...WE HAVE FUN OUT THERE!
GREAT. WHAT A TEAM WE HAVE.
A WEIRDO.
A WIMP.
A COWARD.
AND A LITTLE GIRL.
ADULT WOMAN.
AND A STUPID ASSHOLE.
I ALREADY LISTED YOU AND SAID, "WIMP," PAUL.
I DIDN'T SAY THAT OTHER SHIT BECAUSE I KNOW YOU'RE SENSITIVE.

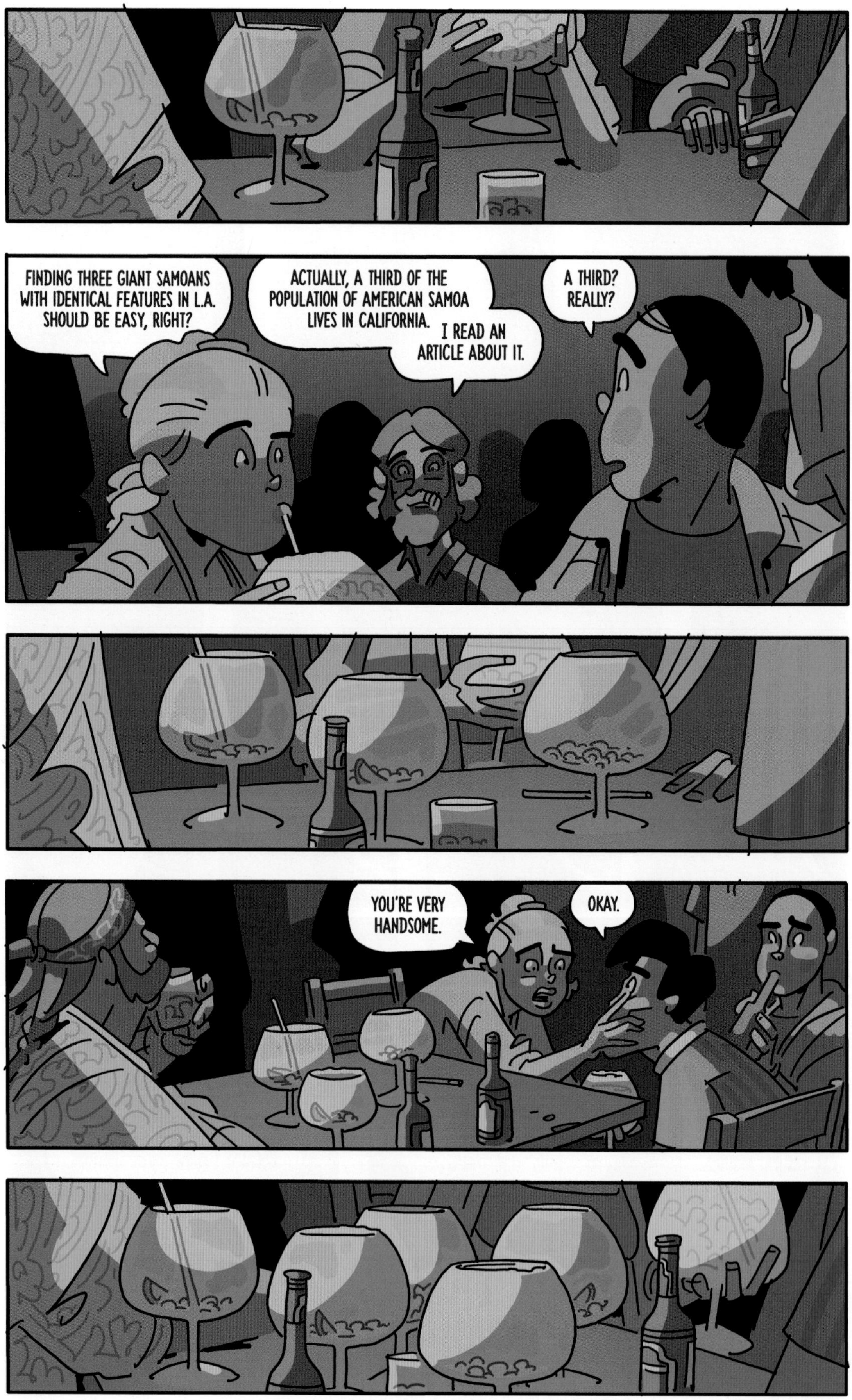

FINDING THREE GIANT SAMOANS WITH IDENTICAL FEATURES IN L.A. SHOULD BE EASY, RIGHT?
ACTUALLY, A THIRD OF THE POPULATION OF AMERICAN SAMOA LIVES IN CALIFORNIA.
I READ AN ARTICLE ABOUT IT.
A THIRD? REALLY?
YOU'RE VERY HANDSOME.
OKAY.

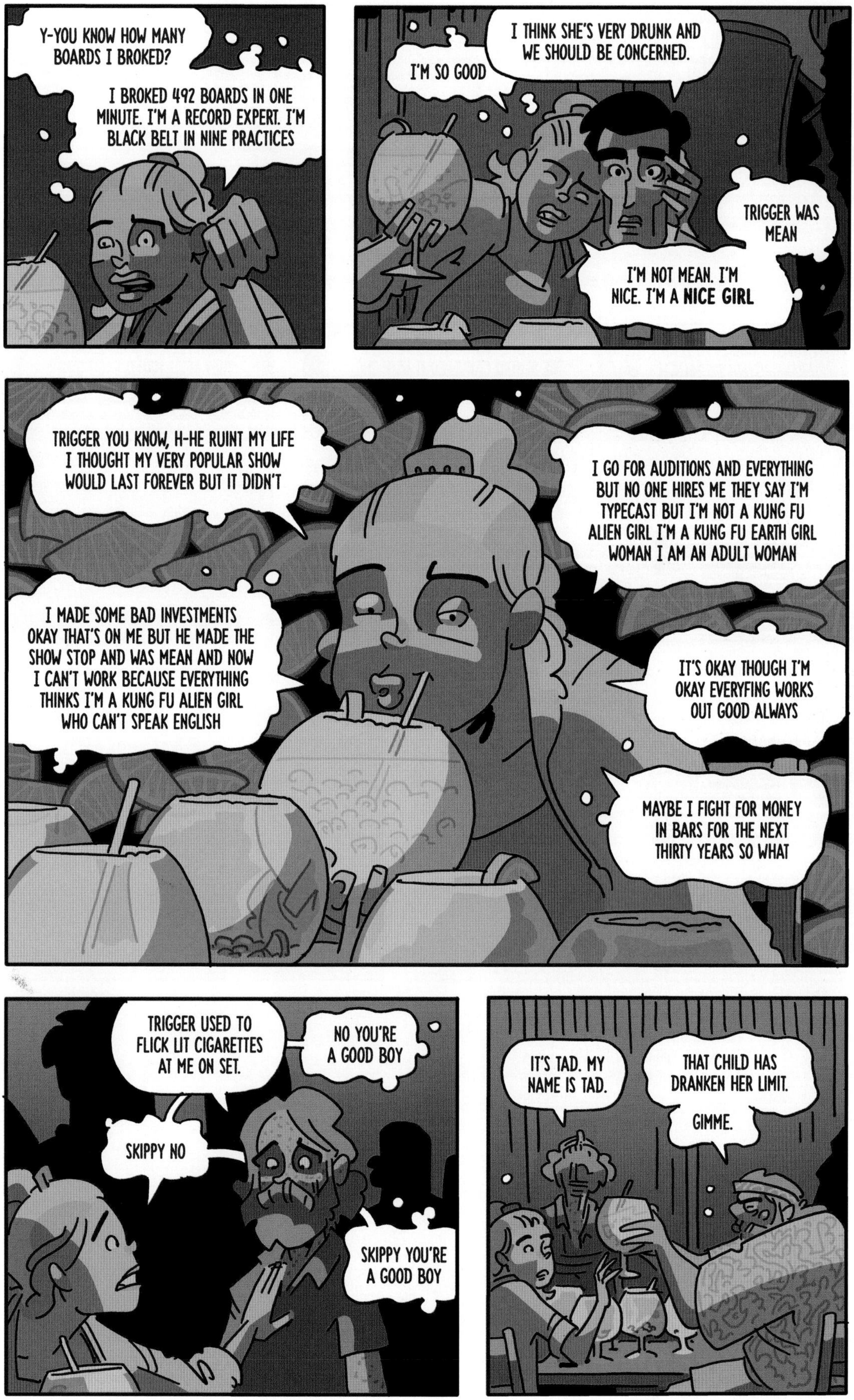
Y-YOU KNOW HOW MANY BOARDS I BROKED?
I BROKED 492 BOARDS IN ONE MINUTE. I'M A RECORD EXPERT. I'M BLACK BELT IN NINE PRACTICES
I THINK SHE'S VERY DRUNK AND WE SHOULD BE CONCERNED.
I'M SO GOOD
TRIGGER WAS MEAN
I'M NOT MEAN. I'M NICE. I'M A **NICE GIRL**
TRIGGER YOU KNOW, H-HE RUINT MY LIFE I THOUGHT MY VERY POPULAR SHOW WOULD LAST FOREVER BUT IT DIDN'T
I GO FOR AUDITIONS AND EVERYTHING BUT NO ONE HIRES ME THEY SAY I'M TYPECAST BUT I'M NOT A KUNG FU ALIEN GIRL I'M A KUNG FU EARTH GIRL WOMAN I AM AN ADULT WOMAN
I MADE SOME BAD INVESTMENTS OKAY THAT'S ON ME BUT HE MADE THE SHOW STOP AND WAS MEAN AND NOW I CAN'T WORK BECAUSE EVERYTHING THINKS I'M A KUNG FU ALIEN GIRL WHO CAN'T SPEAK ENGLISH
IT'S OKAY THOUGH I'M OKAY EVERYFING WORKS OUT GOOD ALWAYS
MAYBE I FIGHT FOR MONEY IN BARS FOR THE NEXT THIRTY YEARS SO WHAT
TRIGGER USED TO FLICK LIT CIGARETTES AT ME ON SET.
NO YOU'RE A GOOD BOY
SKIPPY NO
SKIPPY YOU'RE A GOOD BOY
IT'S TAD. MY NAME IS TAD.
THAT CHILD HAS DRANKEN HER LIMIT.
GIMME.

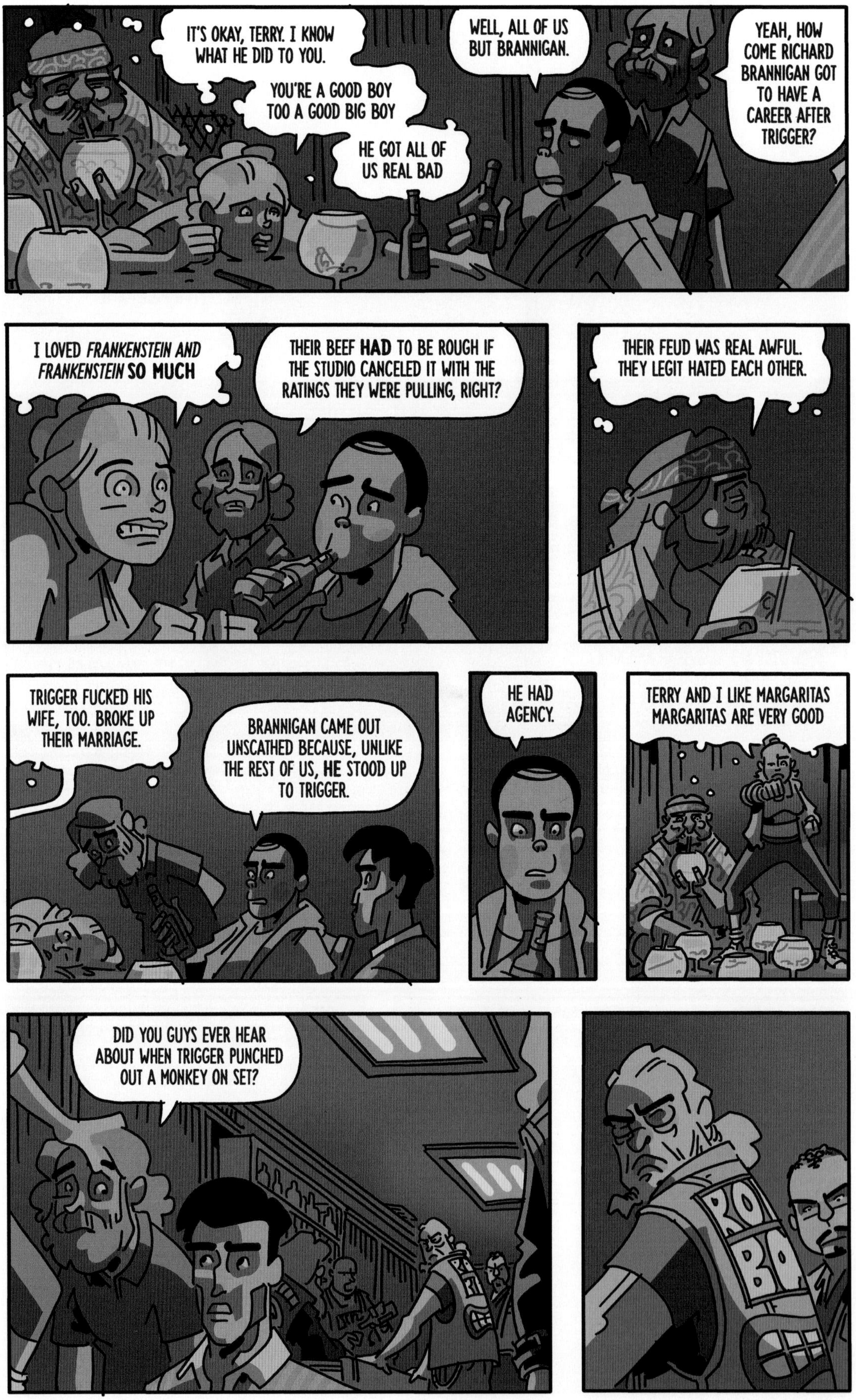
IT'S OKAY, TERRY. I KNOW WHAT HE DID TO YOU.
YOU'RE A GOOD BOY TOO A GOOD BIG BOY
HE GOT ALL OF US REAL BAD
WELL, ALL OF US BUT BRANNIGAN.
YEAH, HOW COME RICHARD BRANNIGAN GOT TO HAVE A CAREER AFTER TRIGGER?
I LOVED *FRANKENSTEIN AND FRANKENSTEIN* **SO MUCH**
THEIR BEEF **HAD** TO BE ROUGH IF THE STUDIO CANCELED IT WITH THE RATINGS THEY WERE PULLING, RIGHT?
THEIR FEUD WAS REAL AWFUL. THEY LEGIT HATED EACH OTHER.
TRIGGER FUCKED HIS WIFE, TOO. BROKE UP THEIR MARRIAGE.
BRANNIGAN CAME OUT UNSCATHED BECAUSE, UNLIKE THE REST OF US, **HE** STOOD UP TO TRIGGER.
HE HAD AGENCY.
TERRY AND I LIKE MARGARITAS MARGARITAS ARE VERY GOOD
DID YOU GUYS EVER HEAR ABOUT WHEN TRIGGER PUNCHED OUT A MONKEY ON SET?

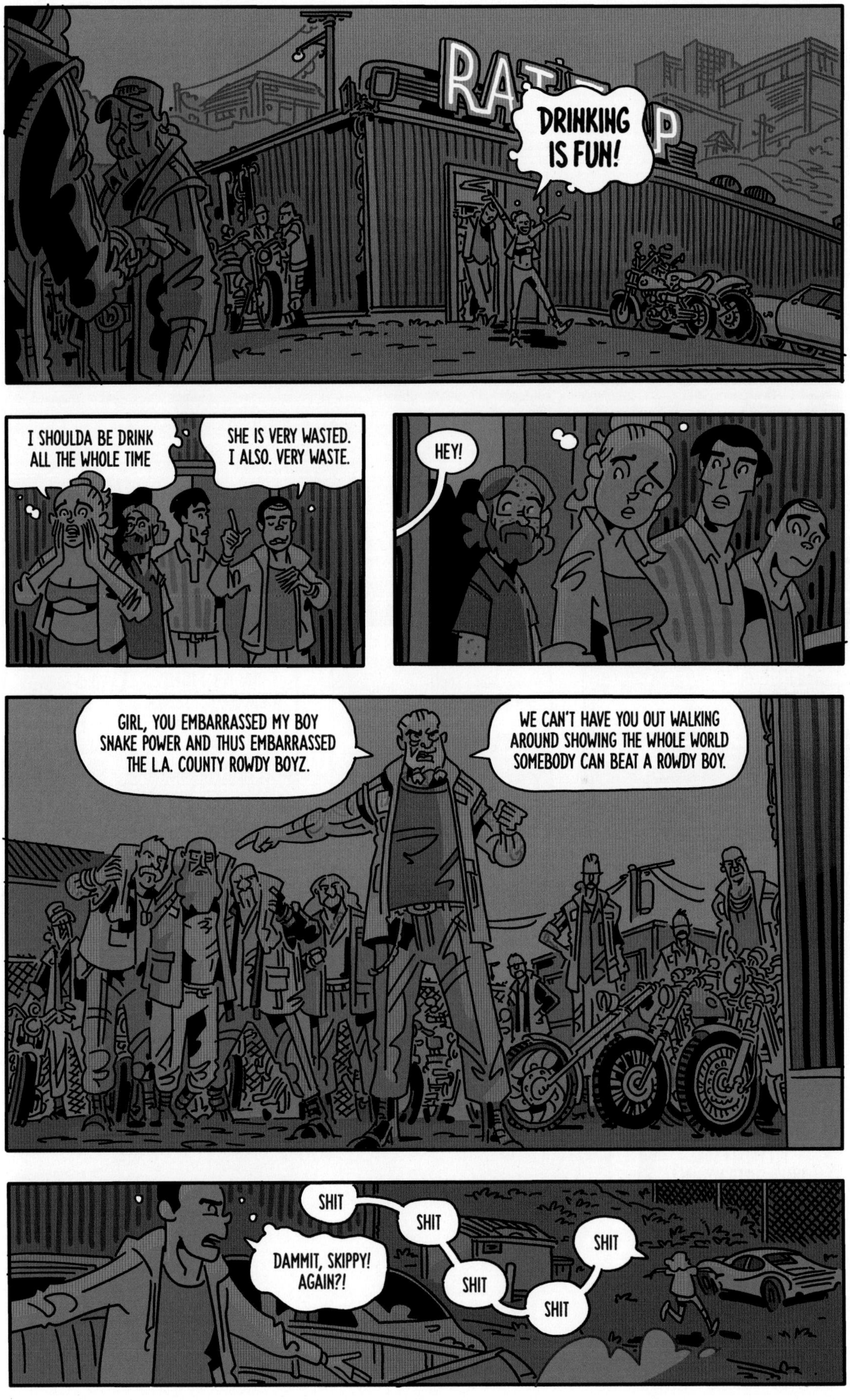

DRINKING IS FUN!
I SHOULDA BE DRINK ALL THE WHOLE TIME
SHE IS VERY WASTED. I ALSO. VERY WASTE.
HEY!
GIRL, YOU EMBARRASSED MY BOY SNAKE POWER AND THUS EMBARRASSED THE L.A. COUNTY ROWDY BOYZ.
WE CAN'T HAVE YOU OUT WALKING AROUND SHOWING THE WHOLE WORLD SOMEBODY CAN BEAT A ROWDY BOY.
DAMMIT, SKIPPY! AGAIN?!
SHIT
SHIT
SHIT
SHIT
SHIT

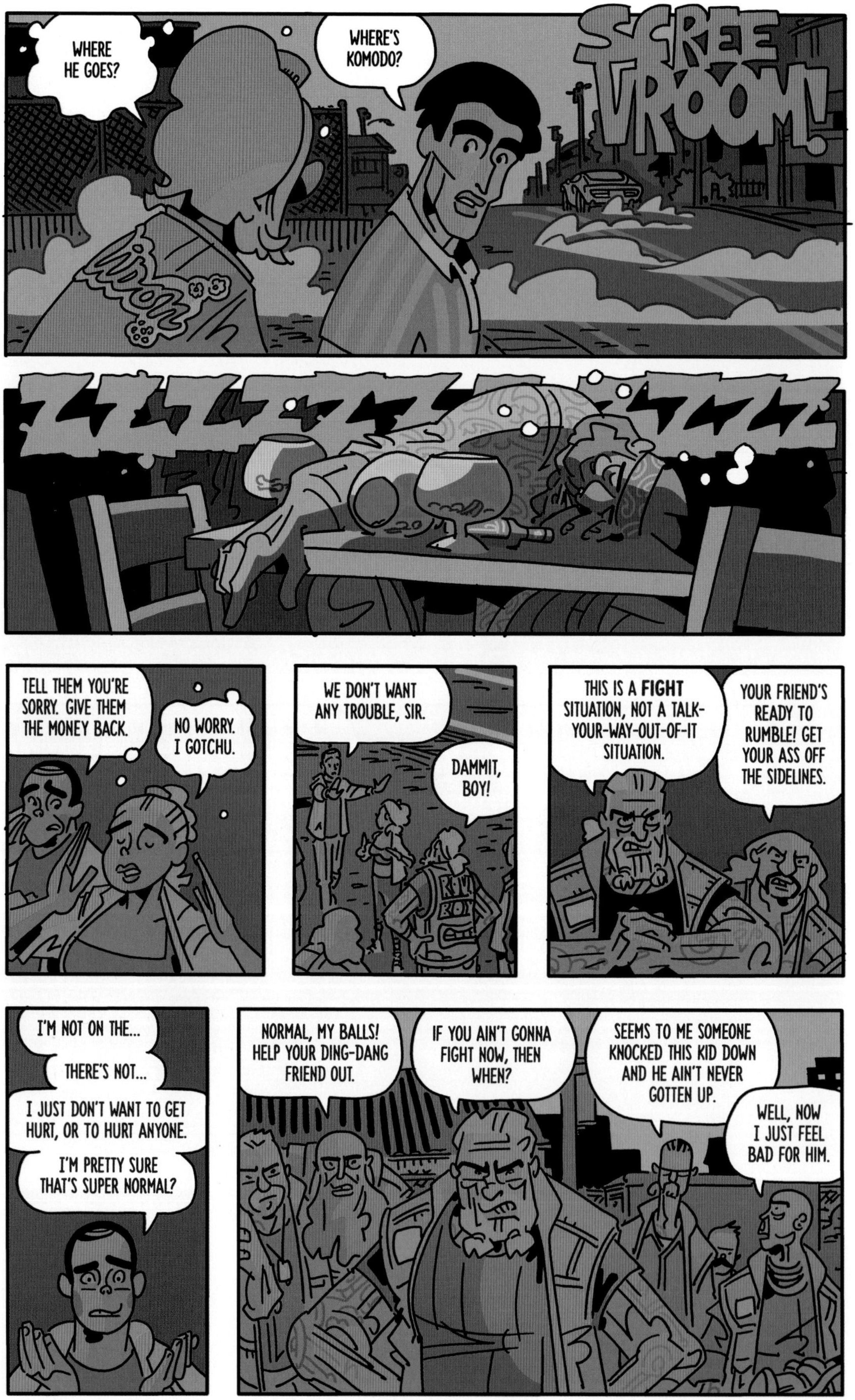
WHERE HE GOES?
WHERE'S KOMODO?
SCREE VROOM!
ZZZZZZ ZZZZZ
TELL THEM YOU'RE SORRY. GIVE THEM THE MONEY BACK.
NO WORRY. I GOTCHU.
WE DON'T WANT ANY TROUBLE, SIR.
DAMMIT, BOY!
THIS IS A **FIGHT** SITUATION, NOT A TALK-YOUR-WAY-OUT-OF-IT SITUATION.
YOUR FRIEND'S READY TO RUMBLE! GET YOUR ASS OFF THE SIDELINES.
I'M NOT ON THE...
THERE'S NOT...
I JUST DON'T WANT TO GET HURT, OR TO HURT ANYONE.
I'M PRETTY SURE THAT'S SUPER NORMAL?
NORMAL, MY BALLS! HELP YOUR DING-DANG FRIEND OUT.
IF YOU AIN'T GONNA FIGHT NOW, THEN WHEN?
SEEMS TO ME SOMEONE KNOCKED THIS KID DOWN AND HE AIN'T NEVER GOTTEN UP.
WELL, NOW I JUST FEEL BAD FOR HIM.

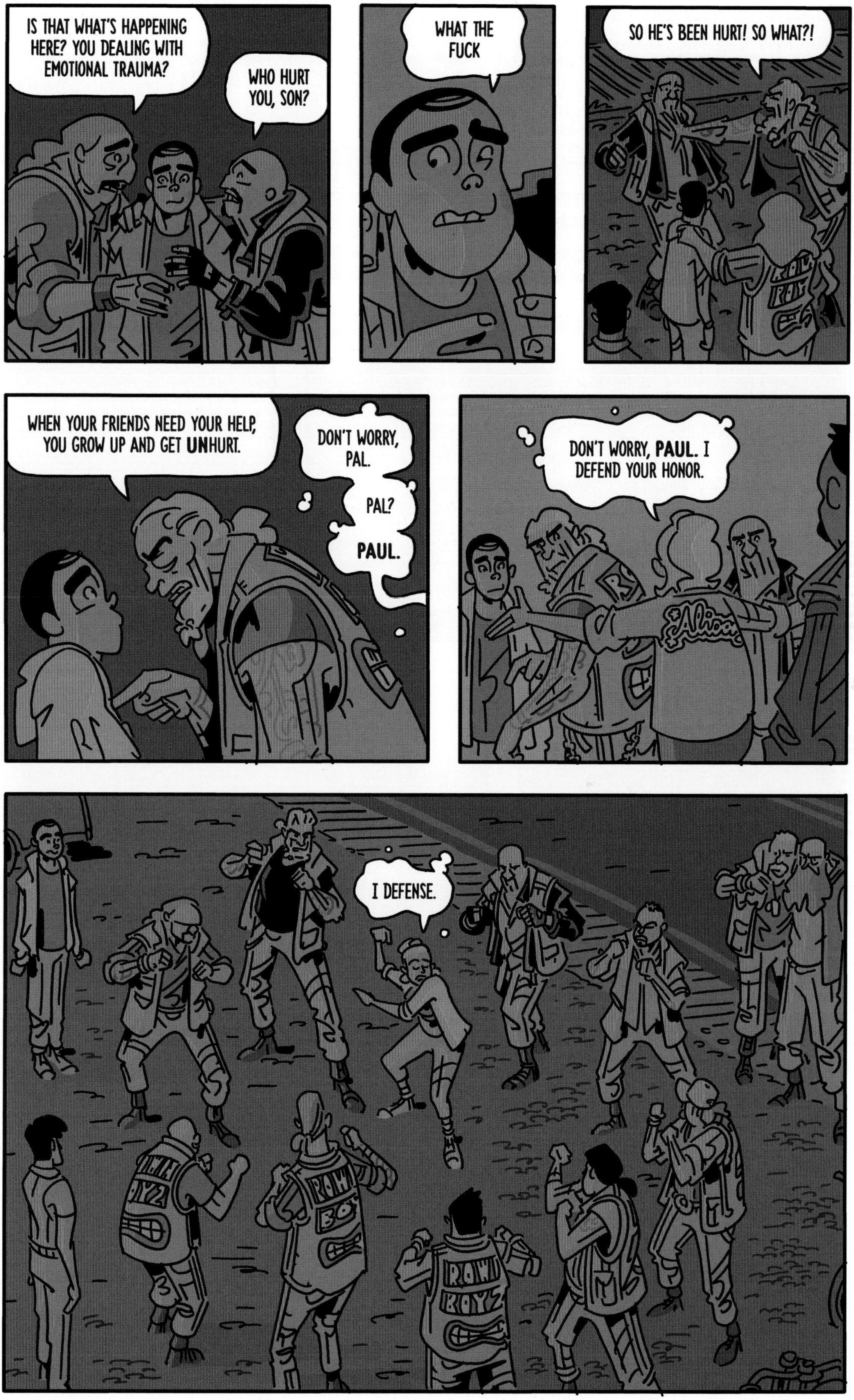
IS THAT WHAT'S HAPPENING HERE? YOU DEALING WITH EMOTIONAL TRAUMA?
WHO HURT YOU, SON?
WHAT THE FUCK
SO HE'S BEEN HURT! SO WHAT?!
WHEN YOUR FRIENDS NEED YOUR HELP, YOU GROW UP AND GET **UN**HURT.
DON'T WORRY, PAL.
PAL?
PAUL.
DON'T WORRY, **PAUL.** I DEFEND YOUR HONOR.
I DEFENSE.

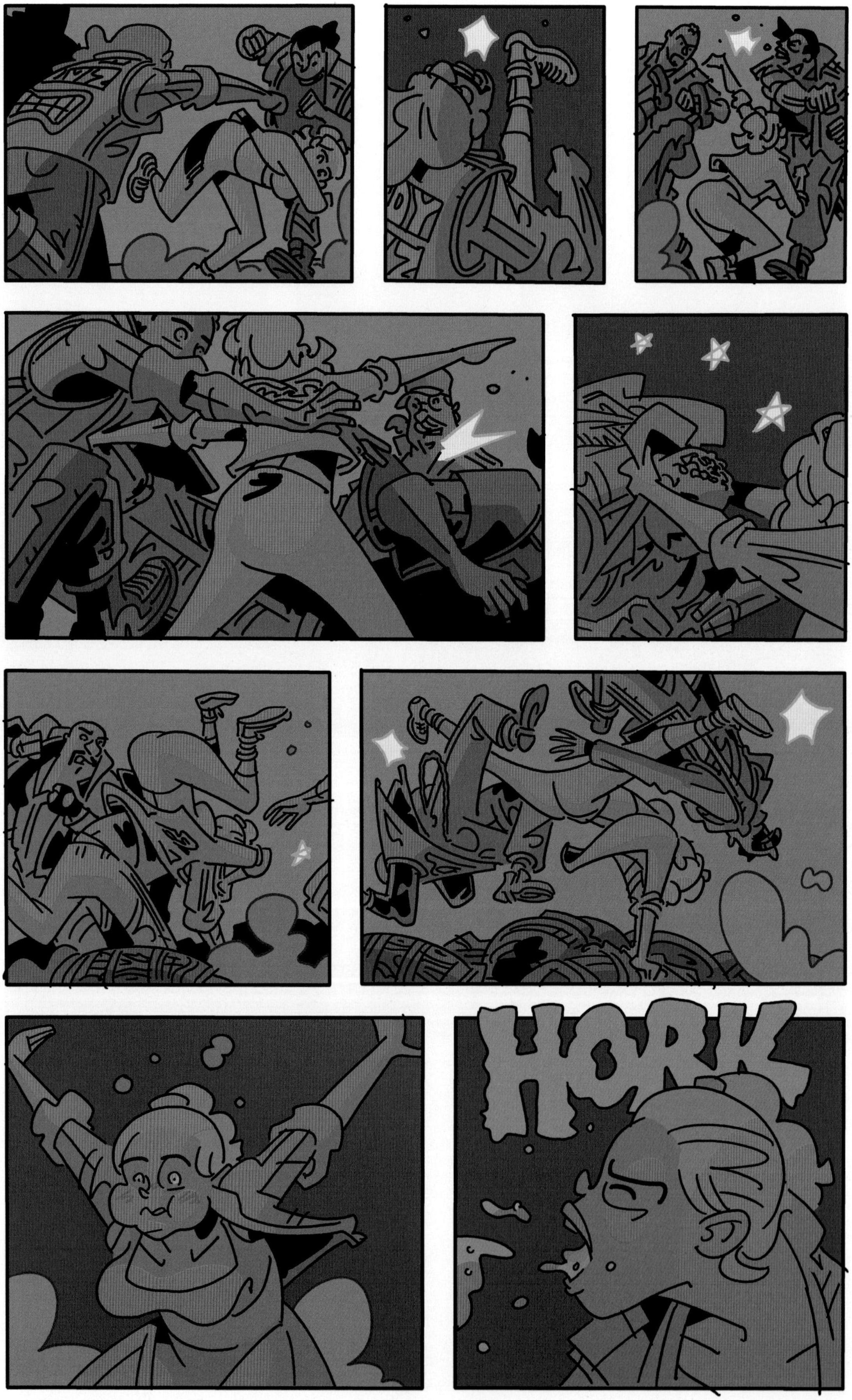
HORK

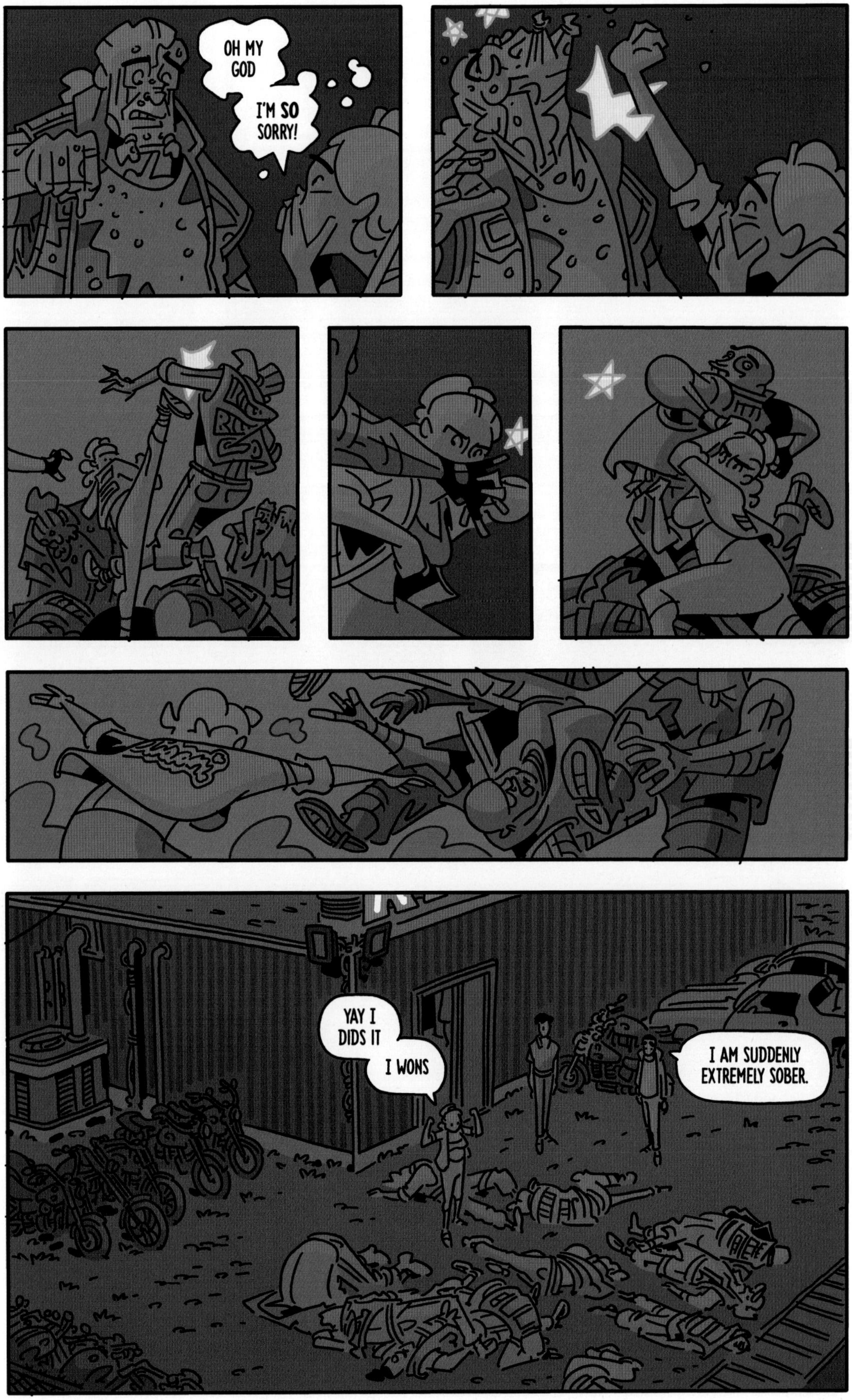
OH MY GOD
I'M SO SORRY!
YAY I DIDS IT
I WONS
I AM SUDDENLY EXTREMELY SOBER.

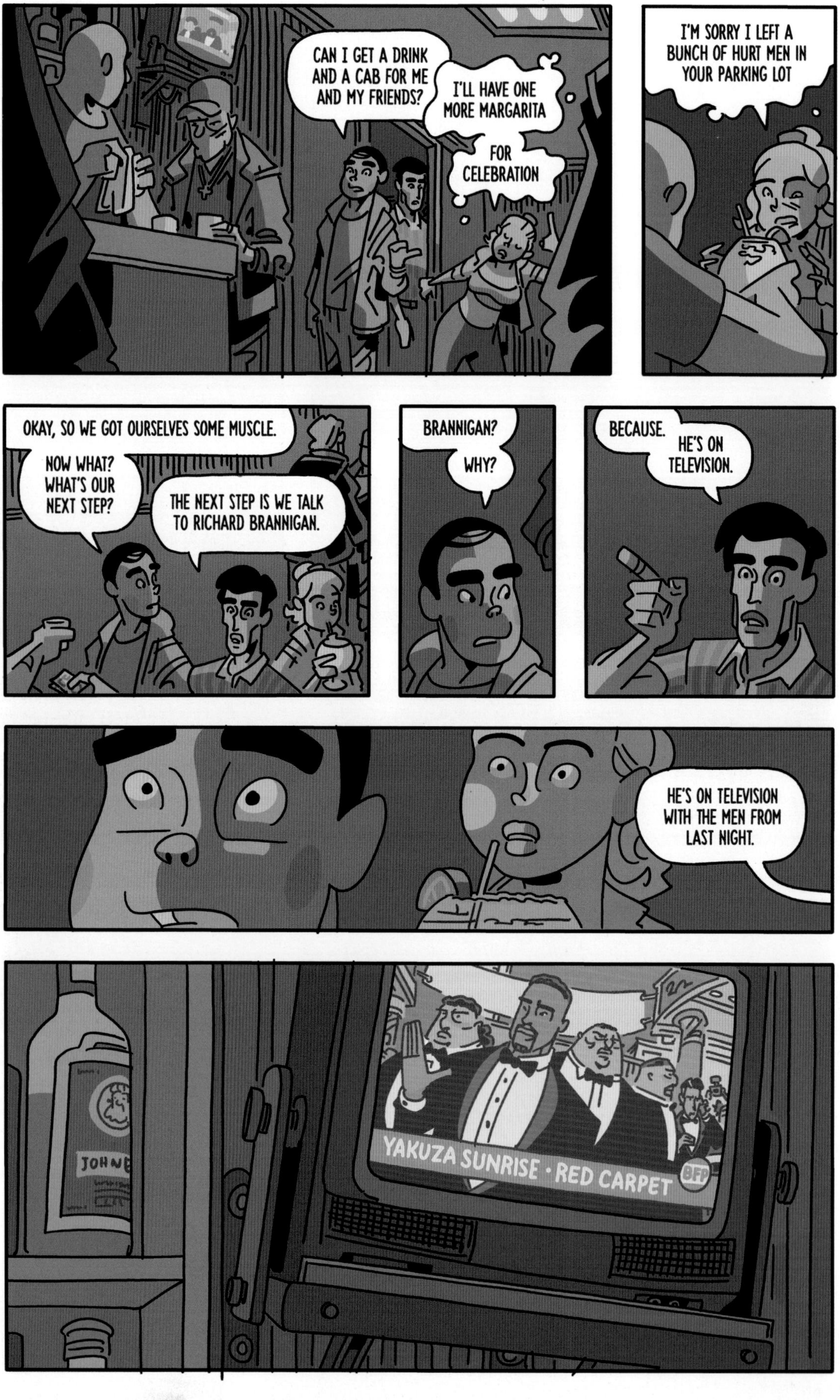
CAN I GET A DRINK AND A CAB FOR ME AND MY FRIENDS?
I'LL HAVE ONE MORE MARGARITA
FOR CELEBRATION
I'M SORRY I LEFT A BUNCH OF HURT MEN IN YOUR PARKING LOT
OKAY, SO WE GOT OURSELVES SOME MUSCLE.
NOW WHAT? WHAT'S OUR NEXT STEP?
THE NEXT STEP IS WE TALK TO RICHARD BRANNIGAN.
BRANNIGAN?
WHY?
BECAUSE.
HE'S ON TELEVISION.
HE'S ON TELEVISION WITH THE MEN FROM LAST NIGHT.
JOHNE
YAKUZA SUNRISE • RED CARPET
BFP

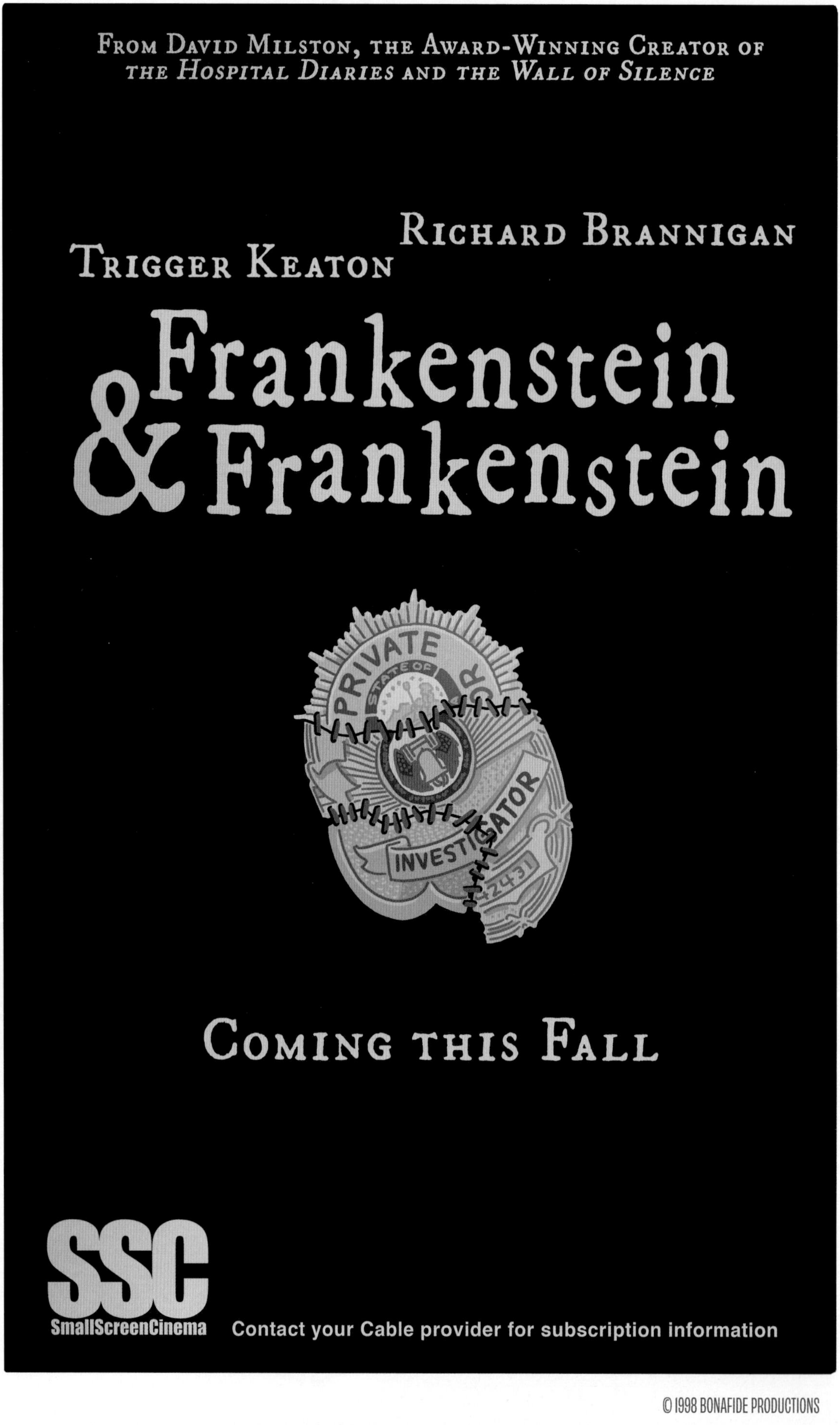
From David Milston, the Award-Winning Creator of
the Hospital Diaries and the Wall of Silence
Richard Brannigan
Trigger Keaton
Frankenstein
& Frankenstein
PRIVATE
INVESTIGATOR
42431
Coming this Fall
SSC
SmallScreenCinema
Contact your Cable provider for subscription information
© 1998 BONAFIDE PRODUCTIONS

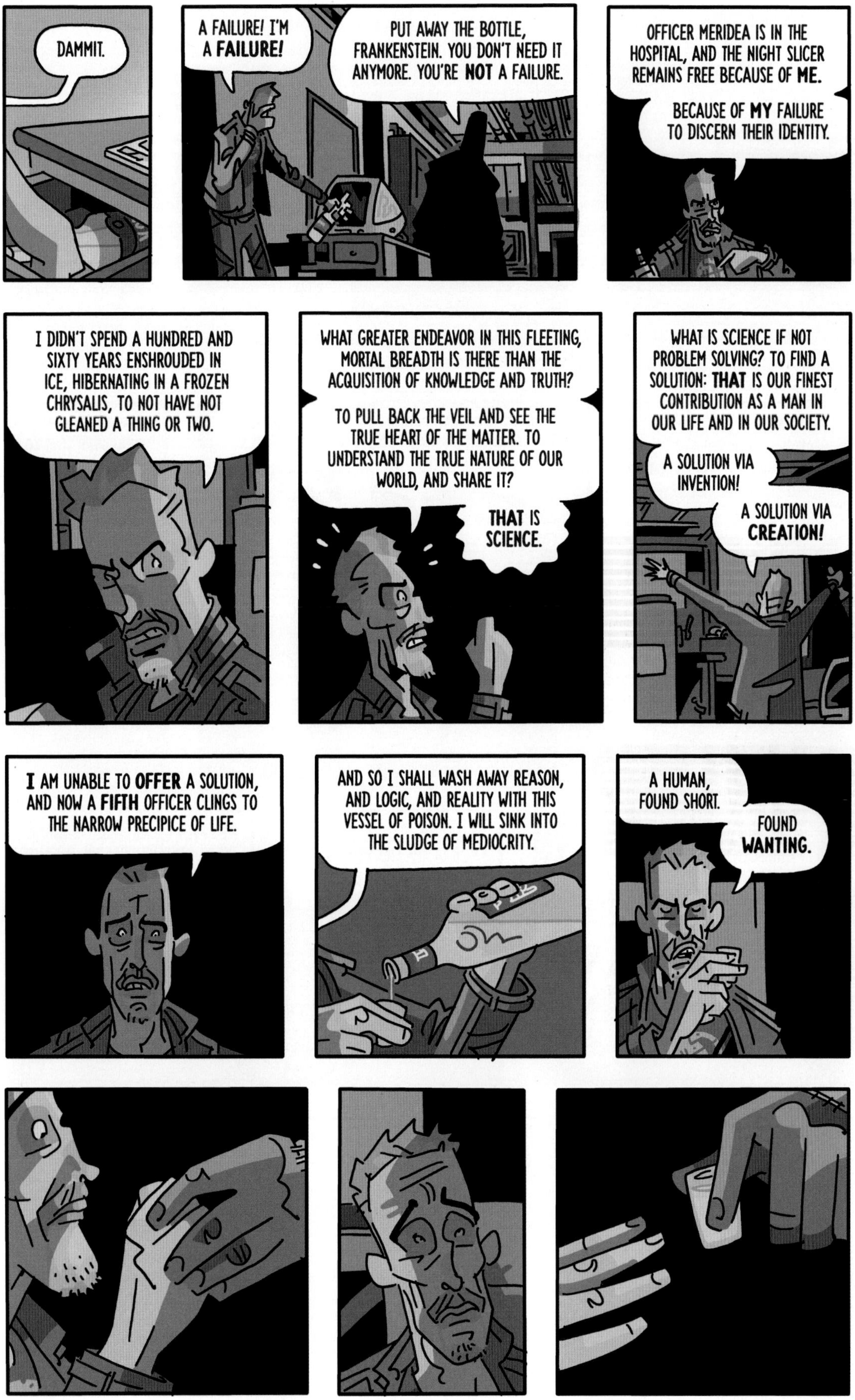
DAMMIT.
A FAILURE! I'M A **FAILURE!**
PUT AWAY THE BOTTLE, FRANKENSTEIN. YOU DON'T NEED IT ANYMORE. YOU'RE **NOT** A FAILURE.
OFFICER MERIDEA IS IN THE HOSPITAL, AND THE NIGHT SLICER REMAINS FREE BECAUSE OF **ME.**
BECAUSE OF **MY** FAILURE TO DISCERN THEIR IDENTITY.
I DIDN'T SPEND A HUNDRED AND SIXTY YEARS ENSHROUDED IN ICE, HIBERNATING IN A FROZEN CHRYSALIS, TO NOT HAVE NOT GLEANED A THING OR TWO.
WHAT GREATER ENDEAVOR IN THIS FLEETING, MORTAL BREADTH IS THERE THAN THE ACQUISITION OF KNOWLEDGE AND TRUTH?
TO PULL BACK THE VEIL AND SEE THE TRUE HEART OF THE MATTER. TO UNDERSTAND THE TRUE NATURE OF OUR WORLD, AND SHARE IT?
THAT IS **SCIENCE.**
WHAT IS SCIENCE IF NOT PROBLEM SOLVING? TO FIND A SOLUTION: **THAT** IS OUR FINEST CONTRIBUTION AS A MAN IN OUR LIFE AND IN OUR SOCIETY.
A SOLUTION VIA INVENTION!
A SOLUTION VIA **CREATION!**
I AM UNABLE TO **OFFER** A SOLUTION, AND NOW A **FIFTH** OFFICER CLINGS TO THE NARROW PRECIPICE OF LIFE.
AND SO I SHALL WASH AWAY REASON, AND LOGIC, AND REALITY WITH THIS VESSEL OF POISON. I WILL SINK INTO THE SLUDGE OF MEDIOCRITY.
A HUMAN, FOUND SHORT.
FOUND **WANTING.**

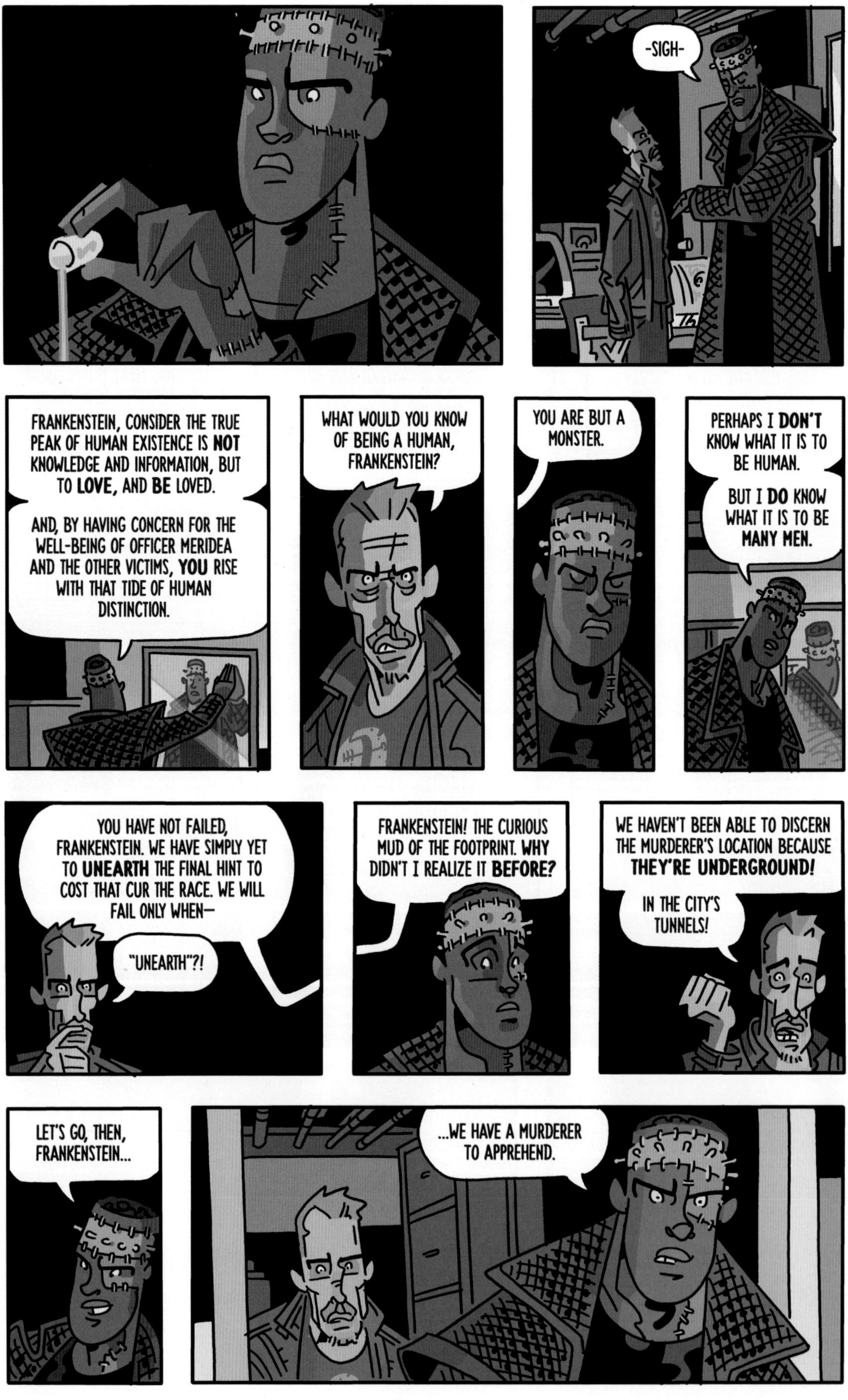
-SIGH-
FRANKENSTEIN, CONSIDER THE TRUE PEAK OF HUMAN EXISTENCE IS **NOT** KNOWLEDGE AND INFORMATION, BUT TO **LOVE,** AND **BE** LOVED.
AND, BY HAVING CONCERN FOR THE WELL-BEING OF OFFICER MERIDEA AND THE OTHER VICTIMS, **YOU** RISE WITH THAT TIDE OF HUMAN DISTINCTION.
WHAT WOULD YOU KNOW OF BEING A HUMAN, FRANKENSTEIN?
YOU ARE BUT A MONSTER.
PERHAPS I **DON'T** KNOW WHAT IT IS TO BE HUMAN.
BUT I **DO** KNOW WHAT IT IS TO BE **MANY MEN.**
YOU HAVE NOT FAILED, FRANKENSTEIN. WE HAVE SIMPLY YET TO **UNEARTH** THE FINAL HINT TO COST THAT CUR THE RACE. WE WILL FAIL ONLY WHEN—
"UNEARTH"?!
FRANKENSTEIN! THE CURIOUS MUD OF THE FOOTPRINT. **WHY** DIDN'T I REALIZE IT **BEFORE?**
WE HAVEN'T BEEN ABLE TO DISCERN THE MURDERER'S LOCATION BECAUSE **THEY'RE UNDERGROUND!**
IN THE CITY'S TUNNELS!
LET'S GO, THEN, FRANKENSTEIN...
...WE HAVE A MURDERER TO APPREHEND.

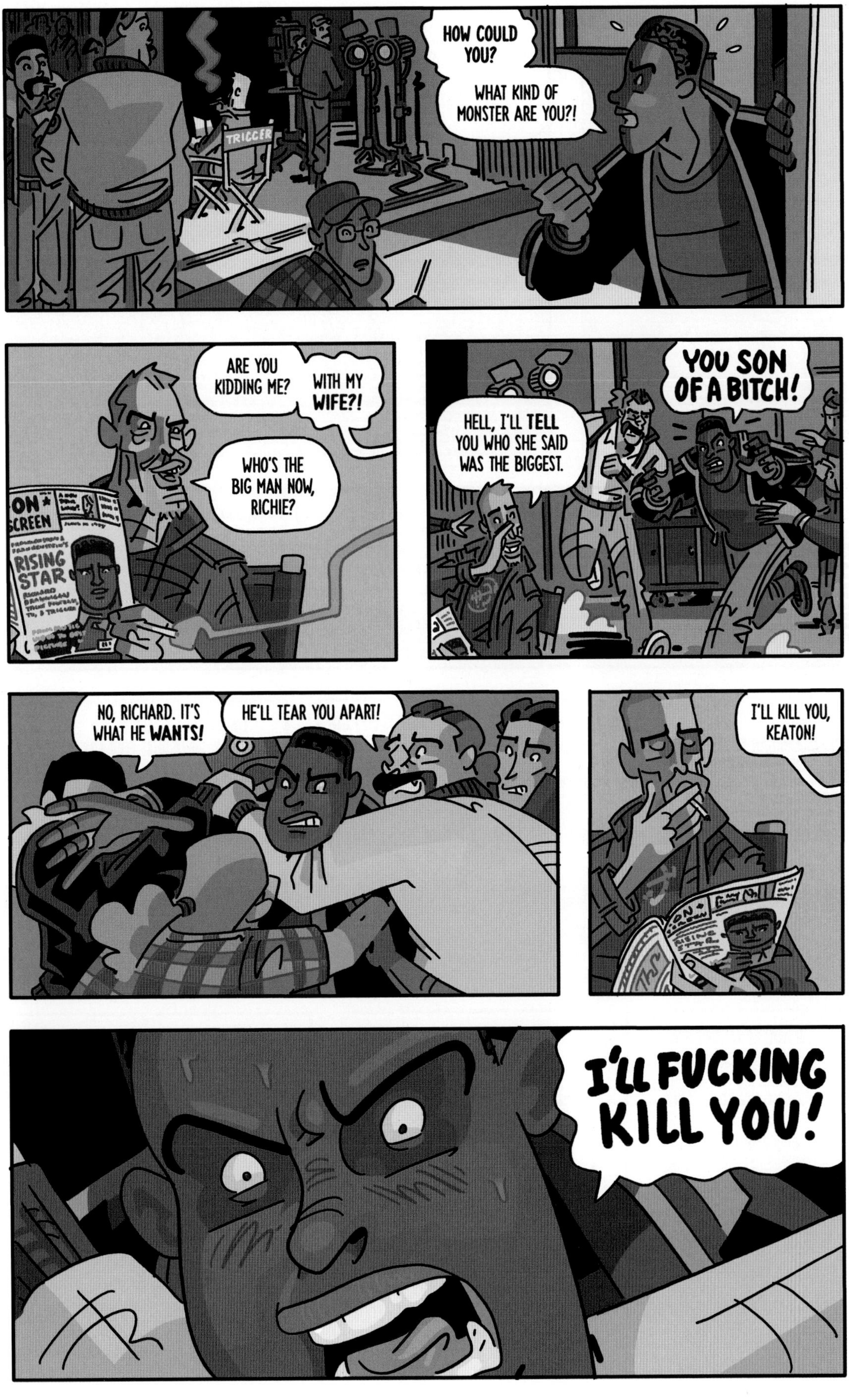
TRIGGER
HOW COULD YOU?
WHAT KIND OF MONSTER ARE YOU?!
ARE YOU KIDDING ME?
WITH MY **WIFE?!**
WHO'S THE BIG MAN NOW, RICHIE?
ON SCREEN
RISING STAR
HELL, I'LL **TELL** YOU WHO SHE SAID WAS THE BIGGEST.
YOU SON OF A BITCH!
NO, RICHARD. IT'S WHAT HE **WANTS!**
HE'LL TEAR YOU APART!
I'LL KILL YOU, KEATON!
I'LL FUCKING KILL YOU!

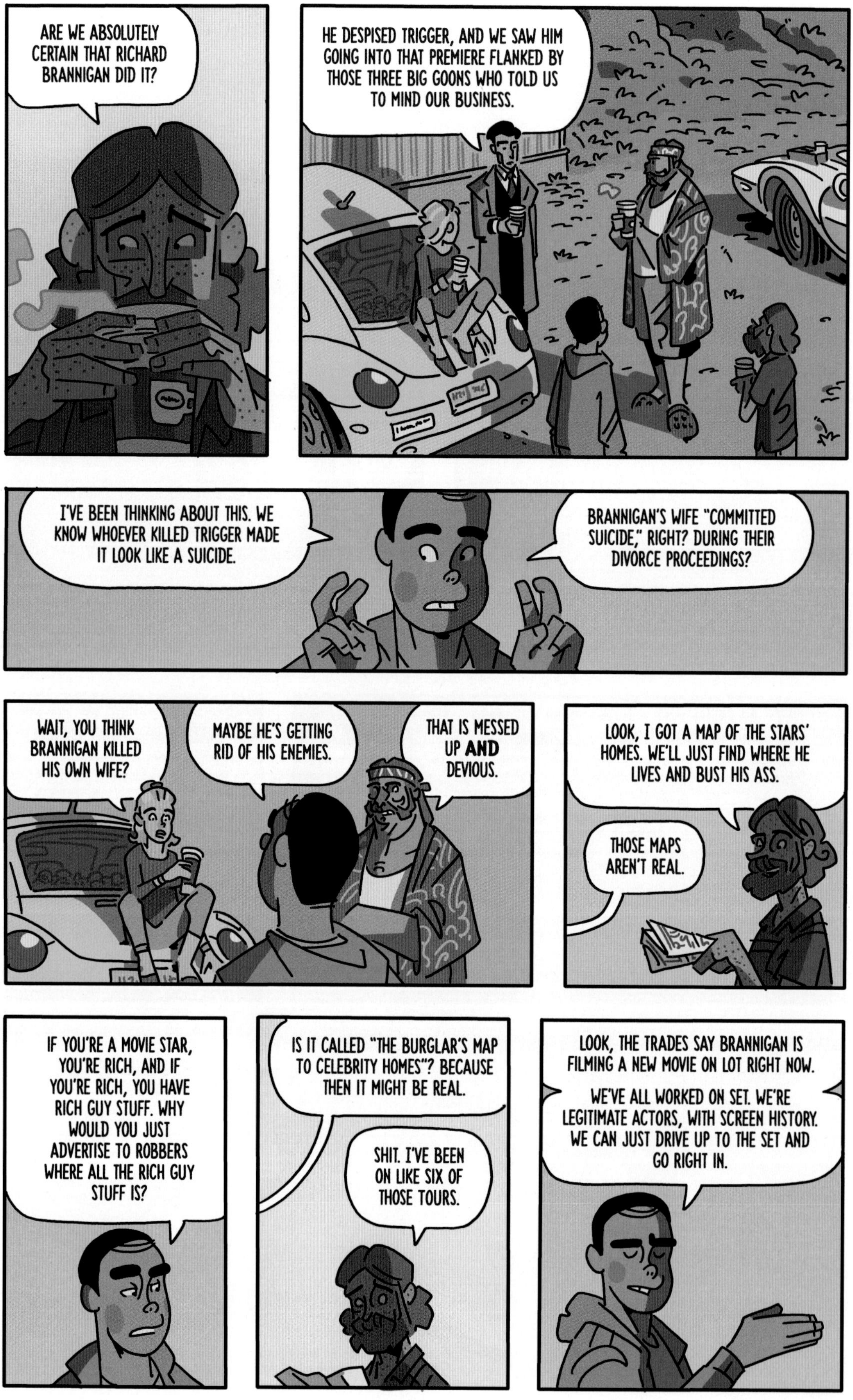
ARE WE ABSOLUTELY CERTAIN THAT RICHARD BRANNIGAN DID IT?
HE DESPISED TRIGGER, AND WE SAW HIM GOING INTO THAT PREMIERE FLANKED BY THOSE THREE BIG GOONS WHO TOLD US TO MIND OUR BUSINESS.
I'VE BEEN THINKING ABOUT THIS. WE KNOW WHOEVER KILLED TRIGGER MADE IT LOOK LIKE A SUICIDE.
BRANNIGAN'S WIFE "COMMITTED SUICIDE," RIGHT? DURING THEIR DIVORCE PROCEEDINGS?
WAIT, YOU THINK BRANNIGAN KILLED HIS OWN WIFE?
MAYBE HE'S GETTING RID OF HIS ENEMIES.
THAT IS MESSED UP **AND** DEVIOUS.
LOOK, I GOT A MAP OF THE STARS' HOMES. WE'LL JUST FIND WHERE HE LIVES AND BUST HIS ASS.
THOSE MAPS AREN'T REAL.
IF YOU'RE A MOVIE STAR, YOU'RE RICH, AND IF YOU'RE RICH, YOU HAVE RICH GUY STUFF. WHY WOULD YOU JUST ADVERTISE TO ROBBERS WHERE ALL THE RICH GUY STUFF IS?
IS IT CALLED "THE BURGLAR'S MAP TO CELEBRITY HOMES"? BECAUSE THEN IT MIGHT BE REAL.
SHIT. I'VE BEEN ON LIKE SIX OF THOSE TOURS.
LOOK, THE TRADES SAY BRANNIGAN IS FILMING A NEW MOVIE ON LOT RIGHT NOW.
WE'VE ALL WORKED ON SET. WE'RE LEGITIMATE ACTORS, WITH SCREEN HISTORY. WE CAN JUST DRIVE UP TO THE SET AND GO RIGHT IN.

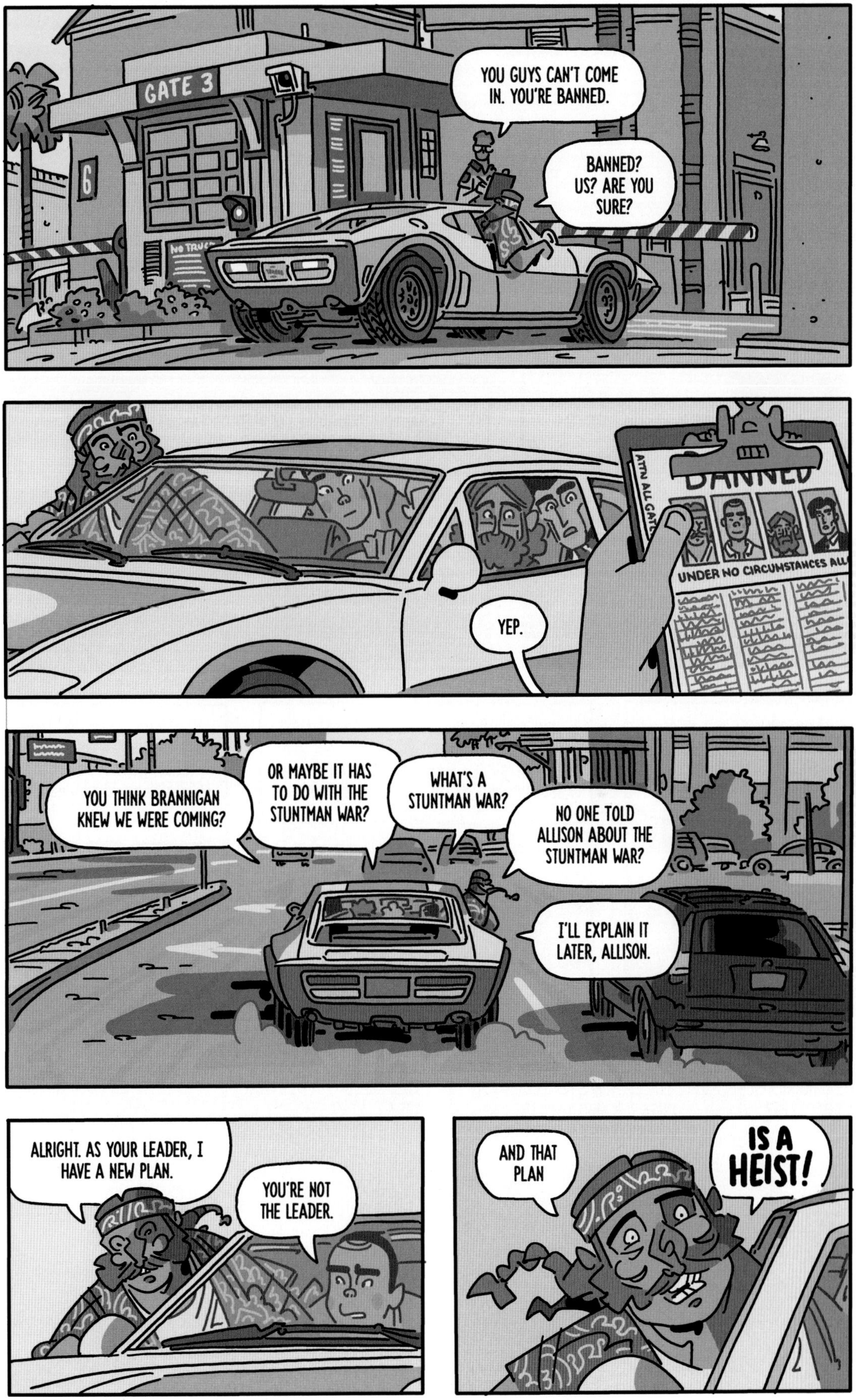
GATE 3
6
YOU GUYS CAN'T COME IN. YOU'RE BANNED.
BANNED? US? ARE YOU SURE?
BANNED
YEP.
YOU THINK BRANNIGAN KNEW WE WERE COMING?
OR MAYBE IT HAS TO DO WITH THE STUNTMAN WAR?
WHAT'S A STUNTMAN WAR?
NO ONE TOLD ALLISON ABOUT THE STUNTMAN WAR?
I'LL EXPLAIN IT LATER, ALLISON.
ALRIGHT. AS YOUR LEADER, I HAVE A NEW PLAN.
YOU'RE NOT THE LEADER.
AND THAT PLAN
IS A HEIST!

I'LL BE PLAYING THE ROLE OF FICTIONAL ITALIAN FILM DIRECTOR, LORENZO FONTORA.

BRANNIGAN'S LAST COUPLE OF FILMS TANKED SO BAD HE WON'T BE ABLE TO RESIST TALKING TO A SUPER SUCCESSFUL INTERNATIONAL DIRECTOR. THEY'LL LET US RIGHT IN.

ALLISON WILL BE IN CHARGE OF MAKING US FAKE I.D.S.

SKIPPY. YOU'RE IN CHARGE OF TRANSPORT. I'LL NEED THE FANCIEST LIMO POSSIBLE TO SELL THE ILLUSION.

PAUL, YOU GET US A MOVIE. BRANNIGAN MAY NEED TO SEE A FONTORA FILM BEFORE HE AGREES TO ANYTHING.

BUT THIS FONTORA ISN'T REAL. HOW AM I SUPPOSED TO GET A MOVIE THAT DOESN'T EXIST?

JUST GET ANY MOVIE, PAUL. QUIT OVERCOMPLICATING EVERYTHING!

BY THE TIME THEY LOAD THE FAKE FILM INTO A PROJECTOR, WE'LL ALREADY HAVE OUR CONFESSION AND BRANNIGAN WILL BE ON HIS WAY TO JAIL.

WHAT ABOUT ME?

IN CASE THINGS GO SOUTH, WE'LL NEED A PLANNED DISTRACTION— PREFERABLY A FLASH MOB.

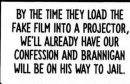

AND WE MIGHT NEED TO BREAK INTO BRANNIGAN'S TRAILER, SO YOU SHOULD PROBABLY MASTER LOCK PICKING.

GOT IT.

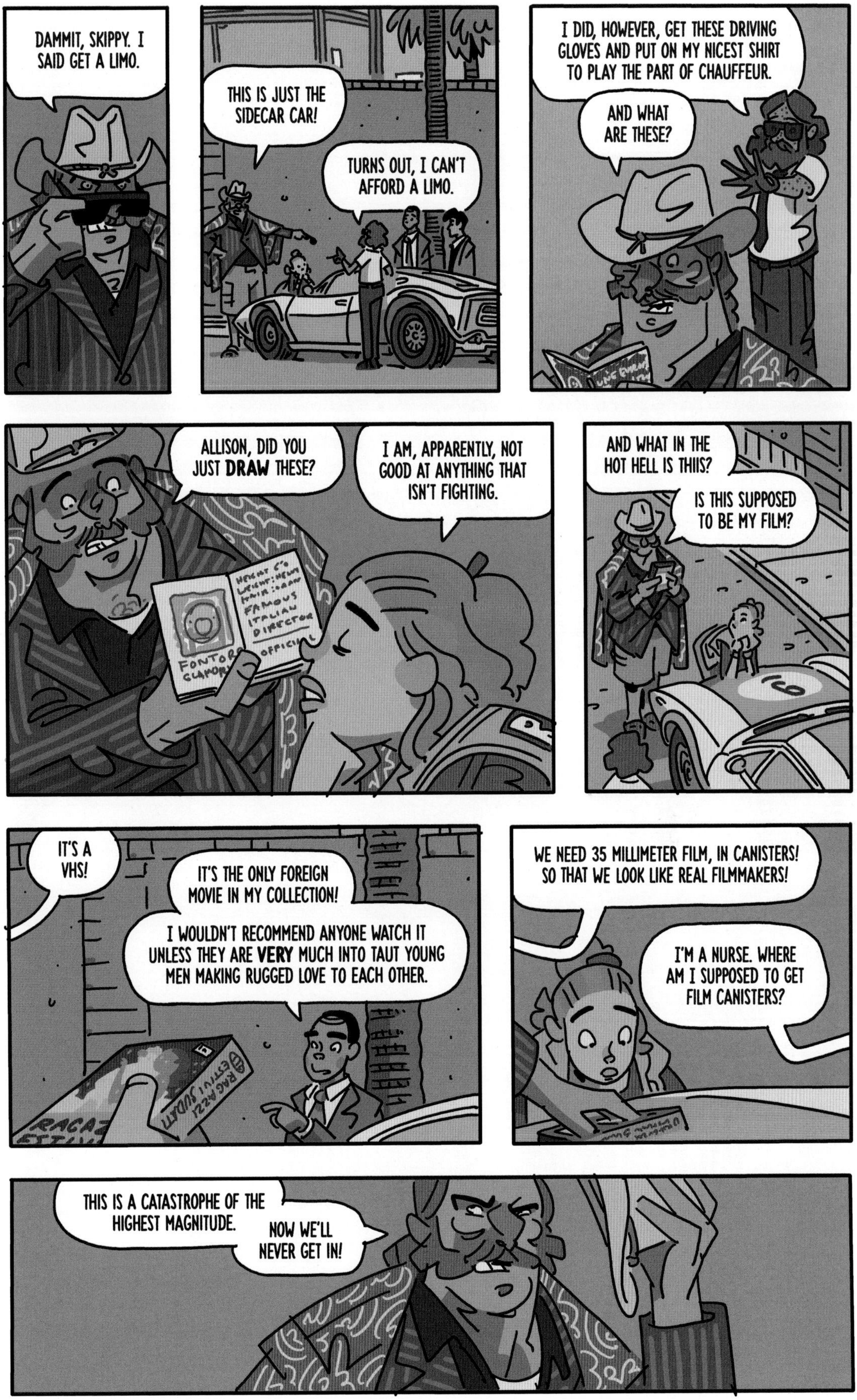
DAMMIT, SKIPPY. I SAID GET A LIMO.
THIS IS JUST THE SIDECAR CAR!
TURNS OUT, I CAN'T AFFORD A LIMO.
I DID, HOWEVER, GET THESE DRIVING GLOVES AND PUT ON MY NICEST SHIRT TO PLAY THE PART OF CHAUFFEUR.
AND WHAT ARE THESE?
ALLISON, DID YOU JUST **DRAW** THESE?
FAMOUS ITALIAN DIRECTOR
I AM, APPARENTLY, NOT GOOD AT ANYTHING THAT ISN'T FIGHTING.
AND WHAT IN THE HOT HELL IS THIIS?
IS THIS SUPPOSED TO BE MY FILM?
IT'S A VHS!
IT'S THE ONLY FOREIGN MOVIE IN MY COLLECTION!
I WOULDN'T RECOMMEND ANYONE WATCH IT UNLESS THEY ARE **VERY** MUCH INTO TAUT YOUNG MEN MAKING RUGGED LOVE TO EACH OTHER.
RAGAZZI ESTIVI SUDATI
WE NEED 35 MILLIMETER FILM, IN CANISTERS! SO THAT WE LOOK LIKE REAL FILMMAKERS!
I'M A NURSE. WHERE AM I SUPPOSED TO GET FILM CANISTERS?
THIS IS A CATASTROPHE OF THE HIGHEST MAGNITUDE.
NOW WE'LL NEVER GET IN!

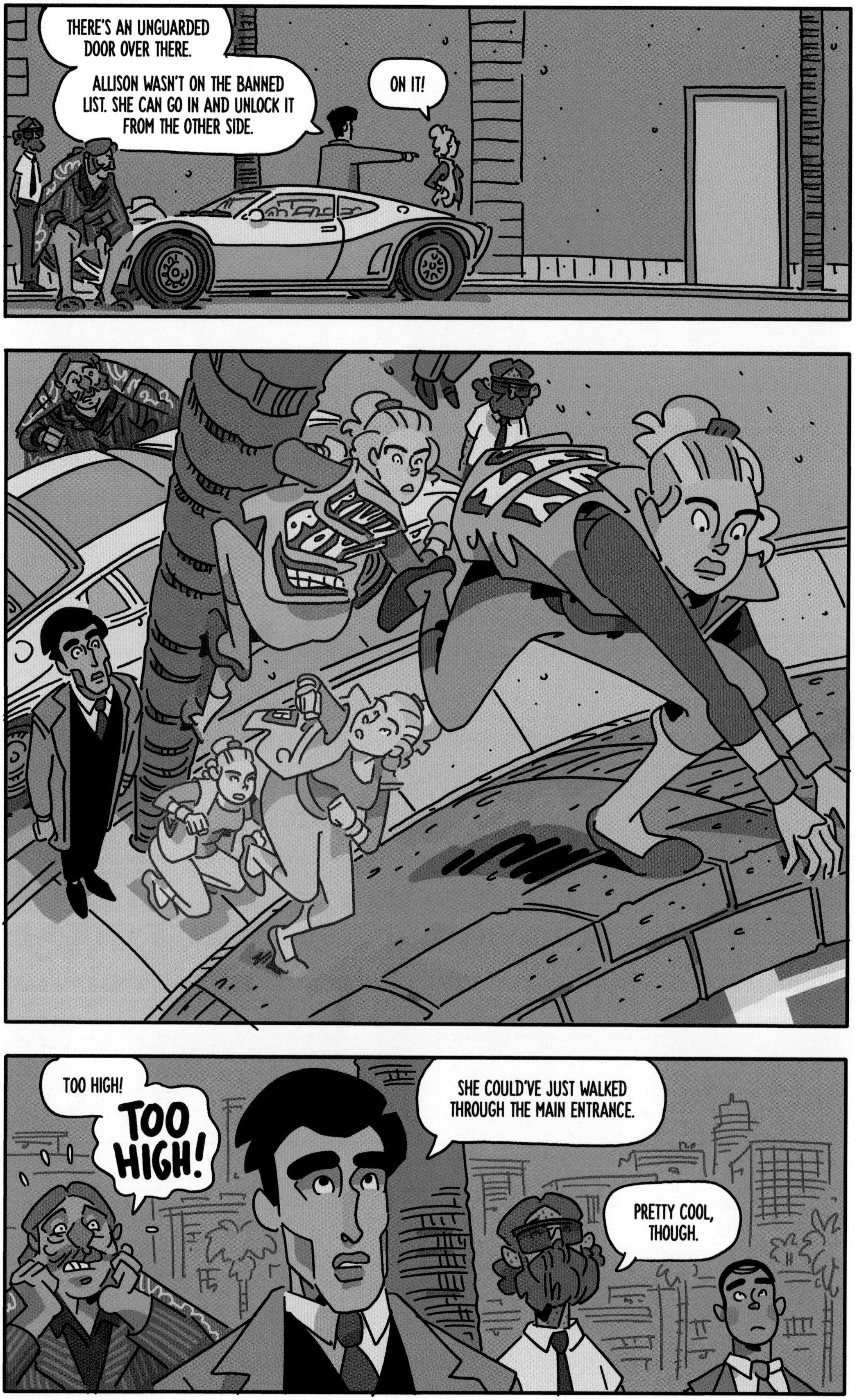
THERE'S AN UNGUARDED DOOR OVER THERE.
ALLISON WASN'T ON THE BANNED LIST. SHE CAN GO IN AND UNLOCK IT FROM THE OTHER SIDE.
ON IT!
TOO HIGH!
TOO HIGH!
SHE COULD'VE JUST WALKED THROUGH THE MAIN ENTRANCE.
PRETTY COOL, THOUGH.

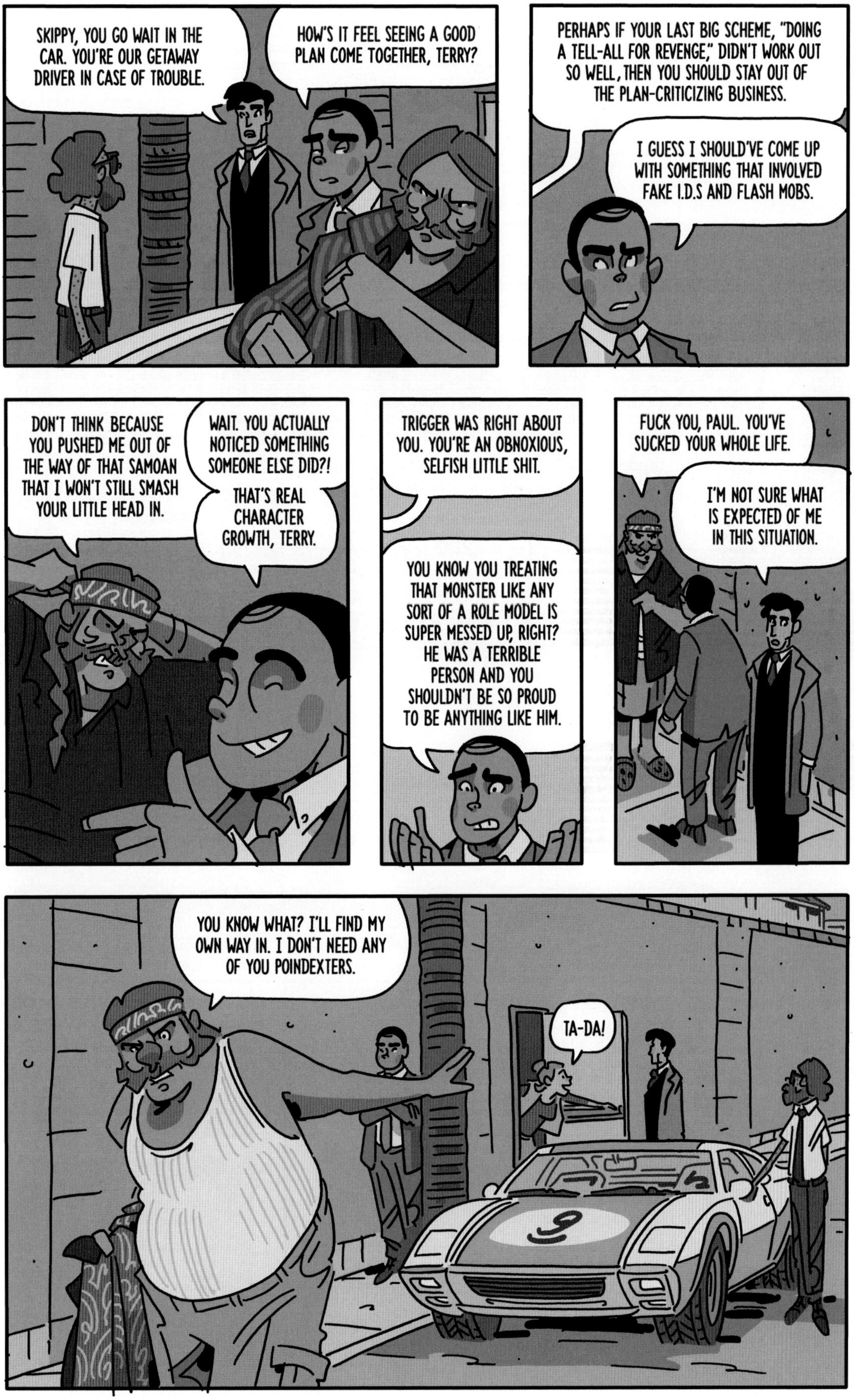
SKIPPY, YOU GO WAIT IN THE CAR. YOU'RE OUR GETAWAY DRIVER IN CASE OF TROUBLE.
HOW'S IT FEEL SEEING A GOOD PLAN COME TOGETHER, TERRY?
PERHAPS IF YOUR LAST BIG SCHEME, "DOING A TELL-ALL FOR REVENGE," DIDN'T WORK OUT SO WELL, THEN YOU SHOULD STAY OUT OF THE PLAN-CRITICIZING BUSINESS.
I GUESS I SHOULD'VE COME UP WITH SOMETHING THAT INVOLVED FAKE I.D.S AND FLASH MOBS.
DON'T THINK BECAUSE YOU PUSHED ME OUT OF THE WAY OF THAT SAMOAN THAT I WON'T STILL SMASH YOUR LITTLE HEAD IN.
WAIT. YOU ACTUALLY NOTICED SOMETHING SOMEONE ELSE DID?!
THAT'S REAL CHARACTER GROWTH, TERRY.
TRIGGER WAS RIGHT ABOUT YOU. YOU'RE AN OBNOXIOUS, SELFISH LITTLE SHIT.
YOU KNOW YOU TREATING THAT MONSTER LIKE ANY SORT OF A ROLE MODEL IS SUPER MESSED UP, RIGHT? HE WAS A TERRIBLE PERSON AND YOU SHOULDN'T BE SO PROUD TO BE ANYTHING LIKE HIM.
FUCK YOU, PAUL. YOU'VE SUCKED YOUR WHOLE LIFE.
I'M NOT SURE WHAT IS EXPECTED OF ME IN THIS SITUATION.
YOU KNOW WHAT? I'LL FIND MY OWN WAY IN. I DON'T NEED ANY OF YOU POINDEXTERS.
TA-DA!

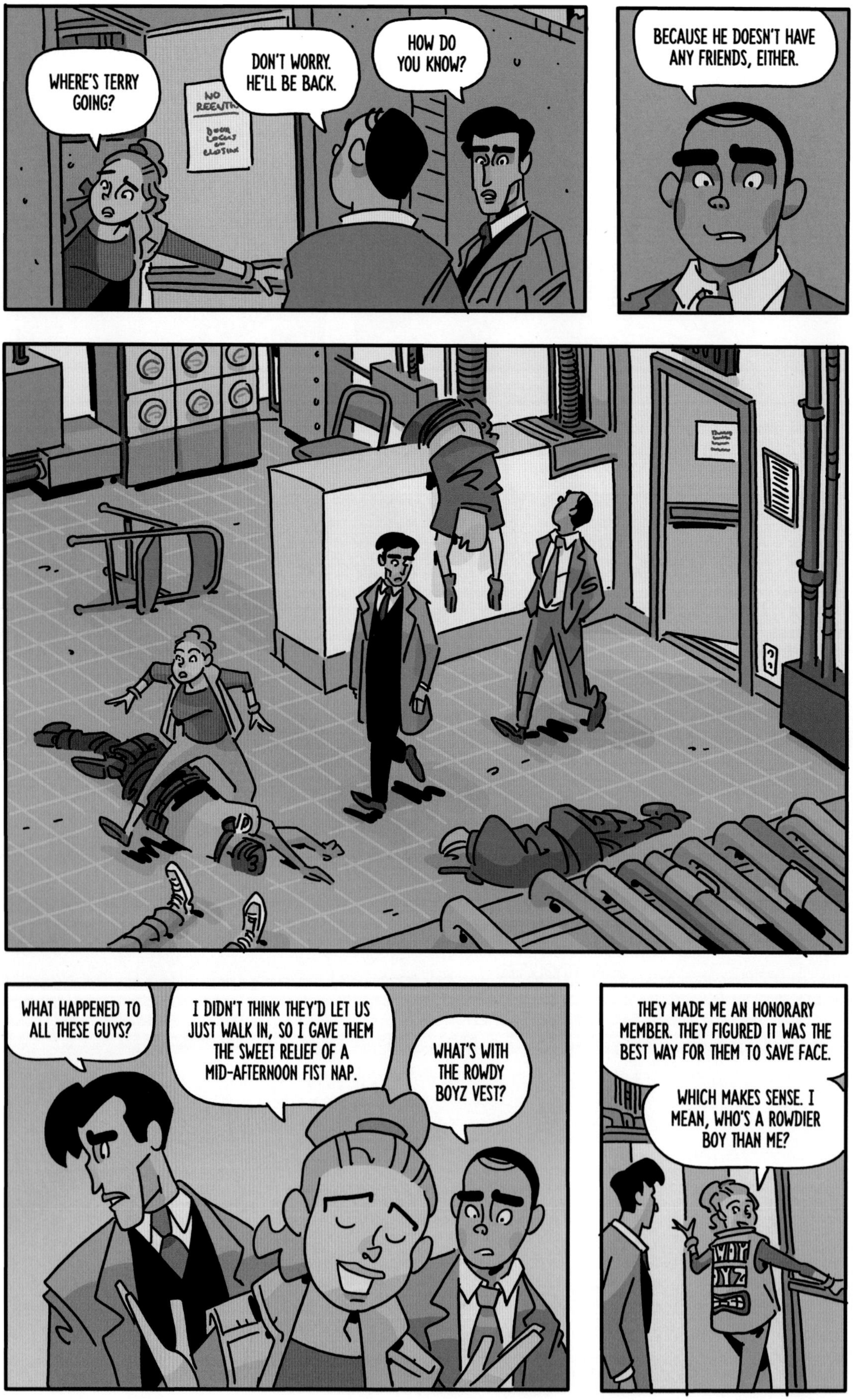
WHERE'S TERRY GOING?
DON'T WORRY. HE'LL BE BACK.
HOW DO YOU KNOW?
BECAUSE HE DOESN'T HAVE ANY FRIENDS, EITHER.
NO REENTRY
DOOR LOCKS ON CLOSING
WHAT HAPPENED TO ALL THESE GUYS?
I DIDN'T THINK THEY'D LET US JUST WALK IN, SO I GAVE THEM THE SWEET RELIEF OF A MID-AFTERNOON FIST NAP.
WHAT'S WITH THE ROWDY BOYZ VEST?
THEY MADE ME AN HONORARY MEMBER. THEY FIGURED IT WAS THE BEST WAY FOR THEM TO SAVE FACE.
WHICH MAKES SENSE. I MEAN, WHO'S A ROWDIER BOY THAN ME?

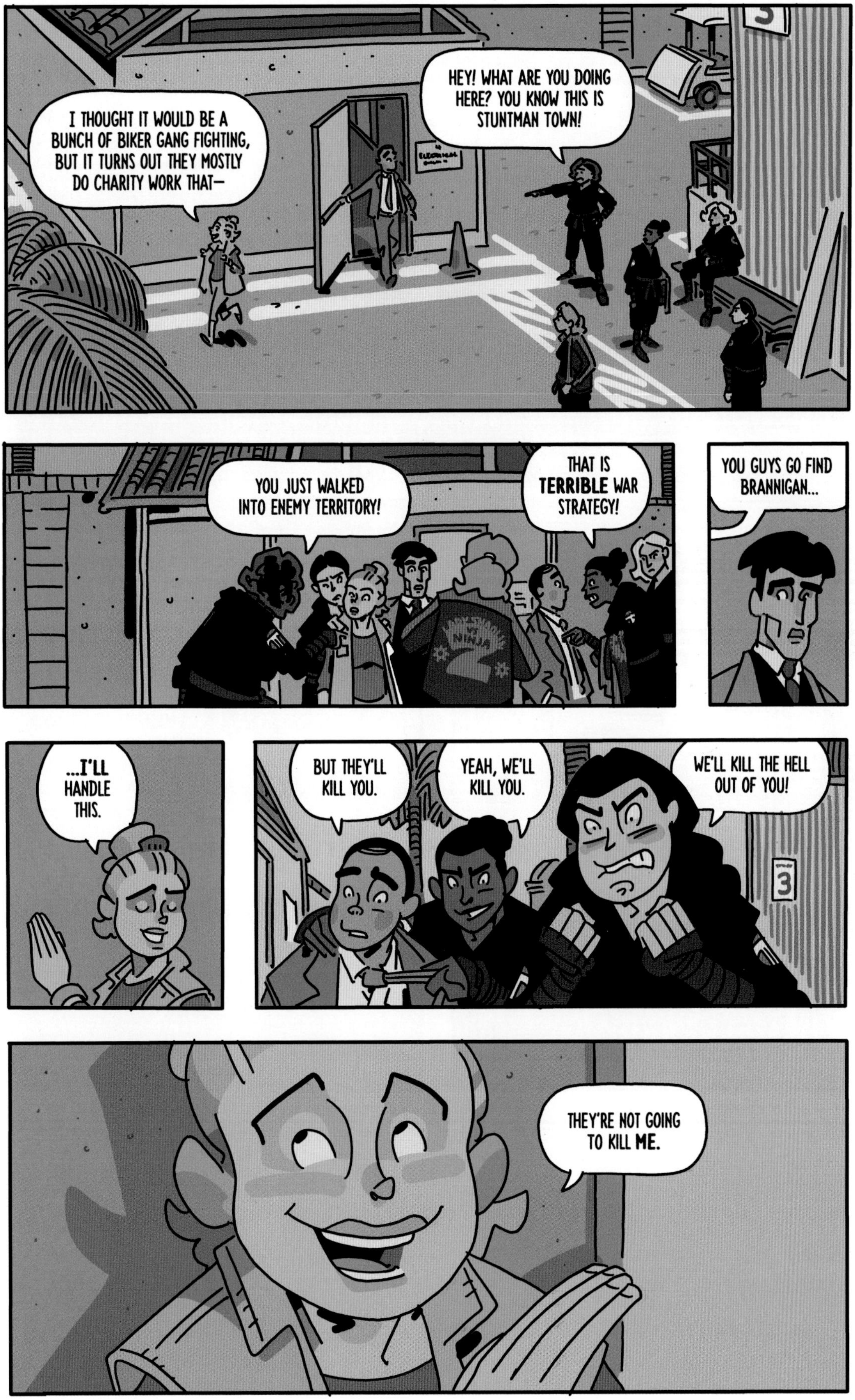
I THOUGHT IT WOULD BE A BUNCH OF BIKER GANG FIGHTING, BUT IT TURNS OUT THEY MOSTLY DO CHARITY WORK THAT—
HEY! WHAT ARE YOU DOING HERE? YOU KNOW THIS IS STUNTMAN TOWN!
YOU JUST WALKED INTO ENEMY TERRITORY!
THAT IS **TERRIBLE** WAR STRATEGY!
YOU GUYS GO FIND BRANNIGAN...
...**I'LL** HANDLE THIS.
BUT THEY'LL KILL YOU.
YEAH, WE'LL KILL YOU.
WE'LL KILL THE HELL OUT OF YOU!
THEY'RE NOT GOING TO KILL **ME.**

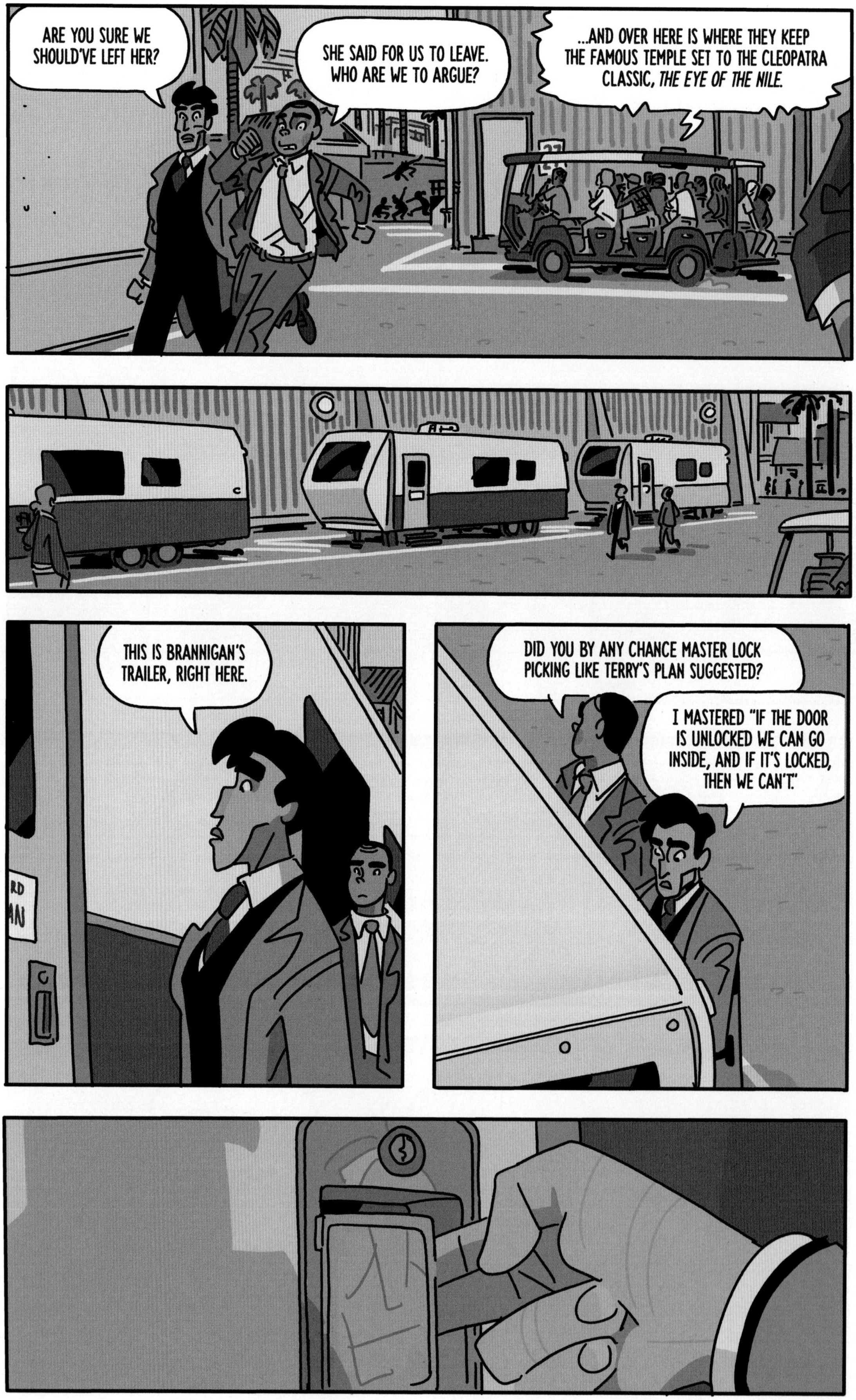
ARE YOU SURE WE SHOULD'VE LEFT HER?
SHE SAID FOR US TO LEAVE. WHO ARE WE TO ARGUE?
...AND OVER HERE IS WHERE THEY KEEP THE FAMOUS TEMPLE SET TO THE CLEOPATRA CLASSIC, *THE EYE OF THE NILE.*
THIS IS BRANNIGAN'S TRAILER, RIGHT HERE.
DID YOU BY ANY CHANCE MASTER LOCK PICKING LIKE TERRY'S PLAN SUGGESTED?
I MASTERED "IF THE DOOR IS UNLOCKED WE CAN GO INSIDE, AND IF IT'S LOCKED, THEN WE CAN'T."

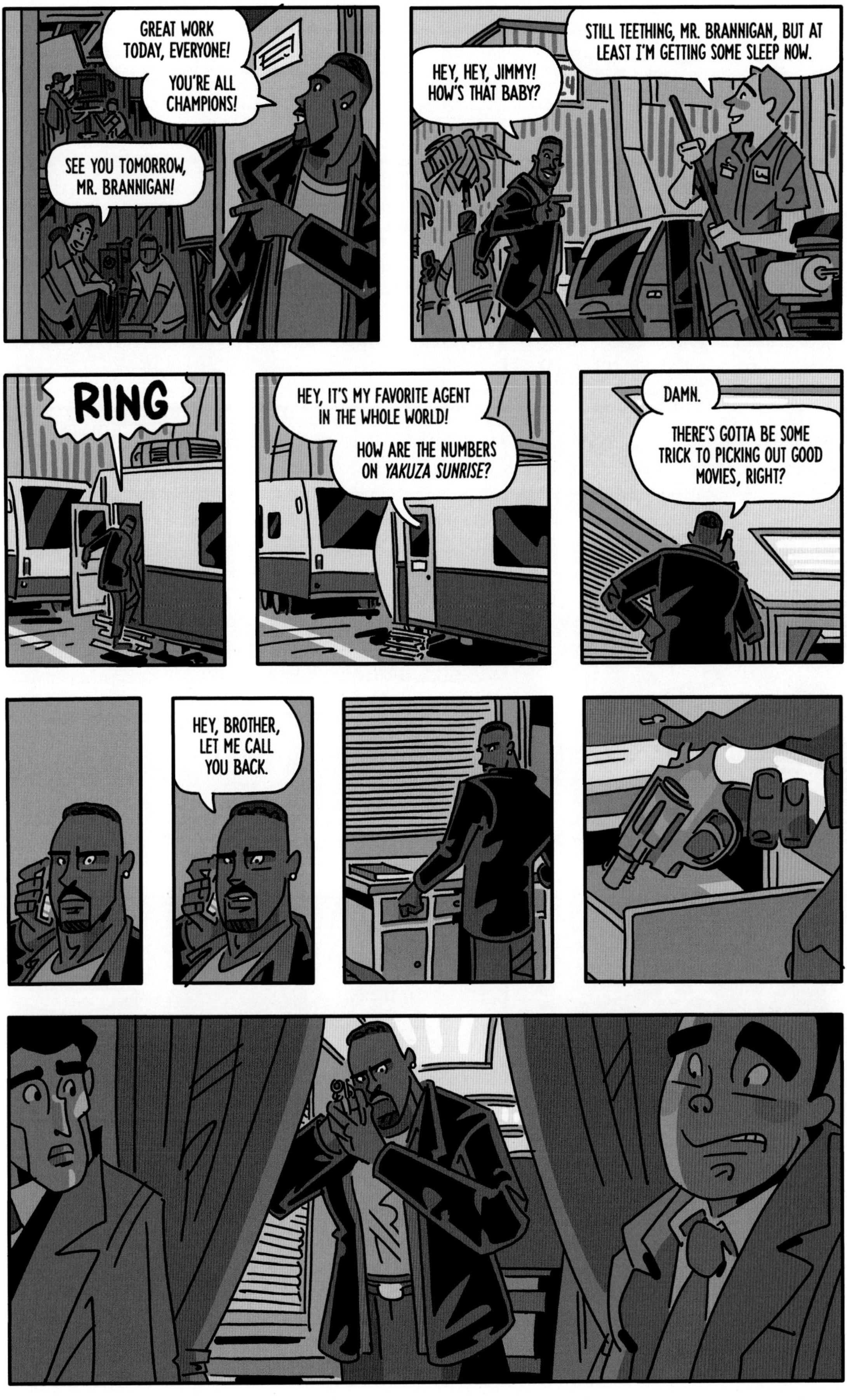
GREAT WORK TODAY, EVERYONE!
YOU'RE ALL CHAMPIONS!
SEE YOU TOMORROW, MR. BRANNIGAN!
HEY, HEY, JIMMY! HOW'S THAT BABY?
STILL TEETHING, MR. BRANNIGAN, BUT AT LEAST I'M GETTING SOME SLEEP NOW.
RING
HEY, IT'S MY FAVORITE AGENT IN THE WHOLE WORLD!
HOW ARE THE NUMBERS ON *YAKUZA SUNRISE*?
DAMN.
THERE'S GOTTA BE SOME TRICK TO PICKING OUT GOOD MOVIES, RIGHT?
HEY, BROTHER, LET ME CALL YOU BACK.

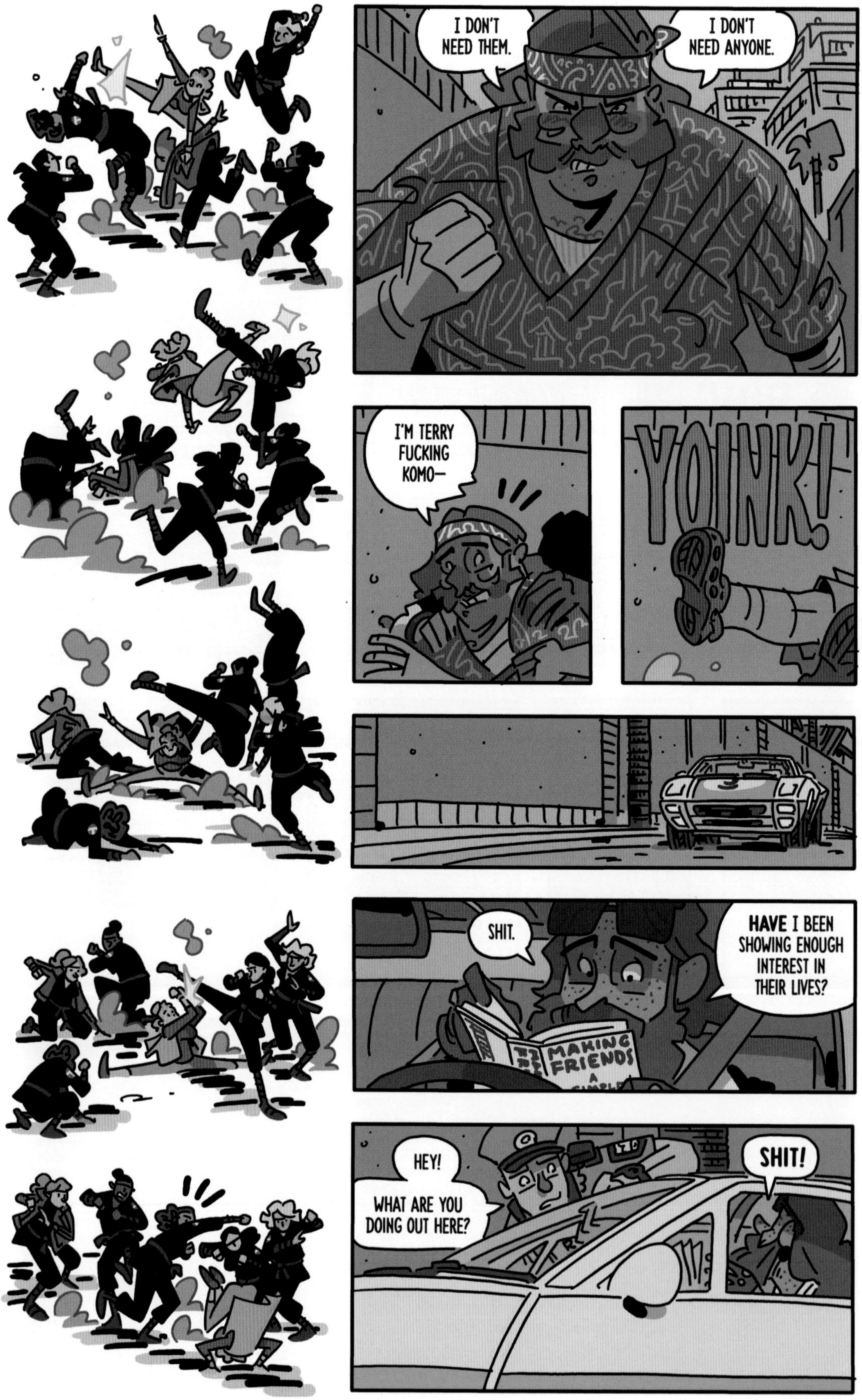
I DON'T NEED THEM.
I DON'T NEED ANYONE.
I'M TERRY FUCKING KOMO—
YOINK!
SHIT.
HAVE I BEEN SHOWING ENOUGH INTEREST IN THEIR LIVES?
MAKING FRIENDS
A
HEY!
WHAT ARE YOU DOING OUT HERE?
SHIT!

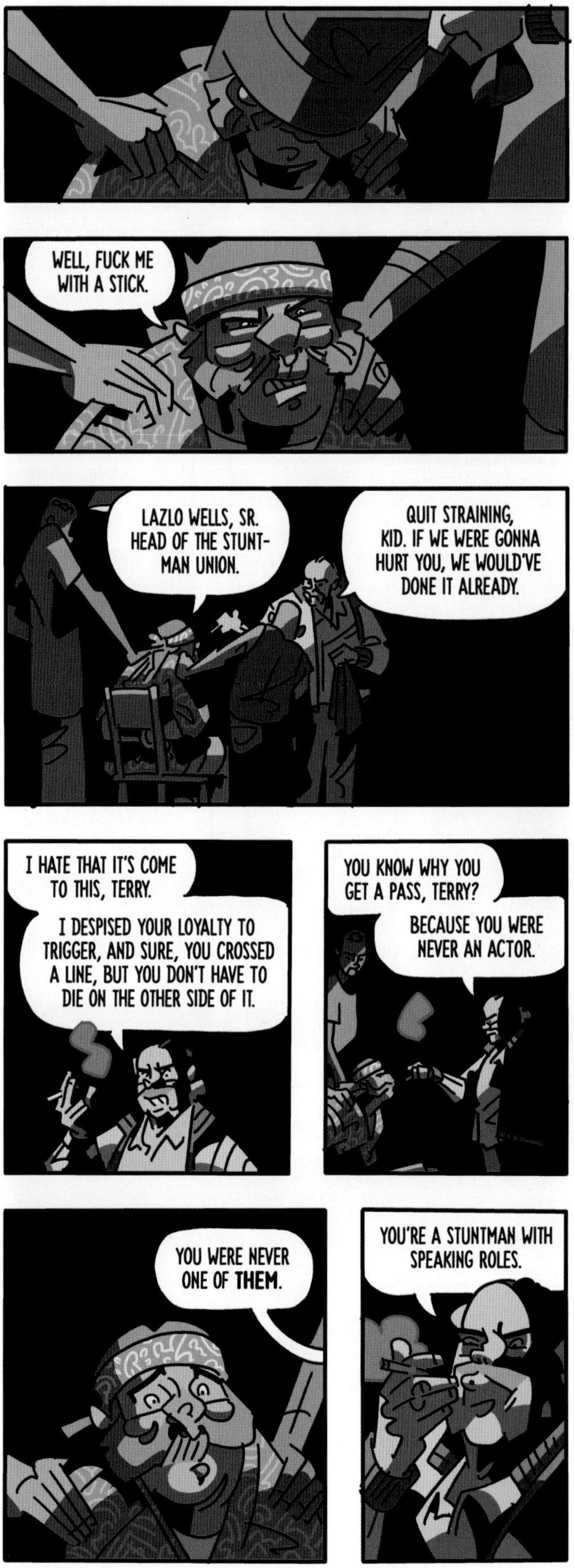
WELL, FUCK ME WITH A STICK.
LAZLO WELLS, SR. HEAD OF THE STUNT-MAN UNION.
QUIT STRAINING, KID. IF WE WERE GONNA HURT YOU, WE WOULD'VE DONE IT ALREADY.
I HATE THAT IT'S COME TO THIS, TERRY.
I DESPISED YOUR LOYALTY TO TRIGGER, AND SURE, YOU CROSSED A LINE, BUT YOU DON'T HAVE TO DIE ON THE OTHER SIDE OF IT.
YOU KNOW WHY YOU GET A PASS, TERRY?
BECAUSE YOU WERE NEVER AN ACTOR.
YOU WERE NEVER ONE OF **THEM**.
YOU'RE A STUNTMAN WITH SPEAKING ROLES.
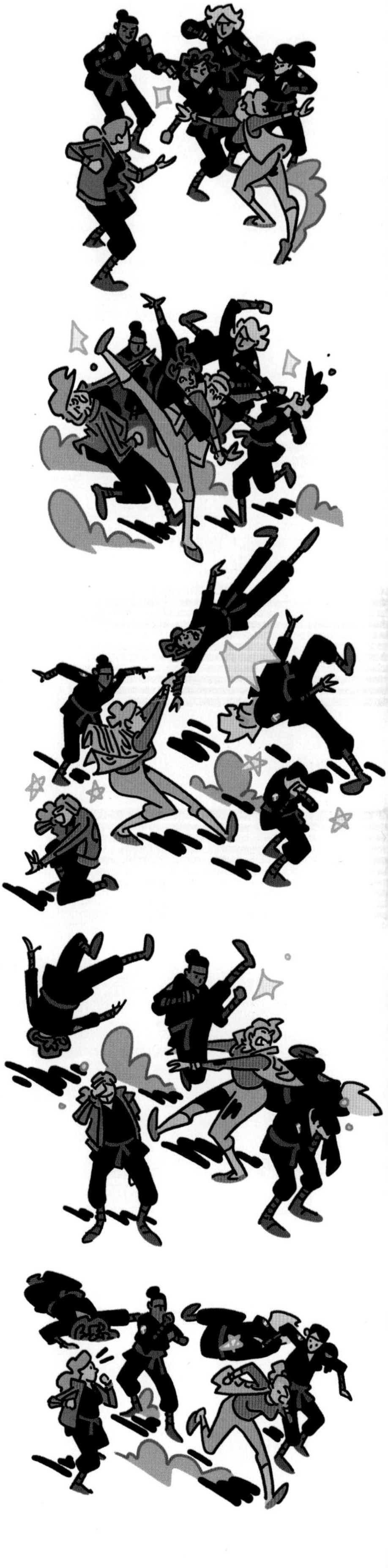

SURE, YOU MAY ONLY BE **HALF** A STUNTMAN SINCE YOU WON'T DO **FALLS**, BUT YOU'RE A GOOD ENOUGH HAND.

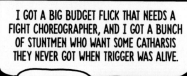

I GOT A BIG BUDGET FLICK THAT NEEDS A FIGHT CHOREOGRAPHER, AND I GOT A BUNCH OF STUNTMEN WHO WANT SOME CATHARSIS THEY NEVER GOT WHEN TRIGGER WAS ALIVE.

CATHARSIS?

THE BOYS WANT THEIR POUND OF FLESH, TERRY.

SO WE'LL GET YOU BACK ON THE JOB. **IF** YOU TELL US WHERE THE OTHERS ARE.

I GIVE UP MY FRIENDS...

...AND I GO BACK TO WORK?

I MEAN, ARE THEY EVEN REALLY YOUR FRIENDS, TERRY?

SOME **ACTORS**?

YOU GOTTA CHOOSE, TERRY. THEM OR US.

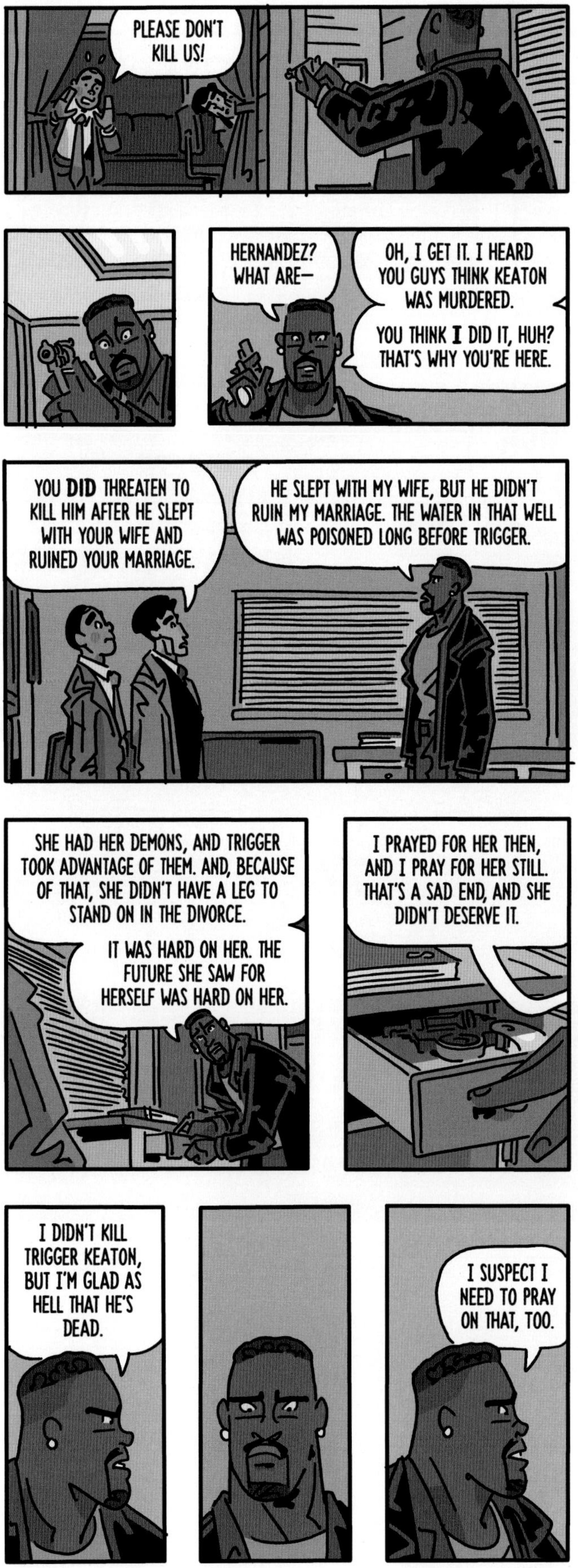
PLEASE DON'T KILL US!
HERNANDEZ? WHAT ARE—
OH, I GET IT. I HEARD YOU GUYS THINK KEATON WAS MURDERED.
YOU THINK I DID IT, HUH? THAT'S WHY YOU'RE HERE.
YOU DID THREATEN TO KILL HIM AFTER HE SLEPT WITH YOUR WIFE AND RUINED YOUR MARRIAGE.
HE SLEPT WITH MY WIFE, BUT HE DIDN'T RUIN MY MARRIAGE. THE WATER IN THAT WELL WAS POISONED LONG BEFORE TRIGGER.
SHE HAD HER DEMONS, AND TRIGGER TOOK ADVANTAGE OF THEM. AND, BECAUSE OF THAT, SHE DIDN'T HAVE A LEG TO STAND ON IN THE DIVORCE.
IT WAS HARD ON HER. THE FUTURE SHE SAW FOR HERSELF WAS HARD ON HER.
I PRAYED FOR HER THEN, AND I PRAY FOR HER STILL. THAT'S A SAD END, AND SHE DIDN'T DESERVE IT.
I DIDN'T KILL TRIGGER KEATON, BUT I'M GLAD AS HELL THAT HE'S DEAD.
I SUSPECT I NEED TO PRAY ON THAT, TOO.

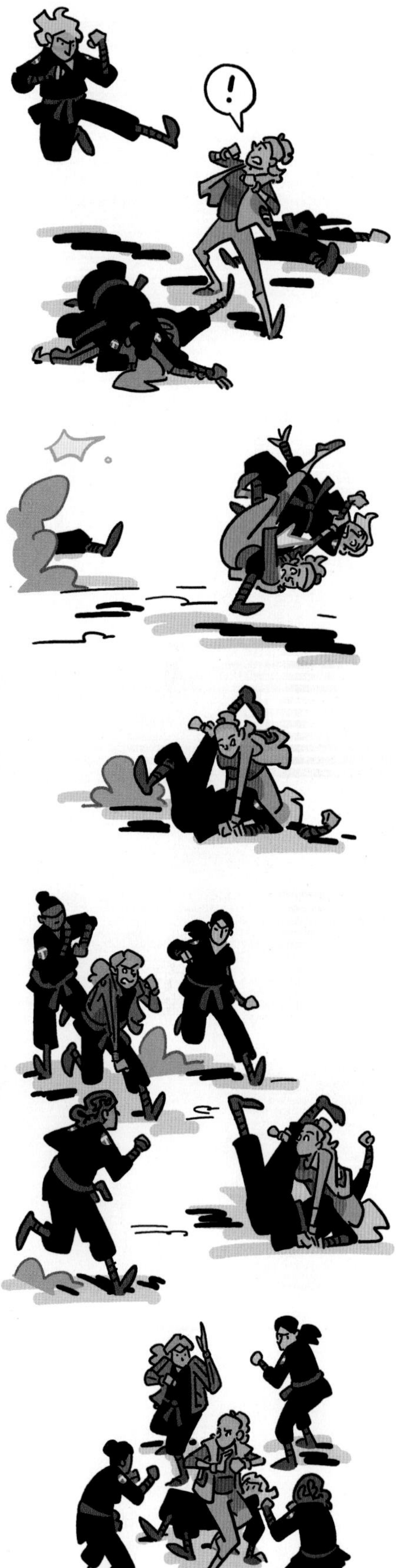
!

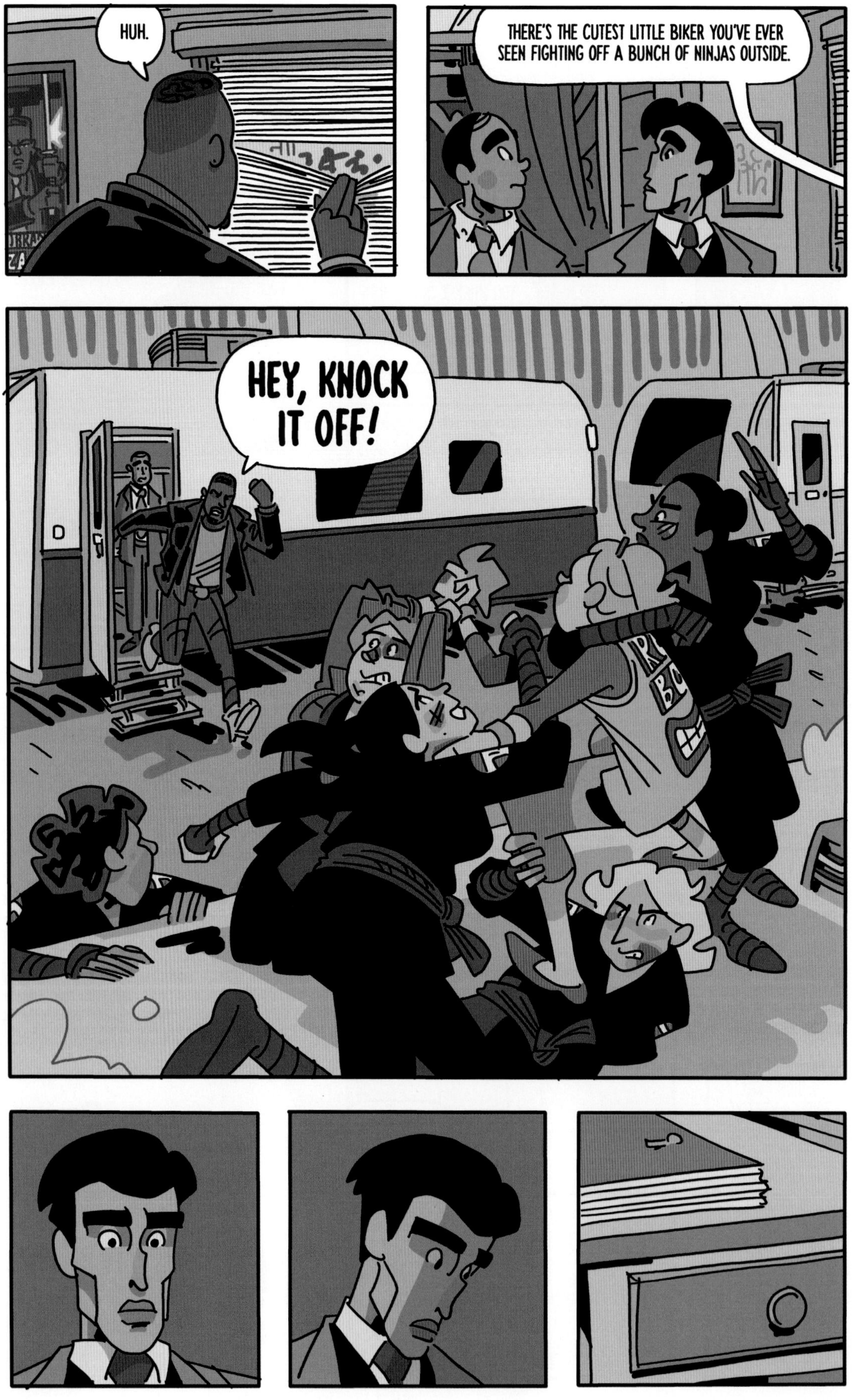
HUH.
THERE'S THE CUTEST LITTLE BIKER YOU'VE EVER SEEN FIGHTING OFF A BUNCH OF NINJAS OUTSIDE.
HEY, KNOCK IT OFF!

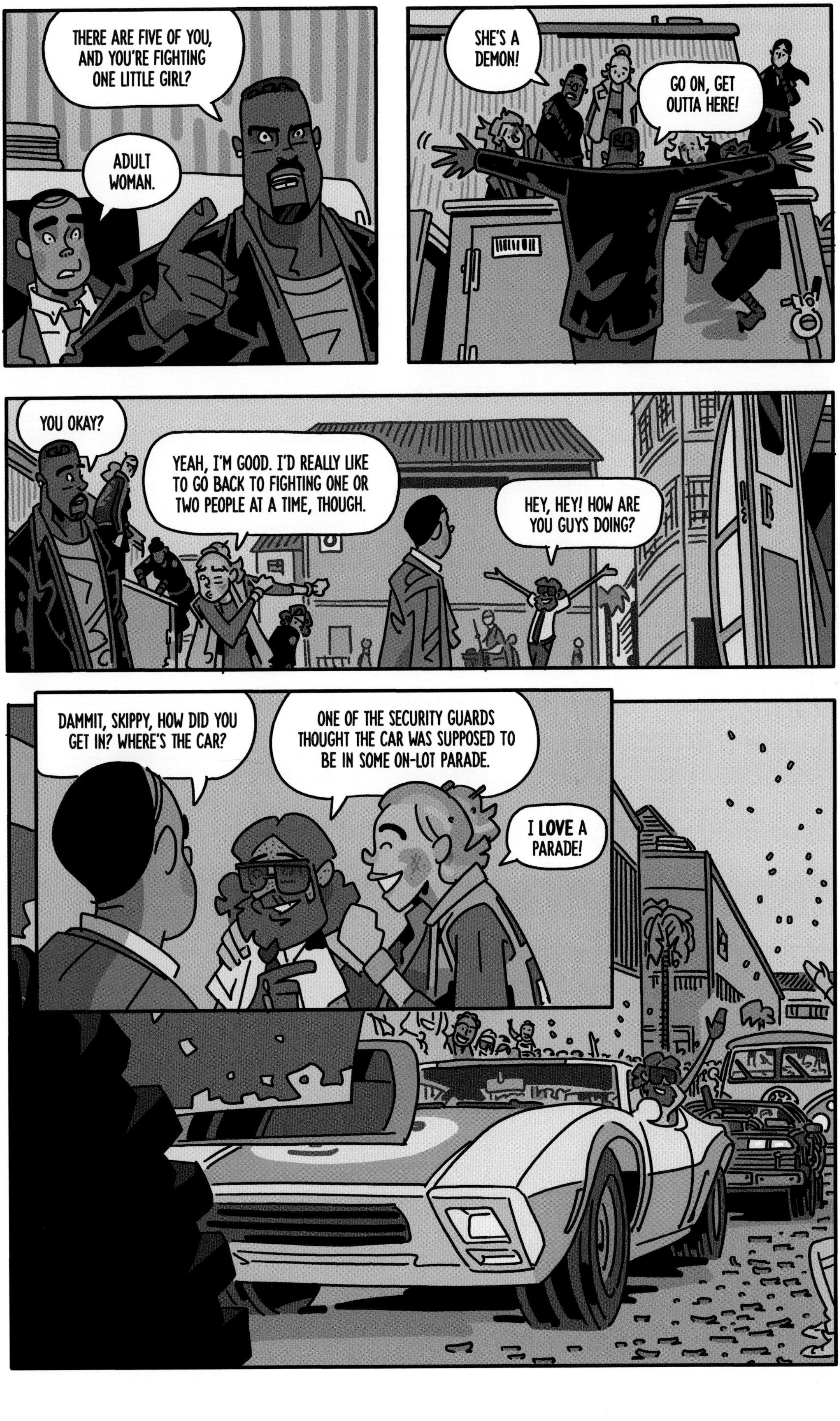
THERE ARE FIVE OF YOU, AND YOU'RE FIGHTING ONE LITTLE GIRL?
ADULT WOMAN.
SHE'S A DEMON!
GO ON, GET OUTTA HERE!
YOU OKAY?
YEAH, I'M GOOD. I'D REALLY LIKE TO GO BACK TO FIGHTING ONE OR TWO PEOPLE AT A TIME, THOUGH.
HEY, HEY! HOW ARE YOU GUYS DOING?
DAMMIT, SKIPPY, HOW DID YOU GET IN? WHERE'S THE CAR?
ONE OF THE SECURITY GUARDS THOUGHT THE CAR WAS SUPPOSED TO BE IN SOME ON-LOT PARADE.
I **LOVE** A PARADE!

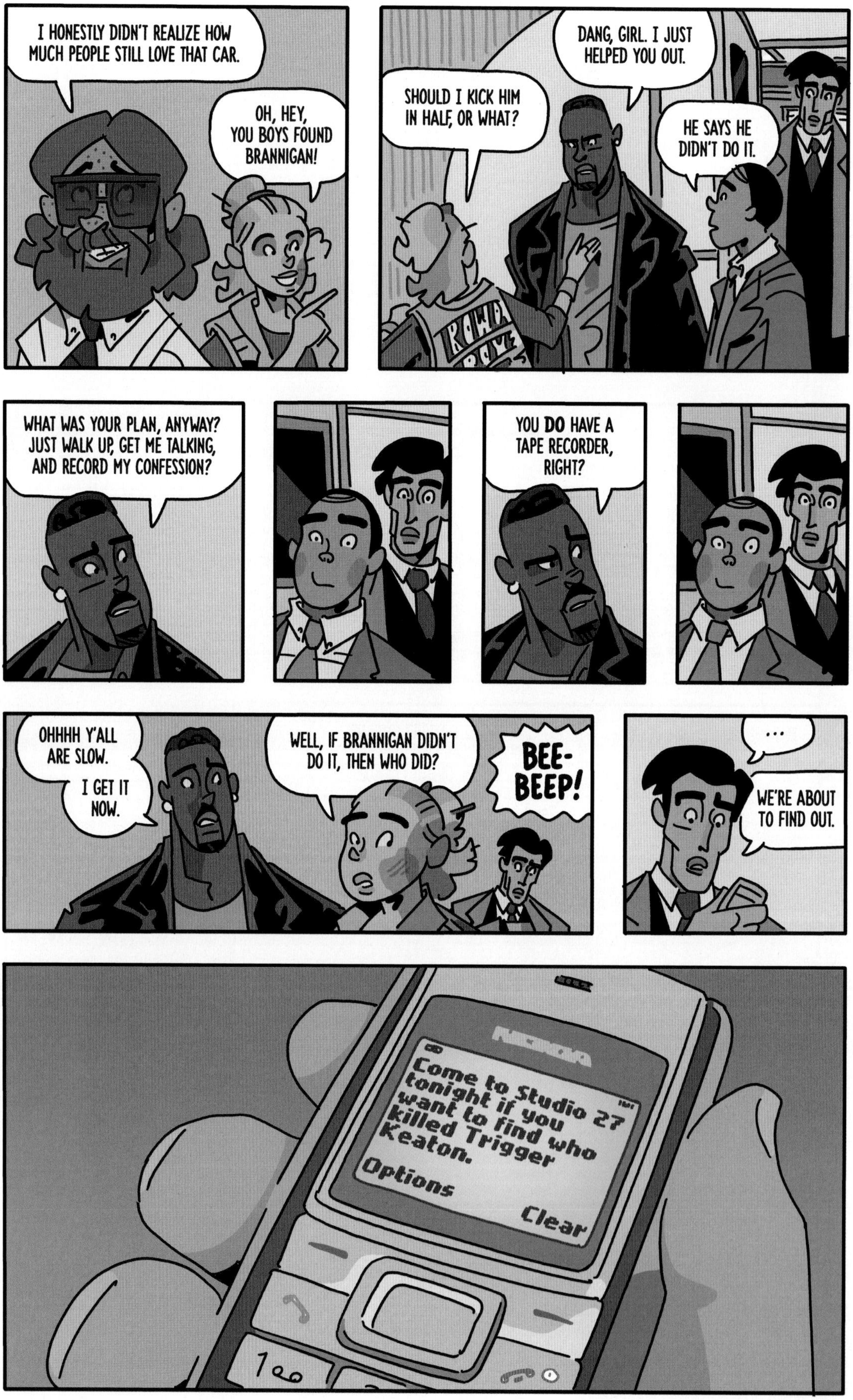

I HONESTLY DIDN'T REALIZE HOW MUCH PEOPLE STILL LOVE THAT CAR.
OH, HEY, YOU BOYS FOUND BRANNIGAN!
SHOULD I KICK HIM IN HALF, OR WHAT?
DANG, GIRL. I JUST HELPED YOU OUT.
HE SAYS HE DIDN'T DO IT.
WHAT WAS YOUR PLAN, ANYWAY? JUST WALK UP, GET ME TALKING, AND RECORD MY CONFESSION?
YOU **DO** HAVE A TAPE RECORDER, RIGHT?
OHHHH Y'ALL ARE SLOW.
I GET IT NOW.
WELL, IF BRANNIGAN DIDN'T DO IT, THEN WHO DID?
BEE-BEEP!
...
WE'RE ABOUT TO FIND OUT.
Come to Studio 27 tonight if you want to find who killed Trigger Keaton.
Options
Clear

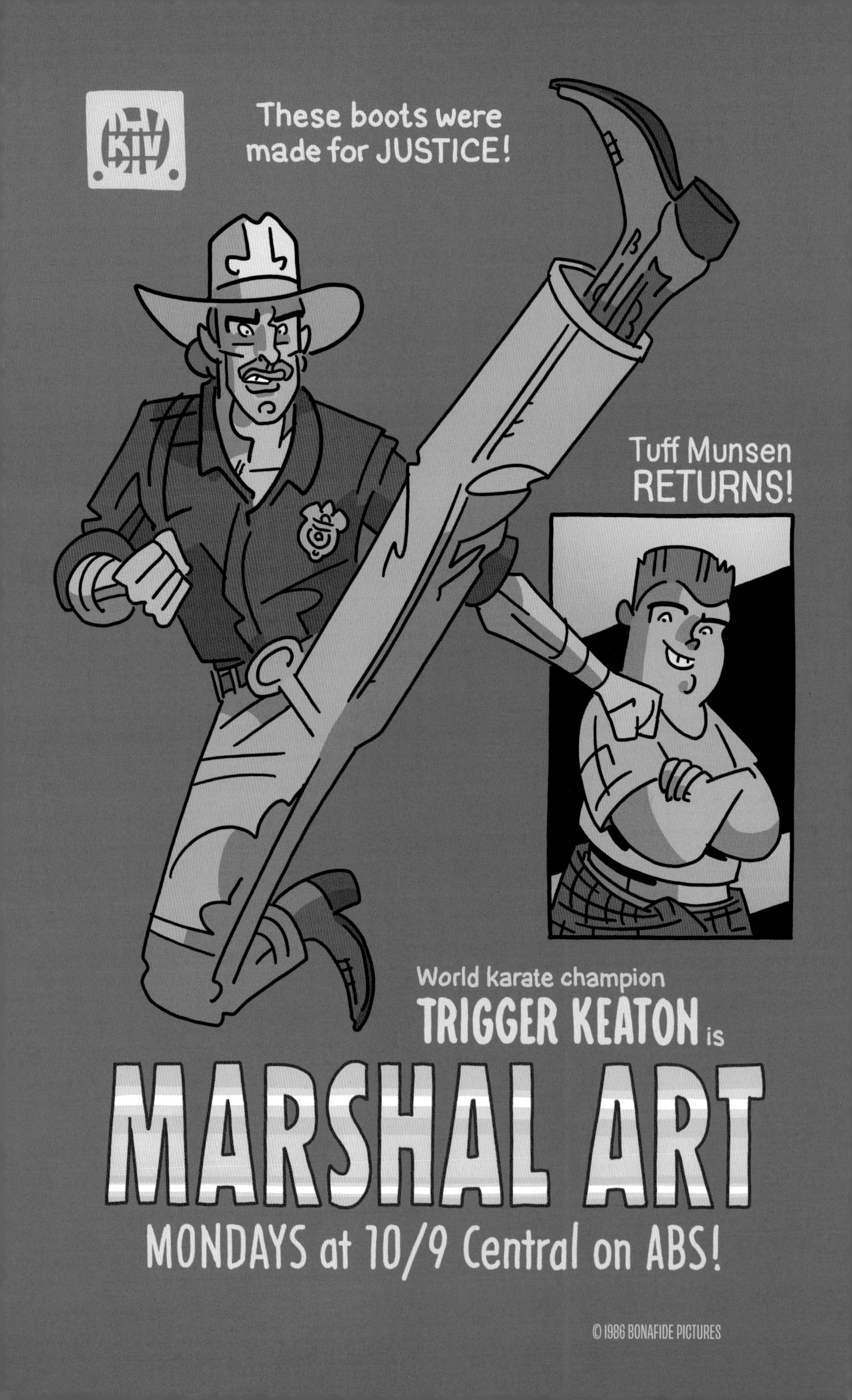
KTV
These boots were made for JUSTICE!
Tuff Munsen RETURNS!
World karate champion
TRIGGER KEATON is
MARSHAL ART
MONDAYS at 10/9 Central on ABS!
© 1986 BONAFIDE PICTURES

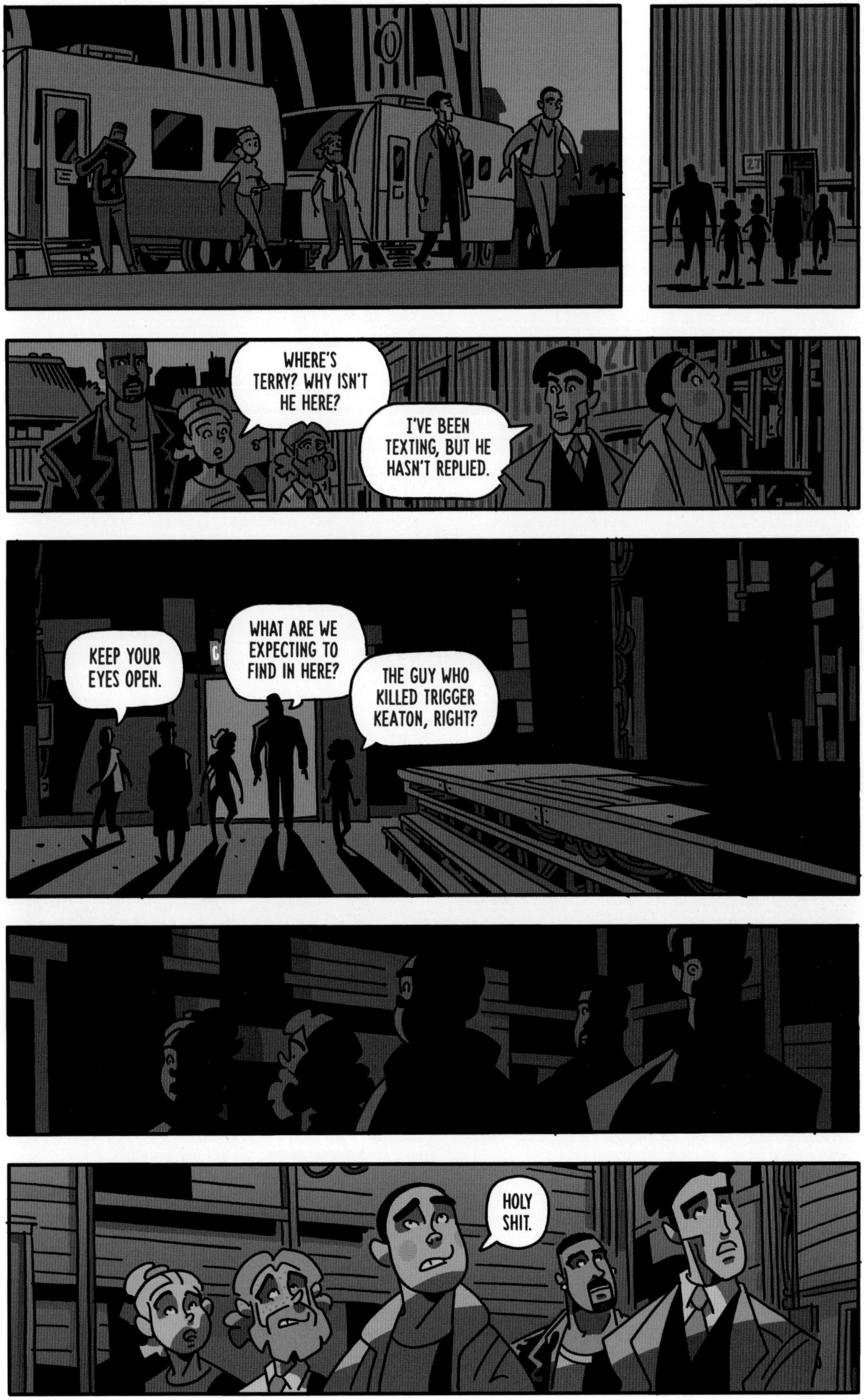
WHERE'S TERRY? WHY ISN'T HE HERE?
I'VE BEEN TEXTING, BUT HE HASN'T REPLIED.
KEEP YOUR EYES OPEN.
WHAT ARE WE EXPECTING TO FIND IN HERE?
THE GUY WHO KILLED TRIGGER KEATON, RIGHT?
HOLY SHIT.

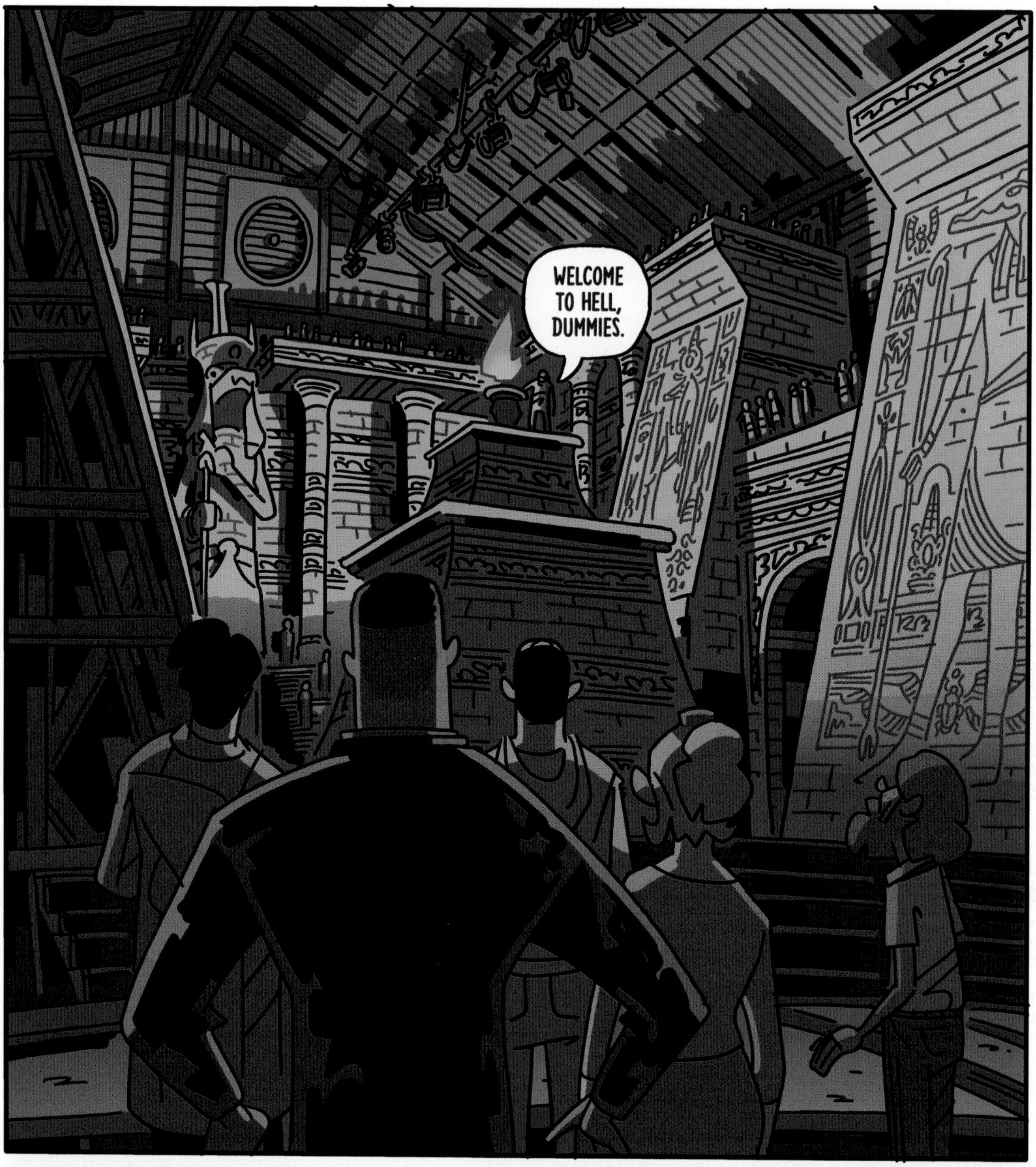
WELCOME TO HELL, DUMMIES.

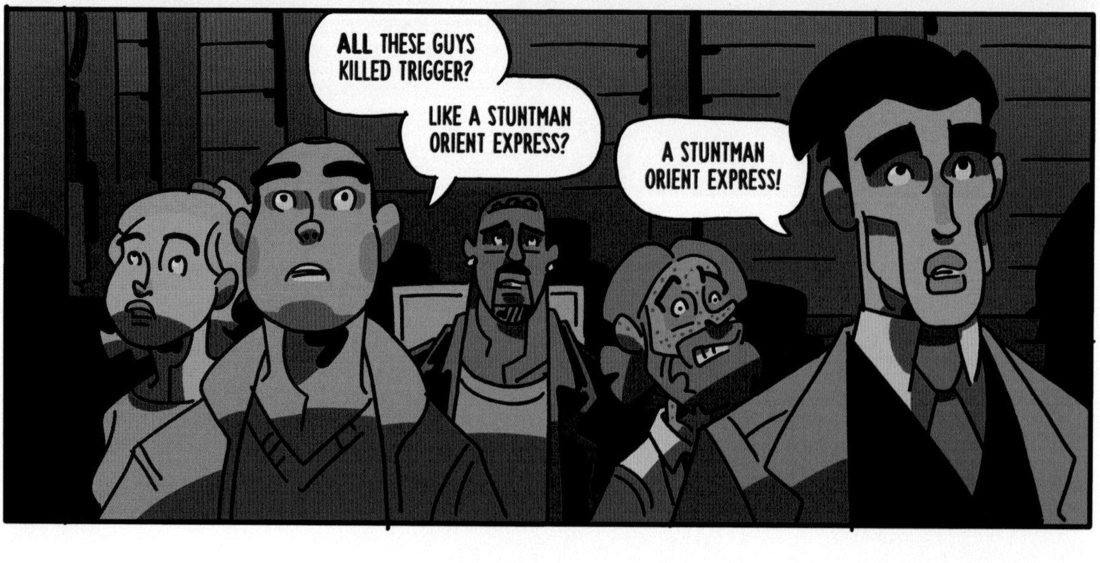
ALL THESE GUYS KILLED TRIGGER?
LIKE A STUNTMAN ORIENT EXPRESS?
A STUNTMAN ORIENT EXPRESS!

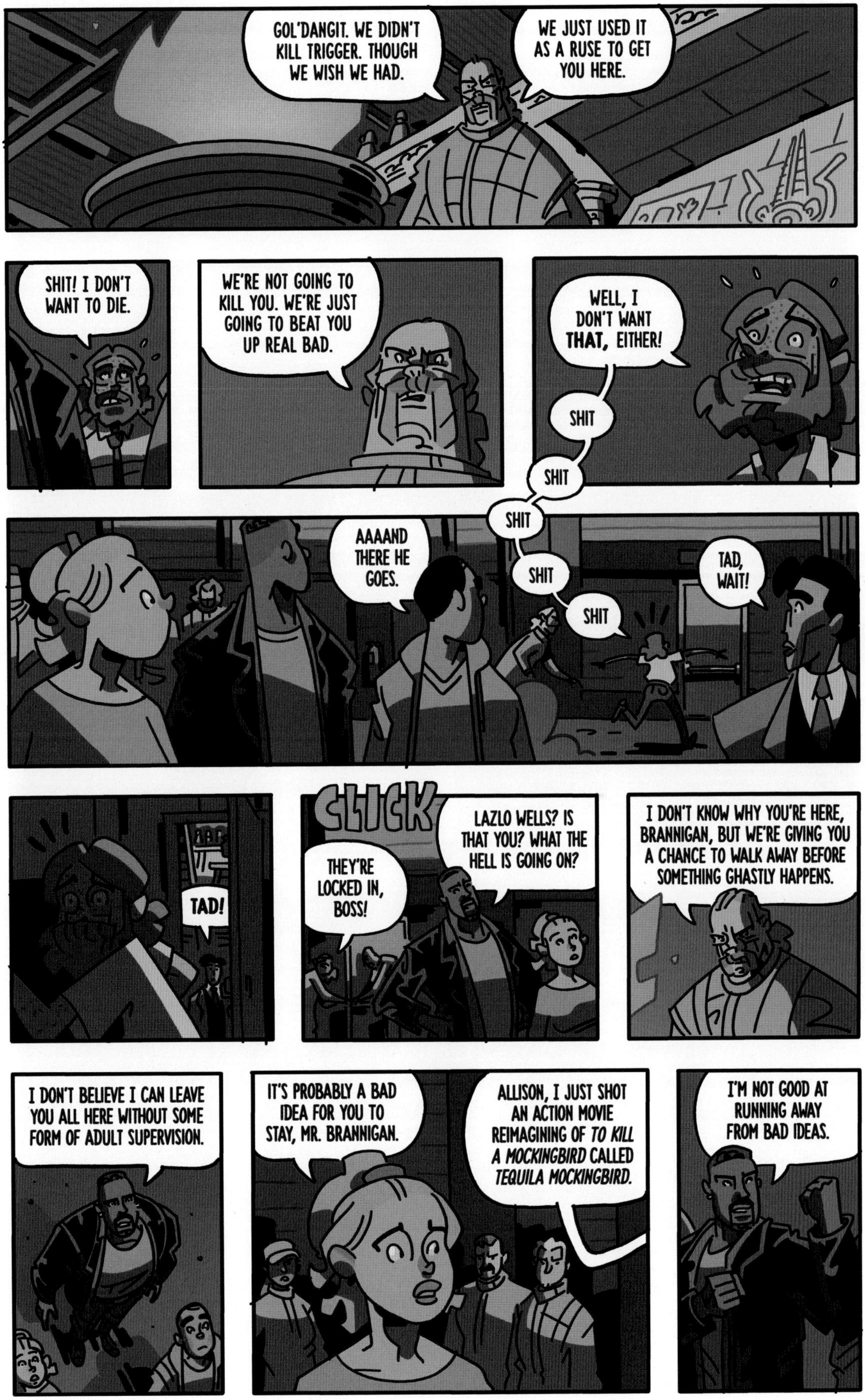
GOL'DANGIT. WE DIDN'T KILL TRIGGER. THOUGH WE WISH WE HAD.
WE JUST USED IT AS A RUSE TO GET YOU HERE.
SHIT! I DON'T WANT TO DIE.
WE'RE NOT GOING TO KILL YOU. WE'RE JUST GOING TO BEAT YOU UP REAL BAD.
WELL, I DON'T WANT **THAT**, EITHER!
SHIT
SHIT
SHIT
SHIT
SHIT
AAAAND THERE HE GOES.
TAD, WAIT!
TAD!
CLICK
THEY'RE LOCKED IN, BOSS!
LAZLO WELLS? IS THAT YOU? WHAT THE HELL IS GOING ON?
I DON'T KNOW WHY YOU'RE HERE, BRANNIGAN, BUT WE'RE GIVING YOU A CHANCE TO WALK AWAY BEFORE SOMETHING GHASTLY HAPPENS.
I DON'T BELIEVE I CAN LEAVE YOU ALL HERE WITHOUT SOME FORM OF ADULT SUPERVISION.
IT'S PROBABLY A BAD IDEA FOR YOU TO STAY, MR. BRANNIGAN.
ALLISON, I JUST SHOT AN ACTION MOVIE REIMAGINING OF *TO KILL A MOCKINGBIRD* CALLED *TEQUILA MOCKINGBIRD*.
I'M NOT GOOD AT RUNNING AWAY FROM BAD IDEAS.

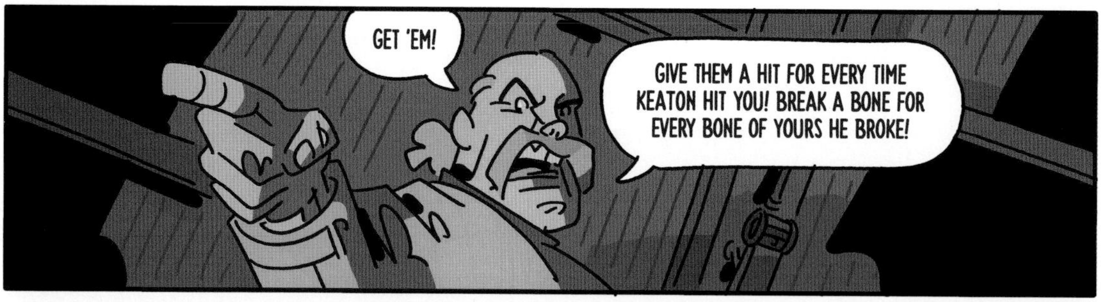
GET 'EM!
GIVE THEM A HIT FOR EVERY TIME KEATON HIT YOU! BREAK A BONE FOR EVERY BONE OF YOURS HE BROKE!

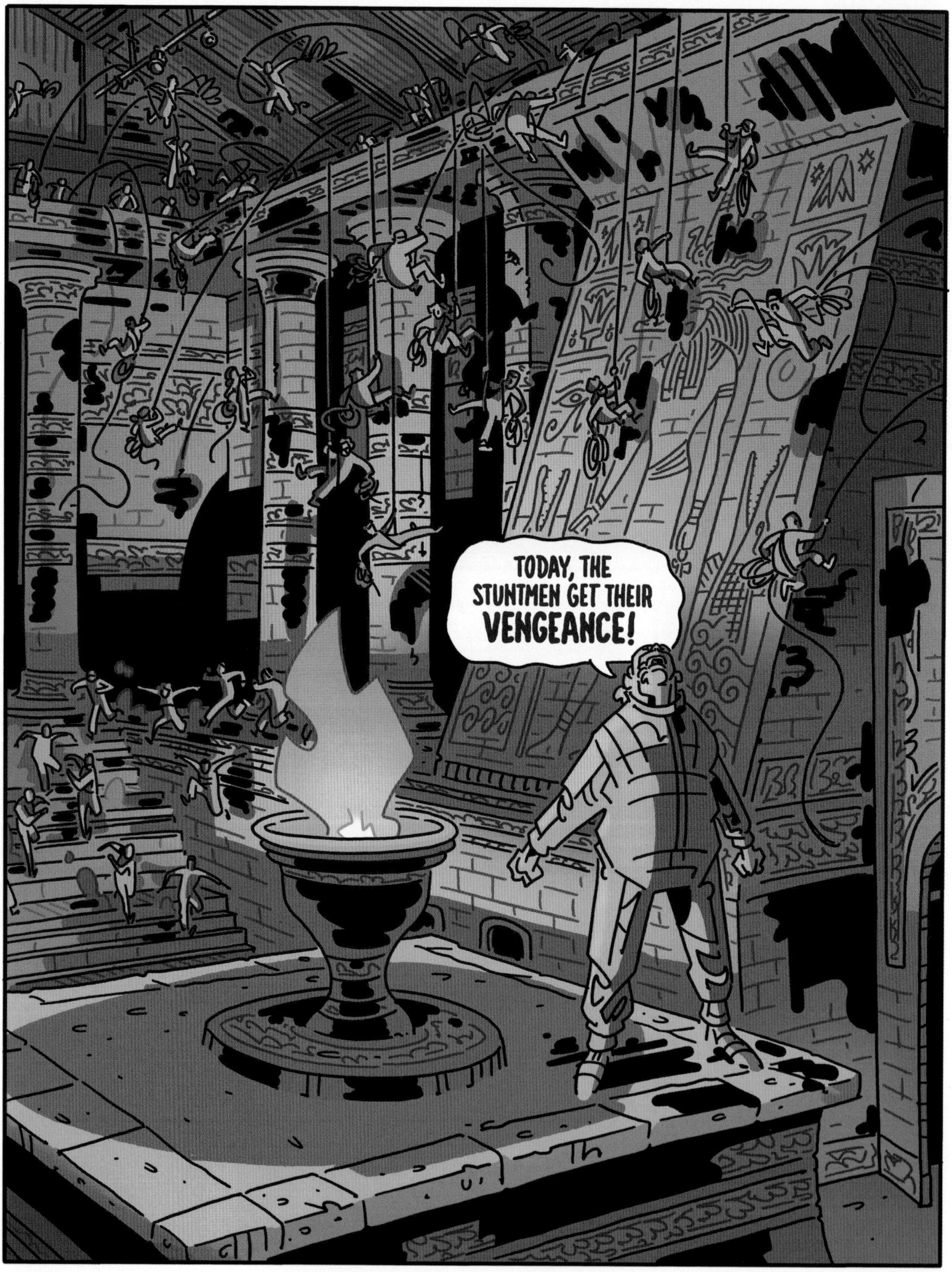
TODAY, THE STUNTMEN GET THEIR VENGEANCE!

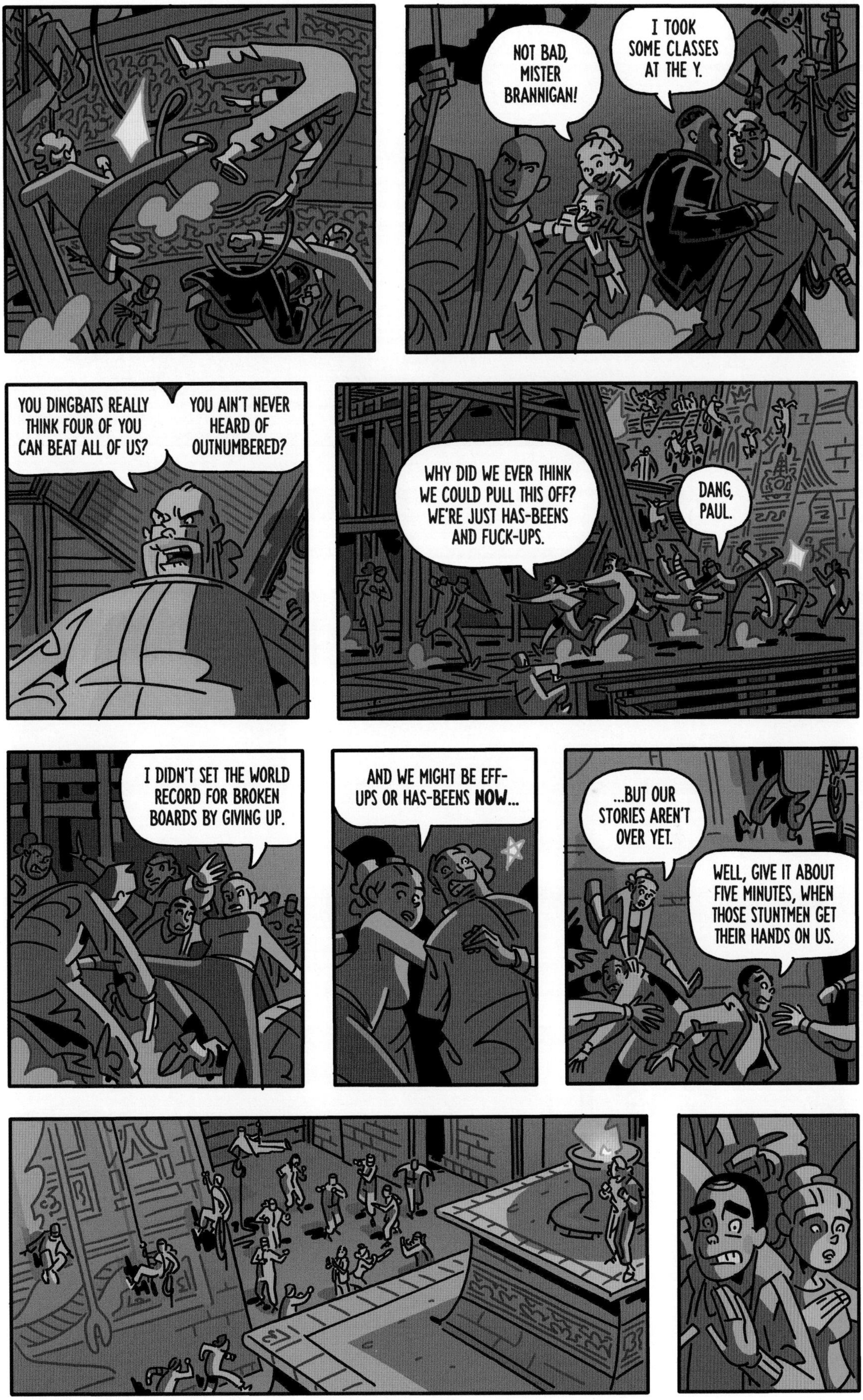
NOT BAD, MISTER BRANNIGAN!
I TOOK SOME CLASSES AT THE Y.
YOU DINGBATS REALLY THINK FOUR OF YOU CAN BEAT ALL OF US?
YOU AIN'T NEVER HEARD OF OUTNUMBERED?
WHY DID WE EVER THINK WE COULD PULL THIS OFF? WE'RE JUST HAS-BEENS AND FUCK-UPS.
DANG, PAUL.
I DIDN'T SET THE WORLD RECORD FOR BROKEN BOARDS BY GIVING UP.
AND WE MIGHT BE EFF-UPS OR HAS-BEENS **NOW**...
...BUT OUR STORIES AREN'T OVER YET.
WELL, GIVE IT ABOUT FIVE MINUTES, WHEN THOSE STUNTMEN GET THEIR HANDS ON US.

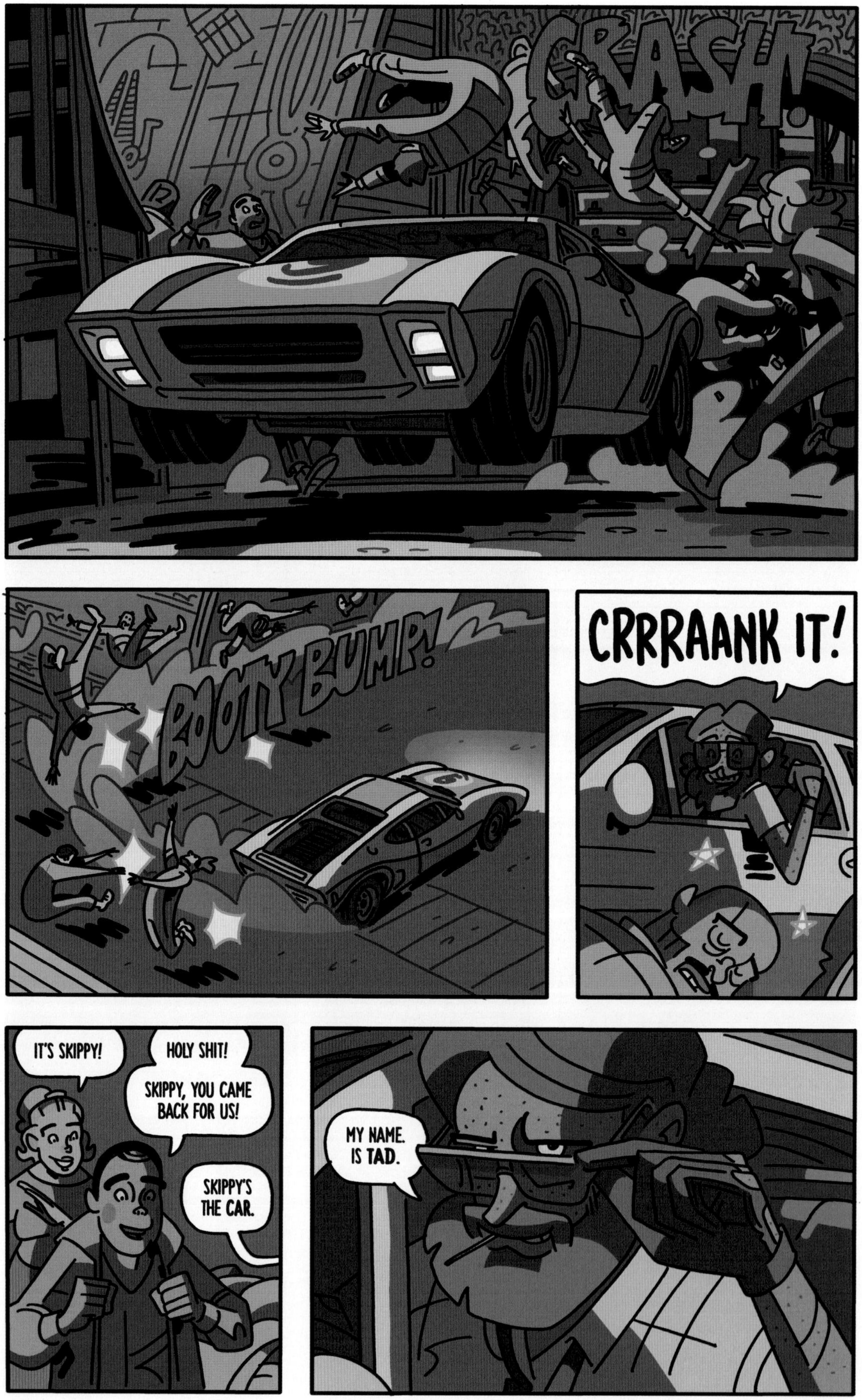
CRASH!
BOOTY BUMP!
CRRRAANK IT!
IT'S SKIPPY!
HOLY SHIT!
SKIPPY, YOU CAME BACK FOR US!
SKIPPY'S THE CAR.
MY NAME. IS **TAD**.

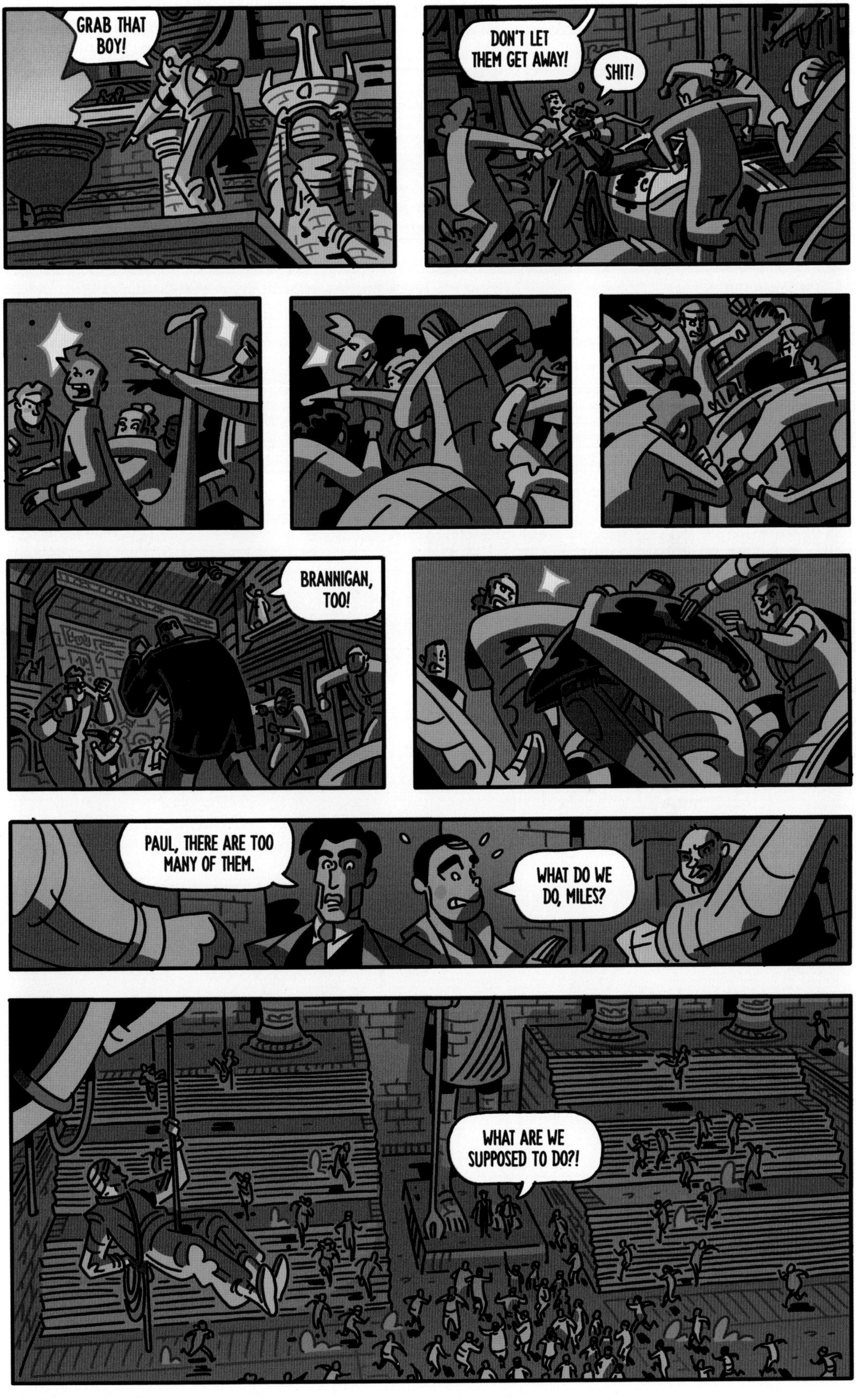
GRAB THAT BOY!
DON'T LET THEM GET AWAY!
SHIT!
BRANNIGAN, TOO!
PAUL, THERE ARE TOO MANY OF THEM.
WHAT DO WE DO, MILES?
WHAT ARE WE SUPPOSED TO DO?!

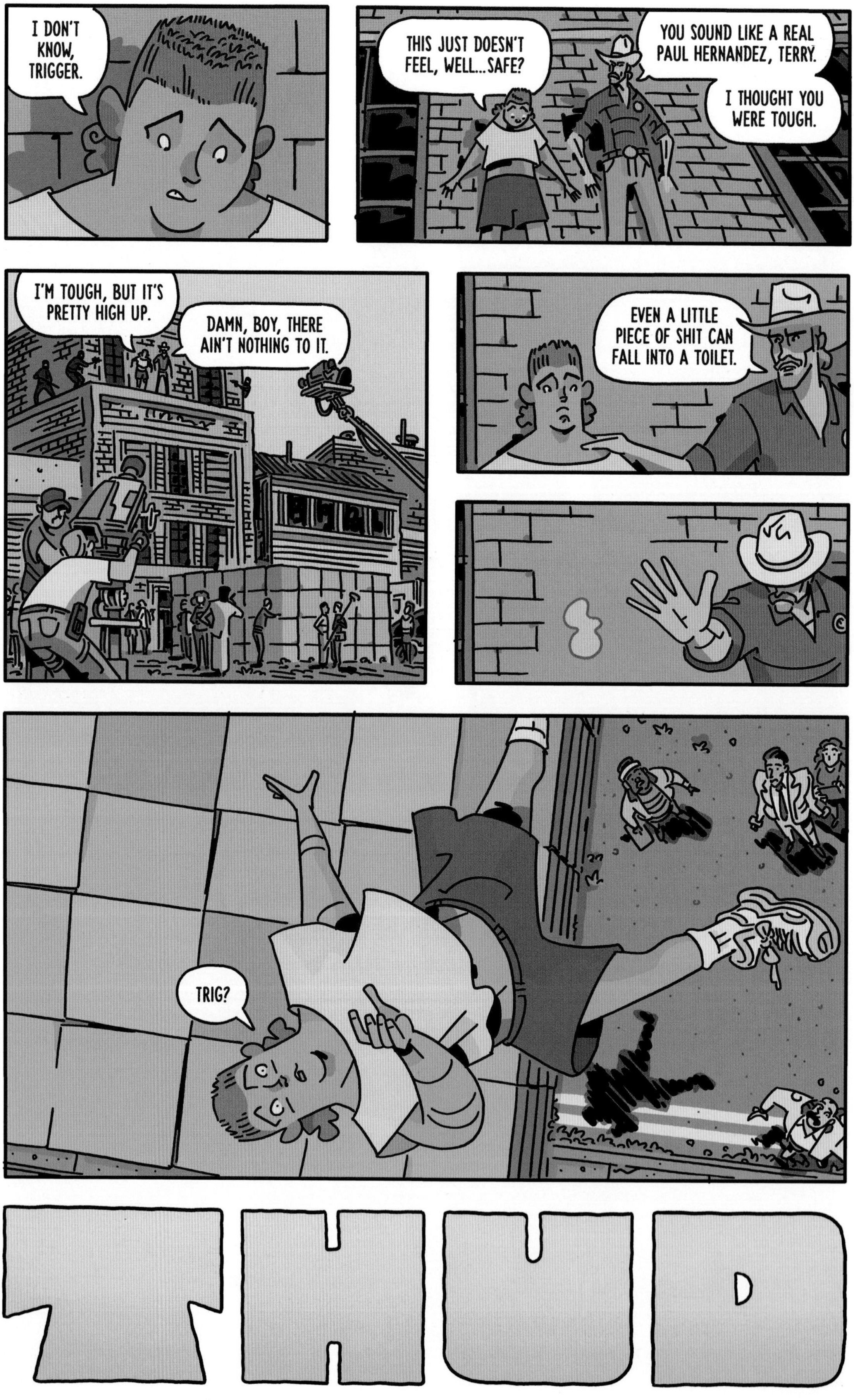
I DON'T KNOW, TRIGGER.
THIS JUST DOESN'T FEEL, WELL...SAFE?
YOU SOUND LIKE A REAL PAUL HERNANDEZ, TERRY.
I THOUGHT YOU WERE TOUGH.
I'M TOUGH, BUT IT'S PRETTY HIGH UP.
DAMN, BOY, THERE AIN'T NOTHING TO IT.
EVEN A LITTLE PIECE OF SHIT CAN FALL INTO A TOILET.
TRIG?
THUD

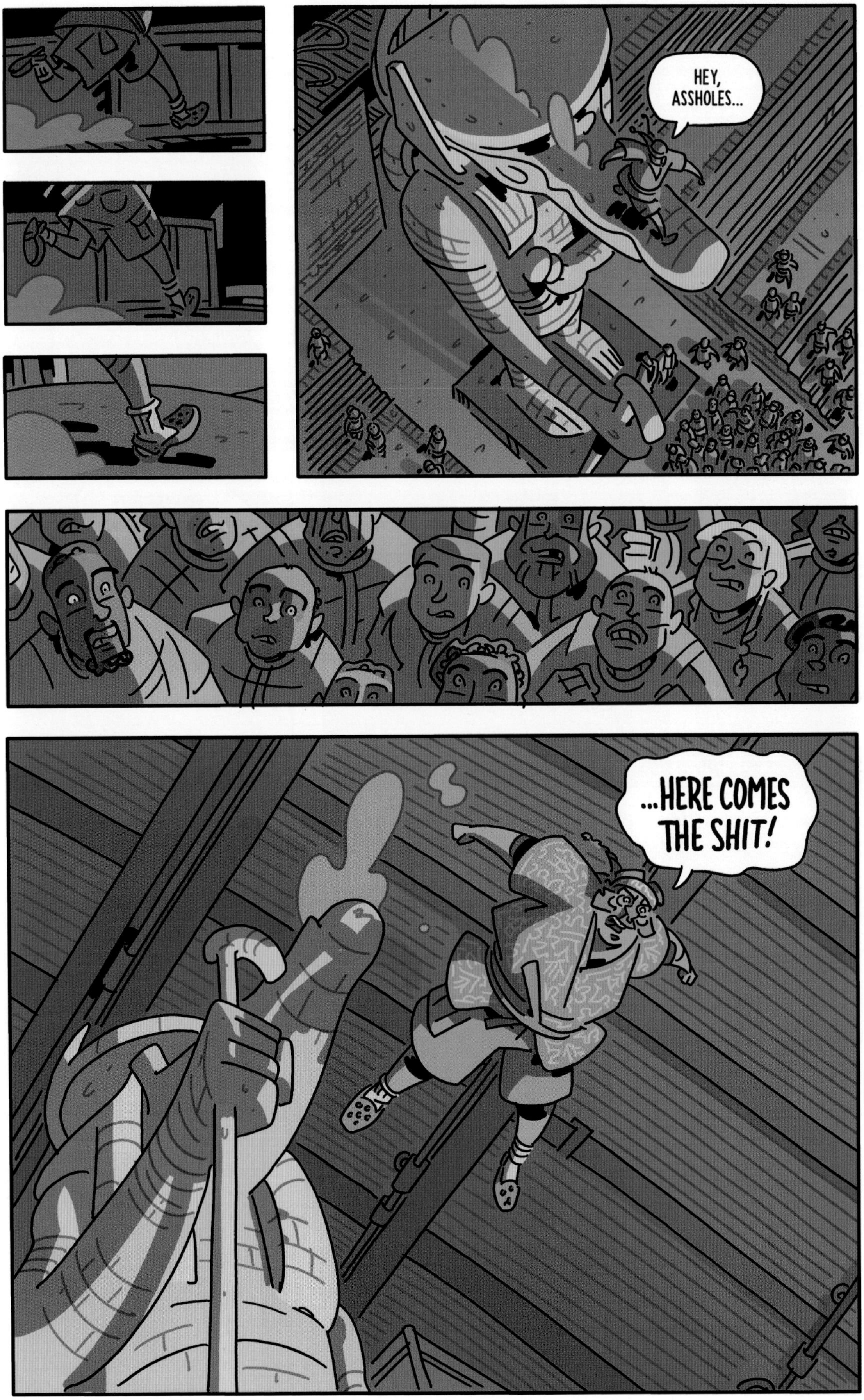
HEY, ASSHOLES...
...HERE COMES THE SHIT!

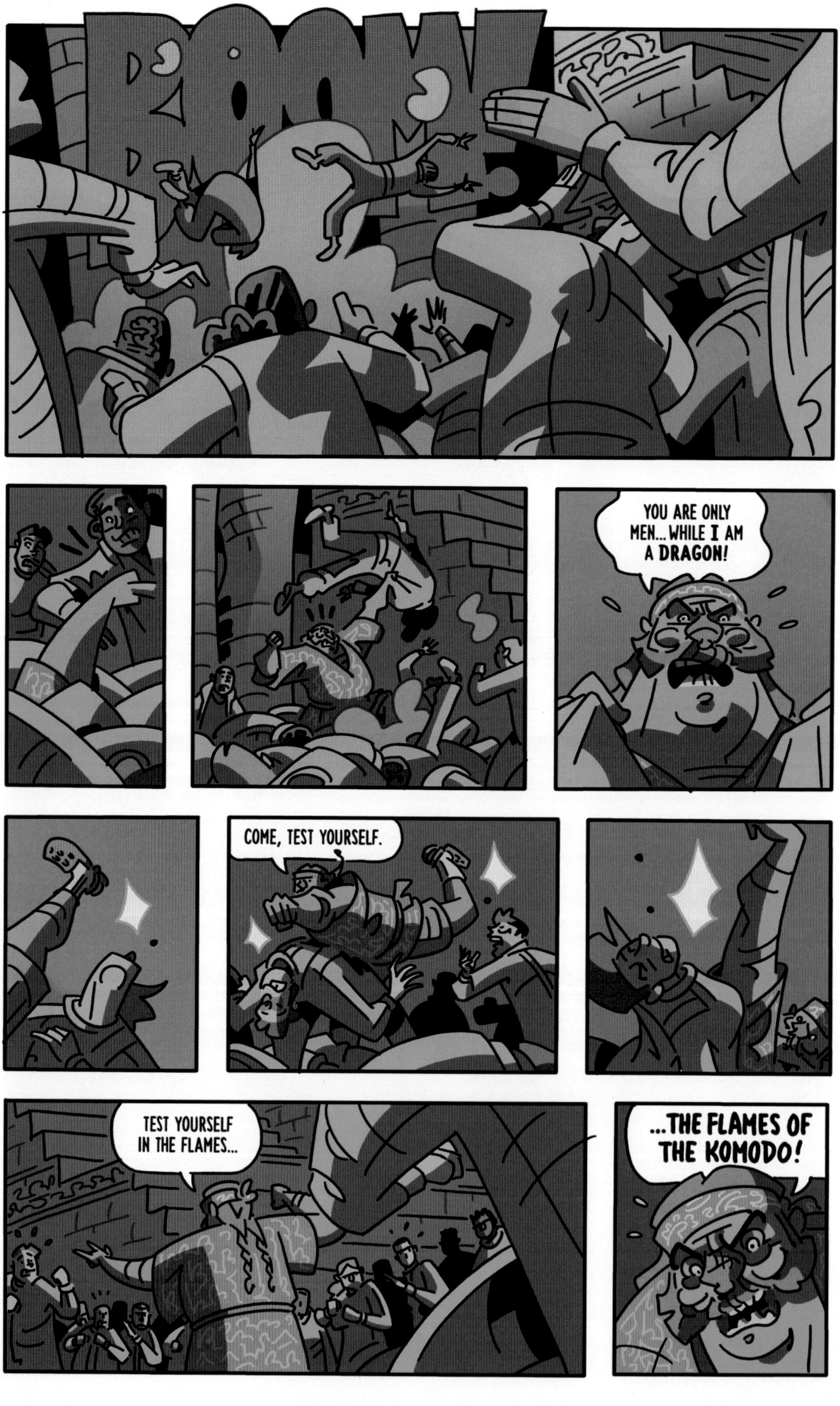
BOOOM!
YOU ARE ONLY MEN... WHILE I AM A DRAGON!
COME, TEST YOURSELF.
TEST YOURSELF IN THE FLAMES...
...THE FLAMES OF THE KOMODO!

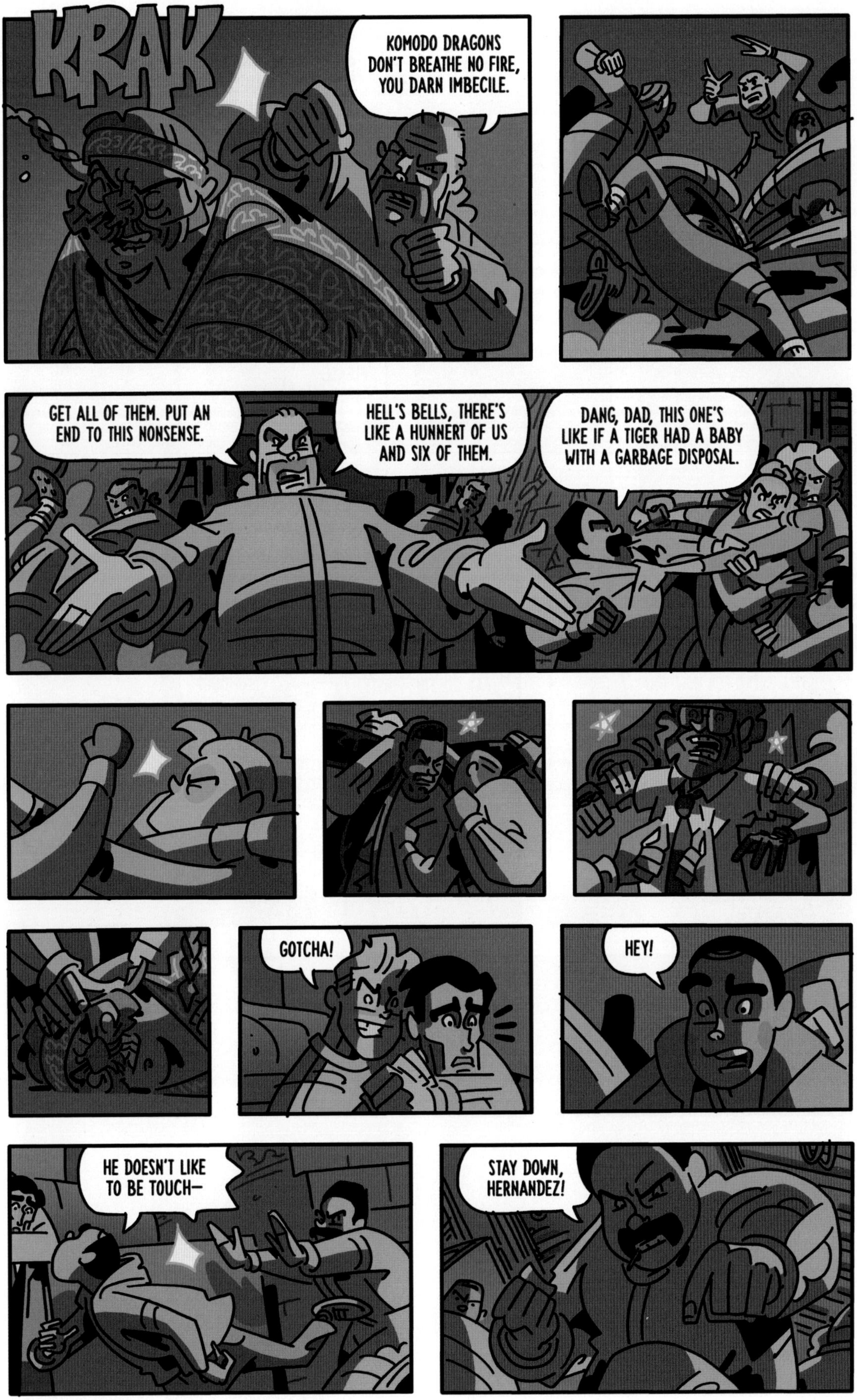
KRAK
KOMODO DRAGONS DON'T BREATHE NO FIRE, YOU DARN IMBECILE.
GET ALL OF THEM. PUT AN END TO THIS NONSENSE.
HELL'S BELLS, THERE'S LIKE A HUNNERT OF US AND SIX OF THEM.
DANG, DAD, THIS ONE'S LIKE IF A TIGER HAD A BABY WITH A GARBAGE DISPOSAL.
GOTCHA!
HEY!
HE DOESN'T LIKE TO BE TOUCH—
STAY DOWN, HERNANDEZ!

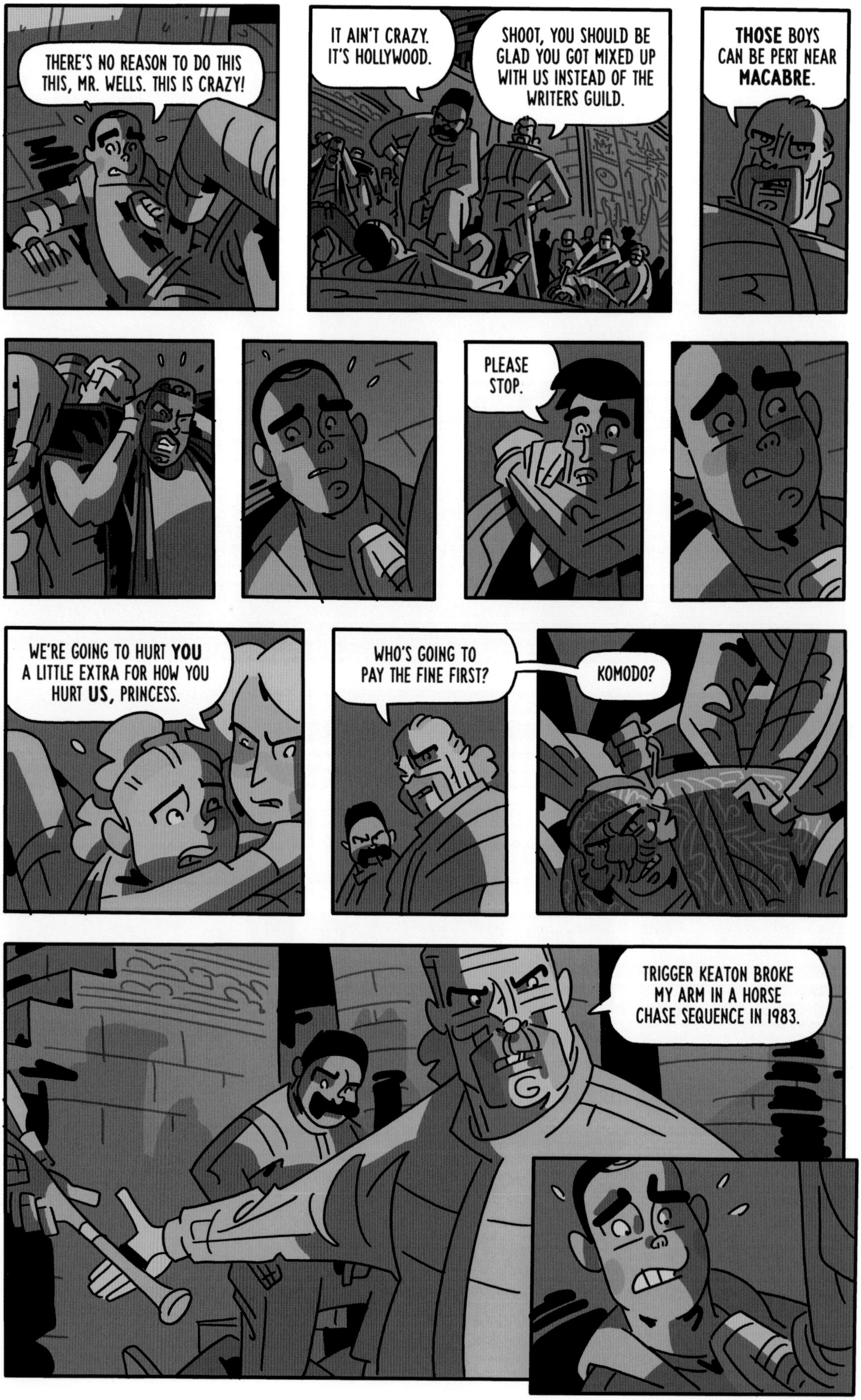
THERE'S NO REASON TO DO THIS THIS, MR. WELLS. THIS IS CRAZY!
IT AIN'T CRAZY. IT'S HOLLYWOOD.
SHOOT, YOU SHOULD BE GLAD YOU GOT MIXED UP WITH US INSTEAD OF THE WRITERS GUILD.
THOSE BOYS CAN BE PERT NEAR **MACABRE**.
PLEASE STOP.
WE'RE GOING TO HURT **YOU** A LITTLE EXTRA FOR HOW YOU HURT **US**, PRINCESS.
WHO'S GOING TO PAY THE FINE FIRST?
KOMODO?
TRIGGER KEATON BROKE MY ARM IN A HORSE CHASE SEQUENCE IN 1983.

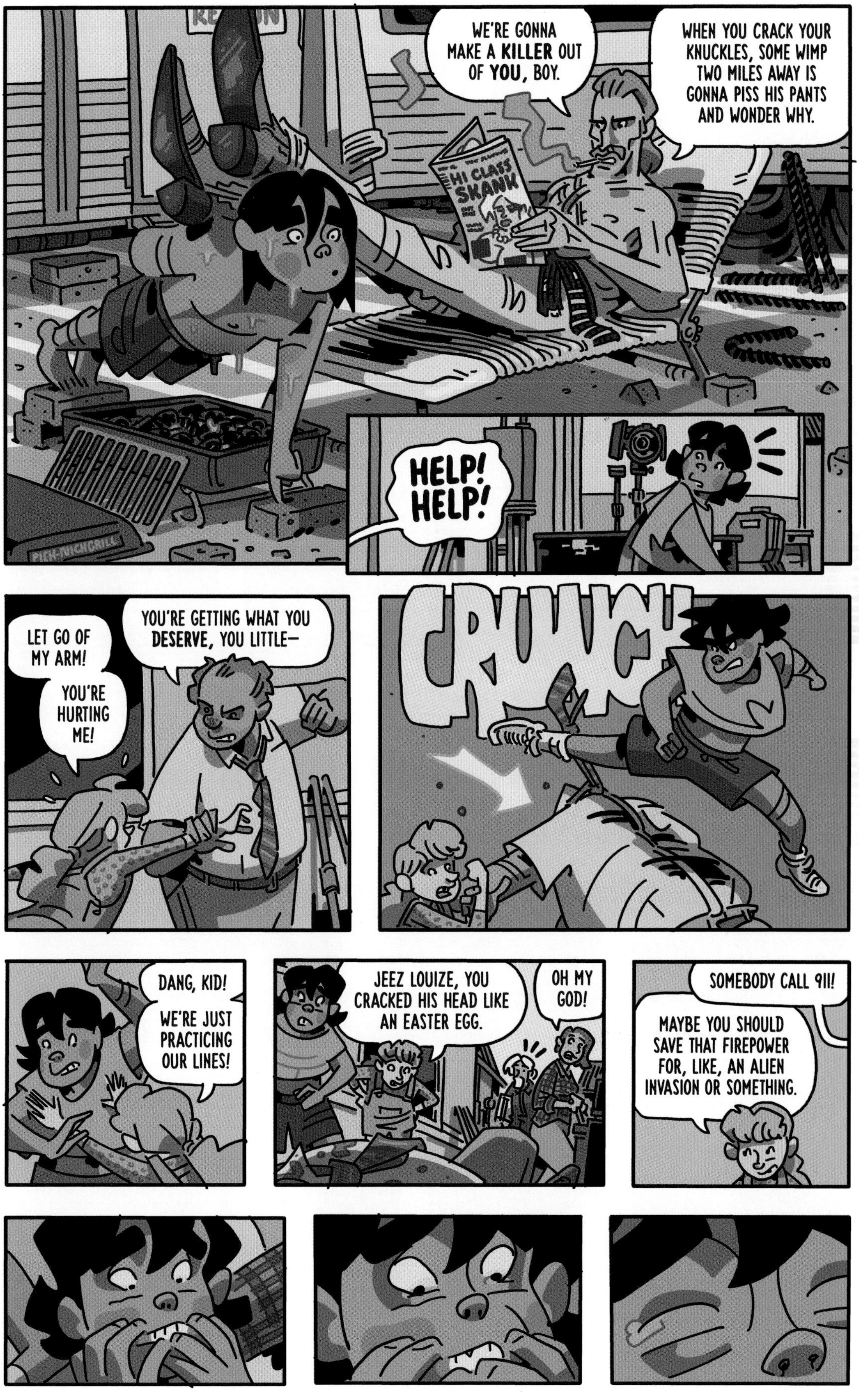
WE'RE GONNA MAKE A **KILLER** OUT OF **YOU**, BOY.
WHEN YOU CRACK YOUR KNUCKLES, SOME WIMP TWO MILES AWAY IS GONNA PISS HIS PANTS AND WONDER WHY.
HI CLASS SKANK
PICH-NICHGRILL
HELP! HELP!
LET GO OF MY ARM!
YOU'RE GETTING WHAT YOU **DESERVE**, YOU LITTLE—
YOU'RE HURTING ME!
CRUUNCH
DANG, KID!
WE'RE JUST PRACTICING OUR LINES!
JEEZ LOUIZE, YOU CRACKED HIS HEAD LIKE AN EASTER EGG.
OH MY GOD!
SOMEBODY CALL 911!
MAYBE YOU SHOULD SAVE THAT FIREPOWER FOR, LIKE, AN ALIEN INVASION OR SOMETHING.

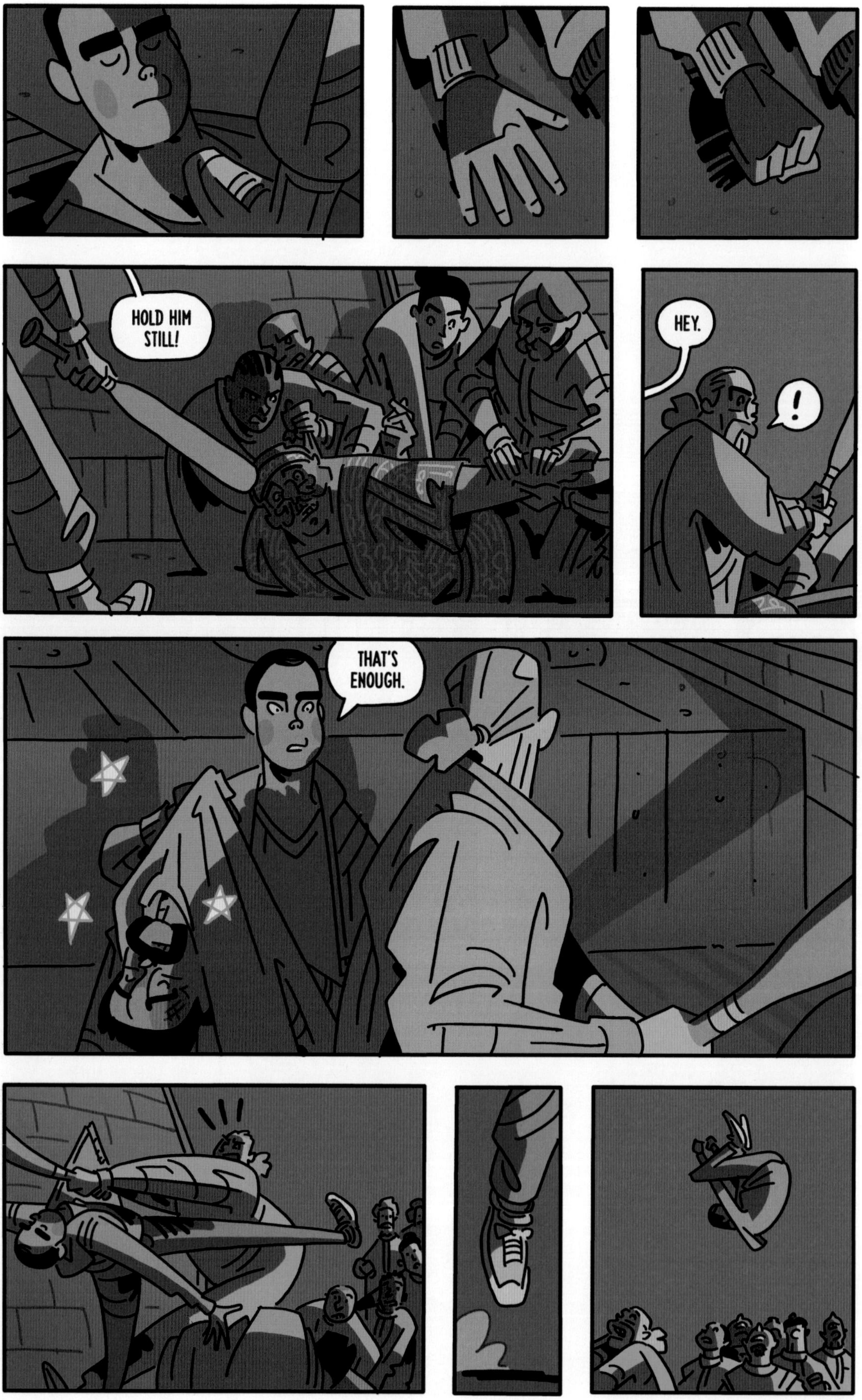
HOLD HIM STILL!
HEY.
!
THAT'S ENOUGH.

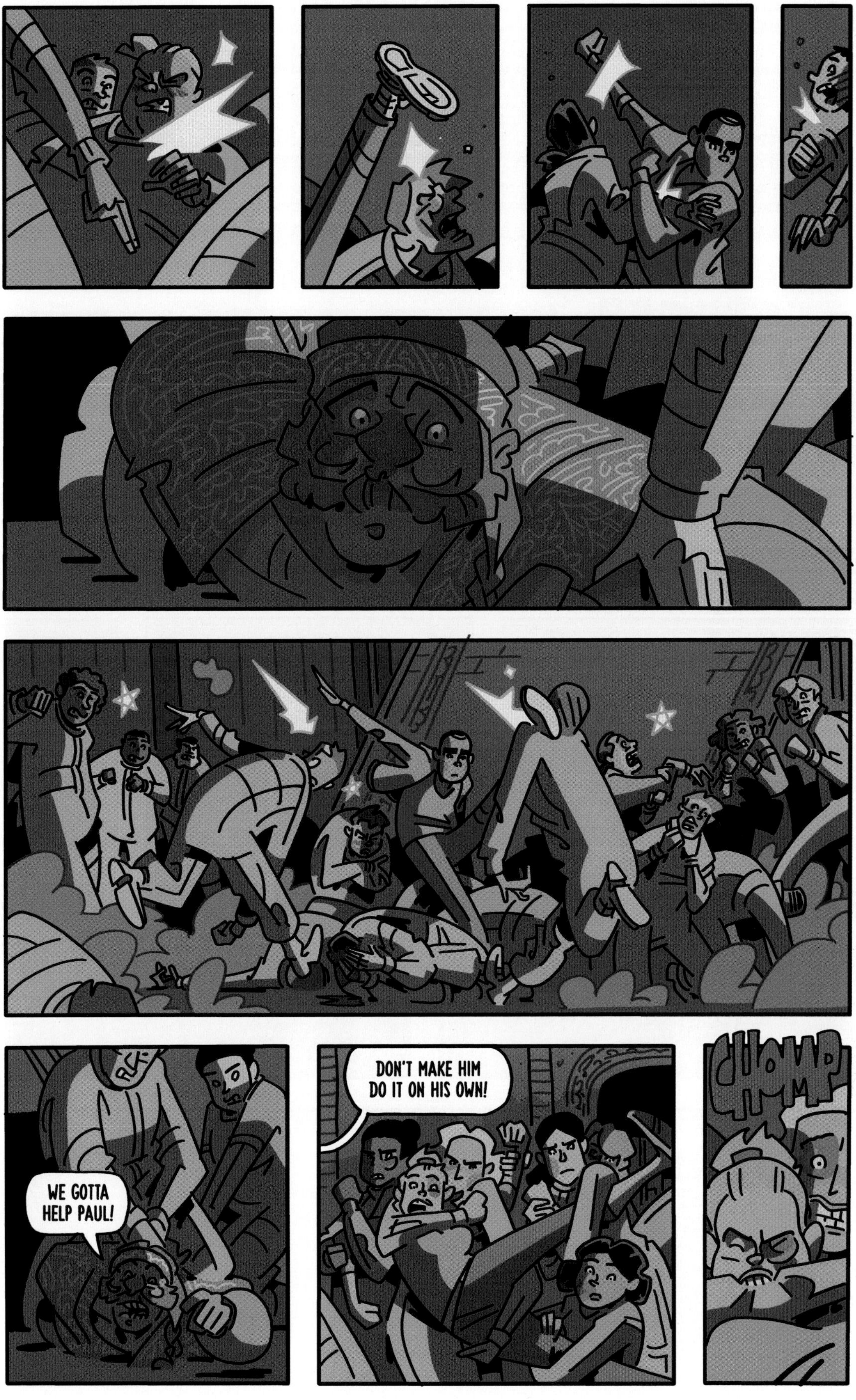
WE GOTTA HELP PAUL!
DON'T MAKE HIM DO IT ON HIS OWN!
CHOMP

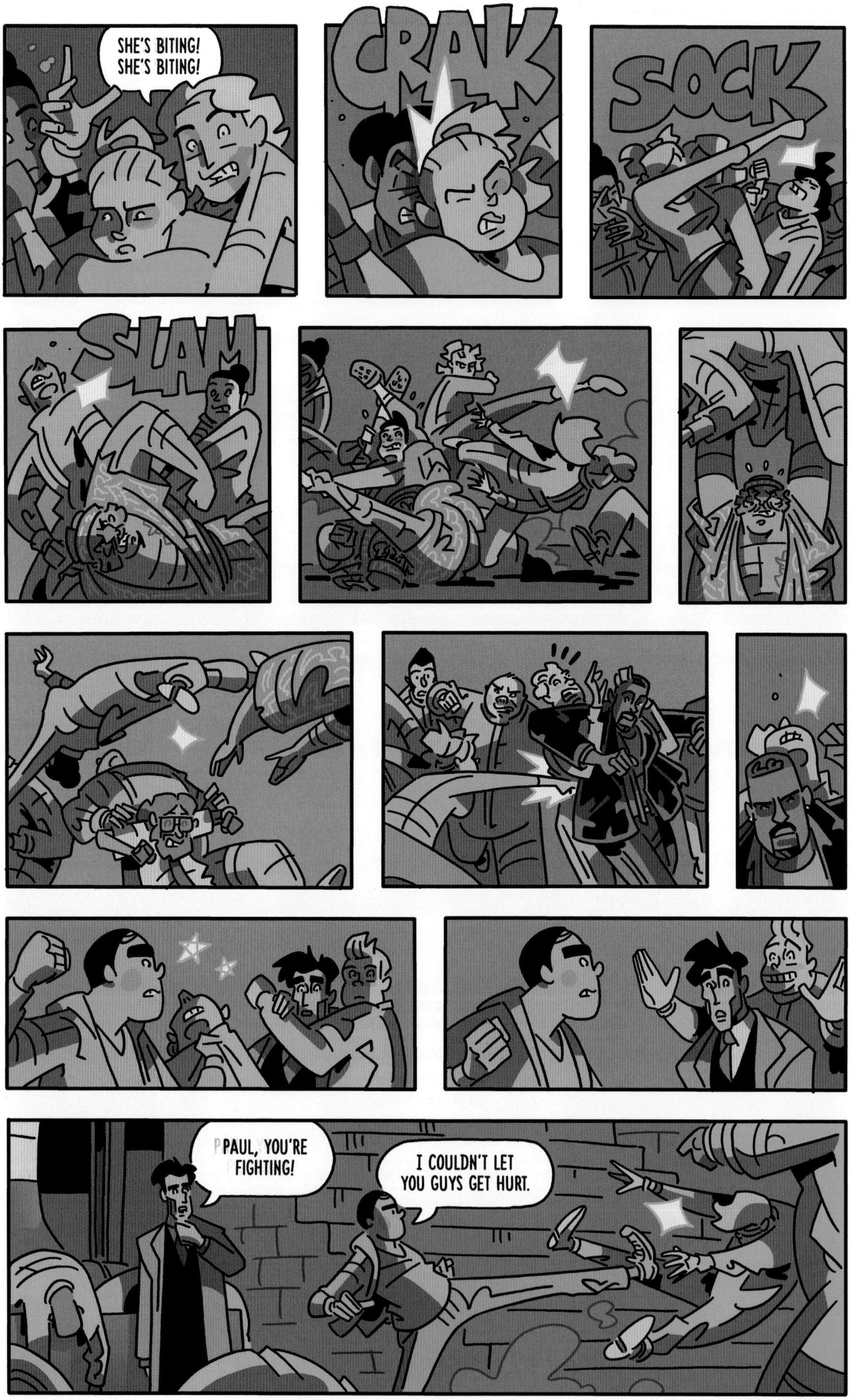
SHE'S BITING! SHE'S BITING!
CRAK
SOCK
SLAM
PAUL, YOU'RE FIGHTING!
I COULDN'T LET YOU GUYS GET HURT.

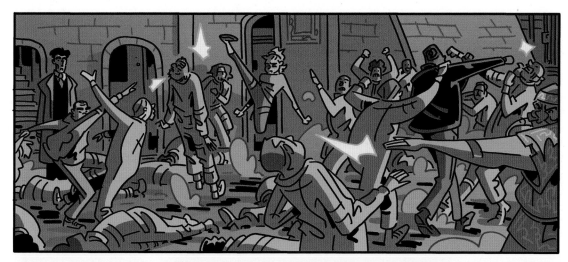

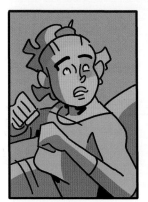

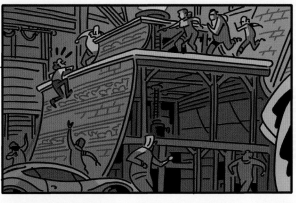

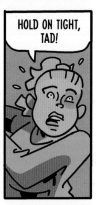

HOLD ON TIGHT, TAD!
CRACK
CRACK CRACK
CRACK
CRACK CRACK
SEPARATE THEM! USE YOUR SUPERIOR NUMBERS!
LAZLO!

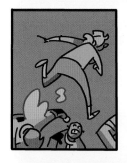

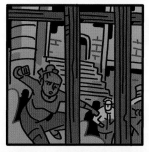

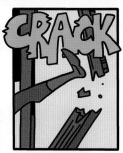

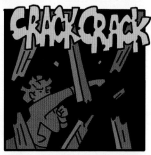

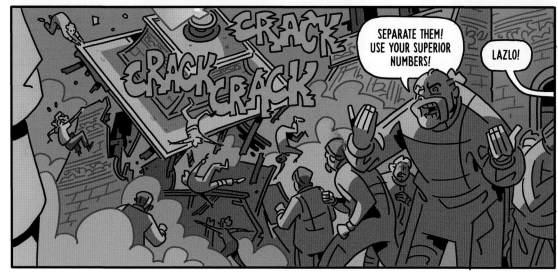

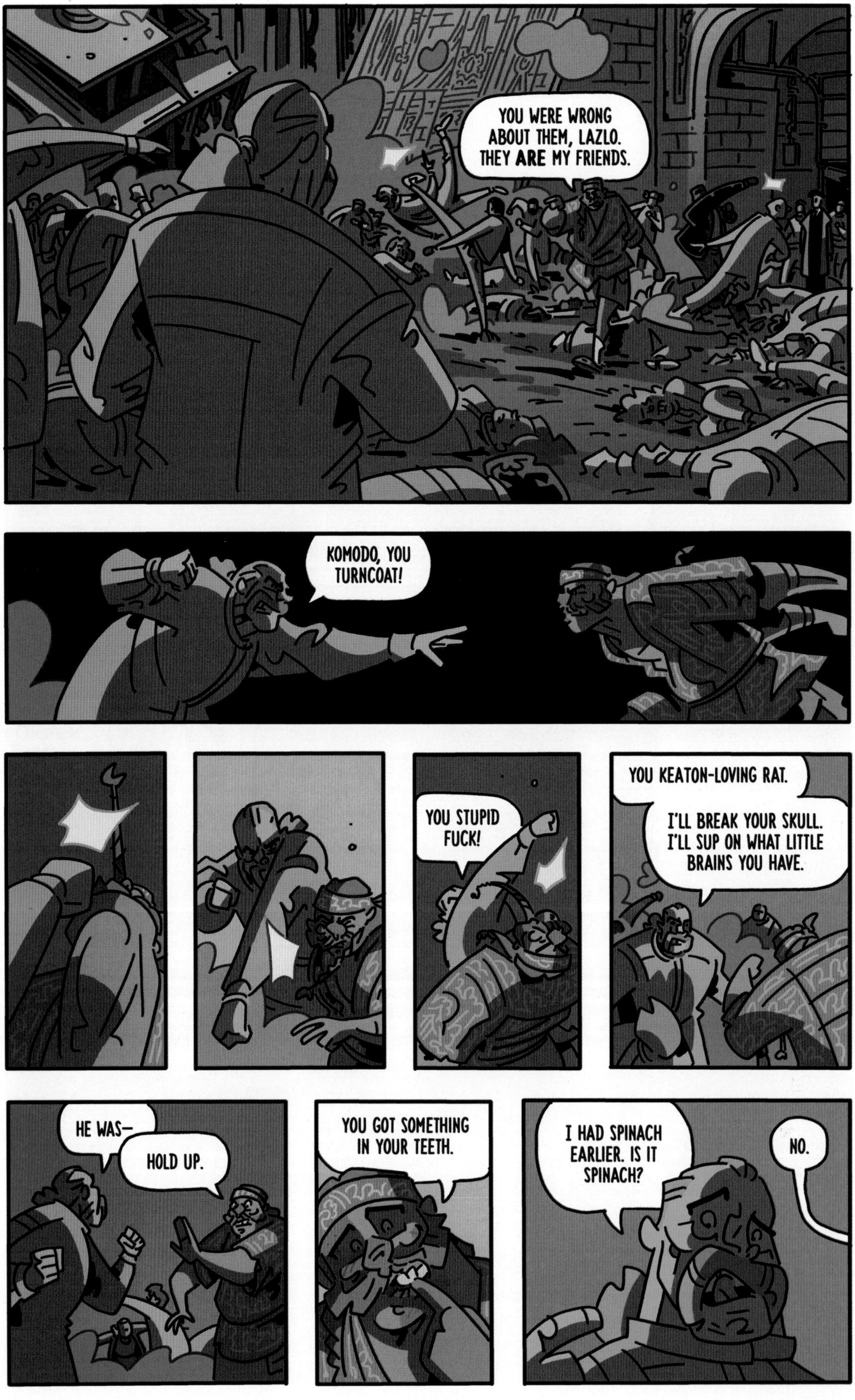
YOU WERE WRONG ABOUT THEM, LAZLO. THEY ARE MY FRIENDS.
KOMODO, YOU TURNCOAT!
YOU STUPID FUCK!
YOU KEATON-LOVING RAT.
I'LL BREAK YOUR SKULL. I'LL SUP ON WHAT LITTLE BRAINS YOU HAVE.
HE WAS—
HOLD UP.
YOU GOT SOMETHING IN YOUR TEETH.
I HAD SPINACH EARLIER. IS IT SPINACH?
NO.

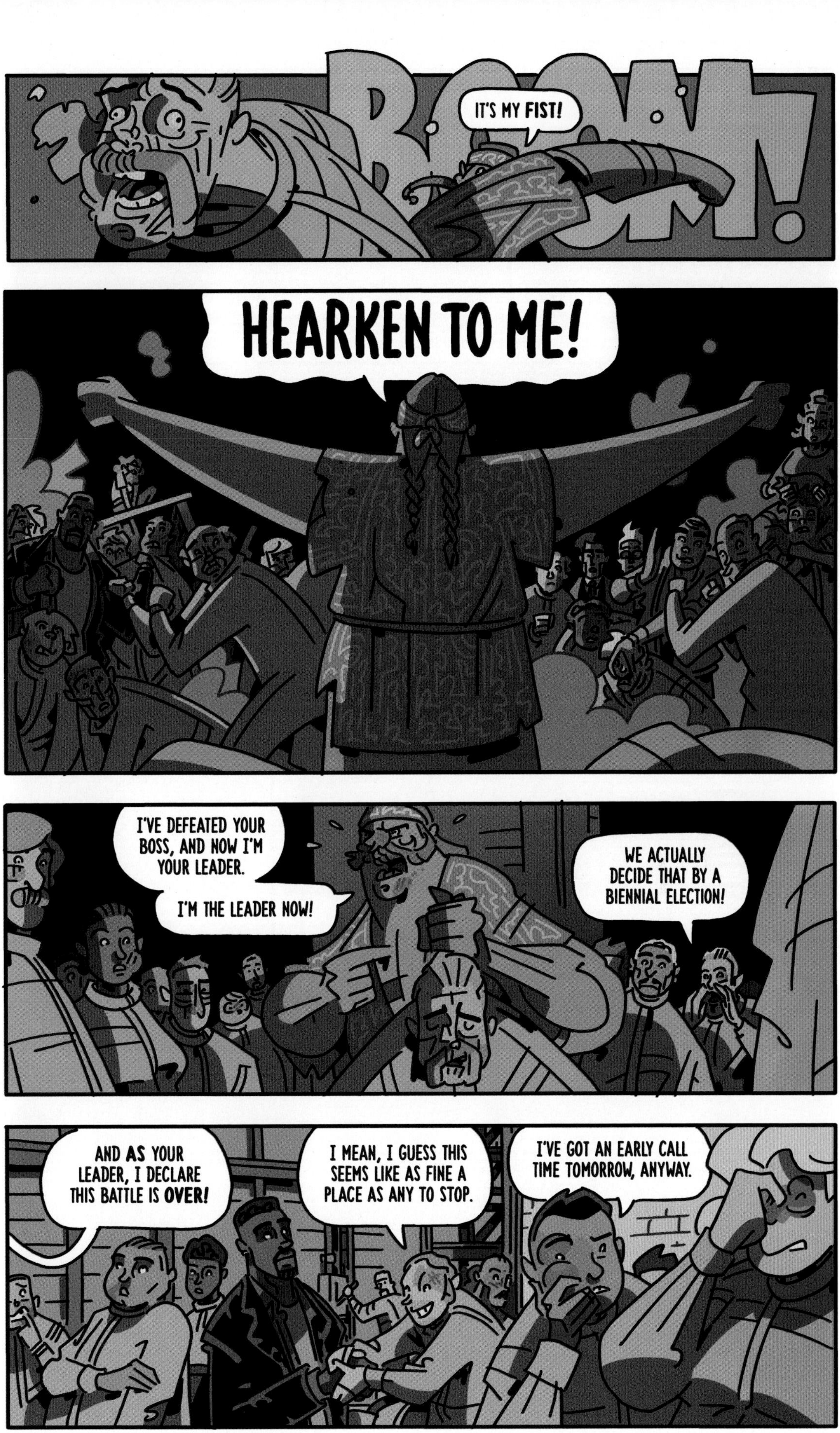
BOOM!
IT'S MY FIST!
HEARKEN TO ME!
I'VE DEFEATED YOUR BOSS, AND NOW I'M YOUR LEADER.
I'M THE LEADER NOW!
WE ACTUALLY DECIDE THAT BY A BIENNIAL ELECTION!
AND AS YOUR LEADER, I DECLARE THIS BATTLE IS OVER!
I MEAN, I GUESS THIS SEEMS LIKE AS FINE A PLACE AS ANY TO STOP.
I'VE GOT AN EARLY CALL TIME TOMORROW, ANYWAY.

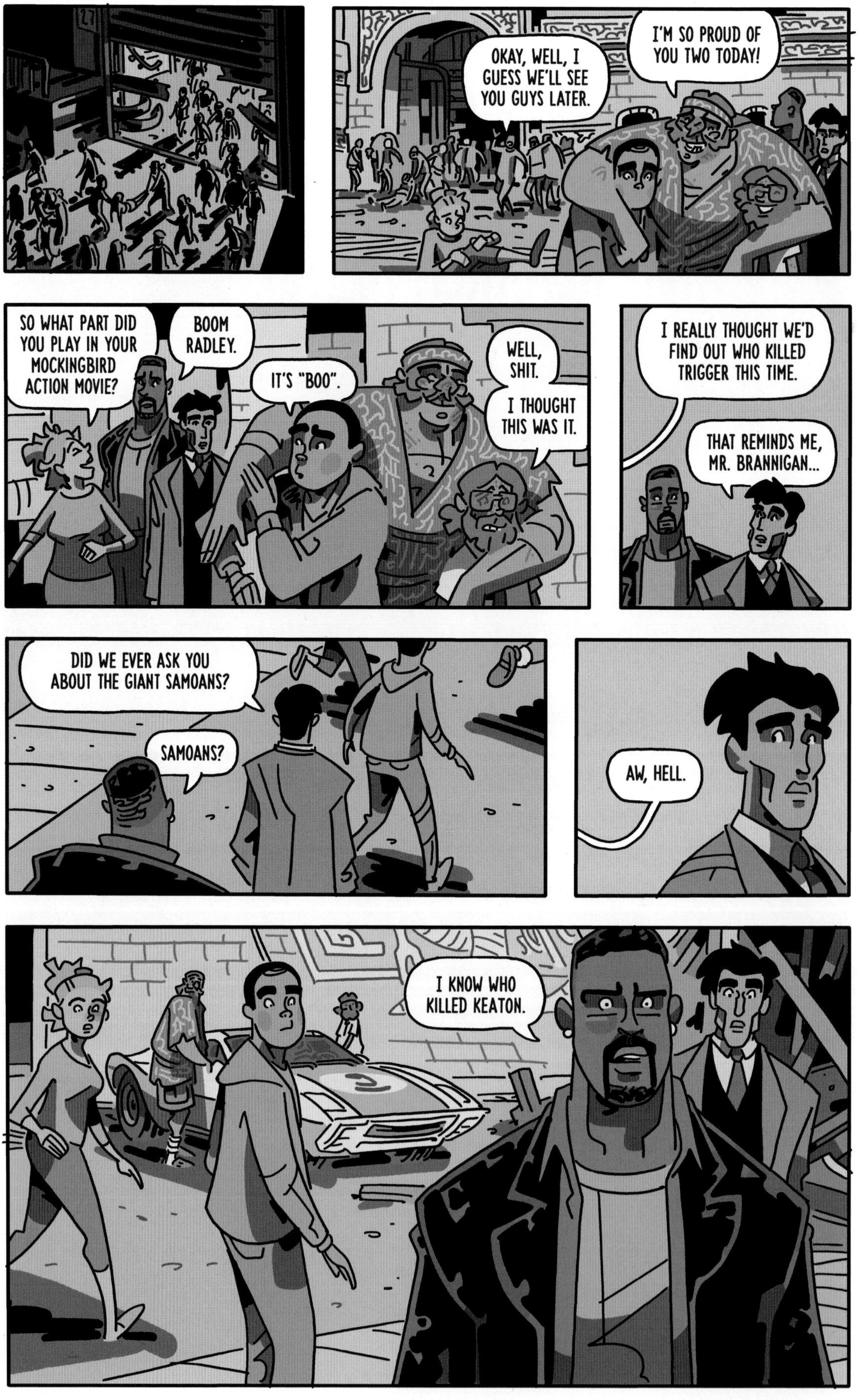
OKAY, WELL, I GUESS WE'LL SEE YOU GUYS LATER.
I'M SO PROUD OF YOU TWO TODAY!
SO WHAT PART DID YOU PLAY IN YOUR MOCKINGBIRD ACTION MOVIE?
BOOM RADLEY.
IT'S "BOO".
WELL, SHIT.
I THOUGHT THIS WAS IT.
I REALLY THOUGHT WE'D FIND OUT WHO KILLED TRIGGER THIS TIME.
THAT REMINDS ME, MR. BRANNIGAN...
DID WE EVER ASK YOU ABOUT THE GIANT SAMOANS?
SAMOANS?
AW, HELL.
I KNOW WHO KILLED KEATON.

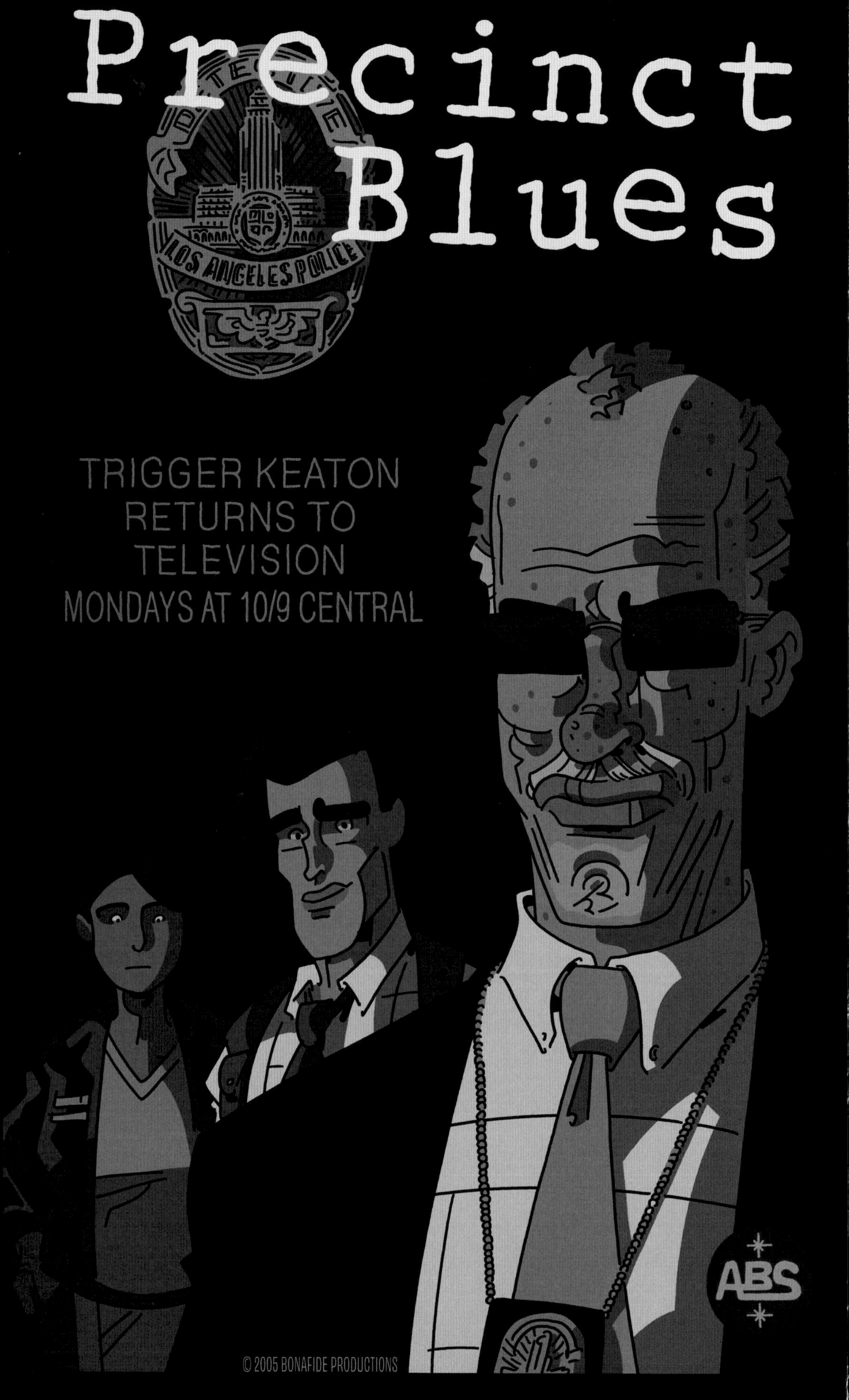
Precinct Blues
LOS ANGELES POLICE
TRIGGER KEATON
RETURNS TO
TELEVISION
MONDAYS AT 10/9 CENTRAL
ABS
© 2005 BONAFIDE PRODUCTIONS

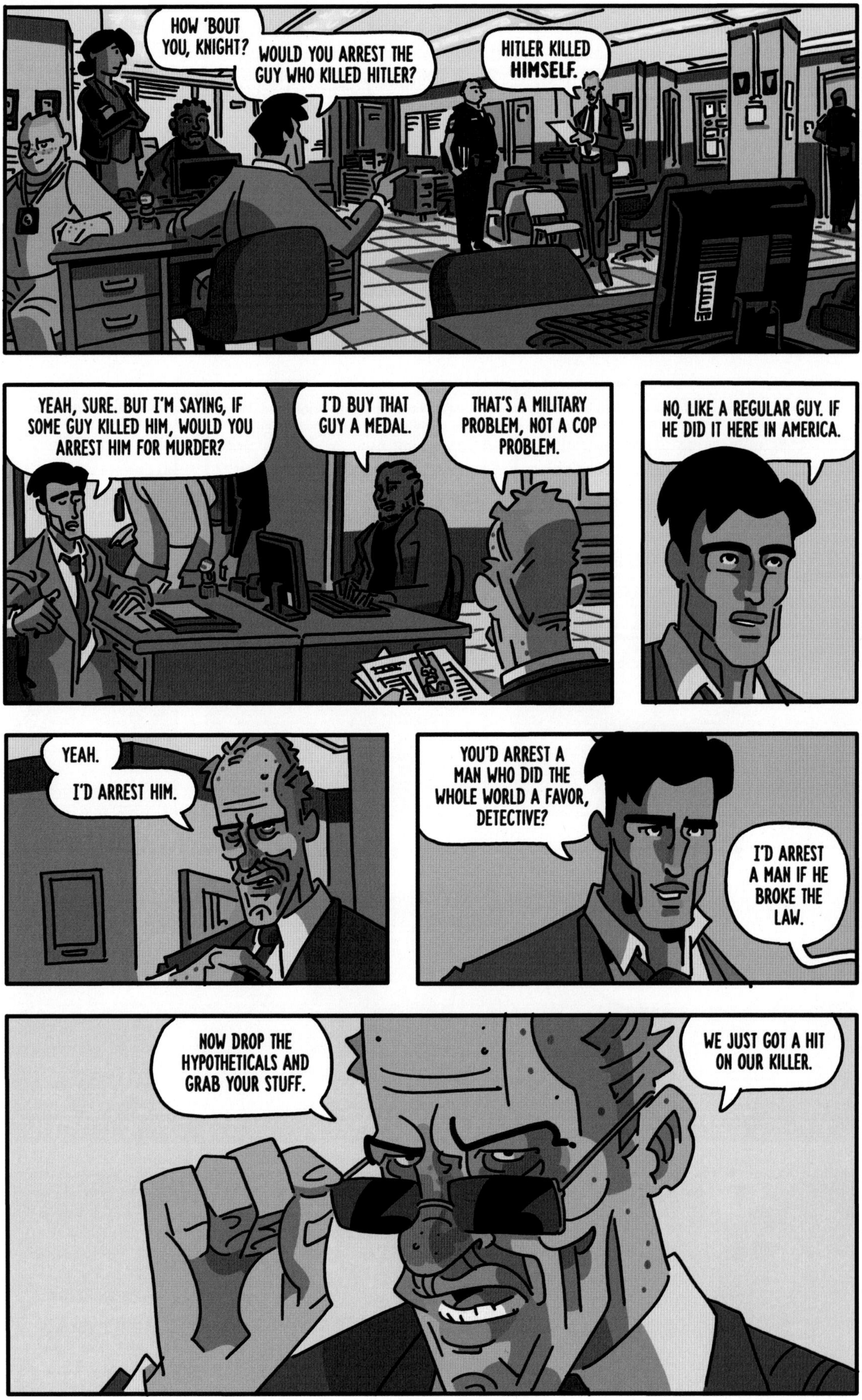
HOW 'BOUT YOU, KNIGHT?
WOULD YOU ARREST THE GUY WHO KILLED HITLER?
HITLER KILLED **HIMSELF.**
YEAH, SURE. BUT I'M SAYING, IF SOME GUY KILLED HIM, WOULD YOU ARREST HIM FOR MURDER?
I'D BUY THAT GUY A MEDAL.
THAT'S A MILITARY PROBLEM, NOT A COP PROBLEM.
NO, LIKE A REGULAR GUY. IF HE DID IT HERE IN AMERICA.
YEAH.
I'D ARREST HIM.
YOU'D ARREST A MAN WHO DID THE WHOLE WORLD A FAVOR, DETECTIVE?
I'D ARREST A MAN IF HE BROKE THE LAW.
NOW DROP THE HYPOTHETICALS AND GRAB YOUR STUFF.
WE JUST GOT A HIT ON OUR KILLER.

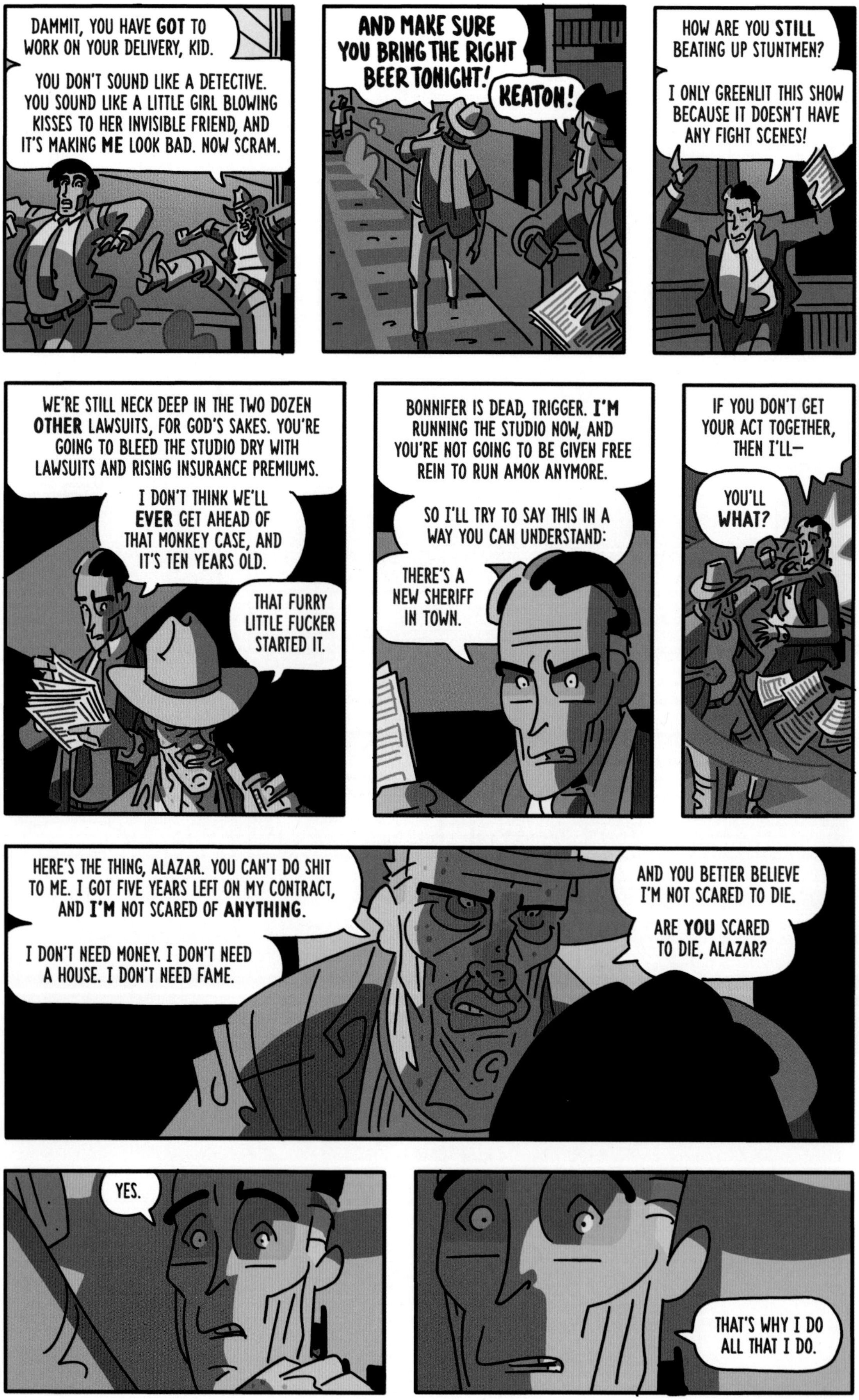
DAMMIT, YOU HAVE GOT TO WORK ON YOUR DELIVERY, KID.
YOU DON'T SOUND LIKE A DETECTIVE. YOU SOUND LIKE A LITTLE GIRL BLOWING KISSES TO HER INVISIBLE FRIEND, AND IT'S MAKING ME LOOK BAD. NOW SCRAM.
AND MAKE SURE YOU BRING THE RIGHT BEER TONIGHT!
KEATON!
HOW ARE YOU STILL BEATING UP STUNTMEN?
I ONLY GREENLIT THIS SHOW BECAUSE IT DOESN'T HAVE ANY FIGHT SCENES!
WE'RE STILL NECK DEEP IN THE TWO DOZEN OTHER LAWSUITS, FOR GOD'S SAKES. YOU'RE GOING TO BLEED THE STUDIO DRY WITH LAWSUITS AND RISING INSURANCE PREMIUMS.
I DON'T THINK WE'LL EVER GET AHEAD OF THAT MONKEY CASE, AND IT'S TEN YEARS OLD.
THAT FURRY LITTLE FUCKER STARTED IT.
BONNIFER IS DEAD, TRIGGER. I'M RUNNING THE STUDIO NOW, AND YOU'RE NOT GOING TO BE GIVEN FREE REIN TO RUN AMOK ANYMORE.
SO I'LL TRY TO SAY THIS IN A WAY YOU CAN UNDERSTAND:
THERE'S A NEW SHERIFF IN TOWN.
IF YOU DON'T GET YOUR ACT TOGETHER, THEN I'LL—
YOU'LL WHAT?
HERE'S THE THING, ALAZAR. YOU CAN'T DO SHIT TO ME. I GOT FIVE YEARS LEFT ON MY CONTRACT, AND I'M NOT SCARED OF ANYTHING.
I DON'T NEED MONEY. I DON'T NEED A HOUSE. I DON'T NEED FAME.
AND YOU BETTER BELIEVE I'M NOT SCARED TO DIE.
ARE YOU SCARED TO DIE, ALAZAR?
YES.
THAT'S WHY I DO ALL THAT I DO.

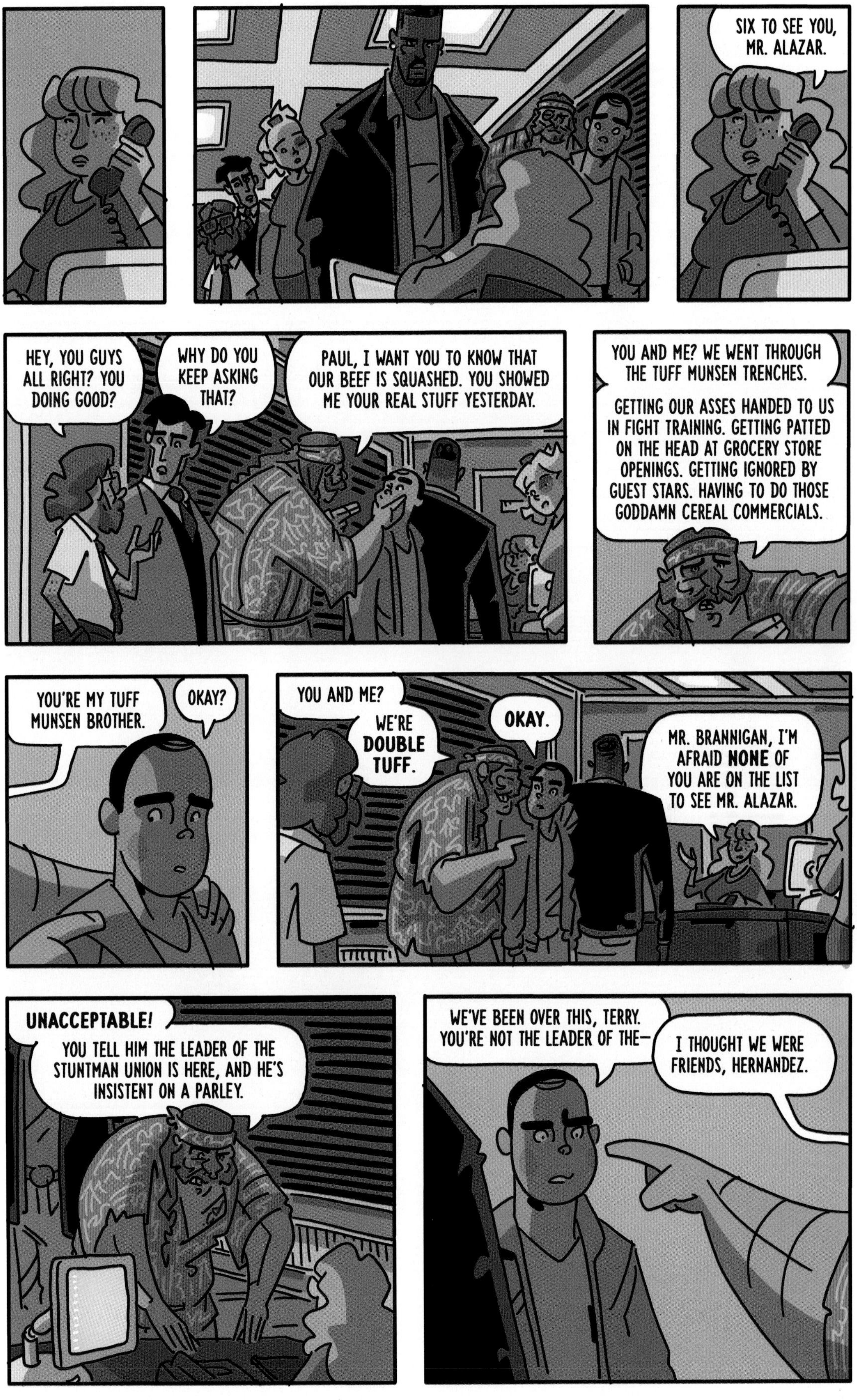
SIX TO SEE YOU, MR. ALAZAR.
HEY, YOU GUYS ALL RIGHT? YOU DOING GOOD?
WHY DO YOU KEEP ASKING THAT?
PAUL, I WANT YOU TO KNOW THAT OUR BEEF IS SQUASHED. YOU SHOWED ME YOUR REAL STUFF YESTERDAY.
YOU AND ME? WE WENT THROUGH THE TUFF MUNSEN TRENCHES.
GETTING OUR ASSES HANDED TO US IN FIGHT TRAINING. GETTING PATTED ON THE HEAD AT GROCERY STORE OPENINGS. GETTING IGNORED BY GUEST STARS. HAVING TO DO THOSE GODDAMN CEREAL COMMERCIALS.
YOU'RE MY TUFF MUNSEN BROTHER.
OKAY?
YOU AND ME?
WE'RE **DOUBLE TUFF**.
OKAY.
MR. BRANNIGAN, I'M AFRAID **NONE** OF YOU ARE ON THE LIST TO SEE MR. ALAZAR.
UNACCEPTABLE!
YOU TELL HIM THE LEADER OF THE STUNTMAN UNION IS HERE, AND HE'S INSISTENT ON A PARLEY.
WE'VE BEEN OVER THIS, TERRY. YOU'RE NOT THE LEADER OF THE—
I THOUGHT WE WERE FRIENDS, HERNANDEZ.

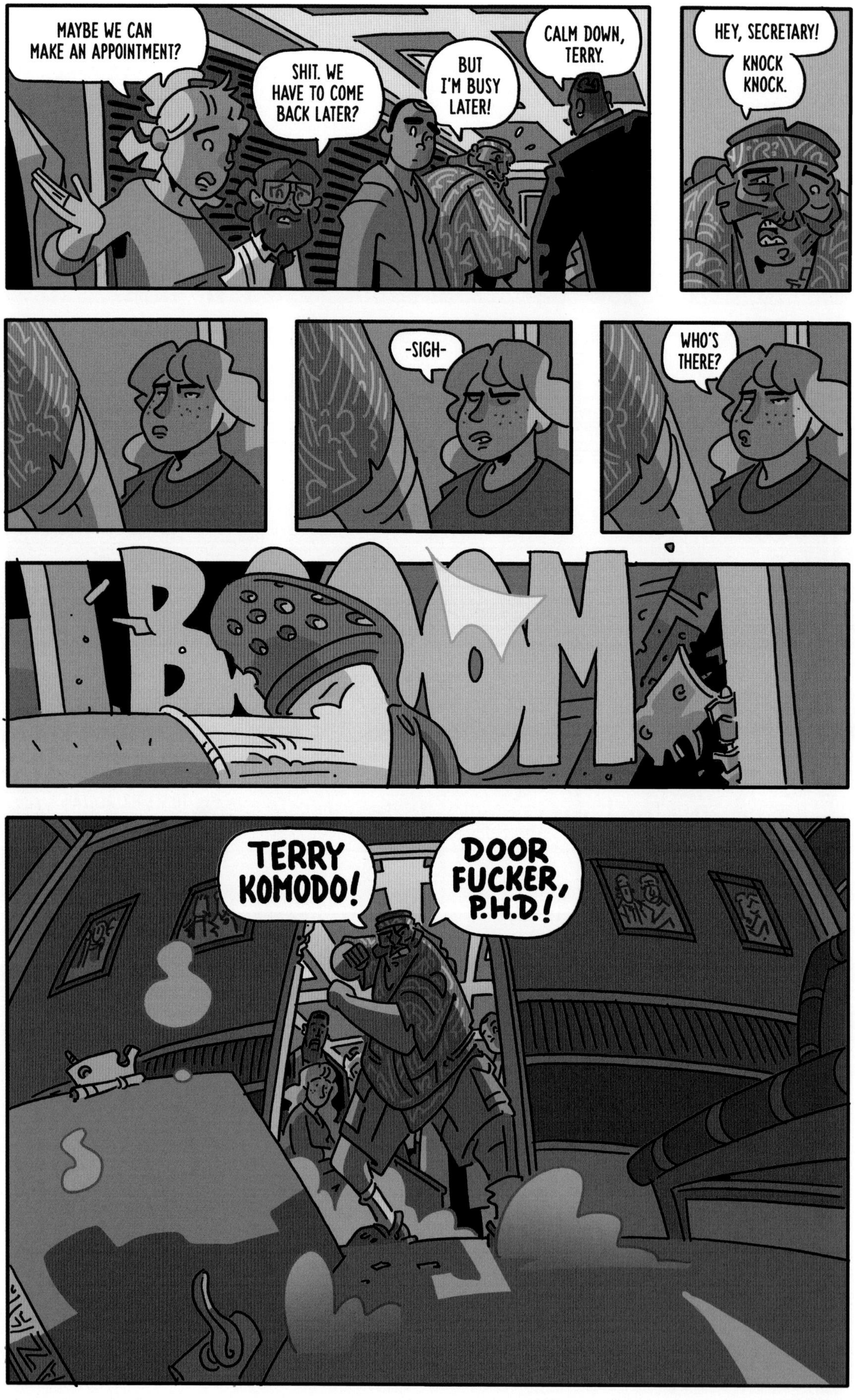
MAYBE WE CAN MAKE AN APPOINTMENT?
SHIT. WE HAVE TO COME BACK LATER?
BUT I'M BUSY LATER!
CALM DOWN, TERRY.
HEY, SECRETARY!
KNOCK KNOCK.
-SIGH-
WHO'S THERE?
BOOOM
TERRY KOMODO!
DOOR FUCKER, P.H.D.!

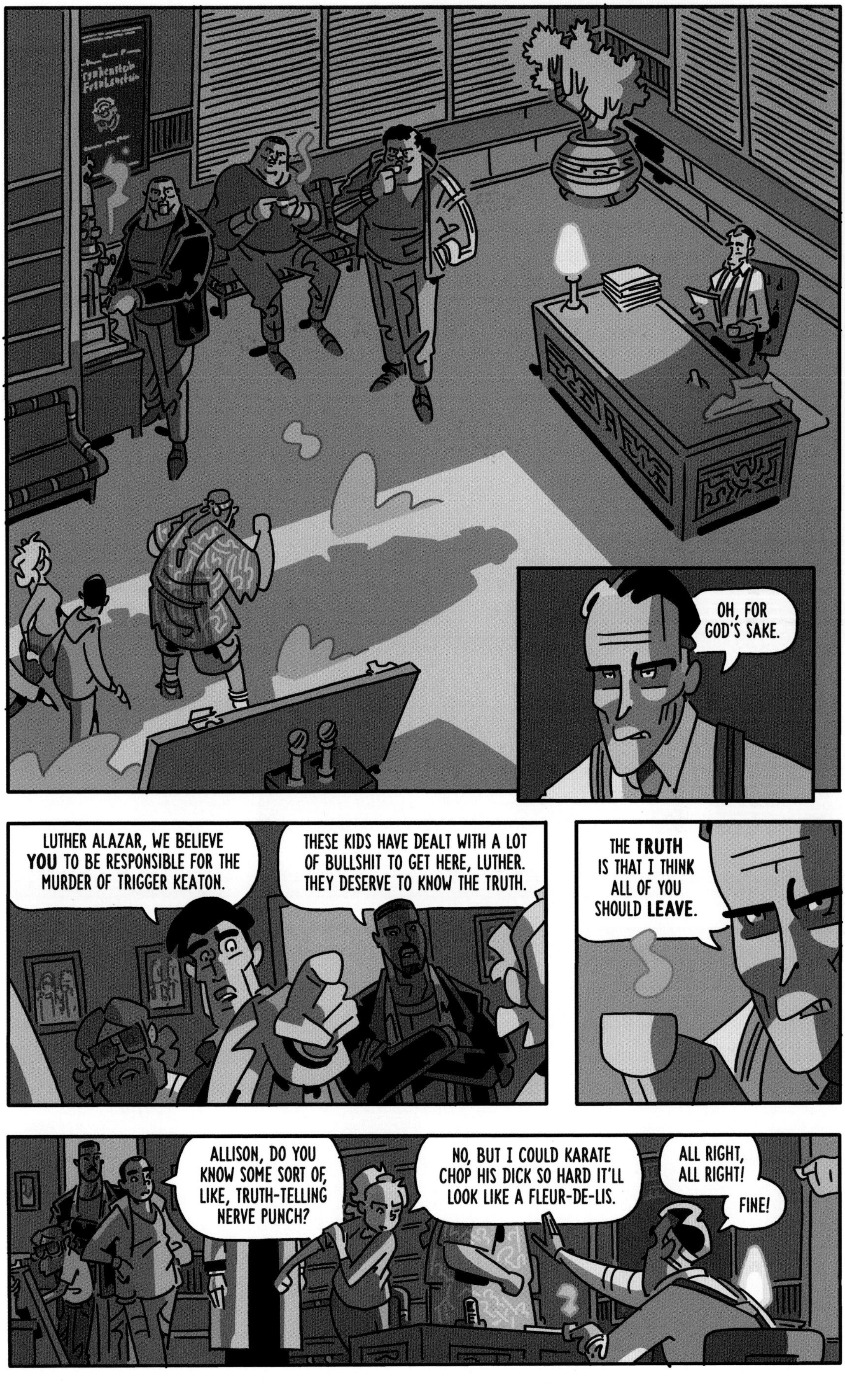
OH, FOR GOD'S SAKE.
LUTHER ALAZAR, WE BELIEVE **YOU** TO BE RESPONSIBLE FOR THE MURDER OF TRIGGER KEATON.
THESE KIDS HAVE DEALT WITH A LOT OF BULLSHIT TO GET HERE, LUTHER. THEY DESERVE TO KNOW THE TRUTH.
THE **TRUTH** IS THAT I THINK ALL OF YOU SHOULD **LEAVE**.
ALLISON, DO YOU KNOW SOME SORT OF, LIKE, TRUTH-TELLING NERVE PUNCH?
NO, BUT I COULD KARATE CHOP HIS DICK SO HARD IT'LL LOOK LIKE A FLEUR-DE-LIS.
ALL RIGHT, ALL RIGHT!
FINE!

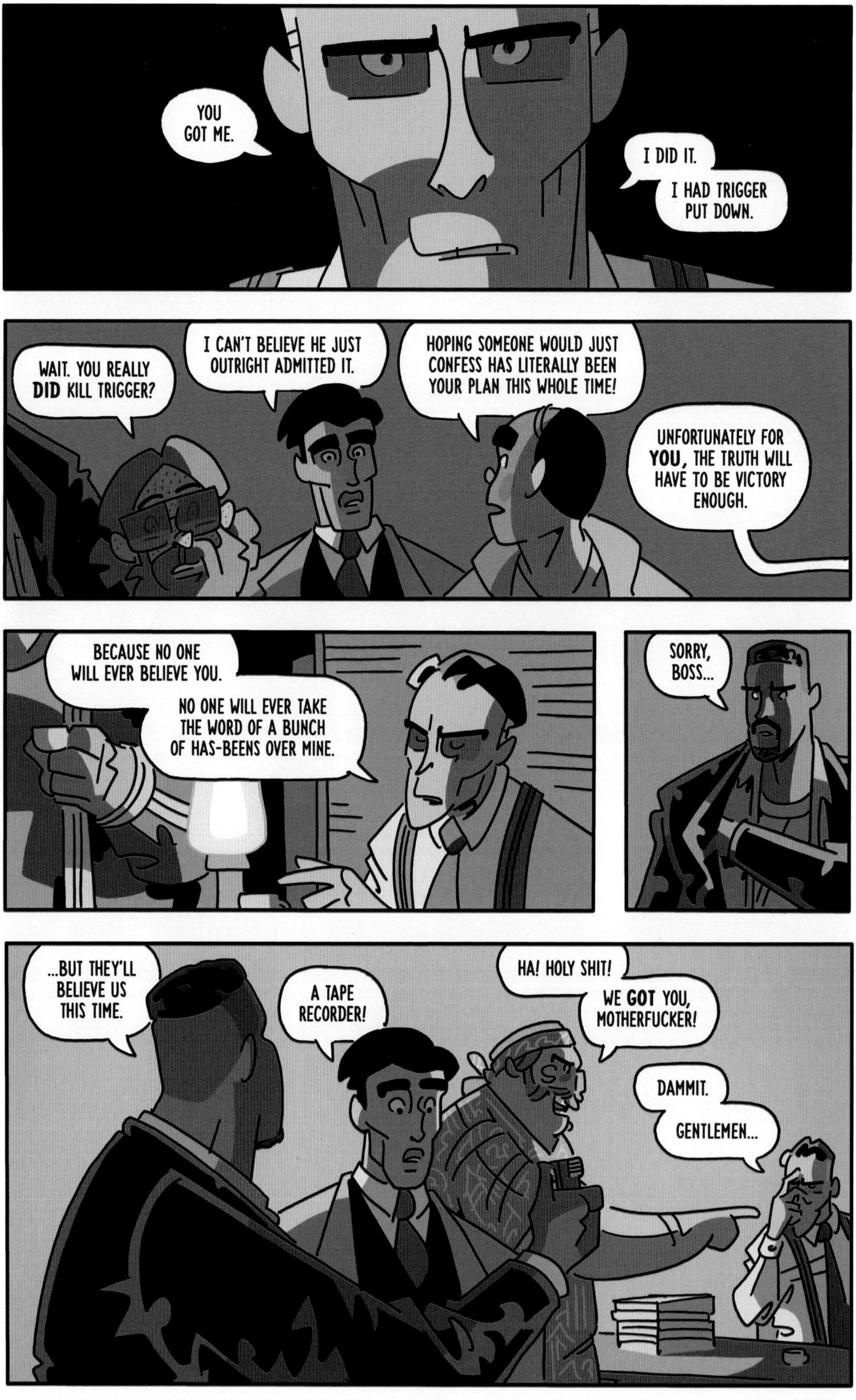
YOU GOT ME.
I DID IT.
I HAD TRIGGER PUT DOWN.
WAIT. YOU REALLY **DID** KILL TRIGGER?
I CAN'T BELIEVE HE JUST OUTRIGHT ADMITTED IT.
HOPING SOMEONE WOULD JUST CONFESS HAS LITERALLY BEEN YOUR PLAN THIS WHOLE TIME!
UNFORTUNATELY FOR **YOU,** THE TRUTH WILL HAVE TO BE VICTORY ENOUGH.
BECAUSE NO ONE WILL EVER BELIEVE YOU.
NO ONE WILL EVER TAKE THE WORD OF A BUNCH OF HAS-BEENS OVER MINE.
SORRY, BOSS...
...BUT THEY'LL BELIEVE US THIS TIME.
A TAPE RECORDER!
HA! HOLY SHIT!
WE **GOT** YOU, MOTHERFUCKER!
DAMMIT.
GENTLEMEN...

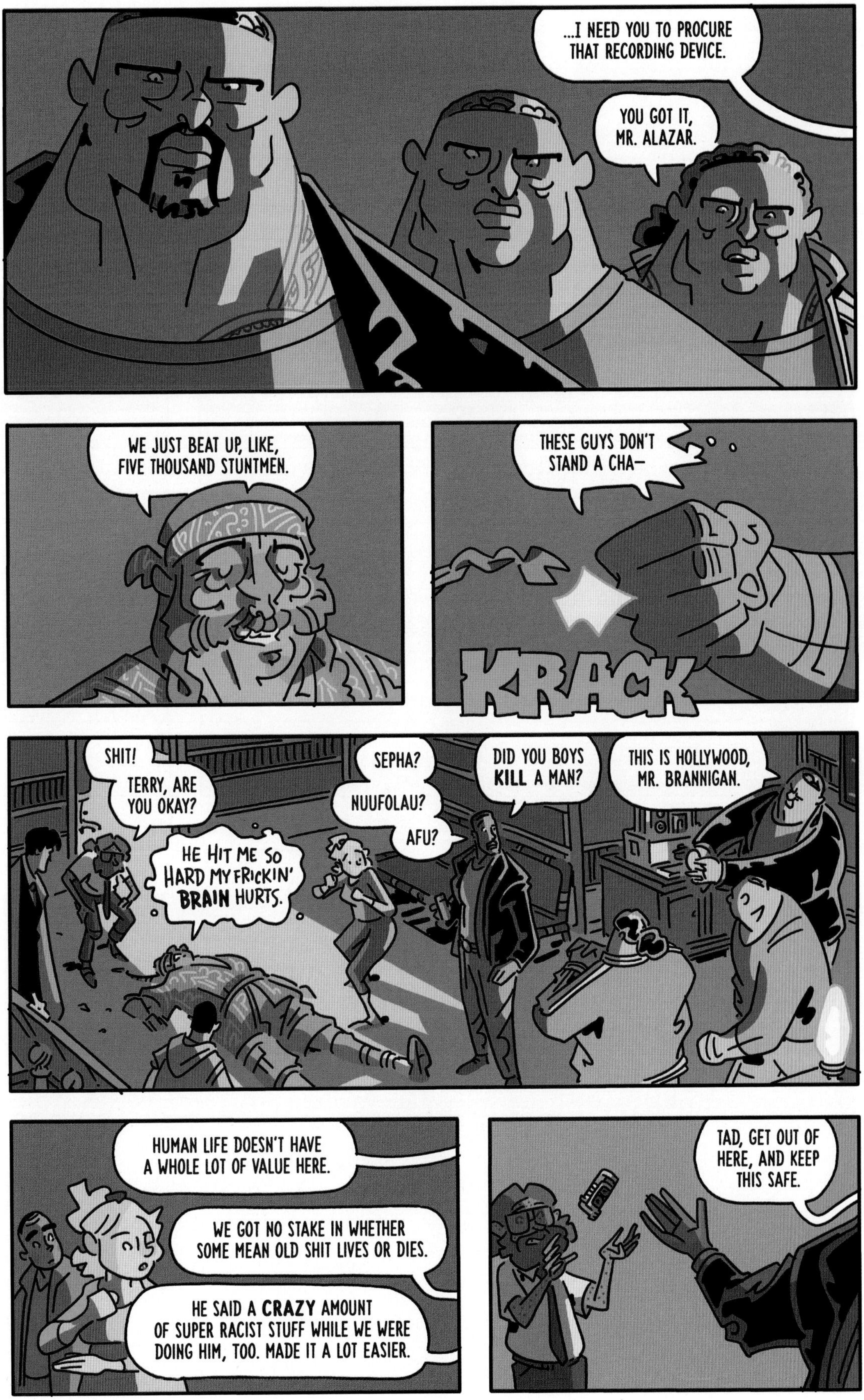
...I NEED YOU TO PROCURE THAT RECORDING DEVICE.
YOU GOT IT, MR. ALAZAR.
WE JUST BEAT UP, LIKE, FIVE THOUSAND STUNTMEN.
THESE GUYS DON'T STAND A CHA—
KRACK
SHIT!
TERRY, ARE YOU OKAY?
HE HIT ME SO HARD MY FRICKIN' BRAIN HURTS.
SEPHA?
NUUFOLAU?
AFU?
DID YOU BOYS KILL A MAN?
THIS IS HOLLYWOOD, MR. BRANNIGAN.
HUMAN LIFE DOESN'T HAVE A WHOLE LOT OF VALUE HERE.
WE GOT NO STAKE IN WHETHER SOME MEAN OLD SHIT LIVES OR DIES.
HE SAID A CRAZY AMOUNT OF SUPER RACIST STUFF WHILE WE WERE DOING HIM, TOO. MADE IT A LOT EASIER.
TAD, GET OUT OF HERE, AND KEEP THIS SAFE.

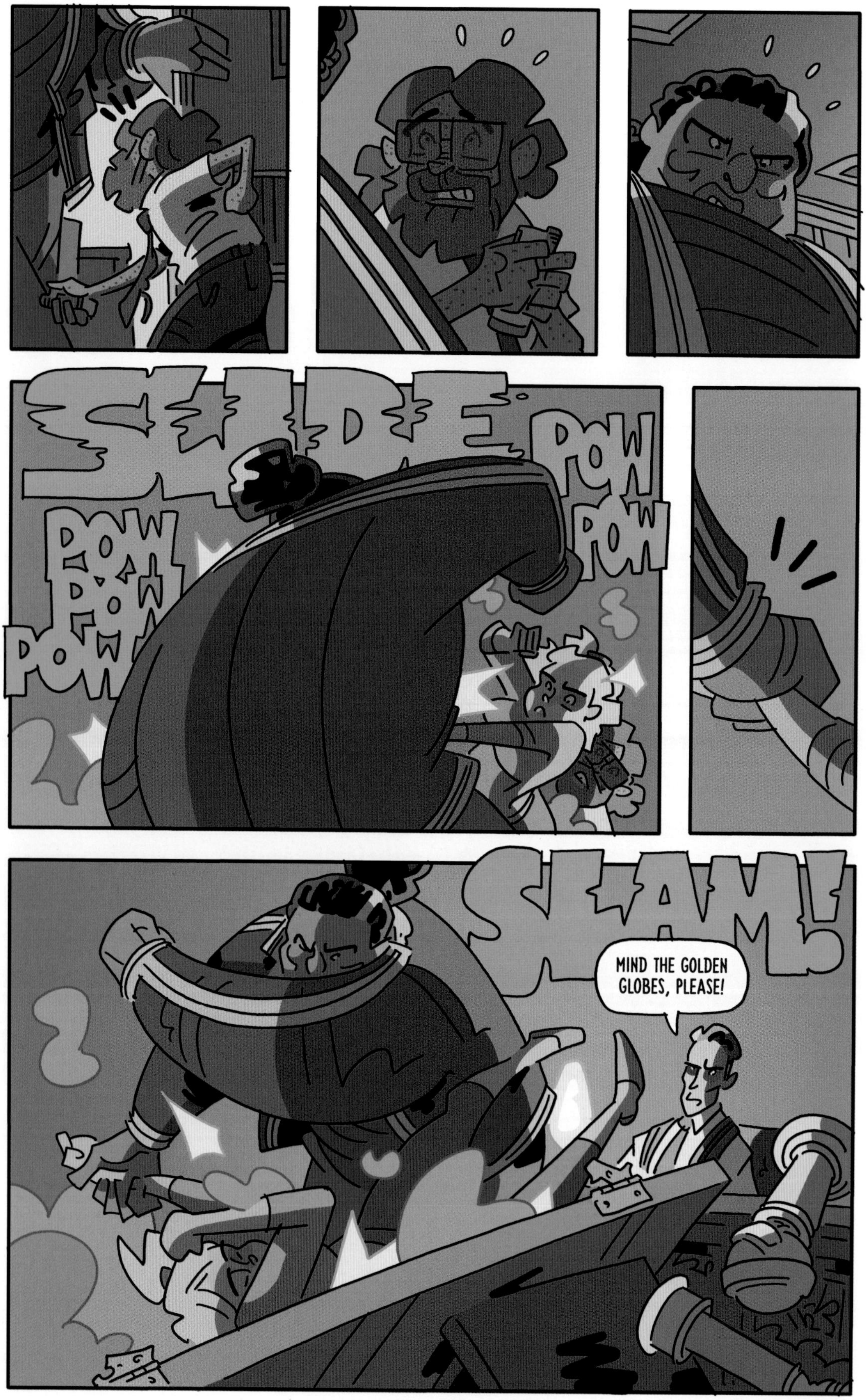
SLIDE
POW
POW
POW
POW
POW
SLAM!
MIND THE GOLDEN GLOBES, PLEASE!

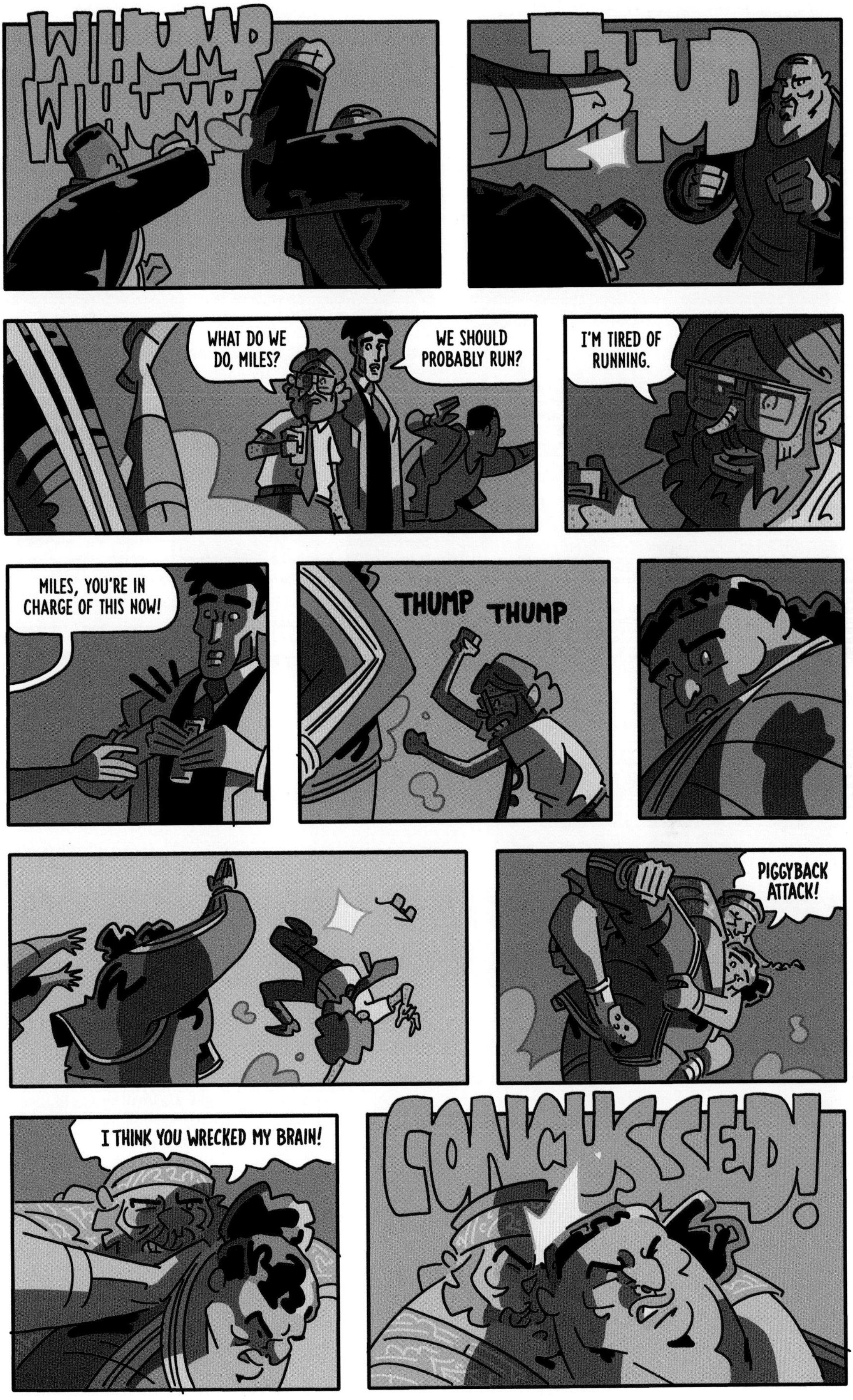
WHUMP
WHUMP
THUD
WHAT DO WE DO, MILES?
WE SHOULD PROBABLY RUN?
I'M TIRED OF RUNNING.
MILES, YOU'RE IN CHARGE OF THIS NOW!
THUMP THUMP
PIGGYBACK ATTACK!
I THINK YOU WRECKED MY BRAIN!
CONCUSSED!

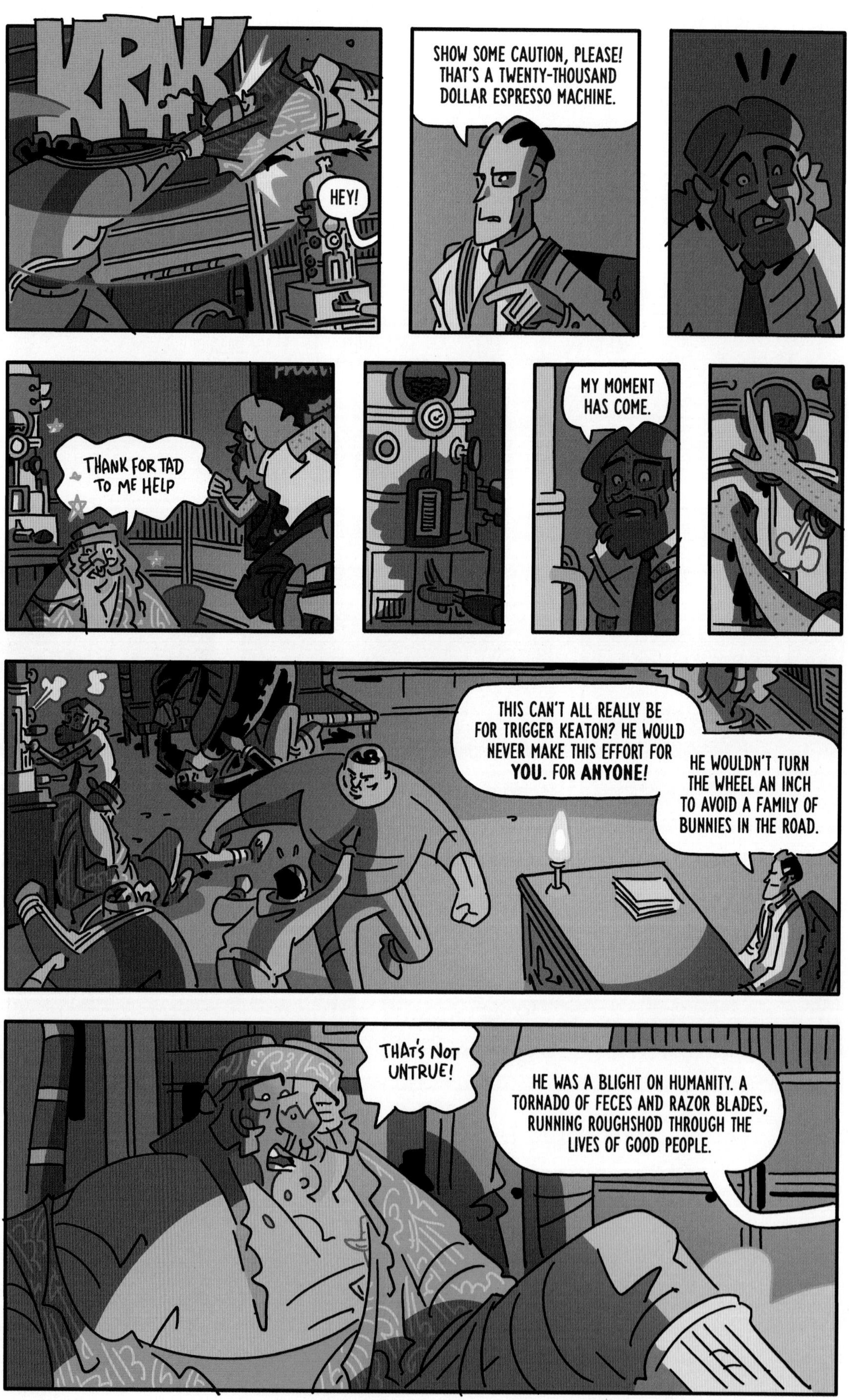
KRAK
HEY!
SHOW SOME CAUTION, PLEASE! THAT'S A TWENTY-THOUSAND DOLLAR ESPRESSO MACHINE.
THANK FOR TAD TO ME HELP
MY MOMENT HAS COME.
THIS CAN'T ALL REALLY BE FOR TRIGGER KEATON? HE WOULD NEVER MAKE THIS EFFORT FOR **YOU**. FOR **ANYONE**!
HE WOULDN'T TURN THE WHEEL AN INCH TO AVOID A FAMILY OF BUNNIES IN THE ROAD.
THAT'S NOT UNTRUE!
HE WAS A BLIGHT ON HUMANITY. A TORNADO OF FECES AND RAZOR BLADES, RUNNING ROUGHSHOD THROUGH THE LIVES OF GOOD PEOPLE.

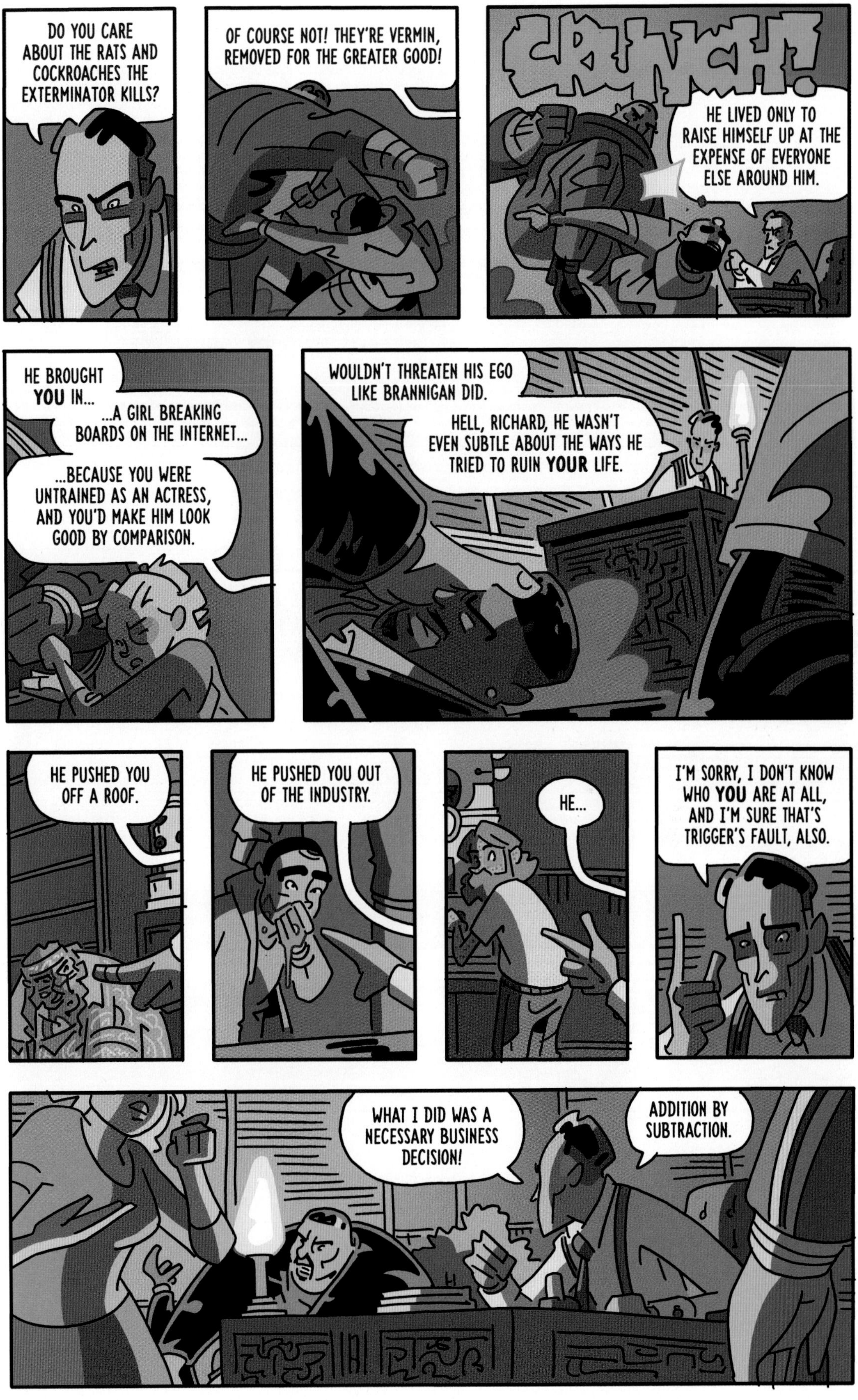
DO YOU CARE ABOUT THE RATS AND COCKROACHES THE EXTERMINATOR KILLS?
OF COURSE NOT! THEY'RE VERMIN, REMOVED FOR THE GREATER GOOD!
CRUNCH!
HE LIVED ONLY TO RAISE HIMSELF UP AT THE EXPENSE OF EVERYONE ELSE AROUND HIM.
HE BROUGHT **YOU** IN...
...A GIRL BREAKING BOARDS ON THE INTERNET...
...BECAUSE YOU WERE UNTRAINED AS AN ACTRESS, AND YOU'D MAKE HIM LOOK GOOD BY COMPARISON.
WOULDN'T THREATEN HIS EGO LIKE BRANNIGAN DID.
HELL, RICHARD, HE WASN'T EVEN SUBTLE ABOUT THE WAYS HE TRIED TO RUIN **YOUR** LIFE.
HE PUSHED YOU OFF A ROOF.
HE PUSHED YOU OUT OF THE INDUSTRY.
HE...
I'M SORRY, I DON'T KNOW WHO **YOU** ARE AT ALL, AND I'M SURE THAT'S TRIGGER'S FAULT, ALSO.
WHAT I DID WAS A NECESSARY BUSINESS DECISION!
ADDITION BY SUBTRACTION.

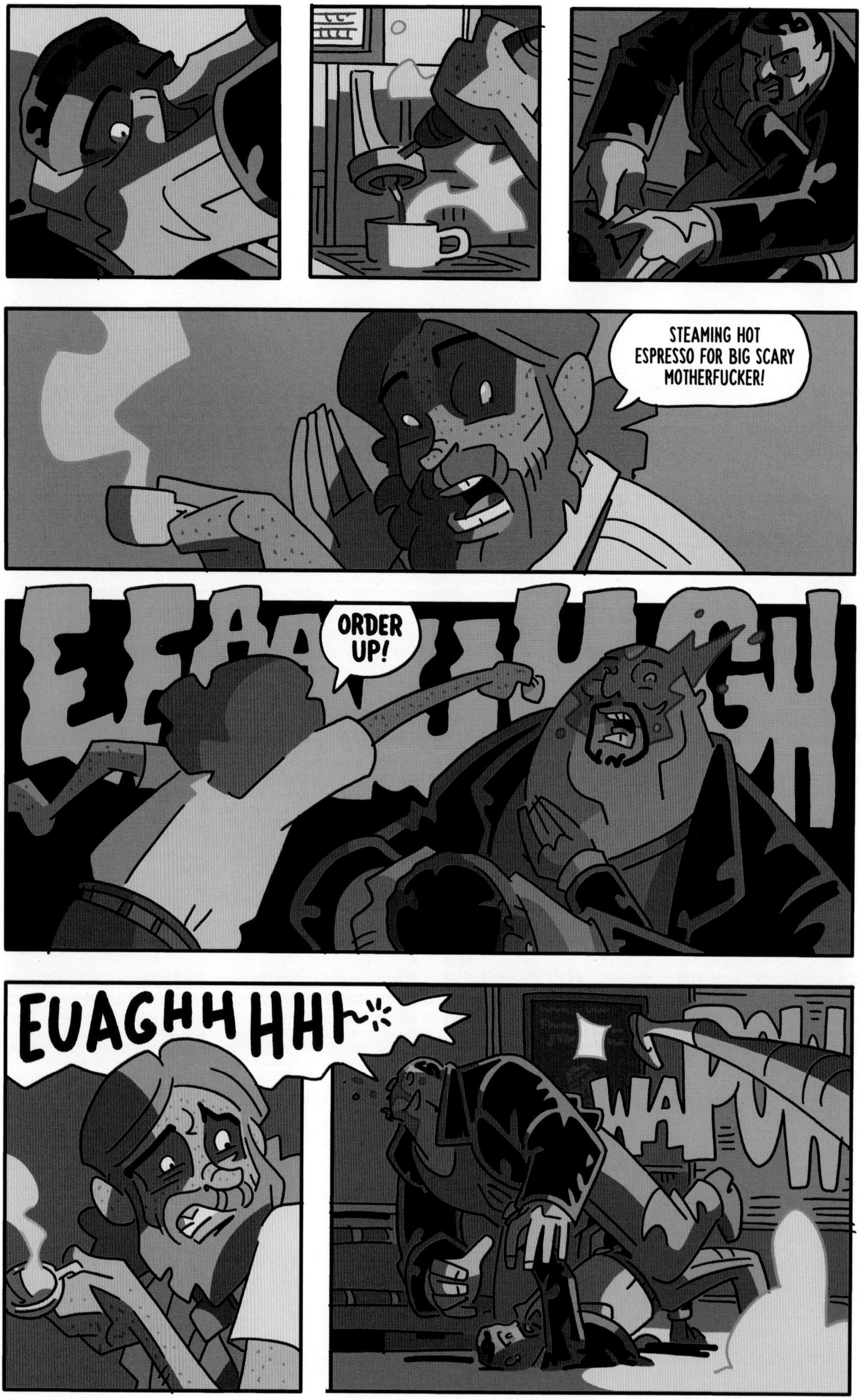
STEAMING HOT ESPRESSO FOR BIG SCARY MOTHERFUCKER!
ORDER UP!
EUAGHHHHH

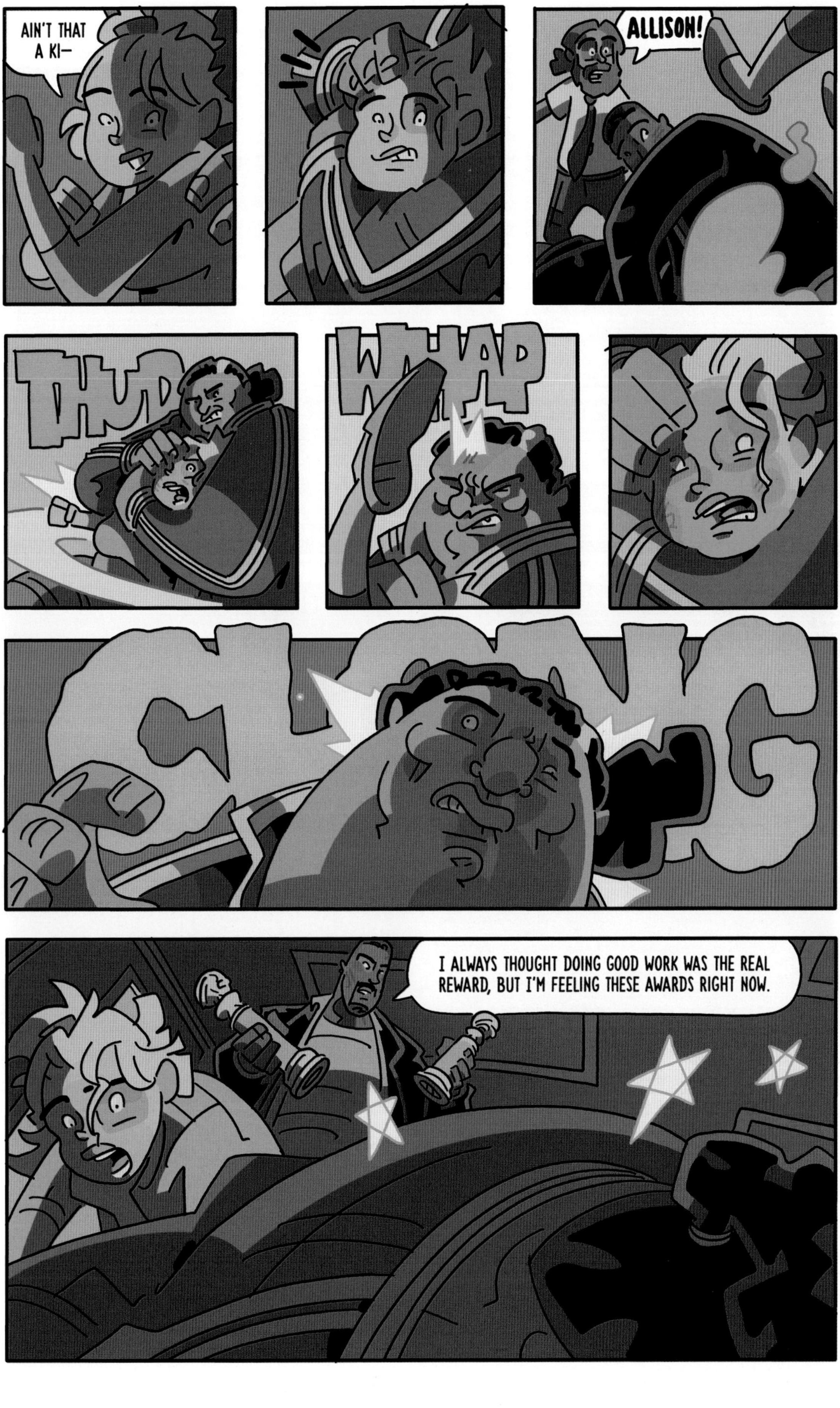
AIN'T THAT A KI—
ALLISON!
THUD
WHAP
I ALWAYS THOUGHT DOING GOOD WORK WAS THE REAL REWARD, BUT I'M FEELING THESE AWARDS RIGHT NOW.

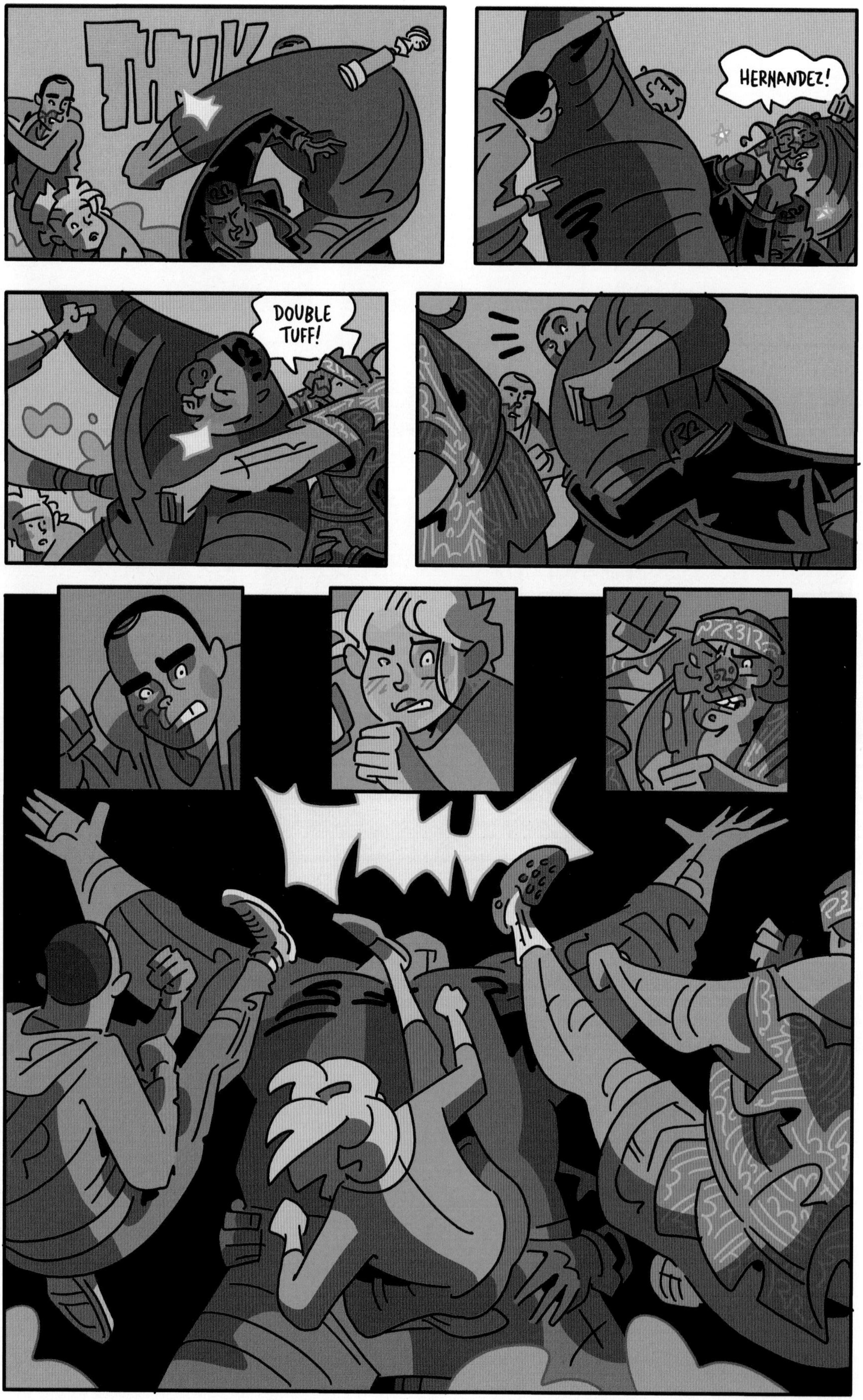
THUK
HERNANDEZ!
DOUBLE TUFF!

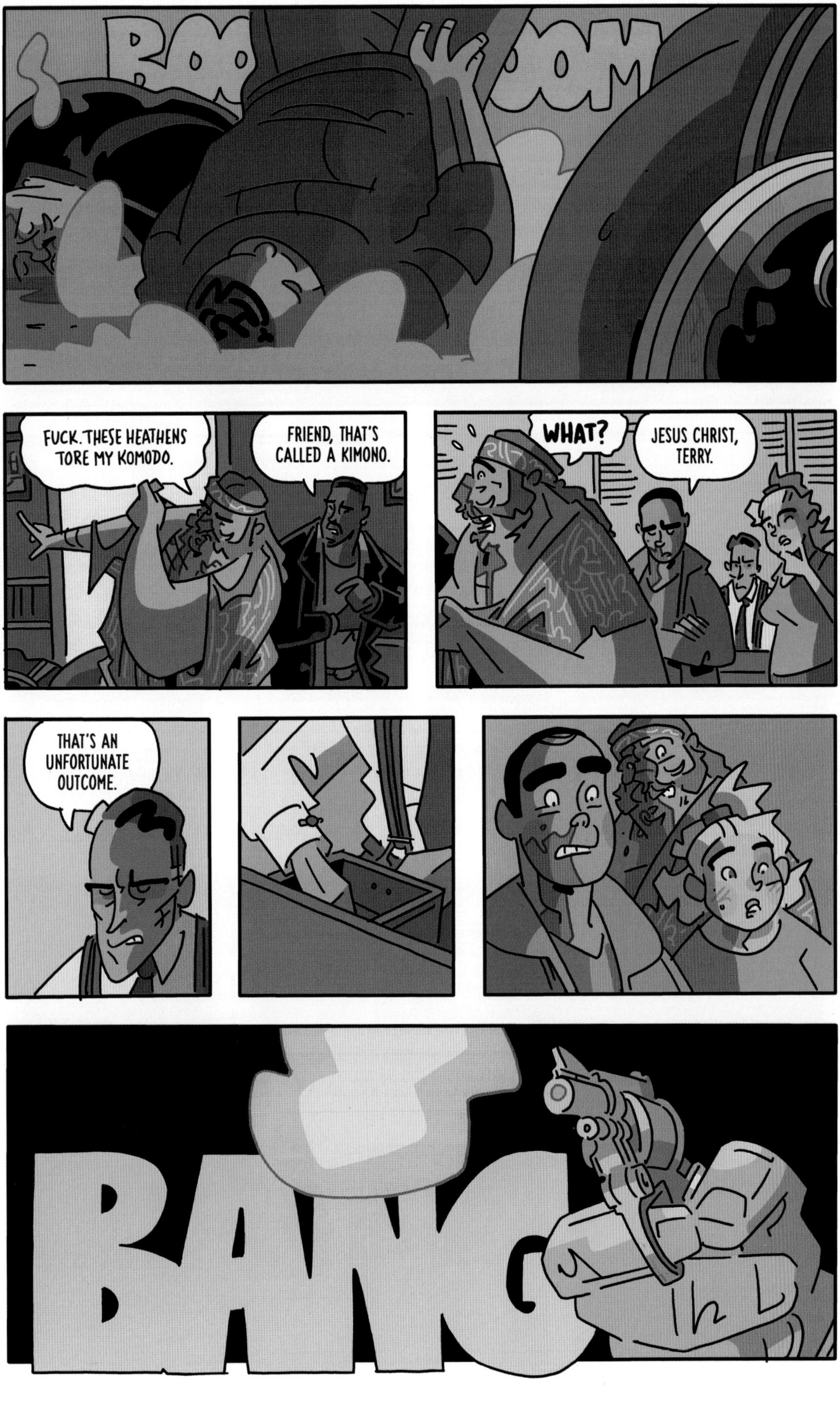
BOOOOM
FUCK. THESE HEATHENS TORE MY KOMODO.
FRIEND, THAT'S CALLED A KIMONO.
WHAT?
JESUS CHRIST, TERRY.
THAT'S AN UNFORTUNATE OUTCOME.
BANG

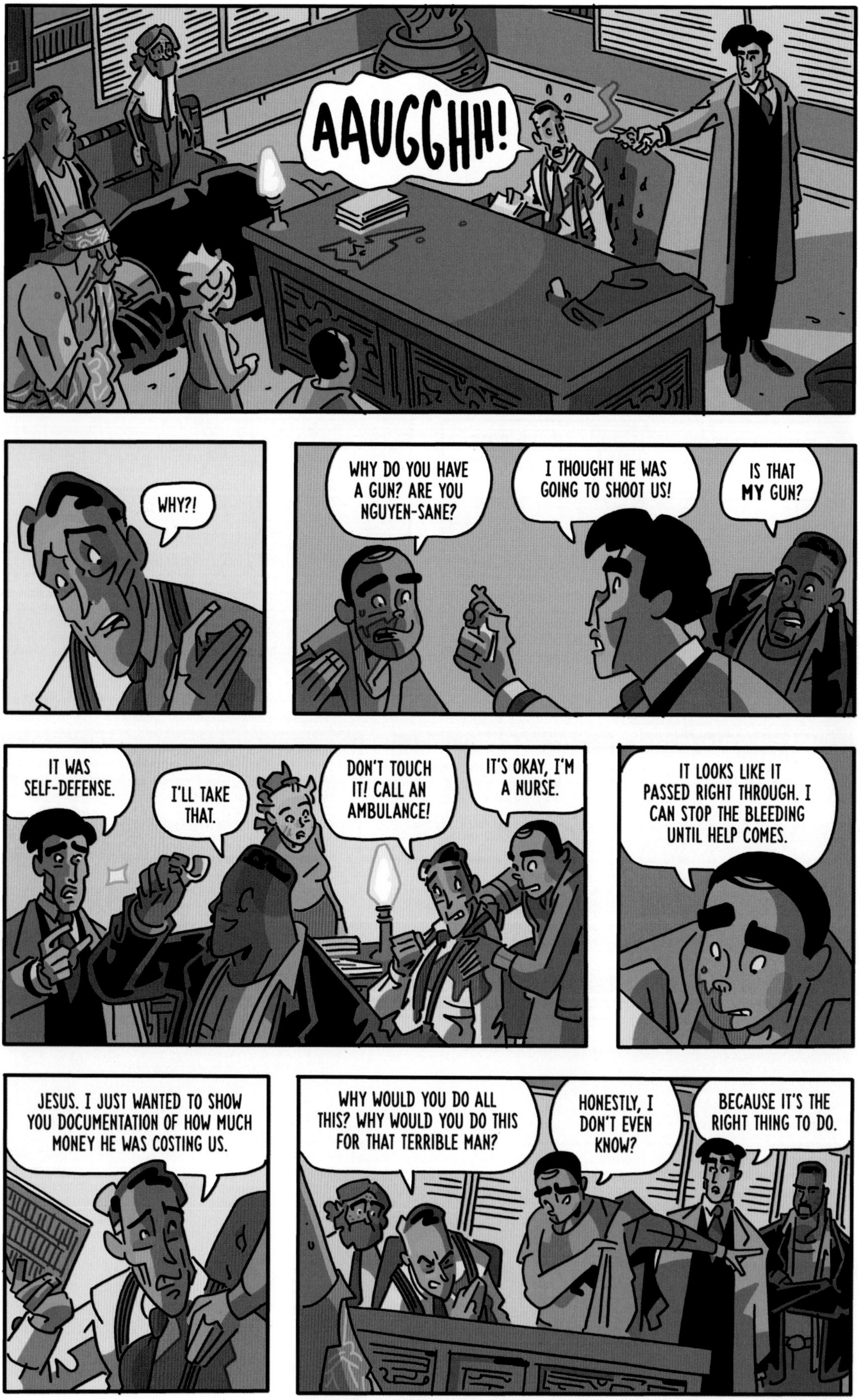
AAUGGHH!
WHY?!
WHY DO YOU HAVE A GUN? ARE YOU NGUYEN-SANE?
I THOUGHT HE WAS GOING TO SHOOT US!
IS THAT **MY** GUN?
IT WAS SELF-DEFENSE.
I'LL TAKE THAT.
DON'T TOUCH IT! CALL AN AMBULANCE!
IT'S OKAY, I'M A NURSE.
IT LOOKS LIKE IT PASSED RIGHT THROUGH. I CAN STOP THE BLEEDING UNTIL HELP COMES.
JESUS. I JUST WANTED TO SHOW YOU DOCUMENTATION OF HOW MUCH MONEY HE WAS COSTING US.
WHY WOULD YOU DO ALL THIS? WHY WOULD YOU DO THIS FOR THAT TERRIBLE MAN?
HONESTLY, I DON'T EVEN KNOW?
BECAUSE IT'S THE RIGHT THING TO DO.

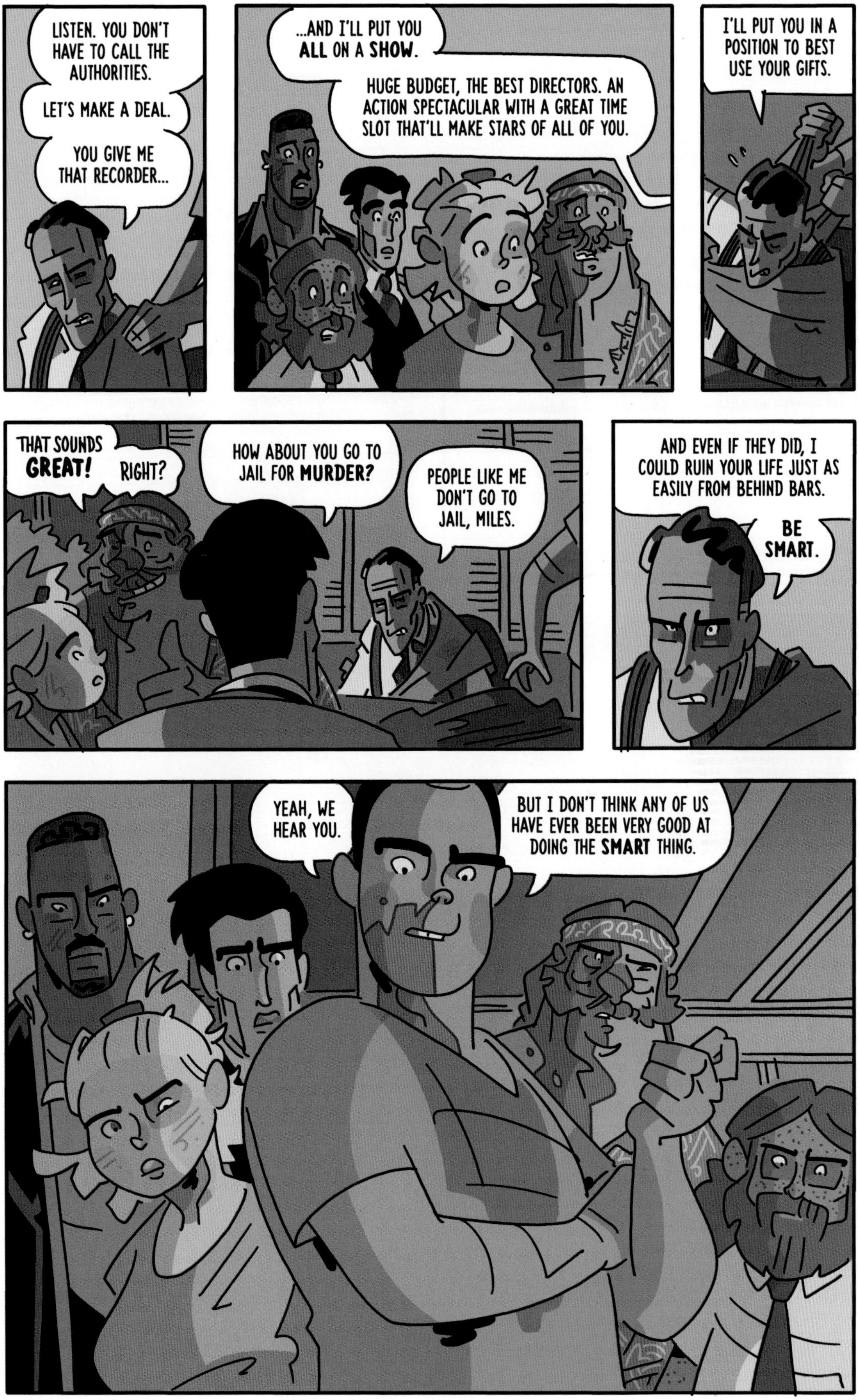
LISTEN. YOU DON'T HAVE TO CALL THE AUTHORITIES.
LET'S MAKE A DEAL.
YOU GIVE ME THAT RECORDER...
...AND I'LL PUT YOU **ALL** ON A **SHOW**.
HUGE BUDGET, THE BEST DIRECTORS. AN ACTION SPECTACULAR WITH A GREAT TIME SLOT THAT'LL MAKE STARS OF ALL OF YOU.
I'LL PUT YOU IN A POSITION TO BEST USE YOUR GIFTS.
THAT SOUNDS **GREAT!**
RIGHT?
HOW ABOUT YOU GO TO JAIL FOR **MURDER?**
PEOPLE LIKE ME DON'T GO TO JAIL, MILES.
AND EVEN IF THEY DID, I COULD RUIN YOUR LIFE JUST AS EASILY FROM BEHIND BARS.
BE SMART.
YEAH, WE HEAR YOU.
BUT I DON'T THINK ANY OF US HAVE EVER BEEN VERY GOOD AT DOING THE **SMART** THING.

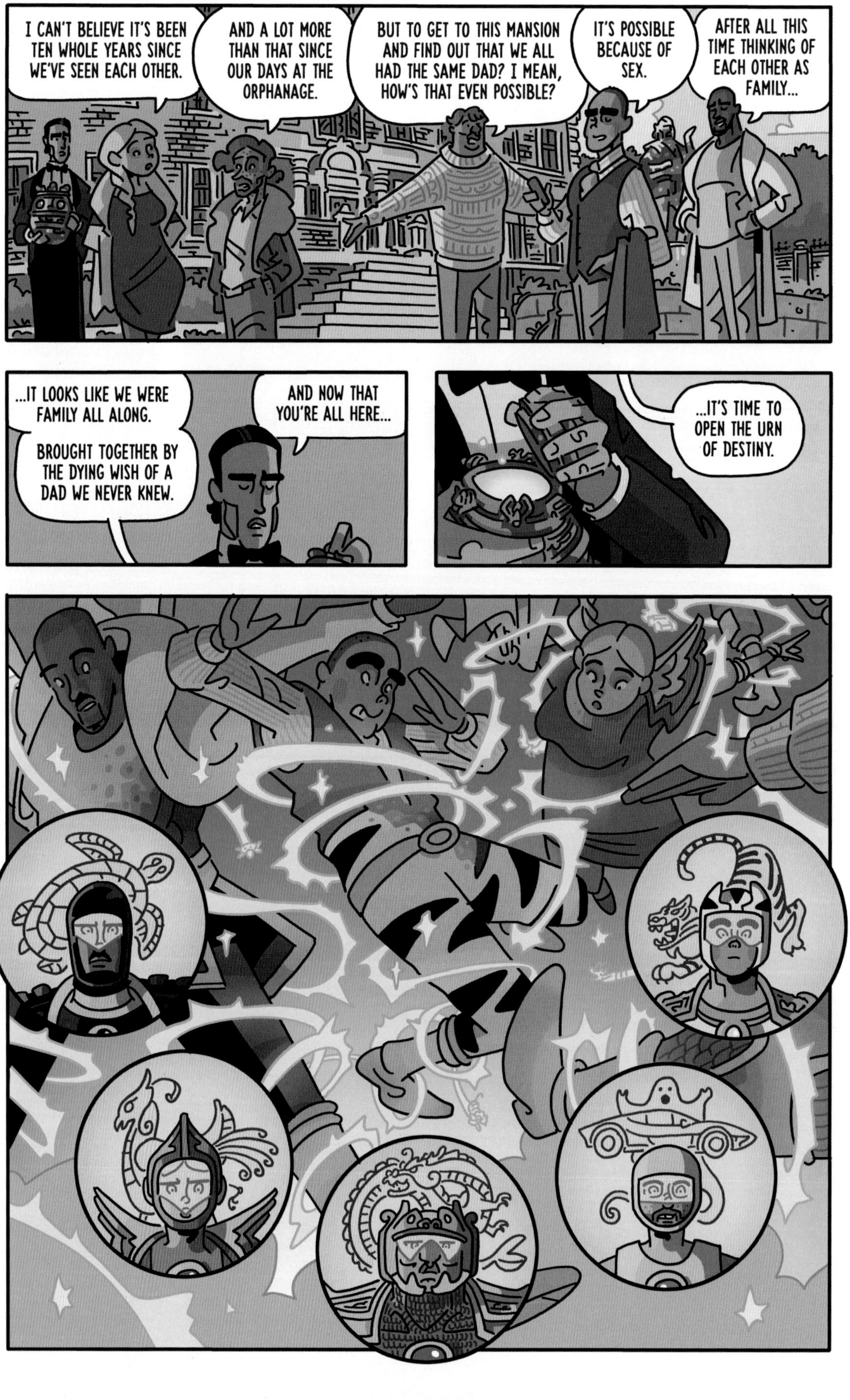
I CAN'T BELIEVE IT'S BEEN TEN WHOLE YEARS SINCE WE'VE SEEN EACH OTHER.
AND A LOT MORE THAN THAT SINCE OUR DAYS AT THE ORPHANAGE.
BUT TO GET TO THIS MANSION AND FIND OUT THAT WE ALL HAD THE SAME DAD? I MEAN, HOW'S THAT EVEN POSSIBLE?
IT'S POSSIBLE BECAUSE OF SEX.
AFTER ALL THIS TIME THINKING OF EACH OTHER AS FAMILY...
...IT LOOKS LIKE WE WERE FAMILY ALL ALONG.
BROUGHT TOGETHER BY THE DYING WISH OF A DAD WE NEVER KNEW.
AND NOW THAT YOU'RE ALL HERE...
...IT'S TIME TO OPEN THE URN OF DESTINY.

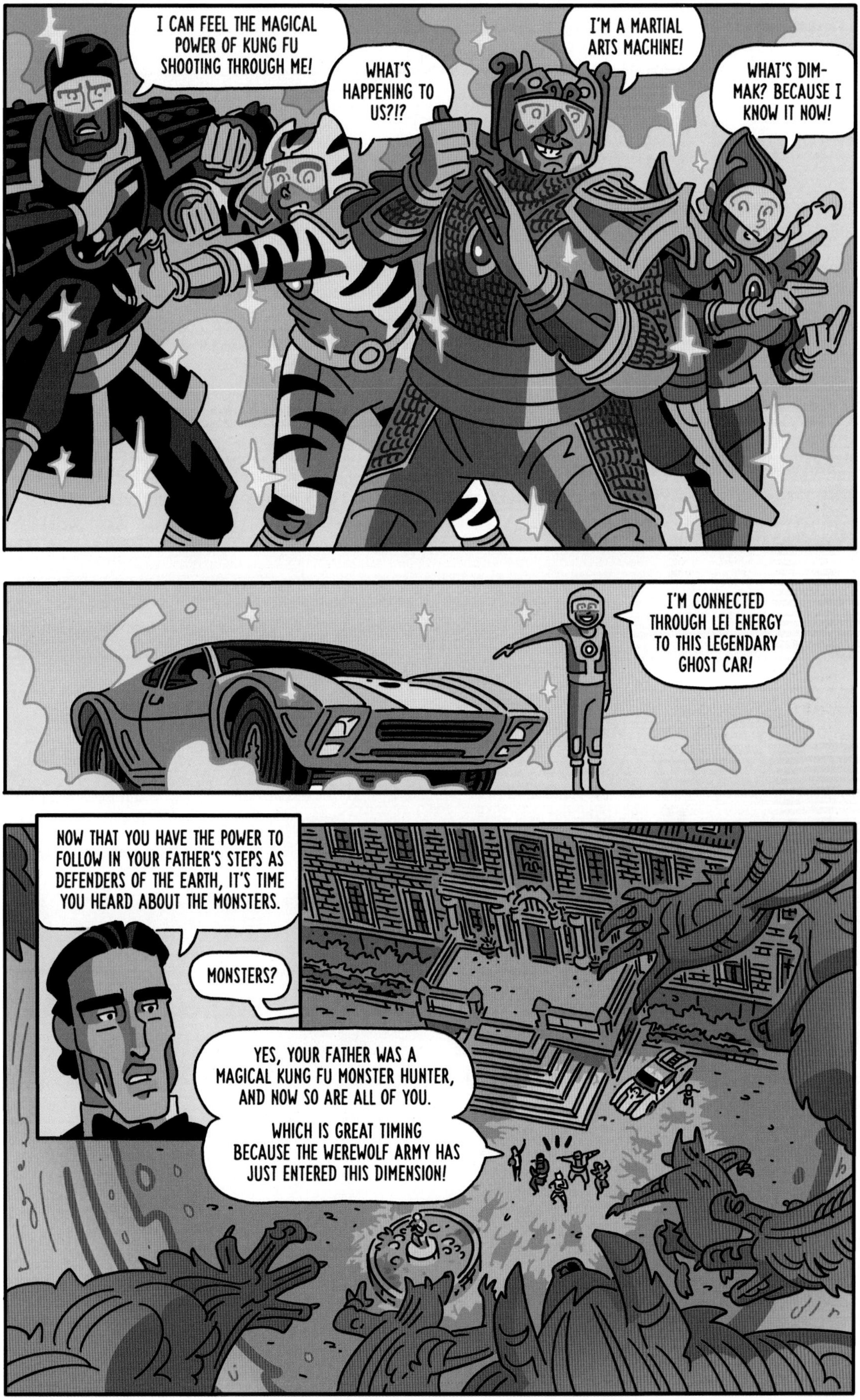
I CAN FEEL THE MAGICAL POWER OF KUNG FU SHOOTING THROUGH ME!
WHAT'S HAPPENING TO US?!?
I'M A MARTIAL ARTS MACHINE!
WHAT'S DIM-MAK? BECAUSE I KNOW IT NOW!
I'M CONNECTED THROUGH LEI ENERGY TO THIS LEGENDARY GHOST CAR!
NOW THAT YOU HAVE THE POWER TO FOLLOW IN YOUR FATHER'S STEPS AS DEFENDERS OF THE EARTH, IT'S TIME YOU HEARD ABOUT THE MONSTERS.
MONSTERS?
YES, YOUR FATHER WAS A MAGICAL KUNG FU MONSTER HUNTER, AND NOW SO ARE ALL OF YOU.
WHICH IS GREAT TIMING BECAUSE THE WEREWOLF ARMY HAS JUST ENTERED THIS DIMENSION!

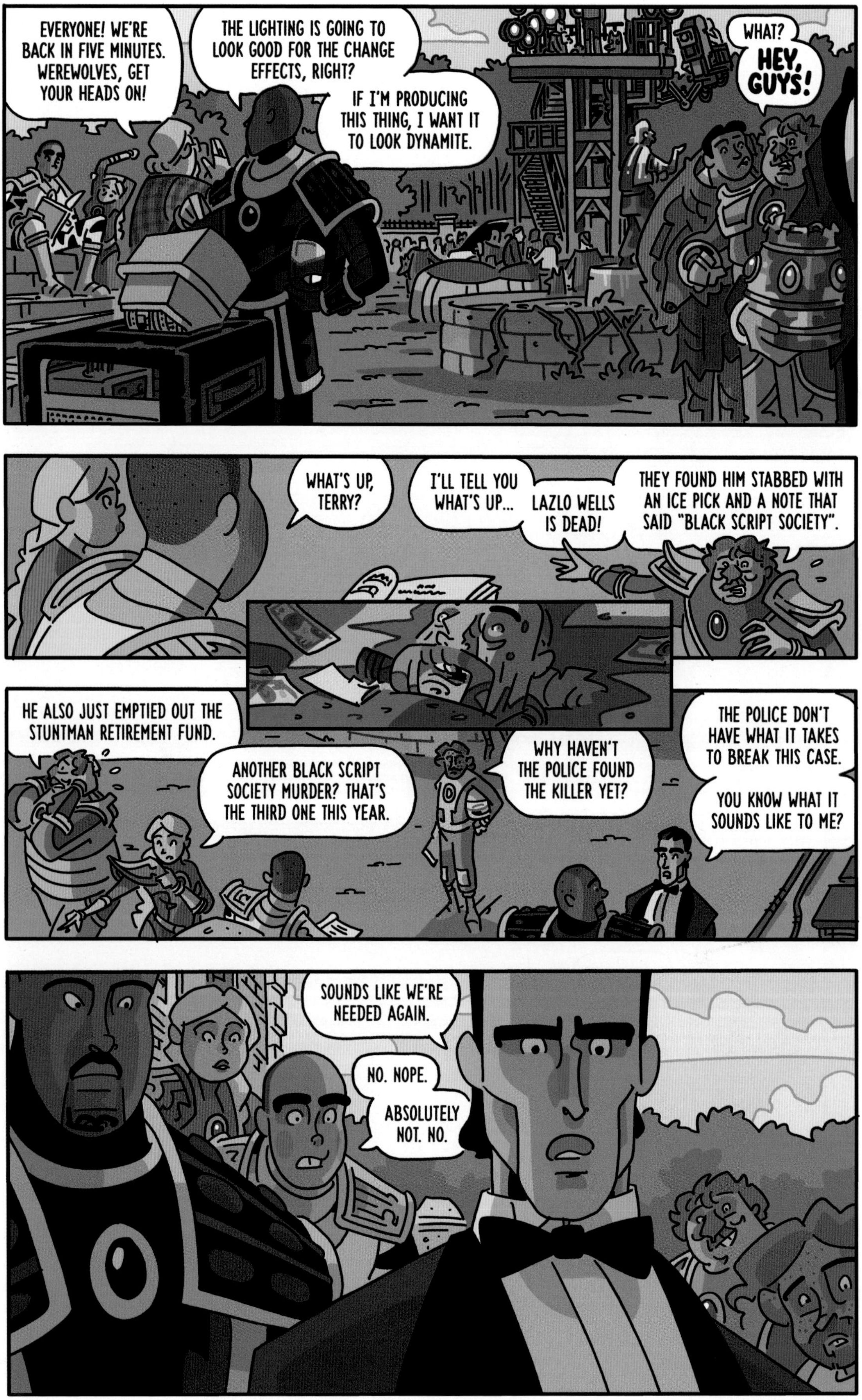
EVERYONE! WE'RE BACK IN FIVE MINUTES. WEREWOLVES, GET YOUR HEADS ON!
THE LIGHTING IS GOING TO LOOK GOOD FOR THE CHANGE EFFECTS, RIGHT?
IF I'M PRODUCING THIS THING, I WANT IT TO LOOK DYNAMITE.
WHAT?
HEY, GUYS!
WHAT'S UP, TERRY?
I'LL TELL YOU WHAT'S UP...
LAZLO WELLS IS DEAD!
THEY FOUND HIM STABBED WITH AN ICE PICK AND A NOTE THAT SAID "BLACK SCRIPT SOCIETY".
HE ALSO JUST EMPTIED OUT THE STUNTMAN RETIREMENT FUND.
ANOTHER BLACK SCRIPT SOCIETY MURDER? THAT'S THE THIRD ONE THIS YEAR.
WHY HAVEN'T THE POLICE FOUND THE KILLER YET?
THE POLICE DON'T HAVE WHAT IT TAKES TO BREAK THIS CASE.
YOU KNOW WHAT IT SOUNDS LIKE TO ME?
SOUNDS LIKE WE'RE NEEDED AGAIN.
NO. NOPE.
ABSOLUTELY NOT. NO.

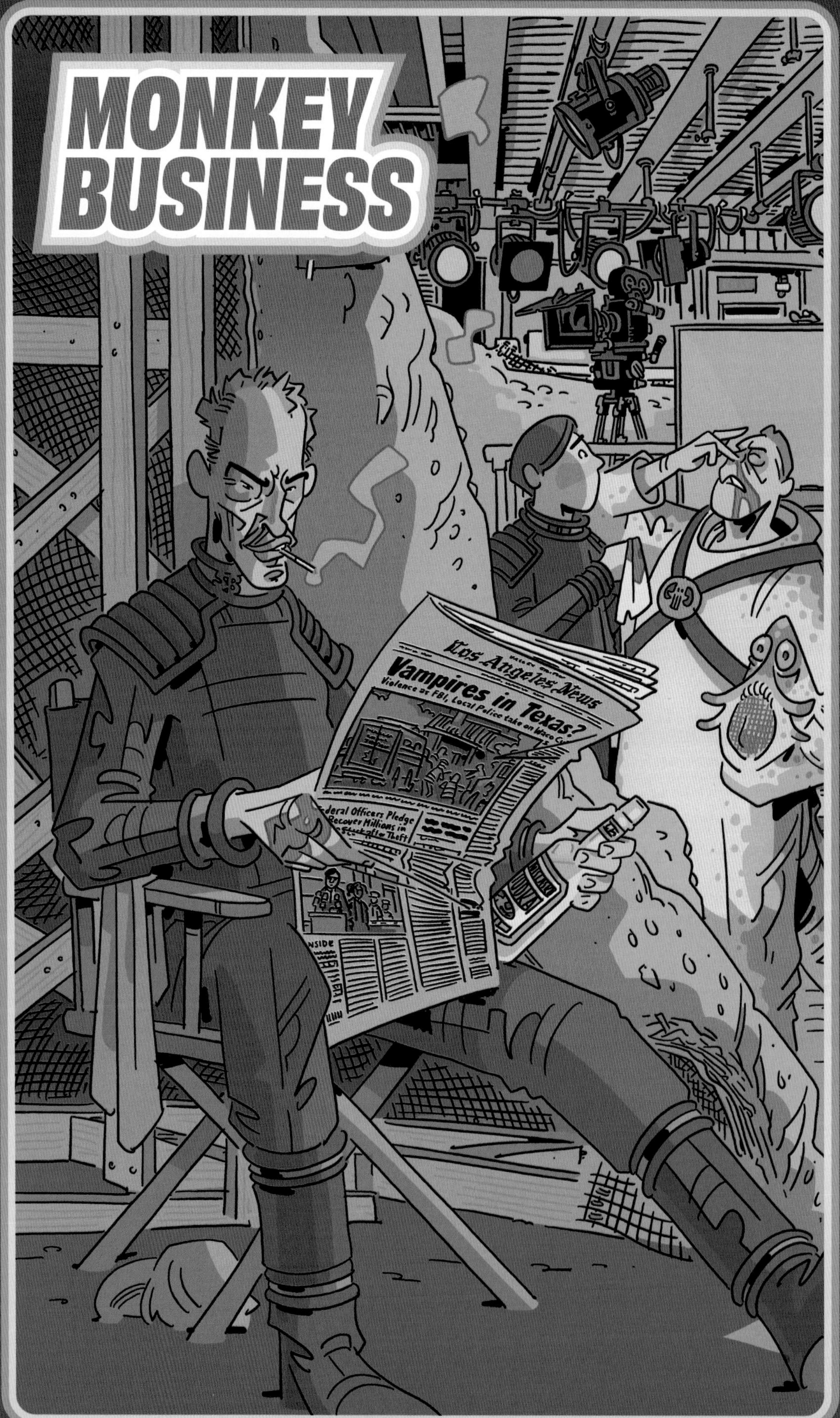
MONKEY BUSINESS
Los Angeles News
Vampires in Texas?
Violence at FBI, Local Police take on Waco
Officers Pledge
Recover Millions in
INSIDE

8PM ⑪ ⑦ ⑩ ⑮ **Sidecar** (cc) 20486
"Banana in the Tailpipe" Carson Gray (Trigg
Keaton) and S.K.I.P.P.Y. help a chimpan-
...cosmetics testing facility.

THE GOVERNMENT LAB THAT WAS TESTING ON OLD DARWIN HERE IS GOING TO BE COMING FOR US FAST, SKIPPY.

WE GOTTA GET TO DR. GALBRAITH SO HE CAN TAKE HIM BACK TO THE JUNGLE AND BE WITH HIS FAMILY.

WELL, CARSON GRAY, I GUESS THAT MEANS IT'S TIME TO...

...CRRRRRANK IT!

AAAANNNND CUT!

CAN WE GET SOMEONE TO AIR OUT THE SIDECAR?

THIS NASTY MOTHERFUCKER SMELLS LIKE A WOOL SWEATER ROLLED IN DIARRHEA.

SO YOU GET TO PLAY WITH THEM ALL DAY?

WELL, I TRAIN THEM AND TAKE CARE OF THEM.

BUT, YES, WE PLAY, TOO.

WHOAA!

HEY, SKIPSHIT!

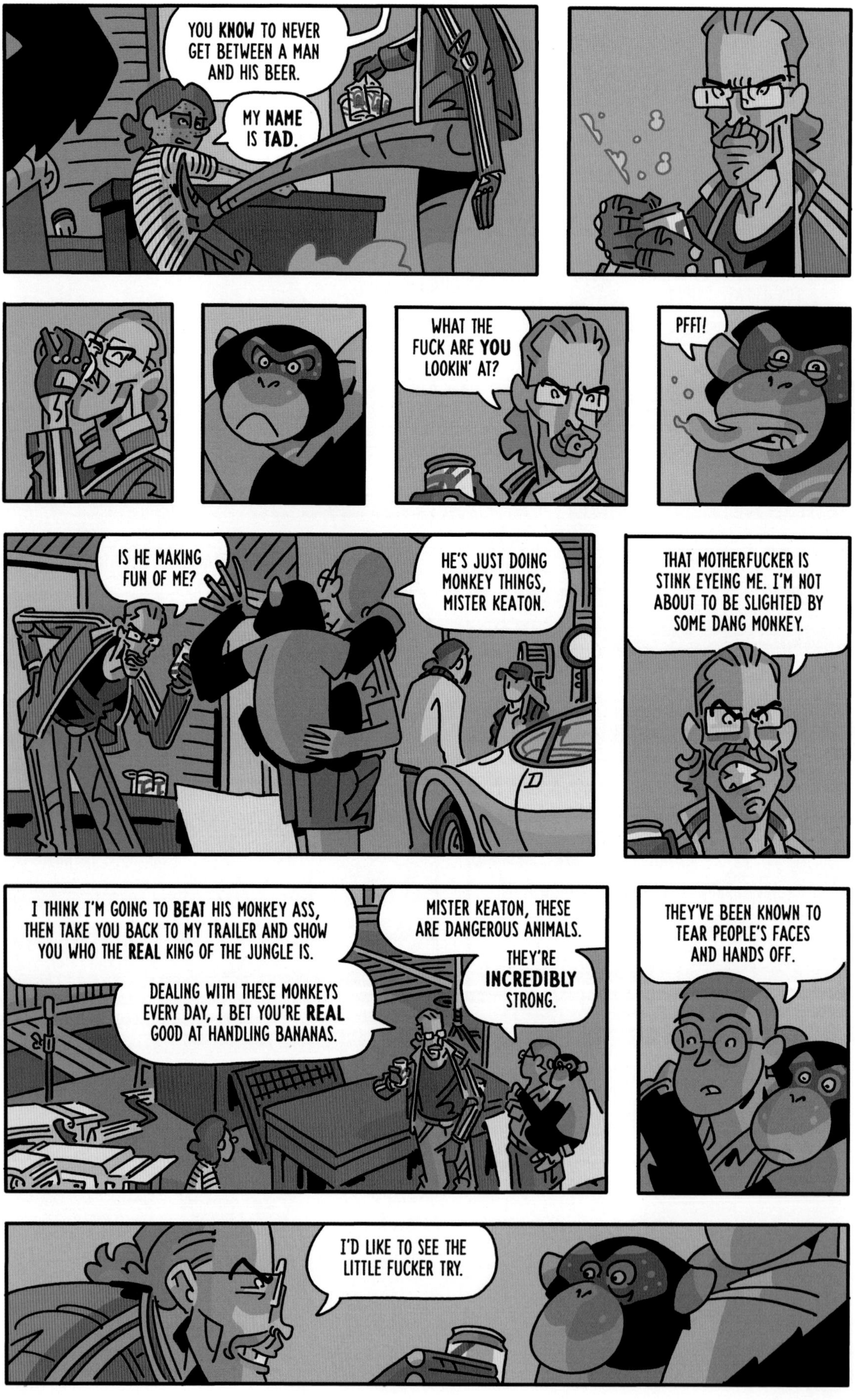
YOU KNOW TO NEVER GET BETWEEN A MAN AND HIS BEER.
MY NAME IS TAD.
WHAT THE FUCK ARE YOU LOOKIN' AT?
PFFT!
IS HE MAKING FUN OF ME?
HE'S JUST DOING MONKEY THINGS, MISTER KEATON.
THAT MOTHERFUCKER IS STINK EYEING ME. I'M NOT ABOUT TO BE SLIGHTED BY SOME DANG MONKEY.
I THINK I'M GOING TO BEAT HIS MONKEY ASS, THEN TAKE YOU BACK TO MY TRAILER AND SHOW YOU WHO THE REAL KING OF THE JUNGLE IS.
DEALING WITH THESE MONKEYS EVERY DAY, I BET YOU'RE REAL GOOD AT HANDLING BANANAS.
MISTER KEATON, THESE ARE DANGEROUS ANIMALS.
THEY'RE INCREDIBLY STRONG.
THEY'VE BEEN KNOWN TO TEAR PEOPLE'S FACES AND HANDS OFF.
I'D LIKE TO SEE THE LITTLE FUCKER TRY.

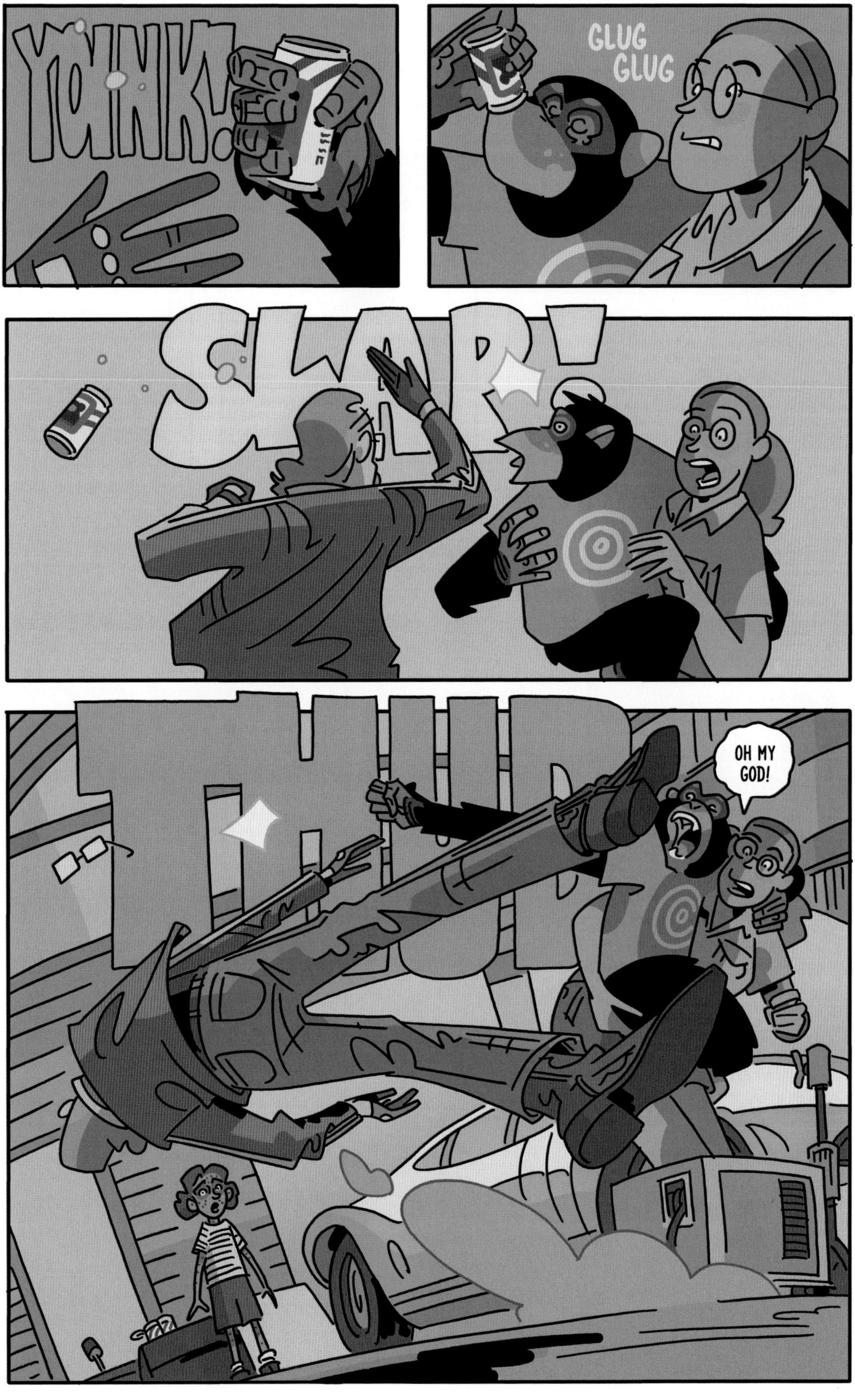
YOINK!
GLUG
GLUG
SLAP!
THUD
OH MY GOD!

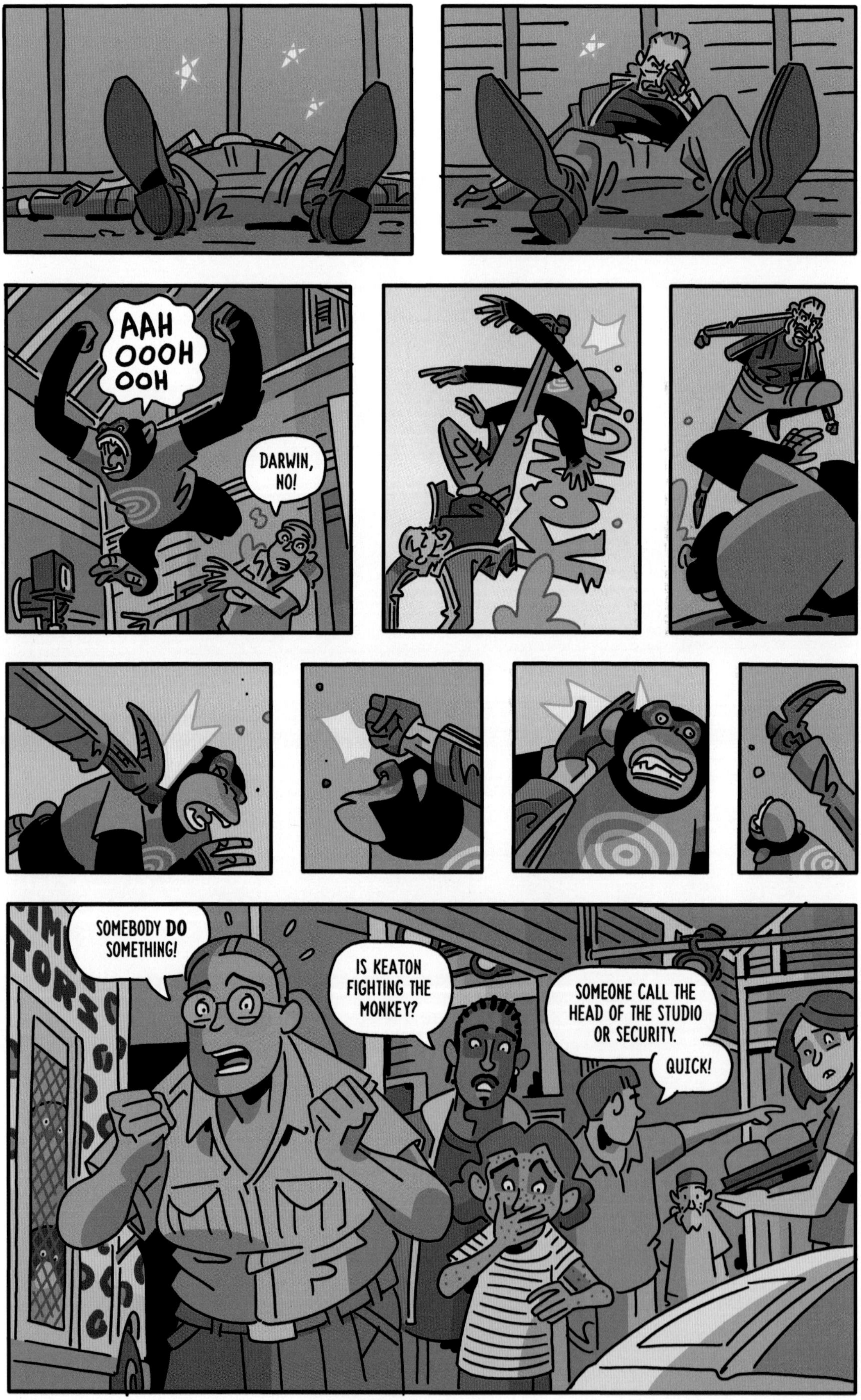
AAH OOOH OOH
DARWIN, NO!
SOMEBODY DO SOMETHING!
IS KEATON FIGHTING THE MONKEY?
SOMEONE CALL THE HEAD OF THE STUDIO OR SECURITY.
QUICK!

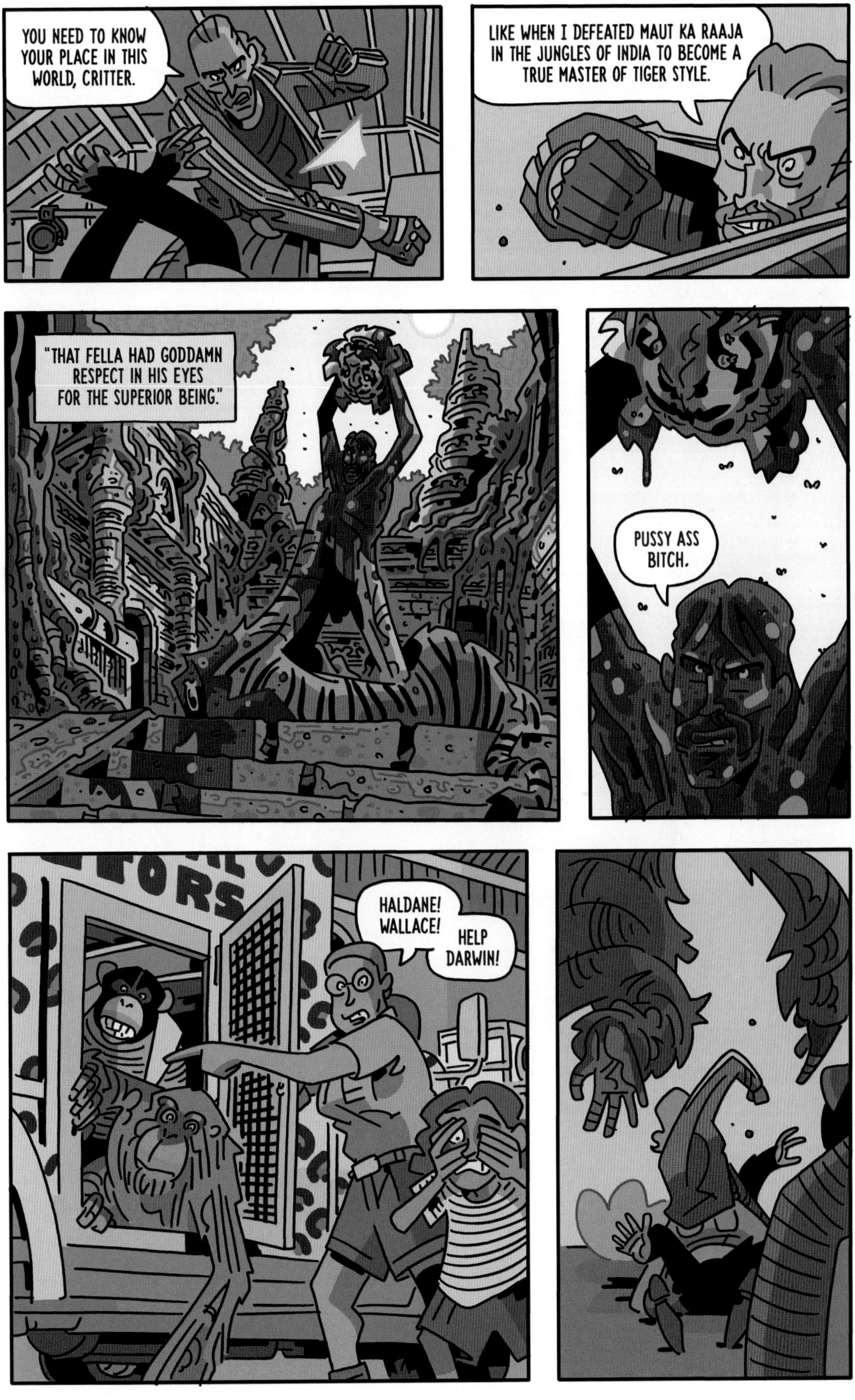
YOU NEED TO KNOW YOUR PLACE IN THIS WORLD, CRITTER.
LIKE WHEN I DEFEATED MAUT KA RAAJA IN THE JUNGLES OF INDIA TO BECOME A TRUE MASTER OF TIGER STYLE.
"THAT FELLA HAD GODDAMN RESPECT IN HIS EYES FOR THE SUPERIOR BEING."
PUSSY ASS BITCH.
HALDANE! WALLACE!
HELP DARWIN!

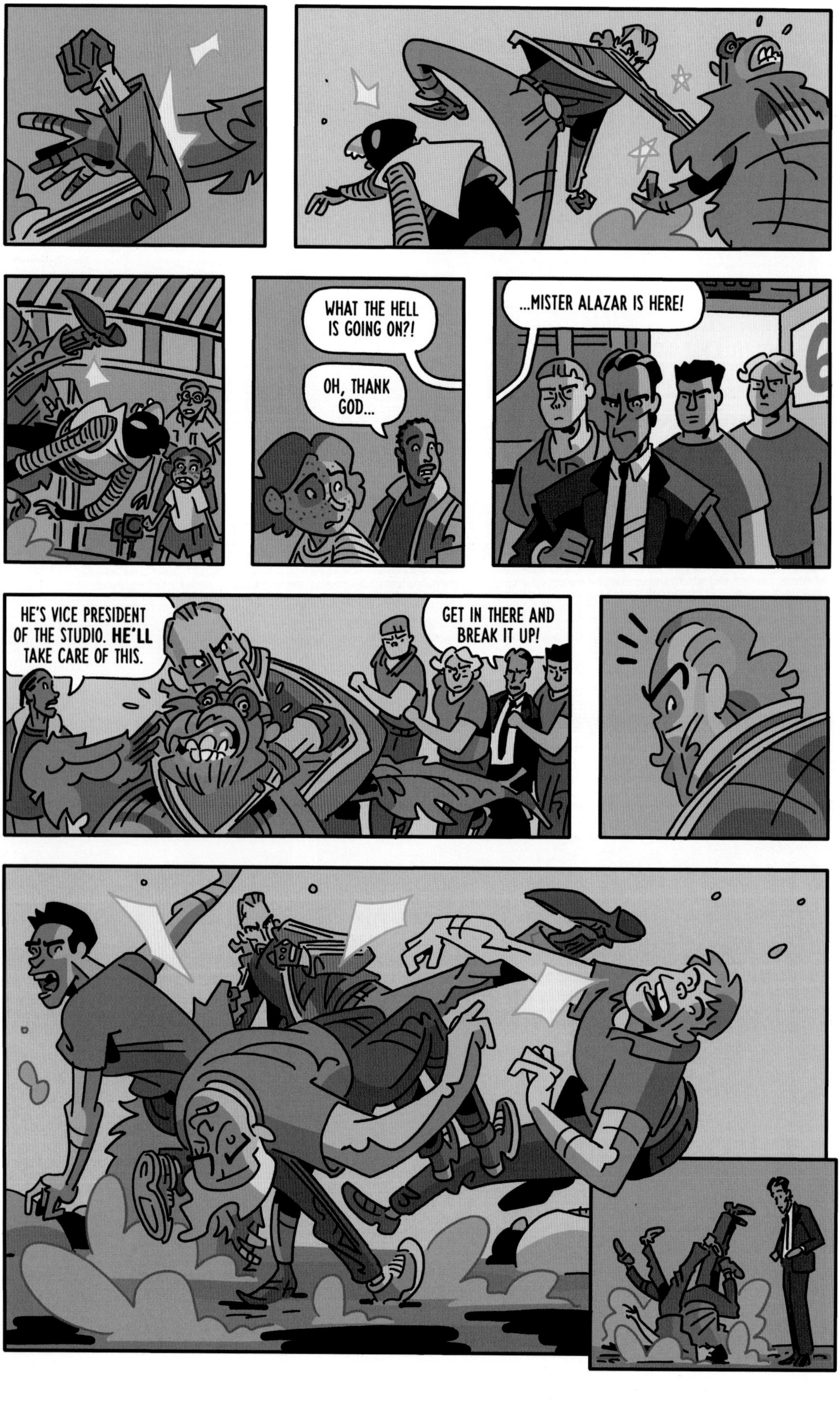
WHAT THE HELL IS GOING ON?!
OH, THANK GOD...
...MISTER ALAZAR IS HERE!
HE'S VICE PRESIDENT OF THE STUDIO. **HE'LL** TAKE CARE OF THIS.
GET IN THERE AND BREAK IT UP!

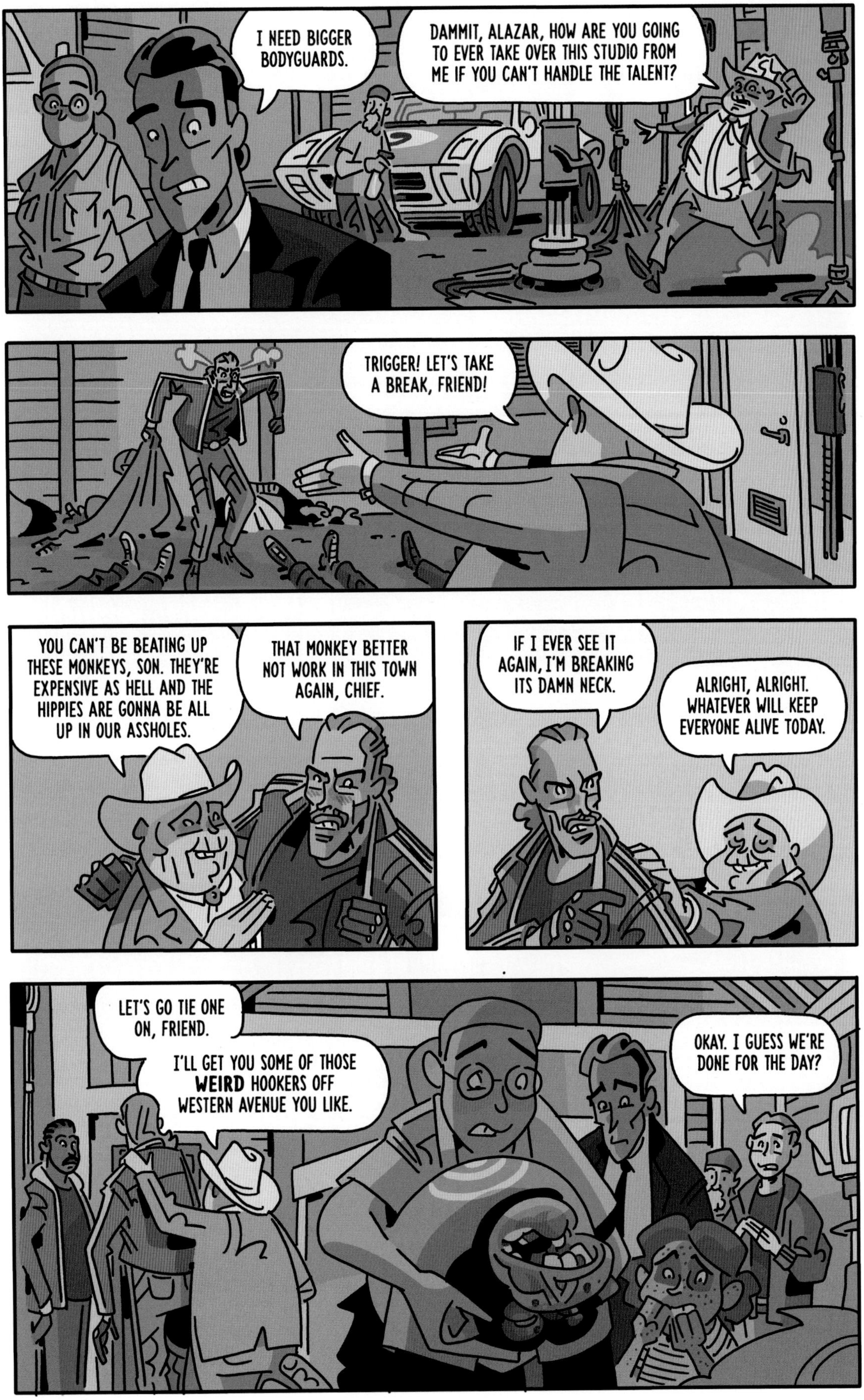
I NEED BIGGER BODYGUARDS.
DAMMIT, ALAZAR, HOW ARE YOU GOING TO EVER TAKE OVER THIS STUDIO FROM ME IF YOU CAN'T HANDLE THE TALENT?
TRIGGER! LET'S TAKE A BREAK, FRIEND!
YOU CAN'T BE BEATING UP THESE MONKEYS, SON. THEY'RE EXPENSIVE AS HELL AND THE HIPPIES ARE GONNA BE ALL UP IN OUR ASSHOLES.
THAT MONKEY BETTER NOT WORK IN THIS TOWN AGAIN, CHIEF.
IF I EVER SEE IT AGAIN, I'M BREAKING ITS DAMN NECK.
ALRIGHT, ALRIGHT. WHATEVER WILL KEEP EVERYONE ALIVE TODAY.
LET'S GO TIE ONE ON, FRIEND.
I'LL GET YOU SOME OF THOSE **WEIRD** HOOKERS OFF WESTERN AVENUE YOU LIKE.
OKAY. I GUESS WE'RE DONE FOR THE DAY?

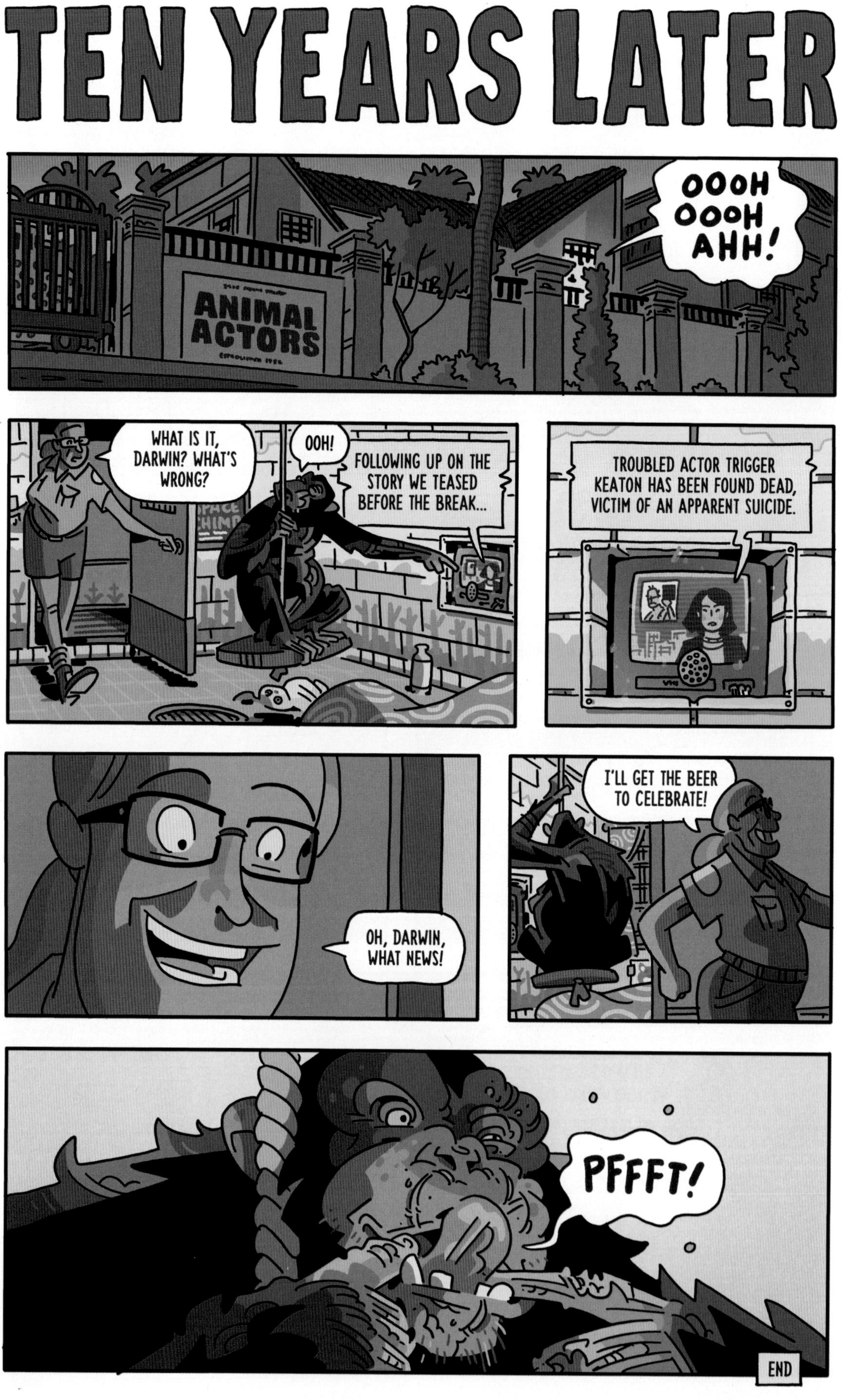
TEN YEARS LATER
ANIMAL ACTORS
OOOH OOOH AHH!
WHAT IS IT, DARWIN? WHAT'S WRONG?
OOH!
FOLLOWING UP ON THE STORY WE TEASED BEFORE THE BREAK...
TROUBLED ACTOR TRIGGER KEATON HAS BEEN FOUND DEAD, VICTIM OF AN APPARENT SUICIDE.
OH, DARWIN, WHAT NEWS!
I'LL GET THE BEER TO CELEBRATE!
PFFFT!
END

TRIGGER FINGER

by STYLE K STARKS

PHOTOS BY SWISS CHRYSLER   © 2003 ABS ENTERTAINMENT

While waiting outside Trigger Keaton's quaint suburban home to begin the only interview he agreed to do about his new police procedural, **PRECINCT BLUES,** I couldn't help but notice through his window I could see a mountain of dead beer cans and a cereal bowl filled with pills--most I recognized from my more gonzo reporting days and the others from when my beloved mastiff hound had a rupture in a disc in his spine.

"*I'll tell you this,*" Trigger said coming out his front door pulling a button-up over a ratty undershirt, "*It's a cop show and there ain't damn near any fighting. They say I'm too old to fight now.*" He flicked his cigarette into his neighbors' yard and immediately lit another one. "*That's all you get. My agent made me do this damn thing. Don't ask me about Brannigan, or that sissy first Tuff, or the monkeys or nothing. I get paid to talk and you can't afford my rate.*" So much for a traditional interview.

Then he had me drive him to a strip club.

It was called THE GLORY HOLE, but my friends, I assure you, there was never any glory here. It looked like a shithole and a condemned doghouse had a kid. It was ill-lit with a gravel parking lot full of motorcycles and that particular air of a place you're not supposed to be.

Trigger walked in like he owned the place.

He slapped the cover charge in front of the bouncer, the largest man I've ever seen by a large margin and tremendously intimidating even with his arm in a sling. Inside, another man--I'd find out later was the owner--when seeing Keaton, his eyes grew big and retreated like the citizens of Tokyo when Godzilla stepped into town. Like he'd seen a ghost.

Something you couldn't help but notice was that Trigger never moved out of the way or avoided contact, and this place was busy. As he bumped shoulders with every big ugly in the place and they sneered or complained, he just kept walking. Midway to the stage he grabbed a waitress by the arm to make an order and saddled up to the stage. Once there, he stamped out his cigarette--directly on the stage, mind you, though an ashtray was two inches to the left. He then looked up at the girl working and said some things so awful I refuse to put them in print.

The girl with the drink order never came, instead it was the owner with a gun and eight men so big it looked like the human equivalent of a monster truck rally. I couldn't help but notice a special forces tattoo on one, the notorious LA County Rowdy Boyz patches on some others.

"I told you, you're not allowed in here." I turned to see the owner looking at Keaton, who responded in no way, a stoic stripper-watching statue you'd think he hadn't heard them. "Get up and get out, motherfucker!" The owner's gun now pointed inches from Keaton's head.

"IT'S A COP SHOW AND THERE AIN'T DAMN NEAR ANY FIGHTING."

Trigger turned slow and then moved as if he was made of lightning.

He slapped the gun out of the man's hand and deconstructed it mid-air before punching this human mountain so hard he crumpled like a Christmas Crown. After that it was chaos. A spectacle.

Have you ever seen an old gal in Vegas holding down a row of slot machines? That's what happened next. In rapid succession he put a coin in the slot and pulled the lever on each of these men. Three apples rolled up in their eyes as they hit the ground unconscious. Eight up, eight down. Trigger kept a cigarette dangling from his lip the entire time. His eyes empty like nothing of real interest was happening.

In the distance there was the din of forthcoming police sirens. Trigger took all the crumpled bills off the counter--the dancers hard-earned wages--and walked out. On the way out he grabbed a patron's drink, flicked a lit cigarette into the bouncer's face and made his way into the night-
Contd.

JOIN THE TRIGGER KEATON CIRCLE OF FRIENDS FAN CLUB

MEMBERSHIP PACKAGE INCLUDES:

AUTOGRAPHED! COLOR! 8X10 TRIGGER PHOTO

QUARTERLY TRIGGER NEWSLETTER

THE SECRET TO AMERICAN KUNG FU BY TRIGGER KEATON

TRIGGER POSTER

TRIGGER BUMPER STICKER

"Remember what old Marshal Art says, kids--respect your elders, study real hard, and knowing how to do a spinning thrust kick never hurt anybody. Except villainy!"

$7.95

plus postage & handling

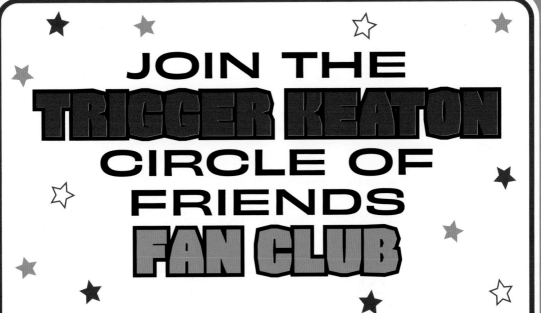

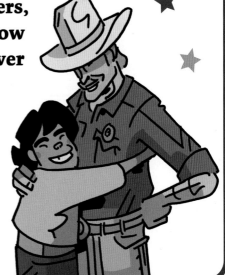

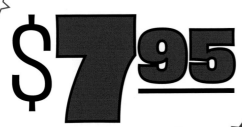

r/sidecar · Posted by u/CarMoisan 4 hours ago

2

What kind of car is Sidecar?

💬 6 Comments Share Save Report

Richard6430 · 3h

A fast one with an onboard computer programmed with the digital imprint of a childs brain. And also cool weapons and stuff.

> **CarMoisan** · 3h
> I mean what model of car, asshole.
>
> > **Richard6430** · 3h
> > Oh, I don't know. Yellow? ⬆ 1 ⬇

WheelMaster4560 · 2h

It's an AMC AMX/3 Prototype. They only made about 6 of them but it was abandoned. Bonafide had a bunch of fiberglass shells for stunts and stuff to be safe but there was one car that was an original. ⬆ 2 ⬇

> **CarMoisan** · 45m
> Oh man I was hoping to get one!
>
> > **CarsonGray1977** · 45m
> > Nope - the only way you'll get one is to steal one from a shady government agency doing sketchy experimental military weapon building but... You'll always be on the run! Looking over your shoulder! Just you and your sidecar! ⬆ 6 ⬇

---

r/sidecar · Posted by u/DarwinFriend08 11 hours ago

6

Do they need to refill the gel?

Hey guys I was just rewatching episode 7: Black Chariot and when SKIPPY drives over that spike strip that the German security guys throw out it's wheels reinflate and I know it's generally believed that it uses a refilling gel technology but we all know that SKIPPY can't go back to the lab where he was made so how would they ever replace those wheels? Surely they're special wheels, right? Is that gel permanent? Do they need to refill the gel?

💬 10 Comments Share Save Report

Richard6430 · 11h

It's not real. It's a tv show.

> **DarwinFriend08** · 11h
> You're not real.
>
> > **Richard6430** · 11h
> > I'm real. Ask your mom.
> >
> > > **DarwinFriend08** · 10h
> > > She said you are real but not real good. ⬆ 1 ⬇

Cheryl994 · 10h

Why do you think Carson Gray is so good at fighting? He's just a race car driver who got tied up in some criminal activities, pulled out of prison to pilot an experimental car.

TrigFan54 · 9h

Because Trigger Keaton is good at fighting so why wouldn't they take advantage of that?

> **Sidebar** · 9h
>
> It's too bad he wasn't as good at driving or sobriety. We might still Sidecar today.
>
> > **Cheryl994** · 9h
> >
> > What?!?!?
> >
> > > **Cheryl994** · 7h
> > >
> > > Keaton had a DUI wreck after the first season. He was in a big drunken police chase through LA that ended when he took out a bunch of cars in an intersection and people were hurt. The studio - correctly - thought it was a bad look to have a car based show where the lead famously caused a lot of damage and hurt a lot of people WHILE DRIVING. ⬆ **14** ⬇

⬆ **3** ⬇

---

r/sidecar · Posted by u/Howdyho_1_1 21 hours ago

Whatever happened to the kid that voiced SKIPPY?

⬆ 13 ⬇

e

💬 5 Comments   Share   Save   Report

Poopdoctor · 21h

I heard he became a prostitute charging by the hour to CRAAAAAAAAAAAANK IT! ⬆ **1** ⬇

> **Richard6430** · 21h
>
> Oh man,I remember yelling this out the window at girls on the strip.
>
> > **Howdyho_1_1** · 21h
> >
> > Oh man, do you remember also how much everyone hated you?

ThatBarristaGuy · 18h

Tad Haycroft is doing okay. He was the voice of Bumthriller the Leprechaun for POT O GOLD cereal and also the voice of Tee-Tee on BEARS? OH MY! He's always looking for more voice work!

> **CarMoisan** · 18h
>
> SKIPPY IS THIS YOU? ARE YOU OKAY? ⬆ **21** ⬇

---

r/sidecar · Posted by u/DarwinFriend08 1 day ago

What do you think the best episode is?

⬆ 2 ⬇

I know most people say BANANA IN THE TAILPIPE but I think it might be OBJECTS IN THE MIRROR because the addition of a car villain to SKIPPY is so great. And MEVO being a truck and SKIPPY being a car is so neat. Do you think they would've brought back MEVO for Season two?

💬 5 Comments   Share   Save   Report

WheelMaster4560 · 1d

MEVO is killed at the end when SKIPPY and Carson Gray trick him into that foundation of wet concrete. I don't think the Agency's scientists would be able to find him.

> **DarwinFriend08** · 1d
> Yeah but maybe they had a backup or something.
>> **Richard6430** · 1d
>> How did a twelve year old ever see an episodes of Sidecar?
>>> **DarwinFriend08** · 1d
>>> I'm not twelve
>>>> **Richard6430** · 7h
>>>> Sorry you just write a like a stupid twelve year old.

---

r/sidecar · Posted by u/MEVOBoss 1 day ago

3

Do they ever explain in show why there's an nineball painted on SKIPPY's hood?

💬 11 Comments   Share   Save   Report

KRider82 · 1d
You know how there's a measurement of cocaine called an eightball? Keaton larger portions he called nineballs. He was coked up for the show.
> **Richard6430** · 21h
> He was he human equivalent of a bunny slope. Frosted up and only going downhill.

Passerby28 · 1d
Doesn't Keaton own the original car?
> **Sidebar** · 1d
> Yeah it was part of his deal to do he show. He chose the car. ⬆ **1** ⬇
>> **MEVOBoss** · 1d
>> Wait. So the eightball thing is real?
>>> **Sidebar** · 1d
>>> Keaton just thought it looked cool and wanted everyone to know he owned a car they only made like six of. ⬆ **3** ⬇

DarwinFriend08 · 1d
In show (Ep 8: Driving Miss Crazy) SKIPPY says it's camouflage to make it look like a normal car but I don't know what kind of normal car has a giant nineball on the hood. (upvote)
> **Richard6430** · 1d
> Also SKIPPY's artificial intelligence is 8.
>> **SidecarGuy** · 1d
>> SKIPPY is 13, an eight year old is useless in a fight.
>>> **CGrayFiancee** · 1d
>>> You fight a lot of eight year olds?
>>>> **SidecarGuy** · 1d
>>>> Hey I gotta do something to make me feel better about myself. ⬆ **1** ⬇

---

r/sidecar · Posted by u/DarwinFriend08 2 days ago

2

Have you seen how Trigger looks now?

💬 3 Comments   Share   Save   Report

An except from the oral biography from

TRAPPED ADRIFT

THE SPACEBOAT 3030 STORY

* * * *

written by Showrunner

Fletcher Newberry

ALLISON SAINTE-MARIE, Lt. ZZrk-Tok: I couldn't believe when they asked me. I was trying to get into acting after my success with professionally kicking things and I grew up watching MARSHAL ART. Trigger Keaton was a hero or an idol to almost anyone who practiced martial arts.

FLETCHER NEWBERRY, Showrunner: Whose idea was it to bring in Allison? It was Keaton's. Honestly.

TRES MATTHEWS, Casting Director: We brought her in and had her do a reading. She was a little rough but Trigger wanted her on the show and, hell, she was playing some alien with this latex hat on so how good of an actress did she need to be?

Rex Dallas, Producer: Some folks believed Keaton wanted her because Brannigan showed him up acting-wise on FRANKENSTEIN & FRANKENSTEIN and I'm sure there's some truth to that. She wasn't going to win any awards for sure but she did a real fine job. Hell, he came up with that stupid Gor A Loo Ra Loo battle cry. He wanted to make sure no one ever took her too serious.

Allison Sainte-Marie, Lt. ZZrk-Tok: Gor A Loo Ra Loo! I like it. It's cute. I love people yelling it at me on the street. It's not annoying at all. It's cute.

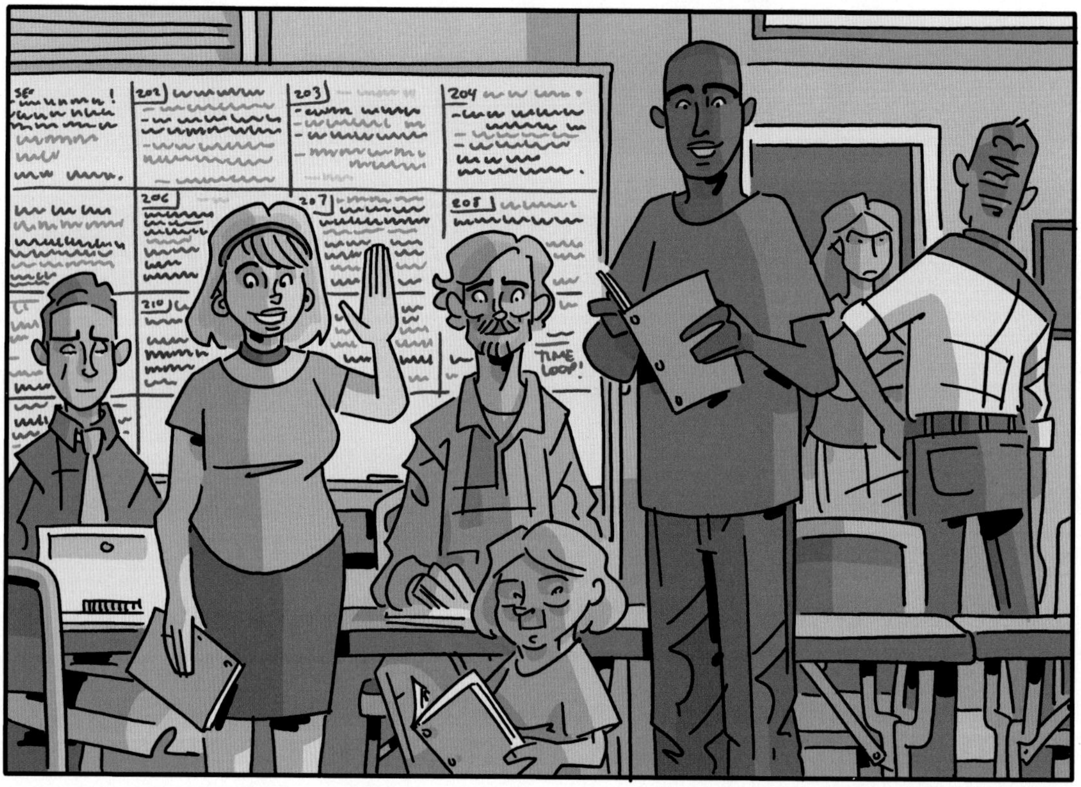
202
203
204
206
207
208
210
TIME LOOP!

Spaceboat Cast Table Read

Fletcher Newberry, Showrunner: I mean, the truth of the matter was that Keaton had just ruined two shows with his antics. He had that wreck with SIDECAR, he had everything you could imagine with his co-host on FRANKENSTEIN & FRANKENSTEIN. He was basically the world's most dangerous diva and it was getting out to the public what a shit-heel of a human he was. Did he suggest Allison? Sure. Allison was a national darling. She had just won "TALENTED AMERICAN" as a martial artist. Her positivity, her joyfulness, it was pervasive. She was the perfect balance to what a terrible, awful, stinky piece of shit he was. We honestly thought maybe she'd even keep him in check. Ying-Yang or whatever.

Terrell Jagger, Grip Seasons 1-2: It was always something with Keaton. He's drunk and disorderly, he's bullying the grips, he's sexually harassing any lady on the set. Shit, he's sexually harassing some of the men, too. Everyone on that set has six crazy Keaton stories. Like shit you can't imagine a person would or could do.

Kurt Dunlop, Gaffer Season 1: One time Keaton comes out of his trailer. His uniform's half on, his face is covered with nose candy. He's yelling at the catering lady because they didn't have barbecue chicken but it was Thursday, you know? Thursday is fucking chicken fingers. Anyway, he's knocking shit over, he's yelling so much he's spitting on her and we thought this was going to be the day Sainte-Marie put his high ass out but she just stood there, you know? Like the rest of us. I guess knowing how to fight doesn't mean you're going to.

Allison Sainte-Marie, Lt. ZZrk-Tok: Ha ha ha. Trigger sure could be a character sometimes alright.

Rex Dallas, Producer: A lot of people figured maybe she was scared of Trigger or maybe didn't think she was up to snuff in comparison. And listen, we were all scared of him. No one ever met him that wasn't scared of him. He was like a human gatling gun. He would tear through everyone and he didn't care, you know? Like, nothing meant nothing to him but whatever the hell he wanted. Anyway, I'll tell you right now I saw her workouts and I saw her win nationals as a thirteen-year-old. She was tough.

Mitch Gerber, Floor Manager Season 2: I saw her break up a gang fight once. We were leaving the set and I don't know why then and why there but two gangs were literally about to throw down. I'm not shitting you! A LA, Bloods versus Crips, honest-to-God gang fight and she snuffed it like human napalm. And afterwards she was SWEET to all of them. Helping them up, patting the dirt off their backs. That girl was that tough. I'm pretty sure if she was really motivated she could have taken him. But hell, you know, that's probably what a lot of those bullfighters thought, too. Right before a horn went up their butthole.

Dan Schmidth, Audio Season 2: I was there for the gang thing. It was surreal. She told the Bloods and the Crips they should be nicer to each other. Like just being a good girl offering up some sweet advice.

Fletcher Newberry, Showrunner: They were two sides of the same coin. Both were so astute at physical combat - their martial arts - that they were without cares, without concerns. Just Trigger's version of that was selfish and destructive and hers was just like no worries, you know?

GREG DALWRIMPLE, Director Season 2: The word on set was she had made some shitty investments and needed the show to do well and didn't want to - pardon the pun - rock the boat so she never did anything about Keaton's antics on set.

TERRELL JAGGER, Grip Seasons 1-2: I feel bad for that girl. She came in and did a helluva a job. Too good, even. No one's ever going to see her as anything but as that stupid alien.

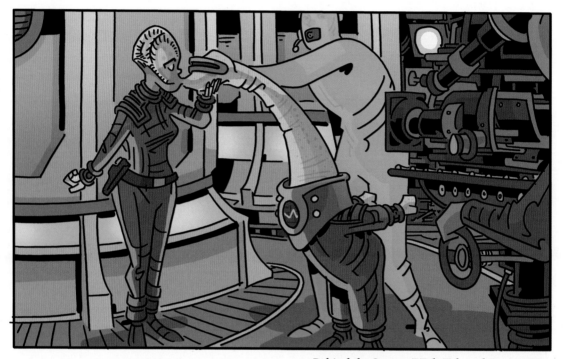

Behind the Scenes, ZZrk-Tok and Fonteni Kiss

REX DALLAS, Producer: I heard that investment thing and I'm sure it's true. I also heard she was sleeping with him. Trigger was a nasty ass human, but the ladies loved him. I mean, then they hated themselves immediately after, but you know girls like a dangerous man and there was no more dangerous man that ever walked this Earth than Trigger Keaton.

FLETCHER NEWBERRY, Showrunner: She wasn't sleeping with him. Trust me, the stuff Keaton was into? A cute, nice, midwestern girl was no way his type. If it wasn't messed up, self-destructive or dangerous he wasn't into it. I don't know where that rumor came from.

ALLISON SAINTE-MARIE, Lt. ZZrk-Tok: People were saying what?

THE ACTOR'S YURT FEATURING RICHARD BRANNIGAN
Transcript from the never-released episode.

Desiderio Fortwidth: Hello and welcome to *The Actors Yurt*. I am your host Desiderio Fortwidth. Today we're joined by former sports standout, turned television wunderkind, who now is, I guess I'd say, attempting to perform theatrically. It's Mister Richard Brannigan.

Richard Brannigan: Thanks for having me, Desiderio. It's a pleasure to be in *The Actor's Yurt*.

So, Richard. (Pause) Tell me about... sports.

Haha ha (Uncomfortable silence) Oh! Really? I mean. They're out there. People are playing them. I had the privilege of sports putting me through college, getting me to the professional level. It was an honor to perform for football fans at USC - Go Trojans - and for the fans of the world.

And at the peak of your powers, your sports momentum building - that was stolen from you?

That's right. I was injured in my third season. I'm sure most people have seen it. I was cutting outside the offensive line and unfortunately my leg and face connected with two lineman who apparently didn't want me to play professional football again.

These gentlemen attempted to intentionally end your career?

Haha, no no. I'm just kidding. It was just a bad play. They're good guys. We're still friends today. I just went to one's wedding. Good guys.

Afterwards you went into acting. Performing on one of my - well, dare I say, everyone's - favorite shows of all time: *Frankenstein & Frankenstein*. A show taken from us too soon. Why acting?

My agent thought, with my football career over, there might be a path for me in acting, and so we tried it out, and the rest is history. And I just fell in love with it. I just love the people you get to work with, the sets, the rehearsals. I love getting that script in my hand, you know? Sitting down and eating it, thinking about who this character is and how they'd do the things.

Did you study the theatrical arts at (squints angrily at papers) the University of Southern California?

No, no. I mostly studied the team playbook and the sorority girls mostly. Ha Ha. I did do a performance of *Brigadoon* in high school though. I've just always been able do things I put my mind to. I'm a hard worker, fast learner. That's how I succeeded in football, and I just applied those practices to acting too.

Your performance in *Frankenstein & Frankenstein* is breathtaking, erudite. It is electric and moving.

Thank you so much.

Let me ask you, Mister Brannigan, why do you think *Frankenstein & Frankenstein* was such a masterpiece, and your cinematic turns have been meaningless fodder? At best an insignificant placation for ignorant masses.

Uh? I'm sorry?

Well, we appreciate the apology, in lieu of an explanation. Do you think it was perhaps because these films lack the tension that the *Frankenstein & Frankenstein* set provided? Not unlike the environments Kubrick created for *The Shining*. Where you and Trigger Keaton's on-set disdain for one another made the performances bloom and grow juicy with the dramaturgical spirit?

I, uh, suppose that is a possible take one could form but-

You and Trigger Keaton fought daily. Some say that he felt intimidated by your breakout role and held it against you. Is that true?

I'd rather not comment on that.

I'm told, screaming fits and death threats were a daily event. I'm told he refused to ever refer to you by your name or address you correctly he had such little respect for you.

I'd rather not comment on that.

Do you think that perhaps, Trigger Keaton cuckolding you with your wife

brought the animus needed to make the Frankenstein creature really come alive?

I'd rather not comment on that.

I see. It's a touchy subject that a man emasculated you and-

He didn't emasculate me. What he did-

Why do you think Trigger Keaton and you never came to blows? Do you think he was scared he would injure you permanently and thus end the show before you could end it by unceremoniously quitting mid-season? Do you feel like the former outcome would be more respectable than the choice you made?

I'd rather not comment on that.

Alright, alright, I see we're going to be a Troublesome Timmy. Let's turn our attention to the fan questions.

Thank god.

From Charlie Mitchell, Grand Rapids, MI. "Who would win in a fight between you and Trigger Keaton?"

SIGH. I'd rather not comment on that.

From Alan Swales, Conway, AK. "Did your wife ever say who has the bigger donger - you or Trigger?"

This is a joke, right? Is this like a hidden camera show or something?

From Desiderio Fortwidth, Beverly Hills, CA -

That is you, mother ******er.

Do you regret that your personal weakness - your inability to withstand the torturous and perhaps criminal behavior of another man - STOLE from us, the audience, the finest television show in years?

I'm not going to sit here and take this.

Do you regret we now live in a *Frankenstein & Frankenstein*-less world because you couldn't simply let Trigger Keaton have the spotlight so that

we could all continue to sup on this delicious feast of perfect television ambrosia?

(Brannigan stands up angrily, leans in to Desiderio's ear and says something we can't make out but makes Desiderio extremely uncomfortable - then Brannigan storms off)

This has been *The Actor's Yurt with Desiderio Fortwidth*. Thank you for joining me.

Director: Cut

I suspect this one isn't making television, hmmmm?

Director: What did he say to you?

I'd rather not say, but also I soiled myself. Can we clear the room post-haste and also have some staff-wide discretion here?

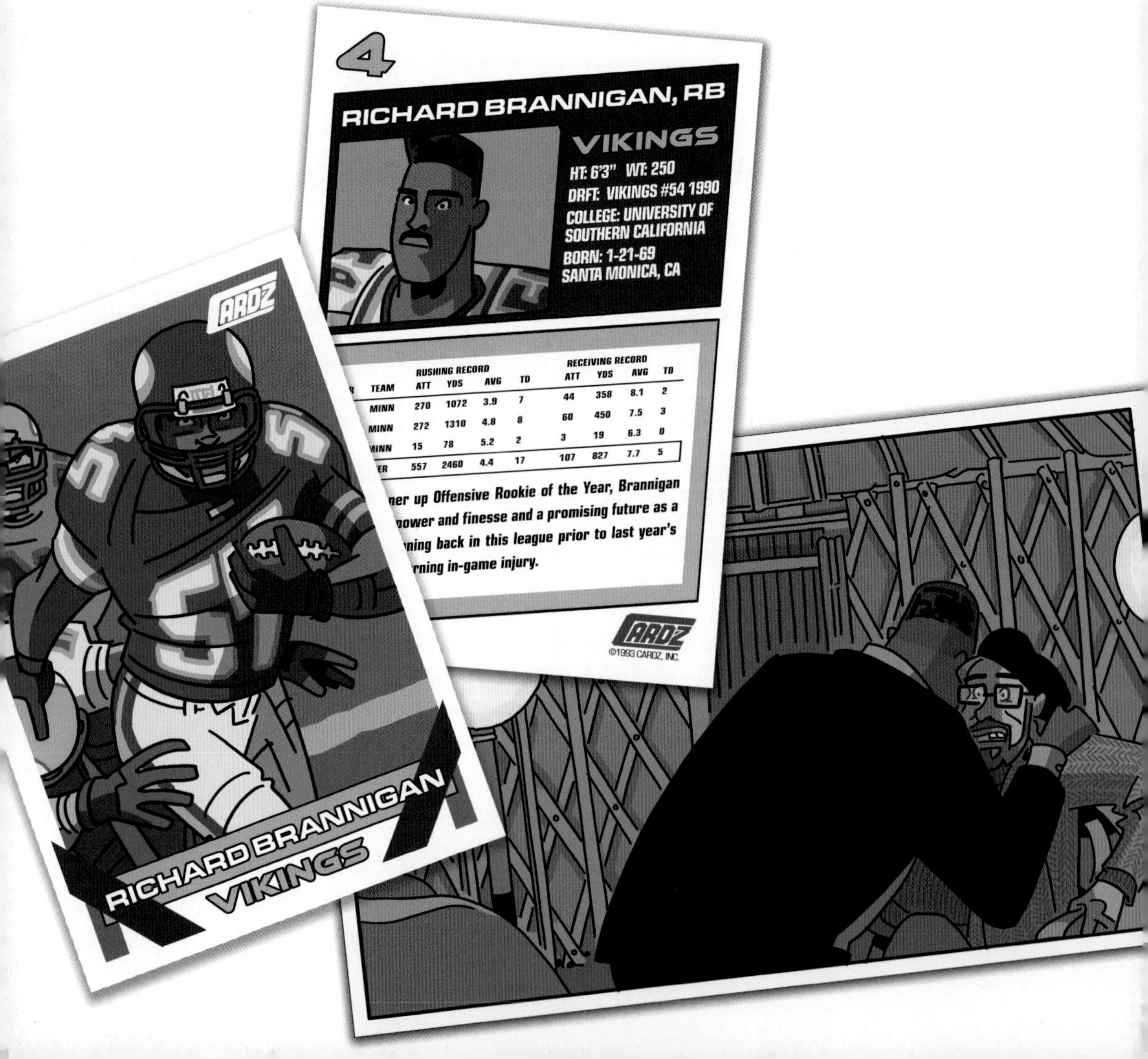
4
RICHARD BRANNIGAN, RB
VIKINGS
HT: 6'3" WT: 250
DRFT: VIKINGS #54 1990
COLLEGE: UNIVERSITY OF SOUTHERN CALIFORNIA
BORN: 1-21-69
SANTA MONICA, CA
RUSHING RECORD
RECEIVING RECORD
TEAM ATT YDS AVG TD ATT YDS AVG TD
MINN 270 1072 3.9 7 44 358 8.1 2
MINN 272 1310 4.8 8 60 450 7.5 3
MINN 15 78 5.2 2 3 19 6.3 0
557 2460 4.4 17 107 827 7.7 5
up Offensive Rookie of the Year, Brannigan
and finesse and a promising future as a
back in this league prior to last year's
in-game injury.
CARDZ
©1993 CARDZ, INC.
CARDZ
RICHARD BRANNIGAN
VIKINGS

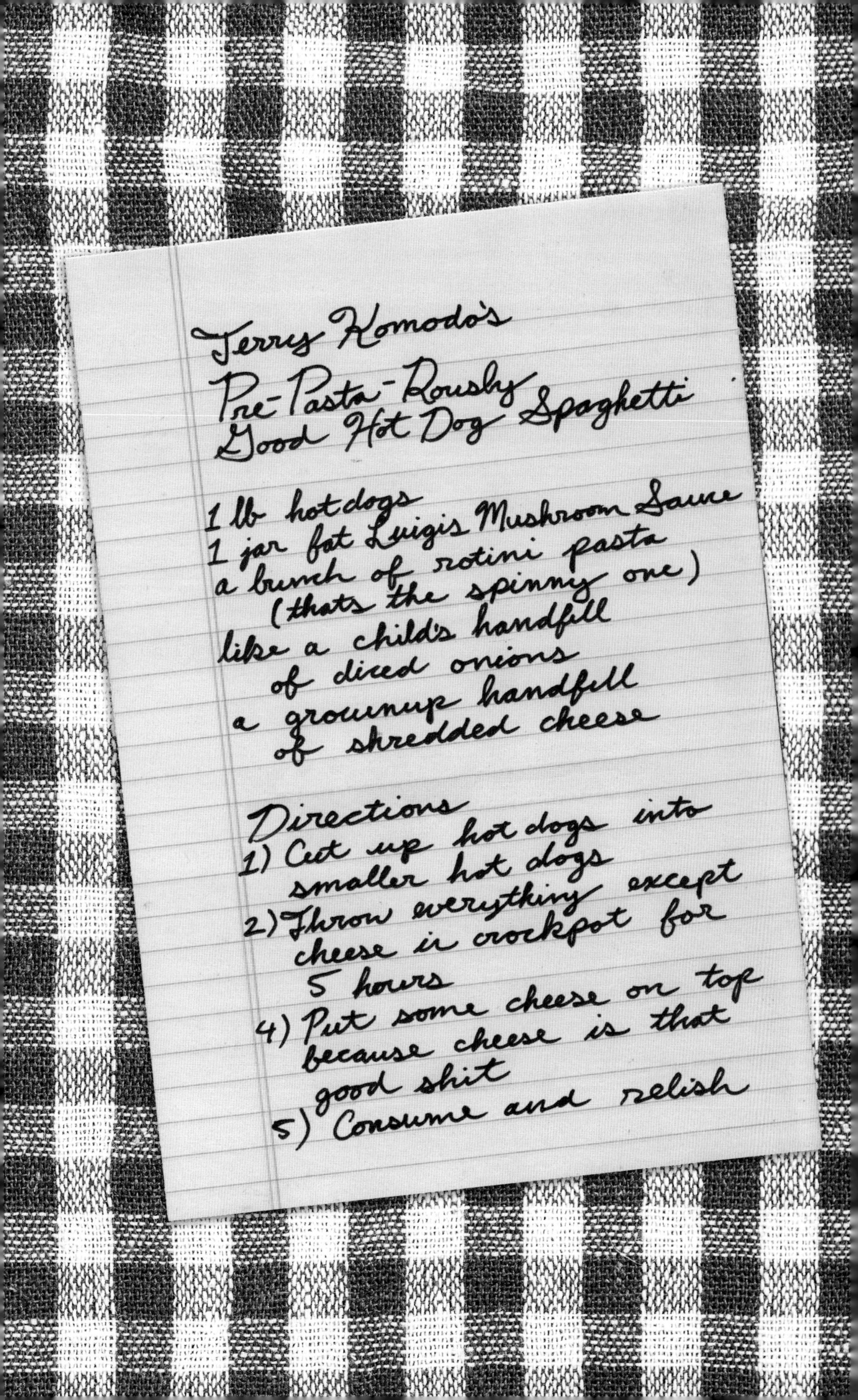

Terry Komodo's
Pre-Pasta-Roushy
Good Hot Dog Spaghetti
1 lb hotdogs
1 jar fat Luigis Mushroom Sauce
a bunch of rotini pasta
(thats the spinny one)
like a child's handfill
of diced onions
a grownup handfill
of shredded cheese
Directions
1) Cut up hot dogs into
smaller hot dogs
2) Throw everything except
cheese in crockpot for
5 hours
4) Put some cheese on top
because cheese is that
good shit
5) Consume and relish

TERRY KOMODO

Stunt Person | Best Fight Choreographer | Child Actor

Hi, I'm Terry Komodo. I've been doing notably dope stunts and incredibly timeless and unforgettably cool fight choreography for nearly my whole life.

You probably have seen me around, I look like someone carved a Stunt God out of a Kung Fu Mountain. I was trained by martial arts and kung fu legend Trigger Keaton to not just be the best around but the best ever. You give me a boring scene and I'll enrich and embolden it with stuntastic flavors of the richest kind. I'll ruin your eyes with pugilistic symphony and you'll be grateful for your newfound weird eyesight.

Here's some of my ackolades:

Selected Stunts

Metal Eagle, 1997:
Big Thug in cavern scene who made everyone else look like schmucks.

Catch These Hands, 1998:
Big Thug in bar scene that made everyone else look like dinky little idiots. I did that spinning scissor kick that made your damn jaw drop.

The Winter Grove, 1999:
The big masked scary guy that made all the masked scary guys look like little masked dopes.

Fallen Heroes, 1999:
I was the big thug soldier that made everyone look like useless paper dolls. I was the one who got ran over by a tank which is bullshit because I was obviously too hardcore and bad-ass to be ever be ran over by a stupid tank.

NOTE: I did like 200 more because I was so bad-ass and good I was in high demand but my agent said don't list everything just the movies people saw and remembered. But I'm a stunt machine, boss. Plug me in and let me stunt you heart into blissful submission.

Selected Choreography

Eight Eagles, 2000:
I hand walked all Eight Eagles through every sequence including that sweet glass ballroom fracas and that bad ass robot ninja rumpus.

Fire Dance In Hell, 2001:
I did all the good parts on this one and none of the bad parts (which was most of it). Yes, people got burnt pretty bad but that wasn't my fault it was the stupid director for not knowing shit about stunts. Directors can be stupid as hell about stunts and they should listen to legit stunt badasses like me when they say all that fire is way too close to dance and fight near.

Mr. Ipsom's Fantastic Journey, 2001:
You remember when Mr. Ipsom goes to TastyLand and that frog boxes that walrus? 100% All Terry Komodo.

The Bad Guy Puncher, 2002:
If a bad guy was punched I choreographed it. Every fist thrown in this flick was a masterpiece of theatrical combat.

Enoughicus Fisticuffs, 2003:
A stunt masterpiece, a kung fu classic entirely put together by me, Terry Komodo, bad ass Stunt Daddy. I birthed raw, unique pugilism into every slobberknocker and brouhaha in this incredible film.

Race Car Man, 2004:
I worked on all the stupid drama baby fights on this one. This flick was boring and stupid. Not enough race cars or fights but I guess it got nominated for an Oscar or something.

Ring Warrior, 2005:
I choreographed all the boxing sequences in this one and they're great even if boxing is the lowest form of fighting set only above two sorority girls drunkenly slapfighting at a light night ice cream parlor.

Cowboy Town, 2005:
I did that rootin'-tootin' brawl in the saloon. It was fucking rad and you know it. Remember when that cowboy does a spinning heel kick and deflects all those sarsaparilla bottles? Hell yeah you do. Terry Komodo made that for you.

Acting *(please don't hold against me I am in the Stuntman Union)*

Boy Who Cried Wolf, 1990:
Terry Komodo played the Boy Who Cried Wolf.

Marshal Art, 1991-1992:
Tuff Munsen (Second one, Best one)

Kung Fu Teenager, 1993:
Terry Komodo played the Kung Fu Teenager's friend Bert Merflin. This movie was stupid and sucked but I ruled in it. Remember when Bert Merflin punched that ski-lodge douche into the hot tub? Hell yeah you do because it ruled.

Special Note: Terry Komodo specializes in fight stunts and fight choreography <u>ONLY.</u> NO FALLS EVER. NO EXCEPTIONS. TERRY KOMODO DOES NOT FALL OFF THINGS OR JUMP OUT OF THINGS. IF YOU HIRE HIM FOR SUCH STUPID NONSENSE HE WON'T DO IT AND YOU STILL HAVE TO PAY HIM BECAUSE THAT'S YOUR FUCK UP NOT HIS.

TMDb
THE MOVIE DATABASE

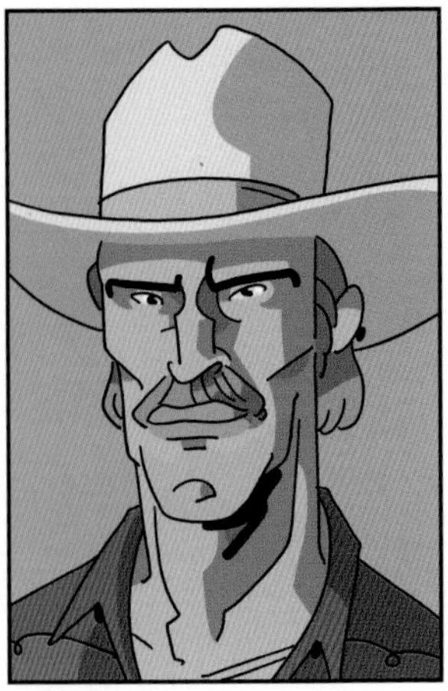

Trigger Keaton | Actor, Director, Stunts

An American action star, Trigger Keaton was a true master of many martial arts and renowned for doing his own stunts and fight choreography. He is now, unfortunately, best known for being the victim of a murder plot and cover-up organized by Luther Alazar, who at the time was president of Bonafide Films. Found seemingly hung in his own apartment, the now famously problematic actor was assassinated by a trio of Alazar's bodyguards ... See full bio »

Born: December 8, 1952 in San Francisco, California, USA

Known For

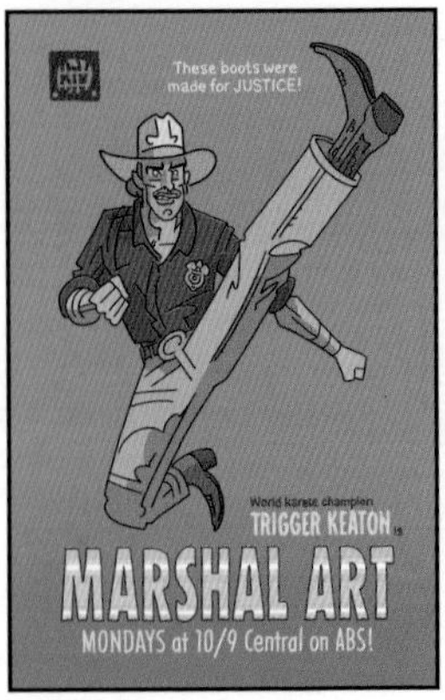
These boots were made for JUSTICE!
World karate champion TRIGGER KEATON
MARSHAL ART
MONDAYS at 10/9 Central on ABS!

Marshal Art
Marshal Art
(1986-1992)

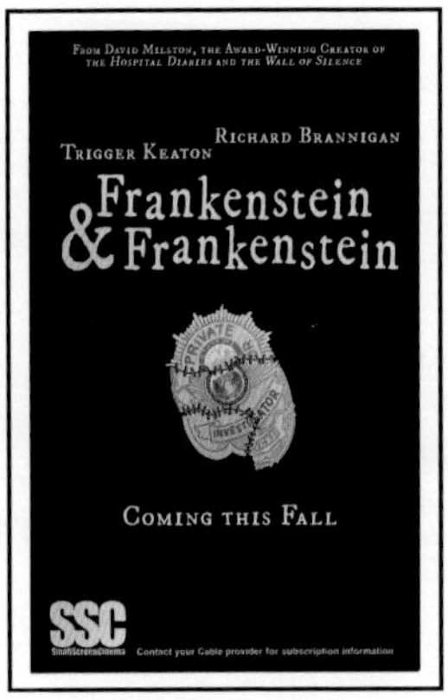
Trigger Keaton
Richard Brannigan
Frankenstein & Frankenstein
Coming this Fall
SSC

Frankenstein & Frankenstein
Dr. Victor Frankenstein
(1998-1999)

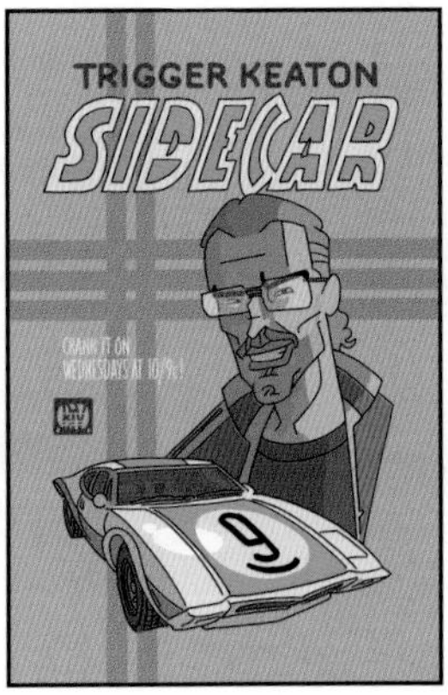
TRIGGER KEATON
SIDECAR

Sidecar
Carson Gray
(1995)

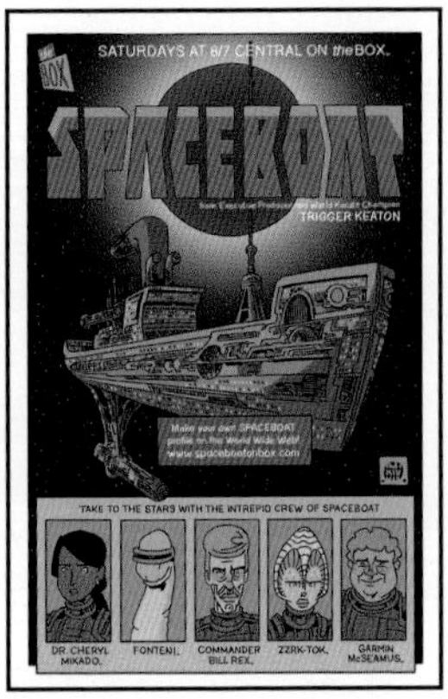
SATURDAYS AT 8/7 CENTRAL ON theBOX.
SPACEBOAT
TRIGGER KEATON
TAKE TO THE STARS WITH THE INTREPID CREW OF SPACEBOAT
DR. CHERYL MIKADO
FONTENI
COMMANDER BILL REX
ZZRK-TOK
GARMIN McSEAMUS

Spaceboat 3030
Commander Bill Rex
(2000-2003)

Filmography

Actor (7 credits)

Marshal Art (TV Series) 1986-1992
Marshal Art
- There's A New Marshal (1986) ... Marshal Art
- Tuff Enuff (1986) ... Marshal Art
- Baby's First Drug Deal Gone Bad (1986) ... Marshal Art

Show All 132 episodes

The Secret To American Kung Fu (Video) 1985
Trigger Keaton (Self)

Sidecar (TV Series) 1995
Carson Gray
- The Car Is Alive (1995) ... Carson Gray
- The Long Road (1995) ... Carson Gray
- Monkey Business (1995) ... Carson Gray

Show All 12 episodes

LA Police (TV Series)   1995
Trigger Keaton (Self)
- Trigger Keaton Public Intoxication and Assault (1995) ... Self

Frankenstein & Frankenstein (Video)   1998-1999
Dr. Victor Frankenstein
- Evil Forebodings (1998) ... Dr. Victor Frankenstein
- Fearless and Powerful (1998) ... Dr. Victor Frankenstein
- Accumulation of Anguish (1998) ... Dr. Victor Frankenstein
Show All 10 episodes

Spaceboat 3030 (TV Series)   2000-2003
Commander Bill Rex
- Encounter at Station X (2000) ... Commander Bill Rex
- Enter...Trycerators! (2000) ... Commander Bill Rex
- Past is NOW (2000) ... Commander Bill Rex/Captain Dave Rex
Show All 52 episodes

Precinct Blues (TV Series)   2005
Detective Roscoe Knight
- City Night, City Beats (2000) ... Detective Roscoe Knight
- The WiFi Killer (2000) ... Detective Roscoe Knight
- Bloody Fingerprint (2000) ... Detective Roscoe Knight
Show All 4 episodes

Stunts (14 credits)

Additional Crew (2 credits)

Director (1 credit)

Self (40 credits)

Personal Details

Publicity Listings: 1 Biographical Movie | 2 Print Biographies | 3 Interviews | 10 Articles | 2 Pictorials | 7 Magazine Cover Photos | See more »

Height: 5' 10" (1.78 m)

Spouse: None

Children: Hopefully None

Parents: Willifred Keaton | Myron Keaton

Star Sign: Sagittarius

Did You Know?

Personal Quote: Yeah, I know my reputation. I know what people think of me. That I'm a mean old grouch, that I'm a hard ass. Maybe I am, I don't give a shit, but people would say, "Trig, why would someone like you want to become an actor?" And I'd say back, "Hell, man, beating ass doesn't pay the bills."

Trivia: In 1987 Keaton was accused by stuntman Lou Reyes of intentionally knocking his eye out with a flaming brand during a fight sequence on tv series Marshal Art. Keaton retorted it's not his fault that Reyes was terrible at his job and that "only having to see half of how shit he is at life now I did him a favor." This would mark the beginning of near countless number of such accusations.

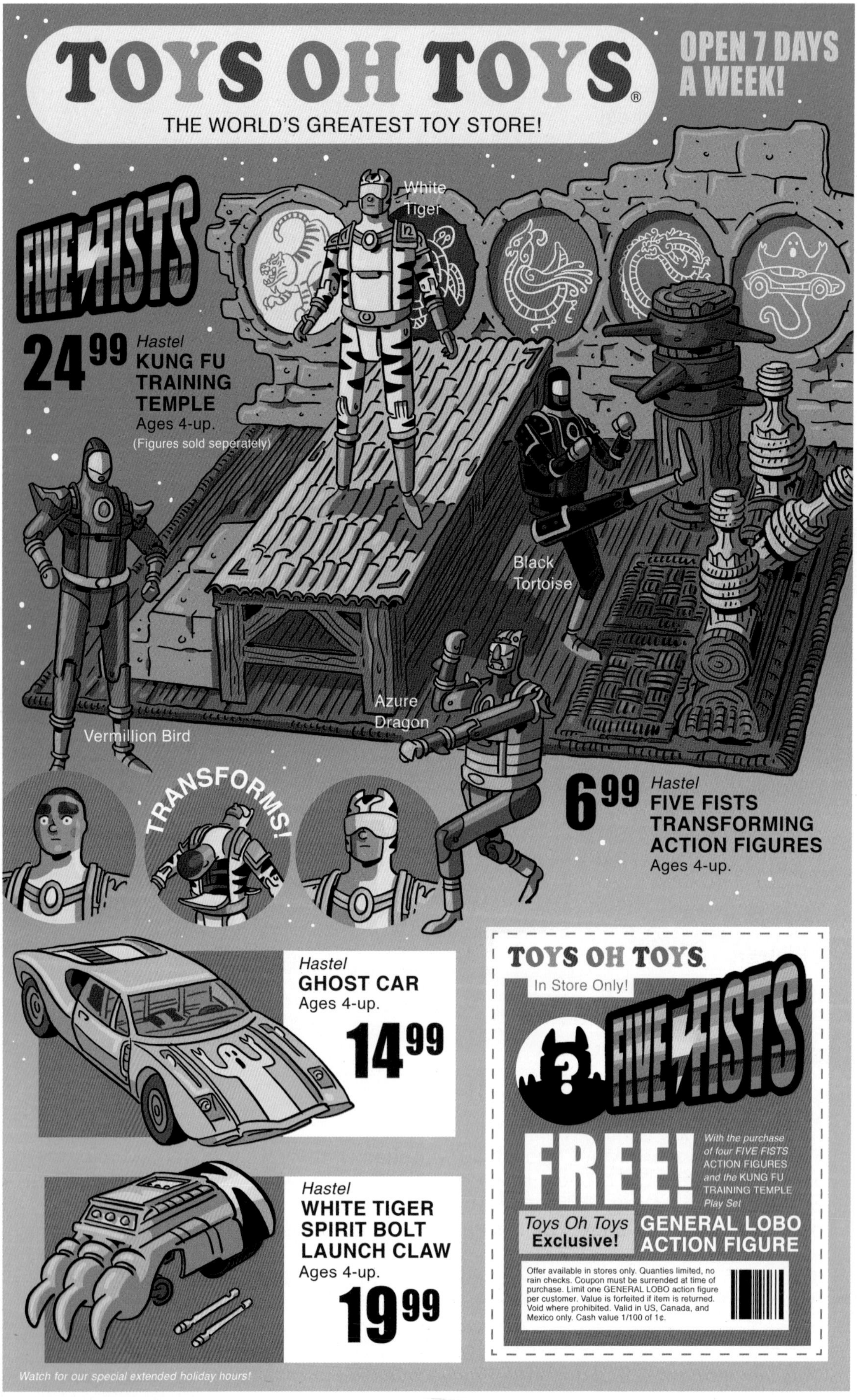

TOYS OH TOYS®
THE WORLD'S GREATEST TOY STORE!
OPEN 7 DAYS A WEEK!
FIVE FISTS
24.99 Hastel KUNG FU TRAINING TEMPLE
Ages 4-up.
(Figures sold seperately)
White Tiger
Black Tortoise
Azure Dragon
Vermillion Bird
TRANSFORMS!
6.99 Hastel FIVE FISTS TRANSFORMING ACTION FIGURES
Ages 4-up.
Hastel
GHOST CAR
Ages 4-up.
14.99
Hastel
WHITE TIGER SPIRIT BOLT LAUNCH CLAW
Ages 4-up.
19.99
TOYS OH TOYS.
In Store Only!
FIVE FISTS
?
FREE!
With the purchase of four FIVE FISTS ACTION FIGURES and the KUNG FU TRAINING TEMPLE Play Set
Toys Oh Toys Exclusive!
GENERAL LOBO ACTION FIGURE
Offer available in stores only. Quanties limited, no rain checks. Coupon must be surrended at time of purchase. Limit one GENERAL LOBO action figure per customer. Value is forfeited if item is returned. Void where prohibited. Valid in US, Canada, and Mexico only. Cash value 1/100 of 1¢.
Watch for our special extended holiday hours!